Dragon Rider

THE ALARIS CHRONICLES
BOOK II

MIKE SHELTON

The Dragon Rider
Copyright © 2017 by Michael Shelton

ISBN: 0-9971900-9-4
ISBN-13: 978-0-9971900-9-0
Library of Congress Control Number: 2017905002
Greenville, North Carolina

Cover Illustration by Brooke Gillette
http://brookegillette.weebly.com

Map by Robert Altbauer
www.fantasy-map.net

For More information about Mike Shelton and his books
www.MichaelSheltonBooks.com

Acknowledgements

This book is specifically dedicated to all my readers. You are what drive me forward in writing new books.

My wife and family have always supported me to the fullest and I couldn't do this without them. I cannot say enough about my editors at Precision Editing, my wonderful beta readers, my illustrator and mapmaker. All have worked hard in helping me make my stories come to light.

The Dragon Rider is a work of fiction. Names, characters, places and incidents are the products of my imagination and are used fictitiously. Any resemblance to actual events, locales, or persons, living or dead, is entirely coincidental. I alone take full responsibility for any errors or omissions in this book.

-Mike-

Books by Mike Shelton

The Cremelino Prophecy:

The Path Of Destiny
The Path Of Decisions
The Path Of Peace
The Blade And The Bow (an e-book prequel novella)

The Alaris Chronicles:

The Dragon Orb
The Dragon Rider
The Dragon King (Summer 2017)

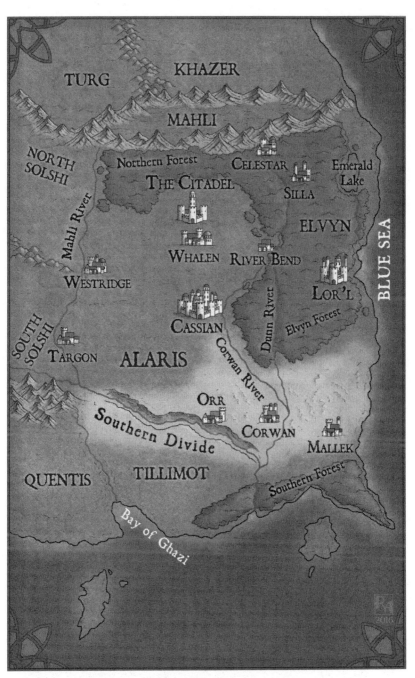

See Color map at www.MichaelSheltonBooks.com

CHAPTER ONE

Riding atop his dragon, Abylar, Bakari grabbed another wooden disc out of his side pack and prepared to fling it down toward the ground. Melded with the dragon's mind, Bakari saw, felt, and knew things his young, fifteen-year-old mind hadn't known even two weeks previously.

Sharing sight with his dragon, he spied the small target his trainer, Zaire, had set up far below. Bakari flipped the disc out forehand and watched as it spun in a graceful and controlled arc. With intense power, it hit the target in the center and fell to the ground. Bakari smiled and steered his dragon back up higher in the air.

Abylar's sleek, blue body had grown a few more feet in the last two weeks—now, Bakari needed a rope ladder to climb up onto his substantial, spiked body. The dragon's wingspan was at least forty feet.

Bakari, who'd become used to the heights, enjoyed flying high over Mahli's countryside. The valley below sat covered in fertile fields and fruit trees and included picturesque winding roads, branching out from the main highway. Seeing the snow-covered peaks of the mountains to the north and to the south reminded Bakari that the fall weather in the valley would soon be colder than in Alaris, the country he had grown up in.

Breathing in deeply, Bakari still relished the newness of the bond with his dragon. He laughed out loud, and Abylar seemed to join in with a loud roar and spit of blue fire across the air in front of them.

Enjoying yourself, Dragon Rider?

Oh yes, Abylar. Bakari held on tighter as the dragon turned in a sharp circle in the air.

As his trainer, Zaire, signaled him to throw again, Bakari nodded, though he knew his new friend wouldn't be able to see his nod from so far below. Grabbing another disc, he took Abylar straight up, higher than before. Leveling out only slightly before the dive, he focused their shared sight on the target and, this time, threw it backhand. The newly made wooden disc spun rapidly, the grained wood causing a dizzying pattern. Signaling to Abylar to follow the disc, the dragon rider and his dragon dove after it, racing it to the intended target.

After a slow fade to the right, the disc came back to the left and hit the target, with Bakari and Abylar only moments behind it. Pulling back his wings at the last moment, the young, intelligent dragon flapped a few times and then lowered the two of them to the ground.

"Amazing, once again!" shouted Zaire. Dark-skinned, like Bakari, Zaire was taller, bulkier, and about ten years older than the young wizard. His size, however, did not appear menacing but rather protective and solid. Long, braided black hair hung down from his head, with the tips resting just above his shoulders.

"I never thought to use something like this as a weapon," Bakari said, patting at his head, even though the wind had hardly messed up his short, dark, curly hair. He absentmindedly put a hand up to adjust his glasses—glasses that were neither there nor needed any longer, due to the increased senses he had received from his dragon. "They could definitely do some damage in battle."

"Not all dragon riders have been wizards, so a unique weapon was developed for them to use." Zaire walked over and helped Bakari dismount. "Although it has been over one hundred and fifty years since the last dragon riders, the craft has been kept up all these years."

Bakari stroked Abylar's nose and, with a silent communication, sent him on his way. A rumbling growl emerged from the dragon's stomach. The growing dragon's appetite was horrendous. Abylar flew up into the air, blowing a strong wind over the two men. Bakari watched wistfully as Abylar shrank into the distance. He was always anxious when his new charge flew too far away.

Freeing Abylar from the Dragon Orb, two weeks earlier in Celestar, a northeastern city in Alaris, Bakari had bonded with the young dragon. Now, this bond remained always present in the back of Bakari's mind, and he spoke to Abylar most anytime he wanted. Upon certain occasions, such as looking at the target from far away, Bakari could actually see and feel what his dragon saw and felt.

"The Mahli ruling council is meeting again this afternoon," Zaire said.

Bakari nodded. "I know. I hear that some of the other searchers have returned."

Zaire patted Bakari on the back. "Bak, you have been prophesied for many years. Fifteen years ago, men left Mahli to search for you. They traveled out to all the neighboring kingdoms, even as far north as the Realm."

"I know." Bakari frowned, not used to being the center of attention. "But I'm afraid they want me to be more than I am. I am just a minor scholar wizard."

"One that also happens to fly on and control a dragon!" Zaire's laugh boomed along the trail they were taking back to the city.

Bakari was indeed the first dragon rider in living memory. Having grown up in the Citadel with the wizards in Alaris for most of his life, Bakari recently served the Chief Judge in Cassian. After he had been sent to investigate the failing of the barrier around Alaris—a barrier that had previously kept the kingdom isolated for one hundred and fifty years—Bakari had discovered and had freed the dragon from its egg. An act that brought down the barrier for good. The failure of the barrier caused others in the land, especially Kanzar Centari, the self-proclaimed High Wizard, to begin to assert power over Alaris. Kanzar's power might eventually reach its neighboring kingdoms. So Bakari had traveled to Mahli, his ancestral homeland, to find out more about who he was and to warn them of the barrier's demise.

Today, as Bakari and Zaire walked through the gates of Amar, the capital city of Mahli, many of its citizens bowed in respect to Bakari, the supposedly prophesied dragon rider that would bring their kingdom out of obscurity and would help to establish peace on the continent. Nodding back, to be polite, Bakari cringed inside once again.

He didn't deserve their bows or devotion. Who was he, to deserve such attention, but a young man in his sixteenth year and of little consequence in the larger world? Many other wizards possessed greater power and deserved much more accolades than he, including his friends—Roland, who ran the Citadel now, and Alli, the newest battle wizard.

Zaire motioned him in through a side door of a three-story building, the tallest one in this small mountain kingdom. The wooden materials used for their buildings seemed appropriate, due to the many forests throughout the mountains here. The city itself, smaller than most in Alaris, sat in a small fertile valley fed by a river running down its center.

Seeing so many of his distant kin around made him think of Kharlia. He moved his head lower to hide the tears now forming at the corners of his brown eyes. Breathing in deeper, he reached out mentally to Abylar for comfort and strength. Bakari didn't know how he could have coped with this loss without their bond.

Bakari had met the young woman less than two months earlier and had quickly developed strong feelings for her. Something that, as a quiet scholar, he never had anticipated finding in his life.

On their way together to Celestar, to discover the secrets of the barrier, a beast had attacked them and their guide, Harley. In the ensuing battle, Kharlia had purposely dropped from a cliff, down into the swiftly flowing Dunn River, rather than let herself be caught and killed by the evil barrier beast. That was the last time Bakari had seen her.

Zaire put his arm on Bakari's shoulder. "Are you all right, Bak?" He was one of the few who treated Bakari with respect but gave him room to be a normal boy also. He preferred being just Bak sometimes to always being seen as *the dragon rider.*

Bakari nodded his head and took control of his emotions. "Just thinking of my friend and wondering if I'll ever see her again."

"Kharlia?" Zaire had been told the story. "Sounds like a strong, independent lady to me."

Bakari smiled. "Ahh. That she was." He let out a small laugh at so many memories of him trying to leave her behind, due to the potential danger. But she had always clung fiercely to him and believed in his quest.

"Perhaps you will see her again," Zaire said.

When Bak and Zaire entered the room, the gathered group grew quiet. The local council and other visitors stood and, once again, gave reverence to their new dragon rider. Bakari noticed one man, someone he hadn't seen before, rising slower than the rest, a scowl on his harsh face, his dark brown eyes shooting daggers at Bakari.

Bakari winced and turned from him to look at the rest of the group. It still seemed strange to see so many dark-skinned people—the predominate color of skin in Mahli. It comforted Bakari in one sense, knowing that he was among his distant family, but he wished some of his friends were here with him also.

"Dragon Rider," said an older man from the gathering, "welcome back to our council." He signaled to Bakari and Zaire to seat themselves around the tables that were arranged for the meeting, with Bakari being given a place of eminence, near Regent Nagasi.

"Sire," Bakari said to Regent Nagasi's welcome.

"Some of our searchers have returned from our neighboring countries to greet you. Their life's work has been in search of you," the regent began. One by one, they came up and greeted Bakari, touching their foreheads and then bowing to him. Bakari copied the greeting back, his face growing hot at all this attention.

The regent continued, "My son Kolo has returned from the northern mountains." He indicated the man in back, whom Bakari had seen scowl at him. "Kolo, please come forward and greet our dragon rider."

Without removing his expression of dislike, Kolo, about a decade older than Bakari, stood and walked in slow steps toward the regent. "Father," he began, "I will greet our visitor, but he has done nothing to warrant my respect or reverence. He is a young boy—and a scrawny one at that."

Silence filled the room, and Regent Nagasi's face reddened. "Is this how you were taught to greet the one we have been waiting for? The dragon rider who will one day be our king?"

Bakari winced at the mention of that idea. He'd heard that prophecy so many times in the last week and was sure they had gotten something wrong. He had admitted to riding a dragon, but, about him being a king—they had indeed made a mistake.

Not one to cause problems, Bakari stepped up to Kolo instead. "I am pleased to meet the son of Nagasi. These events come as a surprise to all of us, I am sure. I hold no ill will toward you." There, that sounded as good as what Roland, his counselor wizard friend, would say in a tough situation.

Kolo only gave a slight nod and then turned away without saying any other words. The meeting continued, and the men returning from other lands, to the north and south, gave reports of what they had found. Soon it was Bakari's turn to discuss the situation in Alaris.

He stood and faced the august gathering, dressed in simple Mahlian robes of green. "As you know, the barrier around Alaris is indeed gone. We in Alaris were taught for one hundred and fifty years that the barrier was there to protect us from other kingdoms. Lately, I learned that this was untrue. One hundred and fifty years ago, some greedy wizards from Alaris began to attack her neighboring countries. So the barrier was put in place by some enterprising wizards that did not agree with Alaris's expansion. Somehow they found a dragon egg— or *the Orb* as it was called—and created the barrier to protect other kingdoms from Alaris's aggressors. This barrier has stood for all this time without us knowing anything about the outside world or you knowing about us."

"And it should stay that way," voiced Kolo.

His father shot him a dark look.

Bakari continued, "Recently, one of our wizards, Kanzar Centari, decided to elevate himself and accelerate the failing of the barrier—a failing that I think would have occurred anyway. Then he displaced our rightful leader, Chief Judge Daymian Khouri, and demanded to be named King of Alaris. He now controls Cassian, our capital, but the Chief Judge is calling men to himself in Orr. Civil war is sure if something doesn't happen fast."

"What should we care about your civil war?" Kolo said. Many of the others in attendance nodded their heads in agreement with this question.

"There is no end to Kanzar's greed, at this point. He is mad with the quest for power." Bakari spread his hands out. "If he wins Alaris, he will turn his plans for conquest to Elvyn, Tillimot, Quentis, Solshi, and, I am sure, eventually to Mahli."

"What about your own wizards?" asked Nagasi. "Is there no way to control him?"

"Many of the older wizards have sided with him," Bakari said. "However, a friend of mine, a newly promoted young wizard, is recruiting apprentices and young wizards at the Citadel. He has not taken sides in the altercation yet, but hopes to remain neutral and to raise his own power base. I don't think he would be a threat to you, but..." Bakari paused. He didn't know what Roland would do. The man wanted power so much that he was sometimes blinded by it. But Bakari hoped, for the sake of their friendship, that Roland would help them keep Alaris in peace.

The regent stood. "Dragon Rider, you have given us much to think about. We will adjourn and discuss this separately among ourselves and will reconvene in a week's time."

Bakari frowned. "A week might be too long, Regent."

The man smiled at Bakari but appeared to stay firm in his decision. "These are not matters to take lightly." With those words, they were dismissed.

As Bakari left, Kolo bumped into him, almost knocking him down.

"Stay out of my way, boy. You are messing with things you are not ready for."

Bakari lifted an eyebrow. "What things are those?"

Kolo shot him a murderous look. "You are not the only

dragon rider prophesied of. I will find an egg and become the prophesied king. Do not get in my way." Then Kolo proceeded to push his way through the rest of the crowd.

Nagasi came up beside Bakari and pulled him to the side. "Please excuse my son. He is a good man. However, he has been trained his entire life so that he can follow me as regent. I think he sees you as getting in his way."

"Sire," Bakari said. "I am new to your prophecies, and, yes, I am a dragon rider, but I do not know if I am *the* dragon rider that is prophesied to be the king."

"You are wiser than many of us, Bakari," Nagasi said. "Being hesitant to take on such a role shows how good of a person you are. Events will prove us out."

The regent moved to walk away, but Bakari called him back.

"Is what Kolo said true?" Bakari asked. "Are there more dragon eggs?"

Nagasi took a moment to answer, and, when he did, his face grew stone serious. "Yes it is, Bakari. It is true. There are records in our books about dragon eggs being in each kingdom, awaiting the day that a rider touches them and they are born and bonded."

"More dragon riders?" whispered Zaire next to Bakari. "What does that mean?"

Bakari's face held a determined look. "It means I need to find them before Kolo or Kanzar does."

CHAPTER TWO

Three days later, Bakari sat neck high in books at the library in Amar. Although not as extensive as the libraries in Cassian or the Citadel, this one held many more books about his heritage and the doings before the barrier arose. It seemed that many times, in the history of Mahli, dragon riders emerged during times of great need. These men and women—some wizards, others not—helped to establish peace in many kingdoms on the Western Continent. The triggering of a first dragon rider—Bakari, in this case—seemed to be the catalyst every time for the emergence of other dragon riders. And, the dragons themselves seemed to hold the knowledge of where the other dragon eggs were.

Bakari rubbed his eyes. It was still hard for him to believe he didn't need to wear glasses anymore. At this thought, he sensed amusement in the back of his mind from Abylar.

Soon Bakari grew weary of reading and realized that he must have missed lunch and that now it was approaching the evening meal. Just a few more books to get through, then he would eat. Bakari sighed and turned back to his reading.

Rider! His dragon screamed in his mind an hour later.

In distress, Bakari threw down his books.

Abylar? He sent his mind out to the dragon as he ran out of the room. Taking the steps two at a time, he descended two flights of stairs and hurried out into the evening. The cool air swirled around him as the sunlight faded behind the mountains.

He sprinted over cobblestone paths, to gravel, then grass, out to where his dragon had called from.

Coming over a rise covered with trees, Bakari glanced down over a small, brown field and looked in horror at the sight below. A group of men, with huge coils of thick rope, had tied Abylar's mouth closed. The dragon tried to claw at them and flapped his wings in a rapid fashion, but another group, of Mahlian wizards, stood around Abylar and hit him with a constant barrage of pain spells. Tears came to Bakari's eyes as the bond exuded the terror going through the young dragon.

Bakari, help me.

This pleading came deep into his soul. So Bakari put his hand against a tree and took a deep breath, trying not to be overwhelmed by the pain of his young dragon. Even though Abylar was huge, by human standards, he was only a few weeks old—a baby still. He was still learning to control his own power, and he wasn't used to having people hurting him.

Bakari ran even faster down this hill, gathering power into himself. Reaching the edge of the group of men, he caught the eye of Kolo, who sneered at him. Then Kolo tied a rope to one of Abylar's thicker spikes and attempted to climb up onto the dragon. Abylar tried to buck Kolo off. But, every time he did, one of the wizards would shoot him with a bolt of lightning.

Bakari threw a bolt of fire himself, at the attackers. He wasn't necessarily strong at that type of power, but the surprise attack from behind did divert their attention enough that Abylar was able to kick over two of them. The wizards then turned their attention to Bakari and shot fire and lightning at him. He had just barely put up a weak barrier in time to stop from being hurt too much, but their strikes did knock him down. He couldn't fight against so many.

Used to having time to studiously figure things out, Bakari had to dig deep quickly into the reserves of his mind. There he found the records he had studied—many of them just that day—about the power of dragons. Dragon riders were known to defy dozens of wizards at once, but Abylar and Bakari were new at their bond. However, Bakari had bonded briefly with other creatures before. So, while running behind a small copse of evergreens, to gain time, he went into a quick trance and entered fully into his dragon's mind.

But Bakari almost fell over and vomited. The terror his young dragon was experiencing was almost overwhelming. Steeling his will against the pain, Bakari again entered Abylar's mind fully. First, he instructed the dragon to buck off Kolo. The man went flying off the noble creature and landed hard on the ground. Now Abylar flapped his wings hard and began to rise from the ground. A group of men, however, held on to the ropes encircling his feet, keeping him from taking off fully.

Bakari needed to touch his dragon physically. Looking around with the dragon's eyes, he found a nearby horse. Calling the horse toward himself, from behind the trees, Bakari mounted it and took off at full speed toward his dragon.

As lightning shot around him, he used his powers to increase his speed and agility on the horse, and the two of them darted through unscathed. He approached Abylar and instructed him to put out his wings to their fullest. After Abylar did so, Bakari then jumped from his horse onto the wing. It sagged for a moment, and Bakari stumbled. Getting his balance, he ran up the wing and onto his dragon's back.

Sitting in the usual soft spot, behind Abylar's neck, Bakari placed his palms on his dragon's neck. This personal contact raised their bond to new levels. The same thing had happened when he had first touched the Dragon Orb. Intelligence, power, and might flowed through Bakari's body. He thrust out his hands, and fire burned away the ropes holding Abylar down. Then, lifting up into the air, Abylar flapped hard and knocked over the rest of their attackers.

Soon the dragon rider and his dragon flew upward into the cloudy skies. Wizard fire flew at them still, and, upon instinct, Bakari reached inside the saddlebag and pulled out a handful of wooden discs. Focusing his dragon sight on each wizard individually, Bakari let go of several discs in rapid succession. With perfect aim, his discs swerved through the air, making a swooshing sound as they hit into each of the powerful wizards, knocking them out onto the ground.

Kolo and a few of the other men stood up and tried to fire arrows at them, but these little sticks didn't damage the majestic, blue dragon hide. Then Abylar opened his mouth wide and let out a stream of blue fire, both loud and ferocious. They were too high up for it to reach Kolo and his men, but the heat from the flames forced them back.

Bakari was euphoric with the power of his dragon. They were invincible. It was incredible. With the power Abylar held, Bakari could perceive each blade of grass and hear each leaf blowing in the breeze of Abylar's wings. The air stirred, crisp with the approaching evening, and it seemed as if power filled his world.

The two, dragon rider and dragon, flew up high into the evening sky, then turned around and returned in a deep dive back toward earth. Kolo and his men scattered before them like ants. They were nothing, compared to the power Bakari held at the moment.

"Bak!" A familiar sound pushed through the fog of his power. "Bakari, stop!"

It was Zaire. He stood on the top of the hill where Bakari had stood just minutes before. Kolo's men stood behind him, looking terrified. Zaire's familiar voice broke the intimate bond Bakari was having with his dragon.

He commanded Abylar to stop the dive and rise back up.

I could have killed them all! Abylar said through their bond. The dragon did not seem happy about Bakari's command, but he obeyed it nonetheless and rose back up into the air.

I know. Bakari patted Abylar and sent soothing thoughts through the bond. *But we must be careful with our power.*

The dragon harrumphed but still obeyed, eventually landing once again at the edge of the field. Then Bakari spoke in a low voice to his dragon with the suggestion that he leave and hunt.

After Bakari jumped off his back, but before Abylar rose, he said into Bakari's mind, *I can find the other riders.*

The thought jolted Bakari back to what he had found while studying earlier. He grimaced and turned back toward the approaching footsteps of Zaire.

"Are you all right?"

Bakari nodded, looking over Zaire's shoulder at Kolo and his men. The regent's son gave him another murderous glare.

Bakari realized then that he couldn't stay any longer. He needed to go and find the other dragon riders. He didn't know if he was the fulfillment of prophecy or not, but he knew that he couldn't let men like Kolo—or, for that matter, like Kanzar—rule the world. They were uncaring and inhumane.

"I will leave in the morning," Bakari told Zaire. "Can you help me gather supplies?"

"Where will you go, Dragon Rider?"

"To visit the elves, then to find the other dragons and their riders."

CHAPTER THREE

Roland Tyre stood in the middle of two elderly Council members. Kanzar Centari, self-proclaimed High Wizard, had left them behind to watch over the Wizard Citadel and over Roland himself. They were too old to travel with Kanzar and his army, made of wizards and mercenaries, when they had gone south to Cassian. But they were still young enough to be perturbed at Roland's quick rise to power.

At sixteen and only a month out from becoming a full wizard, Roland now carried his level four wizard status quite prominently. Many of the young wizards and apprentices had immediately taken a liking to him. His good looks and arrogance annoyed some, but, for the most part, his good nature and his positive attitude made others want to be around him.

Roland pushed a lock of blond hair out of his face, grinned, and, with his sparkling blue eyes, winked at a young woman approaching them. She was one of a few new apprentices who had arrived at the Citadel that week. Tall and curvy, she also carried herself with more authority than the others. She stood in front of them, waiting for introductions.

"My lady," Roland bowed and reached to kiss her hand. "Are you sure you are a wizard? Among these rough heathens, your beauty is a light to my soul."

The young woman stifled a laugh, her eyes looking merry with surprise at Roland's greeting. "I am Celia and hail from a border town in Solshi, just over the Mahli River, west of here." The young woman had dark, wavy hair and had a pouty smile on her full lips. "I heard you are gathering apprentices from all kingdoms."

Roland's royal blue robes stirred around him with a slight breeze in the late-autumn air. "If I knew that ladies from Solshi were so beautiful, I would have broken through the barrier myself years ago."

One of the other wizards cleared his throat and shook his head at Roland.

"Oh, Titus." Roland frowned. "Lighten up, and let us have some fun. What harm does it do? There is time enough for work and formal affairs. Don't you remember being young?"

Titus reluctantly gave a short bow to Roland, acknowledging the young wizard's current preeminence over the other wizards at the Citadel.

Roland turned back to Celia. "Do you know if you are inclined toward any one of the three disciplines yet?"

Celia shook her head. "I'm not sure. Though I doubt I'm a counselor and war is abhorrent, so I must be best suited to be a scholar."

"Ahh, I see." Roland enjoyed talking to this young woman. "Quite boring, all in all, but one of my best friends is a scholar wizard, and now he is riding around on the back of a dragon, so you never know."

"So it's true, then?" Celia stood on her toes and clapped her hands with delight. "There is a dragon rider in the land once again."

Roland frowned for only a moment. With all the power he

held at his disposal, he should be the one riding the dragon, not Bak. Maybe he should find his own dragon. He filed this thought away for later.

"Well, Titus here is also a scholar wizard. I will put you under his fine tutelage, but I hope you will save a dance for me at the autumn ball."

Celia blushed and bowed toward Roland. Then she moved over to stand next to Titus.

One by one, all of the new apprentices met with the three wizards. Titus moved away with one of them in tow, and Eryck, the other old wizard, took a counselor apprentice with him. Then Roland took the two remaining battle apprentices with him and led them down to the training grounds.

He was embarrassed to admit that the Citadel was short on battle trainers. All of its previous battle wizards had traveled with Kanzar to Cassian, in his quest to become king, leaving Roland here with only a few battle apprentices. He himself was quite polished with the sword and other weapons and could hold his own in most battles. But a real battle wizard, like his friend Alli, was a true sight to behold. He became mesmerized each time he saw her fight or train as she created a deadly dance that flowed from one position to another with such accuracy and grace that it almost made him jealous.

Putting the new battle apprentices with experienced ones that had been there for the past year, Roland walked back toward his rooms in the Citadel. Passing through the kitchens, he grabbed an apple. A smile and a wink to the cook's helper enabled him to pass through without any scolding from the cook herself.

He climbed the stairs and entered his office, formerly Kanzar's office. Sitting in the comfortable stuffed leather chair, he studied the richly decorated and overly ornate room. He would need to do something about it. This was Kanzar's way of showing off his power, but Roland didn't need to show off to anyone. His power spoke for itself.

Roland thought about how he had recently risen, in one unheard-of step, from apprentice to level four wizard by beating the wizard test and showing Kanzar and the Council that at sixteen years old, Roland was one of the most powerful wizards in the land. Trained at the Citadel from age thirteen, he had been living in Cassian as the Chief Judge's apprentice counselor wizard for the previous year, and Onius Neeland had been his mentor.

Onius, it had turned out, knew generally of Kanzar's thirst for power and his desires to bring down the barrier and to set himself up as king of Alaris. Onius, Roland's former mentor, had assured Roland that he had things under control and was working to bring down Kanzar from the inside. But Roland was never all the way convinced.

Roland's goals for the Citadel remained for him to stay out of the civil conflict as long as possible and for him to build up his followers—young apprentices that would soon be wizards of their own. But, in the end, he would do what needed to be done to stop Kanzar from becoming king. Kanzar had created the King-men, those men who wanted to do away with the judgeships and reestablish a kingship. Roland didn't care one way or the other who became king. Soon enough, the Citadel would establish its own power base under himself, one that would have influence over many kingdoms, not just Alaris.

* * *

A few hours later, Roland stood up and gazed outside. Lamps were blinking on as the yard quieted down for the night. Then he noticed a shadow moving behind a group of trees. Soon another figure joined the first. Roland reached out his senses to see if he could hear what they were discussing—a magic power he was just learning to use. He couldn't quite hear their words, but he memorized their magic signatures, something that was unique to each wizard. It might just be a clandestine meeting of two lovers, but Roland wanted to make sure that there wasn't any trouble brewing in his Citadel.

"Sir." A servant entered the room. "Dinner is ready. Would you like it brought in here? Or, will you be dining with the others tonight?"

Roland smiled. "With the others, Ollie." This was a tradition he had begun—dining with the apprentices. It made him into their friend and, hopefully, ensured their loyalty to him over their former leader, Kanzar.

The servant led Roland to the dining area, even though Roland knew the way well. He nodded his thanks to the servant and dismissed him to go eat his own dinner. Then, greeting a few of the men by name, Roland seated himself among some of the older apprentices this evening. Soon, a dinner of roast chicken, applesauce, and freshly baked bread was served.

Then one of the men turned to him. "Sir, what news of Kanzar and the Chief Judge?"

Roland turned toward the questioner. "Still at a standoff, it seems. The Chief Judge is receiving recruits from most of the southern cities, and it is rumored that Tillimot might also help him. Kanzar should have moved by now, but I hear there is unrest in Cassian."

"The thieves are running the city, sir," piped up a newer apprentice from one table away. "I escaped from there just last week."

This was news to Roland. "The thieves held their peace when I lived there. They must be getting bolder with the Chief Judge gone."

The man opened his mouth to reply, when the lamps in the room flickered off all at once, plunging the room into near darkness. Then Roland felt a cold breeze stir nearby him, and he shivered. With so many wizards here, the room didn't stay dark for long. Mage lights and small flames popped up all around the room. The men and women began talking at once, and the guards looked to Roland for direction. He nodded for them to search the perimeter. Something was not right.

"My lord," said a husky female voice behind him, making Roland jump. "Are you all right?" Roland turned. It was Celia, the lovely new apprentice.

"I'm fine," he stammered. "But, where did you come from?" She hadn't been standing there before.

"I just arrived," she said with a devious and inviting smile.

Roland frowned. He reached his mind out slightly, as he was wont to do to others, to test her strength. Her mind was strong, and her power seemed somehow *different*. He promptly pulled back, hopefully before she had noticed. For he realized that she had been one of the two shadows he had noticed lurking behind the trees before dinner. He tried to act as if he didn't know anything about her secrets, something his counselor training had taught him to do well.

"You must have been caught up in your studies, to be so late for dinner," Roland said with a neutral expression.

"Yes, all the bookwork is quite distracting." Celia smiled and started to move toward the food. "I better get some, before all the boys wolf it down."

Roland turned around and sat back down.

"Is there something wrong, Wizard Tyre?" one of the apprentices asked.

"How could something be wrong?" said another. "Didn't you see that alluring woman he was talking to? Who is she, sir?"

Roland sat in deep thought, still distracted by his conversation with Celia and her obvious lies to him. He rubbed his arm where he had felt the cold breeze pass by him when the lights had gone out.

"Sir?" the apprentice asked again.

Roland shook himself from his thoughts and turned to his men. "She is stunning, isn't she?" He laughed, and they all joined in, ribbing each other. "Her name is Celia. She says she's from Solshi."

The men continued to talk about the lack of women wizards in the Citadel, but Roland was becoming more and more disturbed by Celia. She was, most likely, a few years older than himself, but she looked and acted the part of an apprentice almost too well. One by one, the men finished eating and then returned to their other activities.

* * *

The next morning, Roland was woken up early by one of

his servants. "One of the wizards insists on speaking to you, sir."

Roland grumbled and rolled out of bed. Quickly pulling on a pair of serviceable pants and a shirt and clasping on his signature blue cloak, he strolled into his ready room. Eryck, the most senior counselor wizard left in the Citadel, sat waiting for him. The man nodded his head toward Roland but didn't stand up. Roland didn't actually care if these men accepted him as their leader or not. The leadership role had fallen to him by virtue of him being the most powerful wizard left in the Citadel. He didn't know if he even wanted to run the place or not, but he did desire to be the most powerful wizard in the land.

"What is it you wanted to see me about, Councilor?" Roland said, deciding to be polite.

"Sir, a few of the apprentices were doing some cleaning and straightening in the basement rooms and found something disturbing." Eryck fidgeted with his hands.

"Go on."

"Well, we, um…There are rooms down there that stay locked for good reasons, sir."

Roland raised his eyebrows but said nothing. Leaning forward on his elbows, he pushed his bangs out of his eyes.

Eryck continued. "As I was saying, we have some rooms locked up with very few people having access to the key. These rooms hold ancient artifacts in them, ones known to cause trouble."

"Trouble?"

"Evil, sir. They exhibit evil magic or have been unstable in the past. Well, one of these rooms was broken into last night, it seems." The man sat back in his chair and took a deep breath, as if to steady himself.

Roland reached over to a nearby table and poured himself some water that had been left for him by one of his servants. No wonder they had left Eryck behind. The man was skittish and prone to fear.

"Anything taken?"

"We have a few of the older scholar wizards looking through the room. We need to take extra precautions. It doesn't look like anything was taken, but someone was definitely looking for something."

"Well, let's go and take a look, shall we?" Roland stood up, but Eryck did not.

"I would rather not, sir."

Roland shook his head again at the timid wizard. "Well, I will go alone then."

"Take someone with you. You don't want to go into those rooms alone." Eryck's face paled again.

Roland peered at him questioningly, but Eryck just shook his head and mumbled something unintelligible.

With a grunt of disgust, Roland stood, grabbed a guard from the hall and an apprentice, and headed down the stairs. Arriving on the main floor, Celia once again crossed his path.

She greeted him with a smile and a bow. "Good day, sir."

Roland nodded his head toward her, and then, to maintain appearances, he took her hand in his and kissed it. "Lovely as always, apprentice." Coming back upright, he dismissed her as he and his two men headed down another flight of stairs.

Somehow he had missed something when talking to Celia. Something felt out of place, but he couldn't identify it.

Two floors lower, they left the stairs and walked down a few long hallways. A group of wizards was still taking inventory of the rooms as Roland approached. They appeared nervous, but not as pathetic as Eryck had.

Roland ran his hand over the doorframe. Down lower, by the floor, something dark and oily dripped to the floor. Bringing it up to his nose, he sniffed it. He wished he possessed Bakari's ability to remember everything. This oily substance had obviously been used to get into the room somehow.

Walking into the room, Roland turned all the way around. It was windowless and held a myriad of shelves. But the room was no more than a few paces wide in either direction. Roland reached his hand toward a random object, but one of the wizards put his arm out and stopped him.

"With due respect, sir, you should not touch anything in here." The elder wizard moved between Roland and the rest of the room. "In fact, you should not even be here. These artifacts are unstable."

Roland grunted. "What harm can they do?"

One of the wizards opened his eyes wide. "Unbearable harm…some of them. One will kill you instantly upon touching it, one will turn you old before your time, one will take your strength away, and one will leave you delusional."

"I get the point," Roland said. "Just make sure nothing is missing, then lock the door again and station guards down here."

The wizards nodded, and Roland walked out of the door.

Looking at the oily substance once again, something clicked inside his mind. *Celia!* When Roland had leaned over to kiss her hand, he had noticed that same oily substance on the hem of her dress. What was the woman playing at? Who was she really?

CHAPTER FOUR

Allison Stenos, who had recently been raised to a full wizard, rode beside Tam Anvil, an apprentice wizard. They were making their way closer to the southeastern city of Corwan. Chief Judge Daymian Khouri had sent the two wizards east from his base in Orr to secure help from the neighboring city. The recent rise of Wizard Kanzar Centari, as he attempted to take over the kingdom, had forced people to choose sides—of either the High Wizard or the Chief Judge—thus preparing for civil war. Corwan was an important city, on the banks of the Dunn River, just across the border from southern Elvyn.

"I'll be glad for winter," stated Tam. "It does cool down here, doesn't it?"

Alli smiled. She understood what Tam meant. Both of them were from the more northern areas in Alaris: her, from the East; he, from the West. They were not used to the southern desert.

"I heard that winter in the desert is like spring in the rest of Alaris—well, spring minus the flowers and green trees and rain." A small laugh escaped her mouth, and she stood up in the stirrups, trying to see farther down the long road. She pushed her dark bangs back from her face. Her hair was getting longer now and stuck to the back of her neck on its way down to her shoulders. Standing five foot and four inches tall at fifteen years old, she figured she wouldn't grow any taller.

Tam just grunted back in reply. A battle wizard apprentice from the Citadel, he had been sent south on Roland's command to accompany the Chief Judge. Tam's dark hair, dark eyes, and bulky build made the older teenager appear more serious than he really was. Alli had met Tam in Orr in the past week and actually enjoyed the company. He was definitely less taxing to be around than Roland. She frowned at the thought of that arrogant boy—why did Roland's face always intrude upon her thoughts? She kicked her horse softly and jumped out ahead of Tam.

"Wait up, Alli," Tam shouted and then raced after her.

They rode that way for the next few miles of open road. Alli reached inside her and felt the familiar magic pouring through her veins. She had sensed her magic almost her entire life. At first, it was just with little things, like running faster than anyone else or hearing sounds from farther away. Then it grew. She had learned to use weapons at a young age. She fought off animals attacking cattle and could lift logs larger than any that the boys could. She also became the town champ in arm and leg wrestling. But her town of River Oak became afraid of her, the little girl who was obviously not like the rest of them. When Alli was ten, her parents sent her off to the Citadel. That was five years ago. Now she rode as a full level three battle wizard.

After a few hours of riding hard, the tall walls and spires and domed rooftops of Corwan came into view in the wavering heat. A fair-sized city, Corwan enjoyed an important river port on the Dunn River. Wood and other goods from up north were shipped there for distribution to Corwan and Orr and the other smaller villages in the area. Now that the magical barrier had come down, Alli wondered how trade with the southern elves and the kingdom of Tillimot would influence the city.

Slowing down a mile or so from the city, they tried to cool themselves off and compose themselves. They would be representing the Chief Judge and needed to look and act the part.

Approaching nearer to the city, Alli saw that a small line of people stood in front of the gates. Guards seemed to be inspecting each person rather thoroughly, probably as a result of the presumed upcoming battle for the leadership of Alaris.

Waiting for their turn, Alli noticed that the people of Corwan appeared similar to those from Orr: not dark-skinned, like Bakari, but a light brown with dark hair and dark eyes. Even though the people had waited a while, Alli didn't notice much animosity—most in the line seemed happy and were talking with their fellow travelers. Alli hoped this peaceful, friendly people would not be destroyed by Kanzar's greed.

Soon their own turn came, and Alli presented their credentials. The guards eyed the pair of teenage travelers with some surprise, but they motioned them into the city nonetheless and provided an escort, who took them to the governor's office.

They waited for a short time in a small but pleasant room. The room's furniture was serviceable, not ostentatious like at the Citadel. It was in a smaller building than what had housed the Chief Judge in Cassian but seemed to bustle with activity around them. City officers and servants moved in quick and efficient strides throughout the three-story stone building.

Soon they were directed into another room. There stood

two men: one, the governor of Corwan; the other, the southern judge of the land; the last remaining judge to show loyalty to the Chief Judge and the current government.

"Welcome, wizards," the governor said, bowing with hands clasped together.

Alli bowed back. "Greetings, Governor Makin and Judge Azeem. I am Allison Stenos, battle wizard, and this is Tamison Anvil, apprentice. We bring you news and greetings from the Chief Judge."

All four bowed to each other again. Alli stifled a small giggle at the inordinate amount of bowing these southerners did. The governor motioned them to a set of chairs. Then, after servants had brought refreshments of drinks and dates for the group, they began to talk.

"Allison," started the judge. "Is it true that Kanzar has replaced all the other judges in the land?"

"Call me Alli, please. Yes. Kanzar, through technically legal means, has appointed his own judges in the North, the West, and the East. You and Chief Judge Khouri are the only remaining judges left out of Kanzar's control. Because of that, we think Kanzar may attack here before taking on the Chief Judge directly in Orr."

"Pardon me for saying, young wizard," Governor Makin said, "but why did Daymian send one so young here on his behalf."

Alli briefly gave him a dark look.

Tam cleared his throat to hide a laugh. "Sirs, I have seen this young woman in practice, but not in real battle, though rumors do abound. She is a marvel to watch, for her fighting skills rival those of the Battlemaster. From among all the Chief Judge's men and women, he has sent you his most prized fighter."

Alli fiercely blushed at Tam's compliments. "I'm just here to help, that's all." She wanted to play down his praise. "One advantage I have is that my size and youth do let me get around easier, and people don't pay me as much attention. What I am here to secure is your loyalty to the Chief Judge." Alli stared at both the governor and the judge, square in the eyes, her bright green meeting their brown. "Are you with the Chief Judge or Kanzar?"

A brief moment of heavy silence settled over the room.

Azeem was the first to speak. "As one of the judges of the land, I do uphold the rightful leader of Alaris, Daymian Khouri."

Alli then turned to the governor for his answer. But his pause did not make her feel comfortable.

"Allison," he began, "I have never had any problems with the Chief Judge or the judges' system. They have ruled fairly for one hundred and fifty years. But many of my people do express the desire to once again have a king. And, now that the barrier is gone and Alaris will be out in the world again, a king will ensure our preeminence once again among the lands."

How could this man sit here and say this?

Alli was about to open her mouth, but then Makin continued, "However, I also hear horrible things about Wizard Kanzar and his treatment of others. His greed knows no bounds. I do not support making him the new king."

Alli relaxed and saw Tam take a deep breath. Playing the

part of counselor, she realized now, was more exhausting than fighting a battle. "I appreciate your candor, Governor. The Chief Judge agreed to allow the people to vote for which form of government they want, and, if they choose to have a king, he will step down peacefully. But—" Alli stood up and pointed with her fingers for emphasis. "He will not, and I repeat, WILL NOT allow Kanzar Centari to be that king."

The governor took a drink and licked his lips. "Then, we are in agreement. I will not fight against the Chief Judge, but I will await the outcome of the vote."

"A vote that Kanzar will not allow, I am sure, or, in the least, one that he will manipulate to support his own doings," voiced Tam. "Will you send men to fight against Kanzar?"

The governor seemed to gather his thoughts. "I will need to meet with my council and decide what we can do."

Azeem didn't look happy with that decision. "I have a battalion of men under my control here. We will fight for the Chief Judge. If the governor wishes to sit by and wait on his fate, that will be his decision."

Alli noticed, for the first time, that there was not peace between the two men. These things had, most likely, already been discussed to some degree.

The governor stood up and put a smile on his face. "We all do what we can. I must protect and support my people. The barrier being down has opened up a whole new world for us. The land of Elvyn and all who control the Blue Sea are now open to endless opportunities for trade."

They all bowed to each other again, and the meeting was dismissed. Then Alli and Tam were shown to the guest quarters, where they relaxed for a bit and were able to clean up. The group would be meeting later in the evening for dinner.

After freshening up and before their late dinner, Alli went for a walk along the upper docks of Corwan. Looking down from her vantage point, she watched the busy fishermen and other dockworkers unloading their last catch for the day.

Corwan sat at the convergence of the great Dunn River and the smaller, but heavily traveled, man-made Corwan River. It was a busy port city, made even more so now by having the magic barrier down.

The late-autumn sun had set earlier, leaving the men now to work by torchlight as they began closing up for the night. Alli gazed east and wondered what it would be like to cross where the barrier had been and stand on Elvyn soil. She had been close to Elvyn in Celestar but had stayed near the city. The elves this far south were, supposedly, different from their northern counterparts.

Over the sounds from the dockworkers, Alli felt something tickling her astute hearing. She closed her eyes and tried to use her growing wizard skills to home in on the interrupting sound. Her hearing and sight had always been better than others'. Some said that this might be due to her growing up close to the barrier, in the Elvyn Forest. Others said that maybe her heritage was mixed with the elves'. Whatever the reason, Alli used these senses now to her full advantage.

The sound was coming from her left, up river, to the north. She scanned that direction more closely. The night sky was growing darker but had stayed clear, and, even though the night was moonless, the stars shone brilliantly. She soon spotted faint points of light in the distance. She tilted her head, trying to make sense of it. Then the lights grew more abundant. All of a sudden, she understood.

Running without hesitation, back along the docks and up the stairs into the city, Alli continued to pick up her pace. She pushed any back that stood in her way and left a trail of yelling people behind her swift movements. Knocking over a young woman carrying a fruit basket, Alli apologized hastily, helping the woman to pick up a few pieces of the fruit. Alli wished she could do more, but she didn't dare waste the time. Luckily, the governor's castle was not too far away.

Alli ignored the guards that tried to stop her at the castle entrance, spinning through them with her unexpected twists and turns, all with very little effort. Then, running up a flight of stairs and pushing past another guard, she burst through the governor's office door and yelled, "We're under attack!" Putting her hands on her knees to cool her breathing, she watched the two men turn to face her. One was the governor, and, standing next to him—with a smirk on his face—was Mericus, one of Kanzar's right-hand men and the newly appointed judge of the West.

A gasp escaped her lips. Then the realization dawned on her.

"My dear, there is nothing to worry about," said the smiling governor. "I said I didn't want Kanzar to be king, and I meant it."

"You?" Alli pointed at Mericus.

"Why not me?" Mericus pushed his smooth black hair

back from his angular face. He stood battle ready in front of Alli. Even though he was powerful, his main discipline was as a counselor, not as a battle wizard. "I am a perfect alternative to both the Chief Judge and the High Wizard. If the Chief Judge sides with me, then together we can vanquish Kanzar's quest for power."

Alli's mind raced. Mericus might be a better option than Kanzar, but she had little faith that Mericus would be a king who would rule fairly and equitably. "How do we know you are not playing us, Mericus? Maybe you are part of Kanzar's plans."

The judge's face grew red, and his lips tightened. "Let me tell you, Apprentice, Kanzar has humiliated me for the last time. Yes, I was one of his men and took advantage of his naming me a judge—legally, I might add, in times of war. But I do not want to live under his rule. The man is a bully," Mericus said with apparent rage.

Alli took a step back, but she couldn't help saying, "I'm not an apprentice, sir. I passed the wizard test." She was proud of this fact and was tired of being underestimated for her youth.

Mericus blurted out a laugh. "You? You are only a girl. How did *you* pass the test?"

"It was administered to me at the Citadel. I can assure you I am more than able. In fact, I am a level three wizard." Alli smirked sweetly.

Tension built in the room, and the governor appeared uneasy to be in the line of fire between two obviously powerful wizards. He took a step back.

"Under whose authority?" Mericus took a step closer to

Alli, his tall frame dwarfing hers.

"Roland Tyre's. He runs the Citadel now."

Mericus blanched and opened his mouth but, apparently, didn't know what to say. Then sounds of fighting erupted outside. All three moved to look out the windows, though Alli was the first to reach them.

Looking down over the town, toward the rivers, she saw two dozen boats, landing along the docks, and armed men jumping out. A few remaining dockworkers tried to fight, but they were subdued without any other loss of life.

Alli turned to Mericus. "This is the way you propose to take over for Kanzar?"

The governor turned to Alli. "It's not what you think. Kanzar sent Mericus here to take the city under his control; however, Mericus has promised me there will be no violence, if the people don't fight back. The city will be on lock-down and this will be his base, until all of this is settled."

Alli frowned. Oh, she could leave anytime she wanted to. That wasn't the worry. But, now there appeared to be at least three people vying for the leadership of Alaris. She hoped Roland wouldn't get greedy and jump in to the race.

Turning to Mericus, Alli studied his face for signs of deception. "Mericus, for now, I will let you and your men stay. However, if I see any trouble, you will see my fighting skills firsthand. Also, Judge Azeem will be allowed to leave with his battalion, to aid the Chief Judge against a potential attack from Kanzar."

Mericus, seeming to now recognize Alli as his equal, as a level three wizard, gave her a slight bow. "You have my word, young lady. But I must ask you to make sure you do not leave the city yourself."

Alli ground her teeth in frustration and then agreed, "I will be glad to stay by your side, sir, and make sure you stay out of any trouble."

"Good then. Now that we are all friends, let's go and eat dinner." The governor clapped his hands and motioned his arm toward the door. "A fine meal is being prepared for us."

CHAPTER FIVE

"We are sorry you need to leave so soon, Dragon Rider." Regent Nagasi stood in front of Bakari. The regent's long braids reminded Bakari of how short his own dark hair still was. Though, in the two months since leaving Cassian, his hair had grown bushier, and he was sure he could get a few inches out of it if he straightened it. The regent gave a grave look toward his son, Kolo. "I also ask forgiveness on behalf of our kingdom for the way your dragon was treated."

Bakari nodded his acceptance of the apology as Kolo's eyes continued to shoot mighty daggers into his own. No matter where Bakari looked, whenever he turned back, Kolo remained staring hard at him.

"I truly don't know if I am an answer to your prophecy," Bakari said. "But I do have a dragon that says he will help me find the other dragon riders. With their help, hopefully I can help my friends in Alaris and, in turn, save the neighboring kingdoms from Kanzar's apparent greed."

Nagasi patted him hard on the back with his heavy hand. "Well, my boy, it seems you carry a good head on your shoulders. I wish your visit to your homeland would have been longer and less dangerous. My ancestral regents and I have waited for over one hundred and fifty years for the return of our king. A few more months or years will not matter."

Bakari's eyes opened wide at this mention of their prophesied king. It was hard not to wonder if it would be him or not. He couldn't deny that he was one of the famed dragon riders, but he was also young and untested in the things of the world. He recognized his weaknesses.

Abylar, flying overhead, landed near the group. He kept a wary and ferocious eye on Kolo and his men. *I can still eat them,* he voiced to Bakari's mind.

Bakari coughed to cover up his surprise. *No, you can't do that, Abylar,* he said back to his dragon.

In response, Bakari felt, rather than heard, Abylar sigh his disappointment. The young dragon knelt down, and Bakari mounted up.

A new saddle was on Abylar, which had been made especially for Bakari. A leather harness wrapped around him and extended down over one of Abylar's scales in the front. In addition, Zaire stepped forward and handed him a few bags the town's leather man had made for Bakari. These fastened to hooks on the sides of the saddle. One bag held the wooden discs, and the other, a few days' rations and some new clothes. Bakari also regarded the newly made robes he was wearing, which consisted of bright green and blue layers of cotton and silk. They were some of the finest clothes he had ever owned.

"Farewell." Bakari nodded his head to the gathering. "I have enjoyed my visit to my homeland." Well, he mostly had, outside of the incident with Kolo. The people were very kind and accepting of Bakari—even with the surprise of him showing up on the back of a dragon. A sight not seen in many generations.

Abylar lifted up into the air amid cheers from the gathering. Children jumped up and down and waved. So Bakari broke into a generous smile and waved back. Turning in a circle, as he flapped his wings a few times, Abylar then shot straight up into the sky. Bakari let out a yell, and the crowd clapped and screamed in delight.

"Return to us, Dragon Rider," Nagasi called out.

Abylar gained some height and then turned southwest, toward Elvyn, flying even higher. Bakari closed his eyes and merged with Abylar. He peered down and ahead at the receding countryside and toward the looming mountains. More peaks sat covered in snow than when they had first arrived, almost two weeks previous—a reminder that fall in the Mahli Mountains would turn into winter here sooner than in Alaris.

On the way to Lor'l, the capital city of Elvyn, Bak would first return to Celestar, a city that, historically, had sat on Elvyn lands. But, when the barrier came up, Celestar was caught on the side with Alaris. Then it became the home of the guardians, who had given their life energy throughout the years to the Orb. The Orb was also Abylar's egg and—unknown to most people—it was what had supplied the barrier its power for one hundred and fifty years.

Bakari realized he would never tire of riding on the back of Abylar. With a few graceful flaps of the dragon's wings, they coasted on the wind's currents for miles before having to flap again.

Does it bother you to have me on your back? Bakari asked Abylar.

To be the carrier of a dragon rider is a grand honor. Abylar puffed out his chest as they flew. *I've never known anything different.*

Bakari sighed and decided to admit his apprehensions to Abylar. *I just don't know what is expected of me, Abylar. Two months ago, I was a scholar sitting in a library, researching, studying, and preparing to pass on my knowledge to others. How can I be a dragon rider?*

Look down, Bakari, Abylar instructed.

Bakari did as his dragon requested and focused his eyes down at the astonishing sight. Flying over the peaks of the mountains, he spotted a few animals just below the snow line.

How many other people do you know who have seen these mountains from this perspective? Abylar asked, his voice deep and smooth in Bakari's mind.

No one, Bakari said.

How many have ridden on a dragon?

Only Alli, besides me.

How many have bonded with a dragon?

No one, Bakari said again. *What are you getting at, Abylar? Why so many questions? You are beginning to sound like Erryl.*

Abylar gave a deep laugh. *Now, that boy I like. He was the only one to hear me when I needed to find you.*

The questions, Abylar?

For one with such a scholarly mind, you are becoming quite impatient, Dragon Rider.

Bakari sighed and kept his response to himself.

What I meant, by all these questions, is to point out that you are already a dragon rider, one who has done things greater than any other wizard in Alaris or in her neighboring lands, Abylar boasted. *Together, you and I will do great things. Don't fear anything. I am here to protect you.*

Bakari laughed. *I'm glad you think so highly of us, Abylar.*

Crossing over the mountain range and then down over the

edge of the Elvyn Forest, Bakari soon spotted the gleaming white city of Celestar. Circling the city twice, they then landed out on a sizable field north of the city, between the inner and the outer walls. They were met by a stream of people, guardians and protectors, with Erryl and Wizard Gorn leading the charge. Bakari climbed down from Abylar and was instantly taken into a warm embrace from Erryl, a young guardian. The boy, hardly younger than Bakari, had an innocent curiosity about the world.

"Erryl, it's nice to see you again," Bakari said.

Looking at Abylar, Erryl exclaimed, "He has grown so big! What does he eat? Where have you been?"

The last time Erryl had seen the dragon was right after the beautiful beast had hatched. Erryl had been instrumental in that event: leaving Celestar and finding Bakari and leading him to the Orb—which happened to be Abylar's egg.

Bakari grinned at the sheltered young man. "Still full of questions, I see."

Erryl's fair face blushed, and he rubbed his hand over his short-cropped hair in embarrassment.

"Keep it up. That's what will make you a valued scholar one day," Bakari remarked before turning to Gorn. "How are things here, Wizard?"

"Some elves stationed southeast of here, in a border village, provided a few men to help us. But I fear we don't have enough if Kanzar attacks." The large battle wizard lowered his voice as he added, "Breelyn and Alair left over ten days ago, and we haven't heard anything from them or from the help they promised to send from Silla, the closest Elvyn city of any size."

Gorn, an elderly and powerful battle wizard, had broken ranks with Kanzar and his wizards and had guided Alli to Celestar at about the same time that Bakari had arrived to study the barrier and the Orb. Bakari still didn't know him too well, but Gorn remained a formidable level four wizard and seemed to know how to fortify the city.

"Breelyn mentioned that Silla was only a few days away," Bakari said. "Help should have arrived by now. Make sure all the guardians are trained." Bakari furrowed his eyebrows.

Gorn nodded his head.

Then Bakari continued, "Kanzar has taken Cassian, and the Chief Judge is in Orr. Also, Roland is now running the Citadel."

The broad-shouldered wizard laughed at that. "The boy sure does have aspirations, doesn't he?"

Bakari smiled and inwardly hoped that Roland's aspirations wouldn't run too high before the political climate of the land was figured out. "I am going to Lor'l to meet with the king and to search for the next egg and its dragon rider."

"That's a tall order, Bak." Gorn smiled and gave him a look of warning. "But, remember, not everyone will be happy to see a dragon rider."

"Don't I know it?" Bakari laughed and then told Gorn and Erryl about his greeting in Mahli and the situation with Kolo.

Someone called to Gorn, and he dismissed himself for a moment. Bakari pulled Erryl to the side. After taking a few steps away, he spoke to his friend.

"Erryl, while Abylar is growing, he still uses the life force of those that gave of it so freely here in Celestar. So he still has a connection to you. Once he grows more, he won't need it. But, please, in the meantime—keep everyone safe."

Erryl nodded his head.

"Also," Bakari continued, "I brought you something." He dug into his robes and pulled out a small book. The leather cover was worn and ancient.

Erryl's eyes lit up. "What is that, Bak?"

"I know you have been schooled in many languages, Erryl. The knowledge you possess made your life force stronger." Bakari ran his hands over the smooth leather cover of the book. "This book holds a prophecy—a special prophecy of the Mahli people, but one that might affect us all. Can you study it? When I return, let me know what you understand from it."

Bakari handed the small book to Erryl, who held it reverently. "Oh, thank you!" His light blue eyes widened. His uncorrupted smile was all the thanks Bakari needed.

"I will also want you to tell me who you think the prophecy is about," Bakari said. Then, pulling himself back on top of Abylar, he waved at the gathering. "I will be back soon."

Lifting back up into the sky, they took off over the Elvyn Forest to resume their journey. Bakari watched in amazement, noticing how incredibly huge the trees grew as they moved deeper into Elvyn.

That evening, they landed on the western banks of Emerald Lake. There was a small patch of land without any trees, just big enough for Abylar to land in. Beside that, the forest stood thick with trees as big around as a small cabin and reaching hundreds of feet into the air. Their branches intermixed, letting very little light down to the ground. The lake itself felt cool to the touch and reflected shades of bright green and orange as the sun slid behind the trees to the west. There was also plenty of water and food here for Abylar.

From a distance, Bakari saw a group of elves, but they refrained from coming closer. He bet that, by the next day, news of the sighting of a dragon would be all over the land.

Settling down on a blanket next to Abylar, Bakari leaned against his immense head. The dragon's yellow eyes peered at him with intelligence and interest. Without thinking, Bak ran his hands back and forth over the dragon's thick blue hide. Then, staring off over the lake as darkness settled in, he let out a great sigh.

What is it, Dragon Rider? Abylar asked.

This is the most peaceful place I have been in since leaving Cassian, almost two months ago. I had thought I was going on a short trip with the Chief Judge to the Citadel and was excited to dig into the books there and find out more about the barrier.

And now, you know more about the barrier than most do, Abylar said, his voice deep and full of understanding.

But, the more I know, the less I feel like I know what to do. Bakari closed his eyes and tried to relax.

Abylar shifted, bringing his tail up around Bakari. *That's how it is with knowledge. The more we know, the more we realize there is so much more to still learn about. Alaris may seem big to you, but think of all the kingdoms in the West, then those in the East, then in the entire world. We could spend a lifetime studying and still not scratch the surface.*

Bakari yawned. *How do you know so much, Abylar? You are barely more than a baby.*

Abylar growled, low and deep. *I am not a baby.*

I didn't mean it like that. Bakari chuckled. *You are less than a month old.*

That is where you are mistaken, young wizard, Abylar said. *I have been out of my shell for only a month, yes. But I was a dragon embryo for much longer. One hundred and fifty years ago, I was placed in Celestar to power the barrier. But, even before then, I was a young, dormant egg. It has been hundreds of years since I first came into being.*

Bakari sat up straighter and opened his eyes. *And all that time you were learning? But how?*

Not all learning is through reading, Scholar.

Abylar had taught Bakari things he had never supposed.

I learn through my spirit. I feel what others around me know, take it in, and remember it. I remember all I see and hear. Much like you, Bakari.

Bakari nodded his head. Ever since he was young, anything he read or saw or heard he could remember clearly. Sometimes it took him a while to access things from his mind. But they were always there. This was the way he had first found out that he could bond with other animals.

We dragons contain the power of the spirit, the power to bind, Abylar continued.

The fourth power? Bakari jumped up off the ground. *I know there were rumors of a fourth power. The power of a dragon is the power of the spirit!*

Yes. It binds all other powers. Using the power of the spirit with earth, mind, and heart together can bring about incredible spells. Abylar stretched his neck up into the air and glanced down at Bakari. *That is how the barrier was created.*

This information was incredible. *Is it only dragons that hold this rare power?*

No. Many other magical creatures hold it. The Cremelino horse and the phoenix are two such other creatures with this power.

Bakari gazed up at the star-filled night. *There is so much to learn.*

Ah, yes, there is. And, as a wizard—and now a dragon rider—you will have many, many years to learn it.

Bakari walked closer to Abylar, lay down, and put his hand on the dragon's giant leg. This touch instantly strengthened the bond, and communicating with the dragon felt like Bakari was having a conversation with himself.

You mean, as a dragon rider, I will live even longer than a normal wizard? Wizards tended to live over a hundred years. There were a few still alive who remembered Alaris before the barrier. *And now I might live even longer than they have.*

If we keep you safe and you don't get yourself killed while bringing peace to the land. Abylar chuckled, and a small puff of fire erupted from his nostrils.

Hey! You almost burned me. I thought it was your job to protect me, Abylar.

Moving a paw and pulling Bakari in tighter, Abylar brought his head down onto the ground. *That it is, Dragon Rider. My sole purpose is to protect you and to see that you live for hundreds of years.*

Bakari snuggled closer to his dragon and drank in the peace and love coming from their bond. It took him a while to fall asleep. But, when he did, he slept soundly with few dreams.

CHAPTER SIX

B reelyn Mier stood in front of a tall, gold-bordered mirror in the governor's compound in the city of Silla. The tree-city was the northernmost major city in Elvyn, a kingdom located just to the east of Alaris. Even though Silla had been a minor city of the elves throughout the centuries, one hundred and fifty years ago, as the magic barrier around Alaris came into being, the city became more important. The governor appointed a barrier watcher in Silla, a role that the city and its people had taken seriously through the years.

Breelyn brushed her long, silky hair—twenty strokes on each side, as was her habit. Her blond hair and upturned ears, characteristics of her race, were only in contrast to the desert elves, who lived in Mallek, in the southernmost part of Elvyn. Their hair grew red.

She briefly wondered what she would look like with red hair. The thought made her smile. She peered into the mirror at her clear, blue eyes, and her thoughts changed from her hair to her mission and the disturbing news she had brought of the barrier coming down.

"Protector," called a voice from the other side of the door, "your escort is here to take you to the governor's table. Are you ready?"

"I will be with you shortly." Breelyn finished the last three strokes through her hair and then put the brush carefully in its place, on the small table in front of the mirror.

King Arrowyn had sent her, one of his five protectors, to perform a random circuit of their kingdom's defenses. Every year, each of the protectors would travel around the borders of Elvyn to help ensure their safety. Extra time was always spent on the western border, the one that had been separated from Alaris by only the magical barrier. This year, she was chosen for this incredible honor. Every year, the protectors looked specifically for any weakness in the barrier.

During her circuit, she and her guard, Alair, were ambushed and captured. If it were not for the barrier weakening briefly and the young Celestar guardian Erryl untying her, Breelyn didn't know what would have happened.

What did happen was that she had helped Erryl find the wizard Bakari. From there, events unfolded quickly. The Orb, which powered the barrier around Alaris, was shown to be a dragon egg, and that dragon had emerged and had bonded with Bakari, resulting in the first dragon rider in over one hundred and fifty years.

She stepped out of the room with a flowing, white robe over her white leather clothing. Her almond-shaped eyes and pale pink lips were the only color accenting her attire. She left the tree that her guest room sat in and walked upon a high bridge to the tallest tree of the grove in Silla.

Upon entering the great tree, it took Breelyn some time to climb even higher, toward the top. The living, wood railings felt good against the palms of her hands. She had missed being up in the trees during her ride from the capital city, when most of her nights had been spent on the ground.

She turned a corner around the trunk, and there stood the

grand ballroom, which had been built overlooking most of the other trees of the northwestern Elvyn Forest. Breelyn's heart sang with joy at the sight. She breathed in deeply and relaxed herself before entering the room.

Elves are big on ceremony, and so, even though she carried important news to share, they would first dine together. A reception had been organized in her honor. The protectors came as an extension of the king himself. Since the beginning of their race, the elves had hailed the protectors as special men and women among their people. Their kings lived long and were well loved, and a protector's job, first and foremost, was to protect the king and his kingdom.

As she entered, the crowd rose to their feet, though she saw a few of the older elves doing it slower than they should. She tried not to furrow her eyebrows in frustration. Candles and lamps, along with a row of mage lights, made the room bright and cheery. Bright ribbons in blue, yellow, and pink hung from the ceiling, and the light wooden walls had been shined to reflect all of the brilliance of the grain in the wood. Polished wooden tables sat in the middle of the floor, with a few dozen men and women standing behind their chairs. So Breelyn made her way to the front table.

Governor Ellian bowed low, but not for as long as protocol dictated he should to a representative from the king. Breelyn noticed how portly he had become since the last time she had traveled to the city, years ago. It was not proper for members of the Elvyn race to let themselves go to such extremes. He also seemed tired, and his smile did not reach his eyes.

Before sending Breelyn on her journey to check out the barrier, King Soliel had voiced his concerns about whether the leaders in Silla would take Breelyn seriously or not. She had insisted on going, though, and he had agreed that she was the best protector for the job. After going through the barrier, meeting Bakari, and seeing the dragon, she had definitely gotten more than she had anticipated on her trip. Now, speaking to the governor of Silla would be her last stop before returning back and reporting to the king all that had happened.

The elderly governor motioned with his meaty hand for Breelyn to sit at his right. Once she was seated, the rest of the crowd followed suit. Then they waited for Breelyn to take the first bite.

Breelyn relaxed and savored the moment as a small breeze stirred the bangs of her hair. Being only thirty years old—quite young in Elvyn culture—she actually enjoyed this attention and the lifestyle of a protector. It gave her a chance to use her talents and growing magical powers for the good of her beloved land.

Elvyn was looked upon highly by all of the other neighboring countries on the Western Continent. Their kingdom enjoyed free trade with Tillimot and Quentis to the south, all the territories to the north, including as far as Gildan and, sometimes, even the port of Mar, in the Realm, with periodic trips by sea to North and South Solshi. Now, she supposed, new trade agreements with Alaris would be forthcoming – including new land routes to many of those other kingdoms.

She motioned to the servant standing at her side, and he

poured her drink carefully into a tall glass. It was a beautiful red color and had swirled into the glass, delightfully reflecting the room's light. She guessed it to be a blend of grape and pomegranate. She took the cool glass in her slender fingers and brought it to her lips, enjoying how the fresh juice ran down her throat.

She lowered it with a smile. She had been correct. She tasted the slight tang of pomegranate, most likely grown in the southern region between the Elvyn Forest and the desert of Mallek. As she touched the glass back down on the table, she signaled the others to proceed.

The meal was delicious, consisting of a broad variety of fruits, vegetables, meats, and breads. Small platters of pork, chicken, and local fowl sat around on the tables, but Breelyn did not touch these. She had found that meat did not settle well with her and made her feel sluggish and tired.

"Protector, how is our beloved king?" asked an elderly man a few seats down from Breelyn.

"He is concerned about the barrier. I am traveling back to see what his recommendations are, now that it is down." Breelyn understood why he had asked about their king's health, as the king had not been well in recent months. However, she had purposefully avoided answering the question and had gone right to the heart of the matter.

The man, the chief watcher in Silla, scrunched up his dark eyebrows at her answer, but proceeded anyway. Even while sitting down, he appeared tall. His hair was graying, but it still hung down long on his back.

"He should have no concern there," the chief watcher

said. "We will continue to watch the border, whether there is a barrier or not."

"You?" Breelyn asked, letting her anger show. "The barrier has been weakening for quite some time, and we had not heard anything in Lor'l from your watchers. You have been derelict in your duties here. So I will recommend that the king send his own troops to protect us along the border."

The chief watcher's eyes popped open wider. He glanced at the governor, who had suddenly taken an interest in the conversation. A few of the other men at the table looked briefly at one another. Breelyn continued to eat pieces of a delicious, juicy melon, pretending she did not see the worry in their eyes.

"We will discuss this in the morning, when the full council of the city meets," the governor said, trying to steer the conversation away from the barrier. "You can make a full report then."

"I will expect the chief watcher to also have a full report ready. I will hear why we did not hear about this sooner."

The chief watcher was new to the role. After an accident happened to the previous watcher, earlier in the year, this man had been named as the chief watcher, a position of power and honor among the northern elves. He glared hard at her now, with a look that spelled trouble.

Breelyn also noticed the cold stares directed at her as she leisurely finished eating her dinner. But she wasn't going to let these rough border elves bother her. The king was correct to suspect that something was not quite right in Silla. They had been left on their own too long.

Lor'l, the capital of Elvyn, was so immense that they

sometimes forgot about their northern cousins, who didn't live as long as they did. So, even though Arrowyn had been king since the barrier around Alaris went up, the governor in Silla had changed four times since then and the chief watcher more times than that. Unlike the rest of Elvyn, the elves here closer to the border lived little longer than their human neighbors.

The rest of the guests filed away shortly, and the servants began clearing away the platters. Each of the governor's council excused themselves, one by one, until only the governor and Breelyn were left.

Then the governor stood. "Protector, would you like to retire and rest now, after your long journey?"

"I think I will spend some time in your library." Breelyn excused herself and left the dining room.

Alair, her guard, fell into step beside her as soon as she had exited the doorway. He was much older than she, and his dark hair was speckled with gray, but his blue eyes still appeared bright. He was dressed darkly and moved smoothly and silently next to her.

"Not necessarily a forthcoming bunch," Breelyn said.

"Did you find out anything more, Protector?" Alair asked, his eyes constantly scanning to take in any potential dangers around them.

Breelyn turned aside and asked a nearby servant for directions to the library and then turned back to Alair. "They are hiding something. I know it. The way they regarded one another when they thought I wasn't watching. But..." she paused as she opened the door to the library.

"But you are always watching," Alair said, finishing the

sentence.

Breelyn smiled. Alair knew her too well. "They did not seem surprised about the falling of the barrier or even concerned. I surmise that they were behind the attack on us at the barrier."

Soon, a young girl in the library inquired if the two visitors needed help with finding something.

"Yes," Breelyn said. "I would like to see some works written during the occupation."

"Oh," the young girl said, raising one eyebrow in surprise, and motioned her to follow.

The library in Silla was small, compared to the one in Lor'l. Breelyn remembered roaming the library tree in Lor'l as she had waited for her father, who was on the council of Elvyn in those years. She specifically liked reading the stories from other countries, which had intrigued her, especially the stories of dragons and of the prophecy that, one day, a new dragon king would return, who could bind all the kingdoms in peace. She laughed to herself about that. The last mention of dragons was written before their lifetimes.

This library only contained two small rooms. But, with it being in an area that was an integral part of the barrier battle, she figured its rooms might contain some additional books about that time frame. The library in Lor'l, for some reason, held very little information about that great battle and the time of occupation. She had surmised that it was an embarrassment, somehow, to their nation to have been partially occupied by the selfish and vicious wizards of Alaris. For, she had noticed that most people tried to ignore her whenever she had asked about it, even the king.

Breelyn took a few books and spread them out on a small table that seemed to be growing from the wall. Then Alair asked to be excused. She saw that he would become restless waiting for her, so she instructed him to talk to some of the servants in the castle and see what else he might hear that would be useful for her meeting the next day.

Alair walked silently out of the room, as was his usual habit as a protector's guard, and seemed to disappear into the surrounding evening shadows.

Breelyn turned her head down, and started reading bits and pieces as she flipped through each book. But she learned nothing new in the first few books.

As the night grew late, Breelyn had to replace the light from the worn-down candles with a mage light of her own. The amount of energy the light took would hardly deplete her. Besides, she was now a level three mage, and she'd been told that, after a few years as a protector and once her powers were honed better, she could be a level four. And, her greatest source of power came from the earth and the nature surrounding her anyway.

Hours later, Breelyn put her hand to her mouth to stifle a yawn and closed the smooth, leather-bound book she had been reading. She needed some sleep in order to have a clear head the next day as she met with the local council. So she left the library, trying to remember which direction her room was in.

CHAPTER SEVEN

Leisurely walking toward her room, Breelyn breathed in the evening air. Before she had walked too far, a young page came up to her and handed her a note. His hair sat disheveled on his head, and he appeared to have been woken up to run this errand. The note stated that the chief watcher wanted to meet with her tonight to give her a more detailed report about the status of the barrier.

It sounded plausible to her for him to want to do this, but something in her senses screamed a warning. Yet, to refuse would seem undiplomatic. So she reached her mind out for Alair, but she couldn't find him.

"That's odd," she whispered out loud.

"Did you say something, Protector?" questioned the young boy. He must have only been ten or so, and he craned his neck up to look at her.

"Have you seen my guard?"

"No, Protector. Would you like me to find him?"

"No. That's fine." Breelyn nodded to him, remembering herself at that age: so eager to do anything to please those above her. "Just take me to the chief watcher." She was confident in her own abilities, and Alair could take care of himself. Besides, the chief watcher wouldn't dare attack a protector in the heart of the city.

They wound their way over and through many branches, bridges, and rooms on the way. She tried to keep track of their path but was wary she wouldn't be able to find her way again. She knew that Alair would have been able to, and, once again, she worried about not being able to contact him. Sometimes he did shut down their mind link to concentrate more fully on something. So he would find her when he was finished. He always did.

The page stopped at a sizable, ornate wooden door in a grouping of rooms a few trees away from the governor's complex. Two men stood guard in front of it. The young boy bowed to Breelyn and left with a smile.

"Guards, where is your master? I am to meet him here."

"He will be along shortly, Young Protector. He invites you to wait in this room until his arrival."

She had raised her eyebrows at the mention of her age once again. It was a definite insult, among a people that lived so long, to be called *young*. It denoted being immature and foolish. Being from Lor'l and being a mage, she should most likely live to be well over a hundred years old.

So Breelyn stood up as straight as she could, held her tongue from firing back insults, and, with forceful words commanded them, "Tell your chief that I will wait for him in this room until I have counted to two hundred…and then I am leaving."

The guard's eyes opened wide at her command, and one left to find his master, while the other guard led her into the room. Internally, she berated herself for sounding so childish in her ultimatum.

Lamps already lit inside gave an eerie glow to the room as she entered. She gasped as she noticed the deadness of the wood and turned toward the guard to ask the meaning of it. But the guard was already outside the room, closing the door.

She pushed her magic out to stop the door, but nothing happened. It closed with his soft touch and left her staring at a room of white-colored wood. She had never seen anything like it in her life. She could feel the wrongness of it. The room was pure white and held no life. These trees had been forced into an unnatural form. A few trees, like birch and aspen, were white on the outside, but there wasn't any tree whose wood grew pure white throughout.

Breelyn pushed out with her powers again and only felt them being pushed back against her from the white walls. She couldn't believe that she had let this happen *again*. In her anxiousness to return to the king, she had let her guard down.

Thinking of the king brought a quick blush to her face: not for the king himself but for his son. She glanced around and tried not to let panic take over. Her powers had always been a part of her since she was young. She remembered moving small objects and opening doors at as young as three years old. The power of earth was strong in her family and worked best on moving objects. She had only been without her power one other time. And that was a few weeks ago, when she and Alair had been attacked at the barrier, before it had come down.

She screamed for help but was sure nothing would be heard outside of the room. The walls seemed to be thick wood, which absorbed any sound from within. She pounded on the walls and the door, but nothing gave.

Anger welled up inside her, for she knew she should have trusted her instincts about this meeting and found Alair first.

What would King Arrowyn think of her after all this? She really was, as the guard had taunted, young and foolish.

A table and two chairs sat in the corner of the small room. She took three steps to reach them. She ran her hand over them and sensed nothing: nothing living, nothing she recognized. Their life force had been tampered with.

She sat down to think, wondering how long they would keep her here and for what reason. It must have something to do with the barrier. Then the door swung open, and, before she could move toward it, the chief watcher himself entered and closed the door behind him.

"Did I arrive quickly enough for you, my dear?" he asked, mocking her with a short bow. His black cape swirled around his tall frame.

"How dare you lock me up in here, in this, this, abomination." She spread her hands out toward the walls of the room. "What have you done?"

"I simply cannot have you traipsing around Elvyn, telling others about the barrier, Protector."

"What do you mean? Watching and protecting the barrier was your responsibility: the duty of every elf in Silla." Breelyn paced the short room, trying to figure out what to do. She could attack him physically. Even without her magical powers, it would be a close fight. She had to be more agile and quicker than him, even if he was stronger. The guards would open the door to check on them eventually.

"You are right, Protector; it was the responsibility of every elf in Silla to ensure that the barrier never fell or, at the very least, to inform the king when it did. However, that does not apply to me, you see." The arrogant chief watcher moved smoothly around the room.

"And, why would that not apply to the chief watcher himself?"

There was something about him that she just couldn't figure out, something different. This tormented room took the power out of her senses. She felt blind and deaf. She had lived with the power for so long, and now, with its loss, everything appeared so dull. Colors and sounds were muted and plain in comparison. She wondered if this was how humans lived.

No wonder they don't live very long.

"Because I am not an elf, I am human." The chief watcher leered at her with his white teeth. Then he reached up and took off a small portion from the top of his ears—a piece that made his ears look pointed.

Breelyn gasped at the implications of a human being in disguise as the chief watcher. "But how? You do not seem to be from Tillimot or even Quentis. Your skin is too light." She knew that, even though humans traded and communicated with the other countries on the continent, very few ever chose to actually live in Elvyn for any length of time. With the elves' long lives and magical natures, it was too uncomfortable for others. "The only country you resemble is…" She stopped and shook her head in dismay.

"You have guessed correctly, my dear. My ancestry is from Alaris. In fact, my line goes back to two of Alaris's wizards— ones that lived right before the barrier went up, generations ago. I am also a wizard."

Breelyn sat down, drained and tired, as if she had used up

her magic—but that wasn't how her magic worked. All of this was very confusing. *How had the chief watcher's family stayed hidden this entire time?*

"What do you want from me?" she asked.

"*Want?* I want nothing from you, except for you to be out of the way while we finish what has been started, with the barrier coming down."

"You have no right to keep me here or to be a watcher. And what does the barrier have to do with this?"

"Why, my dear, I am going to let Alaris in and let them wipe out your smug and arrogant race once and for all, something that should have been done one hundred and fifty years ago."

She jumped at him then, trying to gouge out his eyes with her nails. At the last possible moment, he somehow moved just enough to make her miss. Her fingernails dug into the skin of his right cheek, drawing a deep line from below his right eye to the corner of his lip. He reached his oversized hands toward her, but she kicked up strong and knocked them away.

"What did you do with the last chief watcher?" she demanded.

"I killed him, just like I am going to kill you." She saw him automatically reach for his power, but then his eyes bulged wide. His anger had impeded his thinking.

"You forgot where you were, didn't you? I am guessing that if I can't access my powers here, neither can you." She swirled around in her long robes so fast she became a blur. Her leg came out and caught him in the neck, knocking him to the ground with a loud thud.

Breelyn kicked her foot down at the impostor to make sure he stayed there, but he brought his hand up and grabbed her ankle. He yanked it up hard, pulling a muscle in her calf. She screamed and went down instead, hitting her head against one of the solid wooden chairs. She felt a tingling in her body, and then her eyes began to blur.

"No!" she screamed again and tried to reach for her power. She pushed all she could into it, trying to break the barrier of the white wood. But all she felt was it pushing back, and this weakened her. "What is this wood?" she cried in desperation.

"It took years to form." The watcher stood up and moved over to where she lay on the floor. "And much Elvyn blood. It required the removal of all life and form from the wood. It blocks all magic. It is not living, but dead!"

Breelyn could see the self-confidence in his eyes. He thought he'd won. But Breelyn hadn't become one of the king's five protectors for nothing. Also, she had one more power available to her. She pushed back her sleeve, where her protector's amulet was attached to her upper arm. About three inches wide and made of a silver metal that came from the bottom of Emerald Lake, the amulet was more than mere jewelry. Only six existed in the world, and the king and each of his five protectors held one: forged over a thousand years ago.

It was a relatively simple thing to use, although Breelyn had been directed to use the amulet only in dire emergencies to protect the king himself. They had been used once, at the end of the war, one hundred and fifty years earlier, to save Arrowyn, who was only a young prince then. One of the protectors had been with Arrowyn's father, the king, when he had died. The protector had called forth the power of the amulet to protect the king's son and preserve his own life.

Even though the king's life was not directly in danger at this moment, Breelyn justified her using it because of the fall of the barrier and the chance that the elves could be attacked before they were prepared to respond.

Breelyn turned part of the bracelet a quarter turn and then called forth the amulet's power. She pulled her mind inward as much as possible, ignoring the chief watcher for the moment, as she concentrated hard and tried to get past the white wood barrier. It began to crumble slowly, in her mind.

Then the power of the other protectors' amulets flowed into her. She pushed harder and had almost broken through the magic block, when the chief watcher slammed into her. This impact broke her concentration, and she felt herself weaken.

She knew that she was fading and fainting. If she didn't succeed in the next few moments, she would die, the king would never learn that the barrier had fallen, and Elvyn would be plunged into war once again. So she gathered all the willpower she had developed in her *young* thirty years.

If this last effort didn't work, she knew that she would burn herself out. She began to feel the strength and thoughts of the other protectors and of the king himself. She also sensed Alair, her guard, once again. So she called to him in her mind, and he responded.

The chief watcher smiled as he pounded Breelyn's head against the hard floor. The power of the amulet filled Breelyn, and, with one final effort, she struck out with it, pushing out all the power she had accumulated through the amulet.

The look of triumph on the chief watcher's arrogant face was soon replaced as a sudden shock slammed his body back against the white walls. Blood gushed from his scalp, flowing down the right side of his thin face, and droplets of red stood out in stark contrast on the white walls.

Breelyn stood and pointed all her anger and power at him. White-hot fire erupted from the amulet on her arm and burned into the man, scorching his chest and engulfing his body. He screamed as he tried to get up and run out of the door.

Breelyn jumped, soaring over him, and sent blazing white fire back at him and into the middle of the accursed room, burning away the white wood. Then, just as the ceiling began to collapse, she saw the chief watcher point at her, and wizard fire left his fingertips before his body crumpled. The magical barrier of the room had been broken, so she jumped aside, and the fire blasted open the door, hitting a guard outside of the room.

The lone remaining guard drew his sword and advanced toward her. Before she could do anything, Alair jumped on him from behind and, with two hard hits, knocked him unconscious.

"Are you all right, Protector?"

"No, I am not all right, Alair. These people tried to lock me up and kill me." A glow still surrounded the amulet, and she glared with burning anger and immense power. "It is treason, punishable by death, to touch a protector in this way." She stepped out of the room, gathering more power, and then released it back behind her. The room continued to collapse as white-hot fire engulfed the entire area—and the chief watcher's traitorous body now lay dead beneath the rubble.

Alair shielded his eyes with his hand and grabbed Breelyn. She fought him only momentarily, but then let him pull her away. They ran with rapid strides across a wooden bridge and down a flight of wooden stairs as the fire grew, spreading toward a nearby tree. Then alarms sounded, and they heard men running toward where they had just escaped.

Breelyn, still in a daze, turned around. She had to protect the other trees.

"No, Protector, we must leave." Alair grabbed Breelyn around the waist and then jumped. Free-falling in the air, he eyed a vine and then grabbed it, swinging them wildly over to another tree. From there, he grabbed another vine, and they slid down it together to a smaller tree. And the sounds of others, rushing to the fire, faded into the background as she and Alair entered the dense forest.

Soon they found themselves on the ground in the middle of a grove of trees. It was late, well past midnight. The sounds of night insects and of scurrying nocturnal animals, moving away from the fire, filled the air in front of them.

Alair let go of Breelyn and fell onto his knees, breathing hard. He peered up at his charge, and Breelyn replied with a glare of fierce anger. He had been protecting her his entire life, and she knew he loved her as a daughter. Her rage at him for the moment was matched only by her sense of duty to her king and kingdom.

She remembered how, as she had grown, her powers had multiplied tremendously, until she had become the youngest protector in a thousand years. She loved her powers and enjoyed the pomp and circumstance of this position. But her judgments were just, her treatment of others was fair, and her ability to do the right thing was always perfect—until now.

"The trees…" Breelyn breathed heavily. "Why did you take me away?"

"Breelyn, there is nothing you can do. You set the place on fire. It doesn't matter if you are a protector or not, that is a crime with severe punishments. You may be able to justify it to the king, but here, with these people, they would have taken you into custody or, worse yet, slain you."

She glared at him but said nothing.

Alair stood back up and stepped toward her. "Well, they would have tried to take you into custody, but I would guess that they would find you much more elusive than they think."

Her resolve finally crumbled, and she ran the few remaining steps to Alair, burying her face in his broad, strong chest. "They took my powers, Alair. You don't know what that's like. It was like they stole my soul."

Alair stroked her smooth hair with his gentle touch and let her cry.

A few minutes later, Breelyn backed away from him and wiped her eyes. She lifted a hand up to the amulet. It was still warm.

"I will find a messenger to send to the king," Alair noted.

Still rubbing the amulet, Breelyn communicated with the others and then felt the last traces of the four protectors and the king leave her.

"They already know," she said. "I told them everything through the amulet." Alair handed her his waterskin, and she drank deeply. She handed it back with a smile. "Thank you." She knew that she had lost control at the end and that only Alair's clearheaded thinking had allowed them to escape safely.

He only nodded. Protecting her was his job, and he took it seriously. She was the king's protector, but Alair was hers.

"We must get away fast. They will be following us soon," Alair said. "I fear that the governor is in on this also."

"I think you are right," Breelyn said.

Together, they began trotting south, out of Silla. Soon they found a small road, leading east, back to Lor'l.

CHAPTER EIGHT

It would be only a short flight for Bakari and Abylar from Emerald Lake to the Elvyn capital city of Lor'l. Bakari's feet dangled over the sides as he held on with one hand to the strap around the dragon's sturdy neck, which had now grown larger around than a full-sized man. From Emerald Lake, the dragon flew out over the Blue Sea. It was the first time that either of them had seen the ocean. They were both mesmerized by its enormity.

"Does it ever end?" Bakari asked out loud.

There are other lands across the sea, Abylar mentioned. *The eastern kingdoms, where all magic started.*

Bakari filed this information away for later. It could lead to an interesting conversation with his dragon.

A gleaming city, partially built on the ground and partly up in the trees, soon appeared before them. Elves standing outside by the sea began pointing upward, then scattered. By the time Abylar found a place to land on the shore, a generous number of elves had begun gathering around.

Bakari noticed their similarity to Breelyn, one of the Elvyn king's protectors, who had helped Bakari find Celestar. For the most part, their hair was long and hung straight to either side: both brown and blond. White or gray robes hung from their lean frames. Their skin was pale from the amount of time they spent under the enormous trees they predominantly lived in.

Abylar flapped his wings a few times to settle himself

properly.

The crowd grew quiet, then a lone voice rang out, "Hail the dragon rider."

"Hail the dragon rider," the crowd echoed, and then they bowed themselves reverently to the ground.

Not prepared for such a response, Bakari stood in awe. The people of Mahli had indeed been welcoming, but the respect and honor the elves showed him brought a wash of emotions over him. No one had ever shown him such courtesy and deference before. So he wasn't sure what to do.

Abylar moved his neck around, prompting Bakari to climb down off of the immense dragon. Walking a few steps into the growing crowd, he bade them arise. "My name is Bakari. Thank you for your welcome. I come to speak to your king. The barrier is down."

The people clapped and roared welcoming comments to him, though murmurs about the barrier's demise subdued their cheers. Through the crowd walked a man with authority. The crowd parted for him and nodded their heads with respect. He appeared to be in his forties, with a few lines of wrinkles on his forehead and around his eyes. He wore a light blue robe and brought forth a thin but strong arm to shake Bakari's hand.

"I am Lanwaithian Soliel, son of King Arrowyn Soliel. Greetings, Dragon Rider. It has been many years since a rider has blessed this land."

Bakari nodded his head but was tongue-tied. These elves seemed so formal, and the young wizard didn't know what to say. A low growl from his dragon prompted his reply.

"And this is Abylar."

Lanwaithian turned to Abylar, and a broad smile covered his face, making him look even younger. He turned to Bakari. "May I?" He nodded his head toward the dragon.

Bakari came out of his stupor. "Oh, yes, sir. Of course, you may touch him." Prince Lanwaithian walked forward and reverently touched the blue dragon.

"I can feel his spirit. He is strong for one so young."

"Abylar is pleased to meet such a mighty elf." Bakari walked up next to the man.

The prince turned his head to Bakari. "You can speak with him, can't you?"

"Yes," Bakari said. "Through the bond, we can speak in our minds to each other."

"That is because he has the power of spirit," informed Lanwaithian.

"So he has told me." Bakari nodded his head. "The power to bind."

"A very powerful magic," the prince remarked. "Many mystical creatures hold the fourth power."

"I look forward to learning more about these powers, Lanwaithian."

"You can call me Lan." The prince removed his hand from the dragon and smiled again. "All the knowledge we hold here is yours, Dragon Rider. Nothing would we withhold from someone as mighty as to bond with a dragon."

Bakari reeled for a moment. He could hardly imagine how much knowledge the libraries of the long-lived elves would contain. It was a treasure beyond value that he had been offered.

"I am most grateful for that offer, Lan. We are only here for a short time now, to discuss with your king the doings from Alaris and the other kingdoms, and then we will be off to find another egg and another rider."

The crowd began to disperse. And, with a signal from Bakari, Abylar rose back into the air with a silent thought that he was going to hunt for food but would be close enough to return when Bakari needed him again. *When you are finished here, we will be going northwest, deep into the forest, to find the next egg,* the dragon said to Bakari's mind as he flew out of sight.

Lan led Bakari through a small city built up to the edge of the Blue Sea.

"Why do you have buildings on the land here?" Bakari asked. "I thought elves lived in forest cities."

Lan smiled. "We do live mostly in the trees, but we also trade with other lands, to the north and the south, and they are not as comfortable with climbing our great trees to discuss business."

"That makes sense. The trees do look a little daunting." Bakari tried to observe and then catalog everything into his mind.

"This is where the ancient city of Lor'l begins." Lan motioned ahead as they entered the ancient Elvyn Forest.

"You must have strong legs to climb so much."

Lan laughed good-naturedly. Stopping beneath one of the larger trees, Lan motioned Bakari to a certain spot. Above them, a wooden platform was lowered, held in place by a system of vines.

"We have other means than climbing."

Bakari let out a relieved breath. The two stood on the platform and were pulled hundreds of feet up into the air. Soon they came to a stop. Bakari looked down and was surprised that he didn't feel dizzy.

Lan could probably tell what he was thinking. "Being on the dragon helped you become comfortable with heights. We will make an elf out of you yet."

"I don't see any dark-skinned elves here," Bakari blurted. He silently berated himself for voicing this thought. All the excitement of the day must be getting in the way of his normally rational thoughts.

Lan slapped Bakari on the back jovially. "Don't worry about that, Dragon Rider. We accept everyone here. The elves in Mallek, farther south, in the desert, live in caves and have light brown skin and red hair. Now that's a sight to behold."

Bakari wondered at Lan's humor. It was refreshing here. He breathed in deeply and felt at home.

They soon entered a room, the trees forming beautiful wooden walls on all four sides. Light filtered down through an open ceiling. The effect was magical. At the back of this room stood another door. They entered through it, and Bakari blinked a few times. This second room was much darker, and a feeling of death permeated the air.

Lying on a bed was an elderly man. His face was thin, and graying hair hung over his slanted ears. Light blue robes covered his thin frame.

Bakari moved his eyes from the obviously sick man back to Lan, with a questioning look.

With a look of adoration and love, Lan approached the

man. Giving a light tap on his arm, Lan stood still until the man opened his eyes.

"King Arrowyn," Lan said, "meet Bakari, the dragon rider."

The king? Bakari hadn't known the man was sick and dying. He almost laughed at the irony of this thought. With the barrier in place for one hundred and fifty years, how could he have known anything about the Elvyn king?

The king motioned for Lan to help him sit up. Fluffing additional pillows behind him, Lan helped his father move.

Bakari watched them with awe at the love between the two and then longed for his own parents and their love. There was one other that he thought he loved—Kharlia—but he didn't know now if he would ever see her again. Pushing back his emotions, he took a step closer to the king.

Tears filled the king's eyes, and he opened his dry lips. "Dragon Rider, what is your dragon's name?"

"Abylar, Your Highness."

"Ahh," the old man sighed. "Energy and Life. A good name."

Bakari stood still while the king paused and seemed to compose his thoughts.

"Son," the king continued, reaching over and touching Bakari's arm. "Dragon riders are special. Only in times of tremendous need in the world are they born. I have heard that the barrier is down and that Alaris is getting greedy again. You must not allow that to happen," the king said, his voice becoming more forceful. "You must not."

"I will not, Sire." Bakari meant what he was saying. "I go

now to search out the other dragon eggs and dragon riders. Kanzar, one of Alaris's wizards, must be stopped before he tears apart Alaris and then sets his sights on other lands."

"I have lived long, Dragon Rider. I was a young boy when the barrier was erected, and the war fought before then almost destroyed us," the king said. "How did the barrier fall? I need to know."

"You mean Breelyn hasn't arrived yet?" Bakari asked.

"You know Breelyn Mier?" This time, Lan asked the question.

"She came through the barrier and led a young man to find me and bring me to Celestar, a city in the North, by the Dunn River and the Mahli Mountains. It was there that the Orb was being held."

"That is where Breelyn went?" Lan turned to the king.

"It appears she went to Silla after that and ran into some trouble," the king whispered.

Lan glared at his father. "You didn't tell me that. What kind of trouble? She was too young to send her on such a dangerous journey. An older protector would have been better."

"I did what needed to be done, Lan. And Alair went with her. Now that I know she has met the dragon rider, I am even more sure of my actions," the king said. "She was attacked in Silla by a human wizard pretending to be an elf. She recently escaped but has not returned here yet."

Lan's lips were held tight, but he remained silent.

So the king motioned for Bakari to continue talking about the Orb.

"The Orb was in actuality a dormant dragon egg, taken from Mahli. It was powered by the life force of men and women called guardians. When I touched the Orb, it cracked and the dragon was born. So, in a sense, I took down the barrier."

"Don't be too hard on yourself, Rider. It was meant to be, at some point. A kingdom should not be blocked off from others like that. Creating the barrier had to be done to stop the aggressors, but it was not right."

Bakari only nodded.

"The egg came from Mahli, as did your ancestors," the king stated as a fact.

Bakari nodded again. He found it hard to know what to say in this ancient king's presence.

"You do know of the prophecy, don't you? Their people have been coming here for fifteen years, searching for *the one*." A twinkle shown in the king's eyes. "At about the same time as your birth, I would say."

Bakari sighed deeply. "Sire, I know about the prophecy, but I surely don't know if it's about me or not. I don't feel like some hero or king; I just want to help save Alaris. If you have any knowledge of where the next egg may be in Elvyn, that would be helpful. Abylar says it is northwest of here. He can feel its general presence."

The king coughed a few times, and Lan brought him a glass of water. After a moment's silence, he turned to Lan. "Leave us alone for a moment, my son. I have information for only the dragon rider's ears."

Lan raised his eyebrows questioningly at his father, but

then he bowed his head in deference to the king's wishes. "I will wait outside to escort the dragon rider back down afterward."

The king nodded and then turned to Bakari as Lan left and closed the door. "You hold an awesome responsibility, Dragon Rider. To be the first is to be the greatest. You will gather the others as has happened before. Sometimes, there are two or three; sometimes, four or five. They are always from various countries, but the leader is always from Mahli. That is the burden and the blessing which you carry."

"How will I find them?" Bakari asked with a pleading tone that he hadn't voiced out loud before, but he felt the weight of it in his heart.

"The bond with your dragon will help to guide you. Besides, the person must be found before the egg: a person of valor and strength. Someone who looks out for the good of the people. Some riders may have magical powers; others may not. But, if you are bonded with your dragon, you will know."

Bakari ventured a question. "My dragon feels drawn to go deep into the Elvyn Forest for the next egg. Do you know where the eggs are or who the riders should be? You have lived a long time."

The king laughed. "Yes, a long, long time. Even long for an elf. Soon my son, Lanwaithian, will be king. But my greatest secret in life I now share with you. It is a burden I have carried since the barrier first went up. My father told it to me before going off to the last battle. You see, he was the one who took the dragon egg from Mahli."

Bakari stood still with interest, his mind working overtime

with the excitement of receiving more knowledge.

"It was his idea to create the barrier, and he found others, in Alaris and even in Mahli, willing to help him. He had learned from the ancient histories our libraries hold that the eggs held special powers and that, someday, the dragon riders would return."

"Your libraries must be wonderful to contain so much knowledge." Bakari almost drooled at the thought. But he tried to stay focused on what the king had told him.

"You will return and be given access to all the knowledge you desire, Dragon Rider," the king said, his voice growing weaker. "First, you must find Breelyn."

"Sire?"

"Think about what you know of her. If you have met her, even for only a few minutes, you would know."

Bakari thought about the short time he had spent with her: her striking beauty, strong magic, and sense of duty and fairness. "A dragon rider."

The king nodded and smiled. "If the dragon is willing, I think she would make a wonderful choice. Just don't tell Lan." A small glint came to the king's eyes.

"Lan?"

"They are betrothed, and he is fiercely protective of her," the king said. "She is quite a bit younger than he is."

The king closed his eyes for a few moments, and Bakari grew worried.

"Sire?" He touched the king's arm lightly.

"I'm not dead yet, Dragon Rider," the king said. Bakari saw where Lan got his sense of humor. "Now, lean in closer.

This is the great secret of where the other eggs are hidden. You alone will now carry this burden."

Old King Arrowyn Soliel brought his parched lips close to Bakari's ear and whispered the one-hundred-and-fifty-year-old secret to the young dragon rider. Bakari listened, cataloging all that he heard into his mind, and then nodded. Now he knew the lands where he would need to go to find the other riders.

An hour later, after the king's informative meeting, Lan did not push for details but fed Bakari a short meal and then escorted him back outside.

Soon Bakari and Lan stood once again next to Abylar. Clasping hands, Bakari bade farewell to Lan before mounting. "Prince, I have enjoyed this visit and look forward to returning."

"Good luck, Dragon Rider." The man paused. "And, if you see Breelyn, tell her I wish her well, until we meet again."

Bakari nodded and then mounted Abylar, taking off in a northwesterly direction over the thick Elvyn Forest. He needed to find not only Breelyn but also her dragon egg.

CHAPTER NINE

O nius Neeland walked down the main street of Cassian, his purpose certain. But, somehow, he still dragged his feet. He had donned a nondescript brown robe and had a cowl over his head. His shoulders were drooped down, and his steps shuffled. And he didn't want to attract anyone's attention to where he was going.

Life for the people in this capital city of Alaris had changed in the last few weeks. What used to be a vibrant city— filled with traders hawking their wares, inns busy with boisterous drinking and laughing, and children running underfoot—was now a hollow replica. Vendors still sold their goods, but their voices were more timid, and their inventories were not as full. The inns were filled with more mercenaries and soldiers, from the Citadel, than with citizens of the city. And children—Onius saw very few. The ones he did see were ushered quickly back inside their homes by their protective mothers.

In his lengthy lifetime of almost eighty years, Onius had done some things he wasn't proud of, but these choices had affected a relative few. Now, though, a suffocating feeling of guilt and doom had settled over his aching body. The years were quickly catching up to him, and what had seemed like a good idea decades ago, to promote a king, now seemed like a nightmare unfolding before his eyes.

His years away from the Citadel, serving the chief judges,

had made him blind to the rising greed and power of Kanzar. It was past the time when he should have done something about their self-proclaimed leader. Something that could be dangerous but that, hopefully, would ease his conscience—and help the conflict end sooner.

Looking right and then left, as he neared a small alley on the outskirts of town, the former counselor wizard to the Chief Judge felt like a criminal, sneaking around like this. Years ago, Onius and the local criminal underground came to an understanding in the capital city. That was during the reign of the previous Chief Judge. Onius had brokered an unwritten agreement with their leader about what parts of the city they needed to leave alone and what level of thievery would be allowed. It was not a perfectly honest thing to do, but it had maintained a balance between the government and the criminal underground of Cassian.

Any large city in Alaris attracted its share of criminals. They couldn't be eradicated only, hopefully, controlled. Onius now stood at a knotted wooden door and knocked three times, paused, then three times more. He breathed in deeply and realized he'd just committed himself to a dangerous alliance. He almost turned to leave, before it was too late, but the door creaked open in front of him. A small, thin-faced man stuck his head through to see who had knocked.

Onius stood up straight and uncovered his head. The man's eyes widened and he let out a small grunt of surprise at seeing the old counselor wizard standing in the doorway. Backing up, he opened the door a few feet wider and motioned Onius to enter.

Standing in the entryway of the small house, Onius peeked around in the dim light. Dust covered most of the floor and furniture, and only a few lamps lit the small space around him. The man bolted the door and then walked down a long hallway, obviously intending Onius to follow.

At the end of the hallway appeared another door. The servant knocked twice on the door, and another man peered out. His face was fuller than the first man's and appeared younger, but it was hard to know in the dim light. Upon seeing Onius, he, too, gave a small start, and surprise registered on his face. Onius scowled, and the man opened the door.

This time the room was much brighter, with a row of lamps around the foyer. The room was clean and void of dust, and three doorways branched off from it, each a different color.

Onius was led to the blue door. The second man put his hand on an ornate golden handle and pushed it open. Then Onius took three quick steps and entered the room.

Thick drapes covered a wide window, but lamps were situated artistically around the room, giving it a warm and sunny feel. Tall bookshelves lined one wall, while a beautiful painting of mythical woods adorned another. A costly desk— dark, polished cherry wood—stood in one corner.

However, after a brief glance around the room, his eyes settled on a grouping of furniture in the middle. Two light tan leather couches and two chairs circled a short, brown polished oak table. In one of the chairs facing away from him was a man. But Onius could see only the back of a man's head.

The man took his time standing up and turning around.

His clothes hung loosely on his aging frame, and his hair was thick and gray, but his face was the same one Onius had seen when negotiating with him twenty years earlier. It was the face of a man used to luxury and power—both brought forth through illegal, underground criminal activities. A man that worked outside of the law and within the shadows. A man that Onius turned to now in desperation.

"Hello, Onius," the man said, his voice raspy, but his eyes smiled intelligently. "What brings the mighty wizard counselor to such low levels?"

"Hello, Gideon." Onius tried to look confident, but he was feeling the weight of the kingdom on his shoulders. "I need your help."

* * *

Later that day, Onius sat in a room among other wizards, waiting for Kanzar, their self-proclaimed leader, to show up. Just being in the reception room in the castle in Cassian made Onius feel guilty over what had happened to Chief Judge Daymian Khouri. How many times had Onius and Daymian met in this very room, discussing with others the safety and peace of Alaris?

Onius had told Roland that he had always done what was best for the kingdom, but now he questioned ever having had conversations with Kanzar about the benefits of having a king for Alaris. Onius, younger back then, was anxious to please a fellow wizard that he recognized would be in the high ranks of the Citadel someday. Over the years, Onius had distanced himself from Kanzar, but that didn't make him any less guilty by association.

At the time of their first conversation on the subject, thirty years ago, Alaris had been under the judges system for one hundred and twenty years—a system in which the people chose their local judges for a period of time and those judges would choose one from among themselves to serve as Chief Judge for a period of five years. It was a system that worked well and gave balance to the land. That is, until Kanzar decided that the kingdom needed a king again—and that this king should be himself.

Looking around at the other gathered men and women, Onius saw that most were wizards of medium to high ranks. They had dressed in similar fashion to Onius, with a colored wizard robe over serviceable traveling attire. For, as a wizard, you never knew when you would have to move quickly or go somewhere all of a sudden.

Most of these men and women had ridden on Kanzar's coattails for years as Kanzar rose through the wizard ranks. Onius wondered if any of them were having second thoughts like himself. How many could he trust to turn against Kanzar?

A scuffle in the hall turned everyone's attention toward the door. Two guards opened both of the wooden double doors, allowing Kanzar to enter, dragging a young man behind him. Multiple wizards rushed from their seats to be the first to help Kanzar. It was pathetic. Onius watched them grovel for Kanzar's attention. But Onius stayed seated. He was too high ranking on the Council to grovel at anyone's feet.

"Stand for the High Wizard," instructed one of the younger wizards in Kanzar's close circles. The rest of the room stood and bowed to their leader. With only a slight bow, so as not to appear too defiant, Onius took his thin frame out of his chair and then stood at attention.

"Onius! Come and take this man from me," Kanzar ordered.

Onius gritted his teeth. Why did Kanzar continually pull him into things he didn't want to be a part of anymore?

Onius knew Kanzar was behind the organization of the King-men, mercenaries and others who had voiced their demands around the kingdom for the last few years. But Onius had hoped it was only a phase and that it would die down with time. Then, when the wizards received news of the periodic failing of the magical barrier, Kanzar had put his plans into action. Being away from Kanzar for so long, while serving the chief judges in Cassian, had made Onius blind to the High Wizard's ambitions.

Kanzar pushed the man into Onius's arms. "This man is a thief and has news for us."

The man could barely stand. His dark blond hair was a mess, and his teeth chattered with fear. He might have even soiled his dirty clothes as Kanzar had dragged him in.

"Kanzar," Onius spoke. "What is this about? Why are you dragging thieves into our Council meetings?"

Kanzar stood up and rubbed his hand over his large, bald head. His dark and beady eyes stared down at Onius. "I am in charge here, Onius. I don't answer to you."

The rest of the room glanced around nervously. Kanzar had been acting more irrationally lately, and no one knew what he might do next.

Either Onius was determined not to be intimidated or he

just felt like pushing Kanzar further—he didn't know which. And it didn't really matter.

"You brought the Council together for this man, Kanzar? For a thief? Don't you have better things to worry about? Like a war?"

"I cannot fight a war if I cannot control Cassian!" the High Wizard howled, then he lowered his voice as if he realized admitting that was the same as admitting he didn't have control of the situation.

His wife, Alana, walked up to him and put a hand on his arm. "Kanzar, you are trying to do too much. Let the Council help you. Now, what is the meaning of this?"

Kanzar pulled his arm away from Alana and walked closer to Onius and the thief. "This man was caught deliberately replacing the bottles of wine for our soldiers with bottles of water."

The men and women in the room looked from one to the other. If Kanzar wasn't so angry, what he said would have been funny. Onius had to bite his cheek to keep from almost laughing. His old friend Gideon, head of the thieves' guild, had indeed been doing his part to disrupt the town.

"Sir," began one of the younger wizards on the Council. "Then flog him or fine him. This does not warrant a gathering of the Council."

Kanzar whipped his head toward the man and glared. Then, turning to one of his guards, he ordered, "Take that man out. He is no longer on my Council."

Chaos broke out in the room. These were esteemed wizards not used to being treated so poorly. A majority started leaving the room along with the dismissed man. They had seen enough.

"Where are you going?" Kanzar bellowed. "There is business to discuss."

"Then let's discuss *business*," one of the men said, "and leave the thieves for others to deal with."

Kanzar motioned for the guards to take out the thief instead. "Fine. Onius, where do we stand for an attack on Corwan and Orr?"

Onius needed to tread lightly because Kanzar was ready to burst. But, when he eventually made a move, Onius needed to be sure Kanzar was taken all of the way out. Onius was not there yet.

"The last of the troops have arrived, sir. It has taken a bit longer than anticipated, and food and other necessities have taken longer to procure," Onius reported. "We have heard that the Chief Judge in Orr…"

"There is no longer a Chief Judge, Onius!" Kanzar reminded him and all in the room. "I have declared him a rebel to the kingdom."

Onius gave a nod to Kanzar. "Then, we have heard that *Daymian Khouri* has brought in a battalion of men from Corwan with Judge Azeem and has recruited others from Targon. It is also rumored that he may be in discussions with leaders in Tillimot and some of the elves from Mallek."

This news seemed to be taken gravely by the others in the room.

One man stepped forward. "Kanzar, we need to move against Daymian before he is too strong."

"I have sent men south, with Mericus, to secure Corwan," Kanzar answered. "They won't be a problem anymore, and I doubt that the southern elves are any concern." He paced the room and glared at each man and woman. "Someone here in Alaris, though, is undermining our plans. There is a traitor in our midst."

His fellow wizards, a mistrusting group already, seemed to each take a step away from their neighbors. Onius tried to calm his beating heart. He was afraid the sweat on his forehead would give him away.

Kanzar continued, "The thief I brought in is just one example of the lawlessness this town is facing. Someone is undermining our every move in this city: stealing supplies from our soldiers, moving the horses at night, and stirring up trouble in the common rooms. The thieves' guild is behind this. But someone is behind them. I want the traitor found and made an example of." Kanzar studied each person in the room and then settled on Onius. "Onius?"

Onius's heart skipped a beat as he regarded his leader. "Yes, Kanzar?"

"You will be in charge of finding this traitor. You have authority to use every means possible."

Before Onius could answer, the door slowly swung open.

"Who dares interrupt this meeting?"

In walked Wren, a wizard in his thirties. He looked around the room, and his eyes grew big, as if he'd just realized he had interrupted a Council meeting. The man was worn and dirty. Brushing at his clothes, Wren gave a quick bow to the room.

Kanzar glared at his guards, standing at the door with

questioning looks. No one was ever allowed to enter without his permission.

"Guards, you are dismissed from my service. Report to your captain, and tell him you are to be assigned duties elsewhere. If I hear of any other infractions, I will take your lives from you myself."

The men didn't know whether to bow or to run. But, after an awkward moment, they turned and walked quickly away.

"Wren, this better be worthy news. I am not in a patient mood," informed Kanzar.

At that statement, the wizards in the room nodded their heads and seemed to have pity for the poor fellow.

"Sir, I was with Mericus as we took soldiers in boats to subdue Corwan. I stood by his side when we disembarked in the evening three days ago. I rode back here as fast as I could."

All eyes stared at the man. But Onius knew what was coming. He and Mericus had talked the night before the men left for Corwan.

Now for the next step in breaking Kanzar.

"There was no fight, sir," Wren said.

"What do you mean, *no fight?*" Kanzar asked, taking his powerful frame closer to him. Wren seemed to shrink backward from this intimidation. "You mean the townspeople just gave in? Oh, this is better than I thought." Kanzar gave a booming laugh.

"Oh, no, High Wizard." Wren paused and seemed to be considering what to say. "There was no fighting because Mericus has sided with them."

Onius almost closed his eyes, so as not to see the temper

of Kanzar, but he decided to instead take an inappropriate amount of delight in seeing the man's downfall.

Kanzar pushed out his hands in front of himself, and white-hot fire poured forth, immediately consuming Wren, leaving only a pile of ashes on the ground. Alana reached her hand out to stop him, and he turned toward her, pushing a gust of air, sending her flying through the air halfway across the room. She landed in a heap, and Onius wondered if she still lived.

As other wizards around the room started running toward the doors, Kanzar sent a bolt of fire toward the table in the center of the room, and shards of wood flew everywhere.

"I will destroy Mericus," Kanzar said, "and take delight in burning every inch of his flesh with fire before tearing each limb from his useless body. Ready the troops, Battlemaster," he instructed Geoffrey. "You will march to Corwan at daybreak!"

CHAPTER TEN

Alli was bored. It had been three days since Mericus had arrived with his men, mostly mercenaries. She had hoped Mericus or one of his men would give her an excuse to fight, but, besides the normal bar brawls between the men, nothing exciting had happened. Much to Alli's dismay, Mericus had even proven to be quite charming, though she still didn't fully trust any man who could turn on his own leader so quickly. Though, with a leader like Kanzar, she decided that she might need to make an exception in her way of thinking.

Today, she strode around the marketplace, looking at trinkets to bide her time. The weather had cooled as early fall settled in, but it was still warm and sunny in the southern desert. She spotted a head of red hair up ahead and wound her way through the vendors, selling everything from fruit pies to head scarves, to see the unique phenomenon.

Coming closer, she saw that it was as she had thought. A small group of elves from the southern Elvyn city of Mallek. Their red hair hung straight past their shoulders, tucked behind upswept, pointy ears. They were darker and not as fine-featured as Breelyn, but Alli suspected the king's protector was a rare beauty, even among the fine-featured northern elves.

The elves were talking about trade to a local merchant, trying to work out a deal to bring seafood from the Blue Sea to the market in Orr. The merchant seemed excited about the possibility. With the barrier blocking access to the sea for one hundred and fifty years, it would now be good business to be the first to carry the exotic seafood. Alli smiled with the thought that their world had just grown so much larger.

Hearing a ruckus behind her, she turned to see what the commotion was about. The crowd parted, and Mericus, along with the governor, strode forward to meet the elves.

"Welcome to Alaris." Mericus greeted them as if he held some authority there. The elves moved their attention from the man they had been talking to over to Mericus. Recognizing one that wielded influence, they stepped forward and greeted the wizard and the governor. They bowed and spoke with a slight accent.

"We are interested in developing trading terms with our esteemed neighbors," one of them said. "My name is Calanon, head merchant in Mallek. And this is Ambassador Theolin and our negotiator, Raina."

All three bowed to Mericus. Alli watched the two men and one woman look from Mericus to the governor, obviously trying to figure out who was in charge.

"I am Judge Mericus, and this is Governor Makin." Mericus motioned the three elves to him, away from the local merchant. "Why don't we continue this conversation inside, where we can discuss trading terms for all of Alaris?"

The elves' eyes widened at this unanticipated potential boon to their business; however, the local merchant looked crestfallen and sent dark looks toward Mericus.

"My good man," Mericus said, addressing the merchant. "Once we settle on terms, I will send you a finder's payment. Thank you for your services."

Alli's eyes opened wider. That was not expected. Most men in Mericus's position would have just bullied their way to the business. Rewarding the merchant seemed to set everyone at ease and, in short order, made Mericus out as a fair negotiator.

Mericus turned and caught Alli's attention. "Wizard, you may accompany us also," he said with a smile. "I would like you to observe my intentions firsthand."

Alli didn't know what to say and so followed behind the group. She noticed the other merchants who heard the exchange whispering and pointing to Mericus. They clearly didn't know why Mericus was there, but the whispers Alli heard seemed mostly positive. The man was definitely worth watching over. She picked up her pace and soon came up beside Mericus.

"You do not hold the authority to negotiate for all of Alaris, Mericus," Alli pointed out to him. The three elves were busy conversing with the governor.

"I know," he said, and then the man actually winked at her. She rolled her eyes, thinking about Roland. *Him again!* She pushed that thought farther from her mind.

"But they don't know that, do they?" he continued. "Maybe, by the time the negotiations are final, this war will be done and I will have that authority."

"You presume a lot," Alli said darkly. "What are you doing to help the cause while sitting around here, safe in Corwan?"

Mericus frowned. "Don't lecture me on politics, young lady. You have no idea of the plans that are being carried out right now. Things in Cassian are not so peaceful for our esteemed High Wizard. While he is dealing with local concerns there, we will establish treaties and a base of operations here and in Orr."

Alli grunted. "We'll see. There will be fighting before this is over, I'm sure."

"Speaking of fighting..." Mericus said, sounding calm again. He rubbed his hand over his short goatee and smoothed out his burgundy robes. "I brought a battle wizard with me. Wren is his name. Have you seen him?"

Alli shook her head. "I have not noticed a wizard with your men."

"Hmmm. I'm sure he is around somewhere. After our meeting, could you see if you might find him? I think a battle strategy meeting would be helpful."

"Sure," Alli mumbled. She didn't have much else to do. Though something about Wren's absence started worrying her, but she didn't know why.

The negotiations went longer than Alli thought possible. At first, she was interested in monitoring Mericus and his intentions. But, after a few hours, she became convinced that the man was being truthful about negotiating fairly. Creating a fishers' guild in Corwan to work with the elves from Mallek was their current topic, and the elves' faces were beaming with their success.

"What about protection?" Alli asked. It was her first input in over an hour.

They turned to her with questioning looks.

"While you transport the goods across southern Elvyn, what about bandits and thieves? You will need protection."

Ambassador Theolin spoke up first. "My dear girl," he began, "in Elvyn, we don't have highway robbers and such."

Alli felt silly now, and her face turned red. She didn't know what to say.

"I think Allison here is just being cautious, Ambassador," Mericus jumped in to save her. "With the barrier newly down, there will be many in Alaris, Tillimot, and maybe even in Elvyn looking for new opportunities. Sometimes these opportunities breed problems. It's always better to be prepared."

The ambassador nodded his agreement, and the discussion continued on and on. Alli still didn't trust Mericus. Things were going too smoothly and easily. She stood up to stretch her legs and walked to the nearest window. It looked north, toward the convergence of the Dunn and Corwan Rivers.

It was late in the afternoon, and both rivers glowed like bright orange ribbons of reflecting sun, winding their ways through the brown desert surroundings. Something flashed in the distance and caught her eye. It wasn't in the rivers themselves but on the road that paralleled the Corwan River from Cassian to Corwan.

There it was again: a flash of light, reflecting off of something. Her battle sense took over, and she then grasped the situation.

"Gentlemen," she said, turning around with a grim smile. "We have company."

Mericus jumped from his seat and was the first one of the group to reach the window. The others followed.

"Blast it, Wren!" he said. "Wren was always one of Kanzar's men, groveling for his attention."

Allison raised her eyebrows. "Like you did, Mericus?"

Mericus didn't take this bait and ignored her accusation. "That is why he hasn't been around. He went back to warn Kanzar. Now Kanzar sends his men here to find me."

"Good. I was getting bored," Alli said with a smile.

"This isn't a game." Mericus grew serious. "Kanzar is probably furious at what I did. He will be sending Battlemaster Geoffrey; Alana, Kanzar's wife; and others, I am sure, to take Corwan and apprehend me." He glanced at Alli as if waiting for her to make a comment. "He will then turn his sights to Orr."

"So, we will need to stop him here then," Alli said confidently. "You have the men you brought. The governor has his men. And you have me."

"Kanzar will have wizards also." Mericus ground his teeth. "What about Judge Azeem's men?"

"They will be halfway to Orr by now," stated the governor.

"I will send Tam to get them," Alli added. "We can hold these men off a few days until Azeem's men arrive."

Mericus turned to the three elves, whom had stood silent during this exchange. Then he explained the situation to them.

Raina and Calanon gave questioning glances to their ambassador. He was the eldest and took the lead. They nodded to him, and he then spoke to the group.

"We can help also," he admitted. "Though I am not prepared to offer many men or to commit my land to a war, we do have a small group of elves just across the river that could be persuaded to help our cause."

"It seems ridding Corwan of Kanzar's men would help to solidify our position in these negotiations, wouldn't it?" Raina said, summing it up.

Mericus laughed. "My, you *are* shrewd negotiators. We would be happy to accept your help. I have read books about the fighting prowess of the southern elves. How many do you have?"

Raina actually blushed. "Five hundred, sir."

The governor went into a coughing fit. After recovering, he said, "You mean to say that you had five hundred battle ready elves on my border this entire time?" His voice rose in anger as he spoke.

"With the fall of the barrier and the history of the aggressors of Alaris, it was a prudent move," the ambassador said as he walked back to the table and picked up a glass of wine. "Don't you think?"

The governor grumbled, but Mericus slapped the elderly elf on the back. Turning to Alli, he seemed to become serious again. "I guess we should have held that battle plan meeting earlier."

Alli nodded then walked toward the door. "I will be ready. Meet me with your men at the gates to the city." Turning to the governor, she continued, "Bring your strongest men to the gates. We must stop them from entering the city."

Everyone scattered at once, all going to their men. Alli headed out to find Tam and get him going off toward the Orr-bound battalion of men. She knew they would need all the help they could against Kanzar's wizards and mercenaries.

Two hours later, Alli stood boldly, but alone in front of the heavy wooden gates of Corwan. The doors stood closed and were reinforced from inside. The governor's men sat low on the walls, hidden from view of the approaching army. Mericus and his men were down along a short incline, undetected between the road and the riverbank. The group of elves would be held back until needed—a final surprise for Kanzar's men.

From down the desert road, where dust rose into the air, the sound of the army approached. The march here, even on horses, would have taken them a few days. So they would be tired, but approaching a desert city undetected would be impossible. The sun had set, and evening approached. Kanzar's men most likely would be hoping for a morning battle—with time to rest. But that was not to be so.

As Kanzar's men came around a bend, Alli used her strong eyesight to see Battlemaster Geoffrey and Alana, Kanzar's wife, riding at the head of the group. Kanzar had indeed sent his strongest warriors. Alli kept her stance. Waiting. Waiting.

Then she saw Geoffrey's eyes open wider as he recognized Alli for who she was. A look of worry crossed his face but was soon replaced by determination. She held his eyes in hers. He didn't dare look away first from his prey, and that's what she had been counting on.

He rode closer and closer, the rest of their army turning the bend behind him. Dirty and tired soldiers wiped sweat from across their foreheads. But their numbers could still do a lot of damage. At least a thousand men, with a dozen wizards, rode into view.

A yell, from Mericus's men along the side of the road, sounded loud in the evening air. Then arrows flew out and struck a dozen men. Horses began neighing and scrambling away from the threat. Before organization could take over, a group of men rushed up from the riverbank with swords and began knocking down the Battlemaster's men.

It took a few moments for things to sink in. But, when it did, both Geoffrey and Alana turned and returned fire in a fierce battle with Mericus and his men. Flames flew from Alana's fingers and grazed Mericus's hair. With a loud yell, he cut down two approaching men on horseback.

"Is that all you have, Mericus?" the Battlemaster asked. "A few traitorous men to stop us?" Geoffrey blasted a wave of air into a group of approaching soldiers. They fell without a fight to the hard ground.

With a whooshing sound, arrows began falling from overhead as the governor and his men started shooting from the walls of the city. The approaching men turned away from Mericus to meet this new threat. However, Mericus had kept other men in reserve, and they came up now, from behind, as well.

A few lone horsemen of Kanzar's broke through the line and now raced toward the gate. Alli sneered at these on-comers and tapped a long staff between her hands. She stayed still until the men were almost upon her. Crouching down low and then jumping high into the air, she ran each end of the staff into both of the soldiers' throats, knocking them instantly off their horses. More came, and Alli blasted out a sheet of air, knocking them down to the ground.

In twos and threes and fours, men broke through the line of Mericus's men. Each group met Alli alone in front of the gate, and each group met the same fate. Alli was now in full battle mode: she spun through the air, flying over horses and into men, two and three at a time. She dropped her staff and now used two swords, one in each hand. The torchlight from above the gates reflected yellow on the sharp, spinning blades.

A mesmerizing dance of light ran through the group of men, cutting into some, knocking down others. There would be no mercy. Not this time.

Alli ground her teeth in frustration when, as two soldiers jumped from their horses and approached her, one almost caught her off guard, throwing up a bolt of fire at her. She did not expect *him* to be a wizard. She would need to think more carefully and not get distracted.

Reaching toward the ground, she picked up a handful of desert sand and pebbles. Then, opening her hand in front her, she blew a magical and forceful wind into her hand at the wizard. The sand and rock jetted forward and pelted the man in the face and chest, dropping him in agony to the ground. Without stopping, Alli jumped up high into the air and did a three-hundred-and-sixty-degree turn, battle robes flying out around her. Coming down on top of the other man, she knocked the sword out of his hand and then, with a small knife, pinned his foot painfully to the ground.

With a small break in the action, she looked down the lane and saw that Mericus and his men were tiring, many of them down on the ground. The Battlemaster turned toward her and, through the melee of battle, locked onto her eyes and walked purposefully forward to meet the young wizard. Using the power of his magic, he opened up a path in front of him. He threw both friend and foe to the side as he continued walking toward Alli.

As much as she wanted to take on the Battlemaster himself, she needed to set an example and stick to the plan. Though it did irk her. She jumped up into the air and spun around, her acrobatics distracting him momentarily. Then she landed and ran toward the river. The Battlemaster followed her.

Coming up over a small rise, however, he was met by a sight Alli was sure he had never seen in his entire life. A sight that would be the last one he ever saw. Five hundred fiery, red-haired, thin, and battle-trained southern elves rose from a crouch where they had been hiding and attacked as one. Within moments, they overran the Battlemaster himself, leaving him for dead on the ground.

The tide of the battle seemed to turn with this influx of men, and both Mericus's and the governor's men picked up their paces and began pushing the attackers back down the road.

From the top of the wall, a man yelled and pointed toward the river. So Alli ran to a side gate in the wall and was let in. She ran up a flight of stairs, to the top of the wall, and investigated what the man had seen. Wiping her sticky hair away from her face and brow, she studied what she was looking at and then let out a long-held breath. Warships now sailed in from Cassian also and pulled alongside the docks of Corwan.

A loud cannon boom filled the night air as the naval attack on the city of Corwan began from the river. Alli tightened her mouth and berated herself for not thinking about an approach from the river. She turned her eyes from the road to the docks and then back. In the failing light, it was getting harder to see.

She jumped down from the wall and ran toward the docks, bringing some of the governor's soldiers with her. She hoped Tam had reached Azeem's men quickly, for she didn't know how long they could hold out against this double assault.

CHAPTER ELEVEN

Roland stood in the practice yard and observed the training of the battle apprentices by a few older apprentices. They seemed so young to him. Not that they were much younger than Roland—in fact, a few were even older, but their techniques and abilities appeared so crude and untrained. Roland was positive that he had never been that lame. Having been an apprentice for far shorter of a time than most people were, he supposed watching the apprentices was all part of the responsibility of being so powerful.

Soon a servant brought over a platter of food for him. Roland picked out a few pieces of roast chicken, cheese, and bread and absently chewed on them while he continued watching. The influx of new apprentices continued to grow each week, and Roland now felt the burden of being in charge. He needed to find others he could trust.

A young, promising apprentice, from somewhere northwest of the Citadel, jumped high into the air and kicked out against her opponent. Her moves reminded Roland of Alli. That young wizard was sassy and hard to talk to, but her battle dance was amazing to watch. Alli flowed like the wind, her weapons becoming like extensions of her body. He smiled, remembering her shock when he had allowed her to take her wizard test and be promoted to a full wizard. She deserved it, as did he, even though they were so young.

The young apprentice finished, and Roland walked over to

her. "You did well today. Elsa, isn't it?" He had thought of her as *young*, but, at sixteen, she was virtually his same age.

"Thank you, sir," Elsa said with a blush creeping across her face.

"How did you learn such moves?"

Elsa shook her head and shrugged her shoulders. "It just comes to me."

Roland smiled knowingly and winked at her. "Well, keep it up. We might have you teaching some of the apprentices soon."

The apprentices standing around them looked at her jealously. It wasn't good that their own efforts hadn't been praised by their Citadel leader.

Roland laughed and pushed his blond bangs back from his face. "Don't look so dispirited. There is reward enough for all who work hard. We are building the grandest collection of magic and wizards in the West. Keep practicing."

As Roland turned around to return to the building, he saw a shadow move around the side of the courtyard, toward the stables. The figure had seemed to be clothed in black robes with a hood over its face: not the kind of attire for the middle of the day. Roland thought about motioning for a guard to accompany him but then figured there wasn't much he couldn't handle.

So Roland picked up his steps, leaving puffs of dust in the area behind him. Coming to the corner, he looked around carefully only to find the figure sliding around another corner, closer to the stables. He shouted out for the person to stop, but he or she either didn't hear him or didn't want to, and the person didn't stop. Roland now started to run.

Turning around the last corner before the stables, he stopped and scanned everywhere around him. "Strange," he whispered to himself. There was no way someone would have outrun him in that short distance.

A scattering of other small buildings stood around the stables, and Roland investigated in each one. While there, he decided to stop by and see the stable boys.

Entering the stable, his nose twitched at the odor of horses: their excrement and food mixing into a smell that never went away. Then he heard a small sound.

Turning back around, he almost ran into someone. Catching himself on a nearby post, he barely kept from falling down. "Hey, watch yourself—" he began to say, and then stopped himself. "Celia?"

The new apprentice from Solshi gazed boldly into Roland's eyes, her lips holding a small grin, her eyes glittering, as if with a secret. "My lord." She gave a short bow, her chest heaving with labored breath.

"What are you doing out here in the stables?" Roland asked. There were too many suspicious things happening lately, and, even though she appeared quite innocent, he didn't trust her.

Celia's eyes turned down, as if in embarrassment.

Roland sighed. Maybe he had come across too harshly.

"I miss my own horse, back home," Celia said in a somewhat softer tone than Roland had expected.

Roland relaxed. That did make some sense. "You didn't bring it?"

"No," she said. "My family needs her to help with the farm."

"Boy!" Roland yelled to the nearest stable boy. "Saddle up two of our spare horses. Our pretty apprentice here misses riding. I will take her out for a ride."

The young boy bowed briefly, then ran to get the horses ready.

Celia clapped her hands in delight. "Oh, thank you. Thank you."

Roland's mouth opened with a grin as he watched her soft hair bounce around her shoulders in her enthusiasm. This was definitely going to be more fun than the paperwork he had planned on returning to. He would act the part of the gracious Citadel host and try to draw out what she was hiding; he knew there was something he was missing about her.

A few minutes later, they took the horses out of the stables, and Roland led them onto a trail that would wind its way around the back of the Citadel. Then he decided to venture a question to gauge her response.

"Celia, when you came into the stables, did you see anyone with a dark hood and cloak?"

Celia thought a moment. "No. Only the stable boys. Why?"

Roland shook his head. "Oh, nothing. I just thought I saw someone sneaking around."

"There isn't trouble, is there?" Celia opened her eyes wide and moved her horse closer to Roland's.

"Nothing for you to worry about," Roland said. "Follow me." With that, Roland galloped quicker, and Celia pushed her horse to catch up.

With a brush of air, she raced past Roland with a laugh. "Care to race?"

Roland was surprised at her riding abilities and competitive nature. It was refreshing, and he took the challenge.

Side by side, they raced down the trail. Winding intermittently through tall pines and soft grasses, they made their way around the back side of the Citadel. Roland watched Celia, noticing her joy as her dark hair bounced back behind her.

About three-fourths of the way around, they came to a halt by a small bridge leading across a narrow stream. They dismounted and let the horses move down to the water and drink their fill.

Their chests heaved with the exertion of riding, and Roland enjoyed looking at her rose-tinted cheeks. Her lips were full and seemed inviting.

A few inches shorter than Roland, she gazed up at him with a devious look in her eyes. Then, with determination in her pale green eyes, Celia leaned in and gave Roland a warm and lingering kiss.

The move surprised Roland. Usually, he was the one chasing the woman, not the other way around. He didn't know quite what to think about it. His lips, however, brought hers back in for another kiss, this one longer and harder. In the distance, Roland heard faint voices from the Citadel but pushed them out of his mind. A few minutes' respite and some enjoyment away from his duties would be welcomed.

Finally, Celia stepped back first, her pupils large and

dilated. She let out a throaty laugh, and Roland joined in. They mounted their horses and, without much talking, resumed the ride back around toward the stables.

Celia rode out in front this time. Every once in a while, she would look back, her lips pursed, as if inviting Roland for more. Roland sighed and kept riding.

Arriving back at the stables, Roland found an uproar of voices.

"Sir," called one of the stable boys.

Roland jumped off his horse and walked over to the worried boy. "Someone left some of the stalls open, and quite a few horses are now missing."

"When did this happen? I was just here." Roland turned his head to take a quick look around the stable.

"Based on what the other boys have said, sir, it seems it must have been right before you arrived."

"Whose horses are they?" Roland turned his head toward Celia and then surveyed the stables.

"Each one belongs to one of the wizards still here at the Citadel, sir," the stable master said, appearing nervous. "I sent men out to find them and gather them back. This is the third time this week something like this has happened."

Roland arched his eyebrows in a question. "I haven't heard anything about this."

"We didn't want to worry you, my lord. Thought it must be just a couple of lazy boys. But things do seem a little stranger than usual: first, some tack and gear went missing; then, some food; and now, these horses."

"Either someone is packing for a trip, or they are trying to take away our ability to leave," Roland said. He thought back to the other, seemingly separate happenings inside the Citadel that week. There were complaints of food missing from the cook, of clothes missing from the laundry, and of footsteps from someone sneaking around at night.

Roland turned back, to ask Celia a question, but she had left. *Strange,* he thought. She had said she was positive she hadn't seen anyone in the stables, but he wanted to make sure. There was definitely something off about her. And, if she wasn't the one who did this, she was definitely involved somehow.

He gave instructions to the stable master, to inform the captain of his guard to set extra men over the stables. Then Roland walked back toward the Citadel. During the brisk walk, he tried to piece things together. Someone was undermining his authority at the Citadel. That's what it must be. Someone was trying to make him look bad.

As he climbed the wide, curved staircase to the second floor, the immense candelabra that hung down from the ceiling caught his eye. Each night, one of the wizard apprentices was given the chore to light it. But it was not lit yet, and the time for the evening meal was approaching.

His mouth tightened. Approaching Titus's rooms, he knocked twice before someone answered the door. It was a servant.

"Fetch Wizard Titus for me," he informed the servant.

The servant's eyes went wide, and she curtsied and then went into another room.

Soon Titus emerged. "Am I to meet you for dinner

tonight, sir?" the elder wizard asked, holding a book in his left hand. "I'm afraid I lost track of the time."

Roland rolled his eyes. How could these scholars read so much when there was so much more to do? Getting straight to the point, he asked, "Are you and the other wizards behind the Citadel pranks?"

"*Pranks*, sir?" Titus furrowed his bushy eyebrows and stroked his long beard. "I'm not sure I understand you."

"Missing clothes, food, and now horses," stated Roland. "Are you trying to undermine my authority here?" Roland asked, raising his voice at the level three wizard. His patience was being stretched thin. "And is the apprentice Celia part of your plans?"

The old man seemed affronted by Roland's attitude. "No one is doing anything to usurp your authority, young man, whatever authority that is. You do know you have no formal title here, don't you? You rule this place under the guise of being *the most powerful*. That is not anything official, and I'm sure this will be rectified when Kanzar and his council return."

Roland was genuinely surprised at the backbone the old man had. It caught Roland off guard, and he believed the man. "Nice to see the bookworm wizard has some mettle."

Titus glared at Roland, but Roland waved his hand in the air, the accusation already forgotten. He sighed a bit and then admitted, "Sorry, Titus. These things worry me, that's all. I meant no direct offense to you."

"None taken, sir," Titus said, backing down a bit. "In fact, to be honest, you are not doing a half bad job here."

"Not half bad, huh?" Roland laughed.

Before anything else could be said, a scream echoed down the hallway. Both men sprinted to the door. Not seeing it clearly or for sure, Roland thought he saw a hooded figure jump off the stairwell below. He stared in that direction, but his attention was then pulled back down the hallway by another scream.

Instead of following the figure, Roland raced back down the hallway, Titus on his heels. Entering Eryck's room, they saw that a servant was kneeling down next to the old counselor wizard. The man was still conscious but looked pale, and he tried to push away the servant.

Roland leaned down and ran his hands over Eryck's body. Then he closed his eyes and delved deep inside. It was a poison, but it hadn't gone through the man's body too far yet. Concentrating hard, Roland reached his powers inside the old wizard. He felt after the poison and began pushing it outward, through the man's pores. It was thick and moved slowly. But, eventually, this worked and Roland opened up his eyes.

Eryck's face cleared, and he took a deep breath. Roland and Titus helped him sit up. Then he pointed a bony finger at his servant.

"She poisoned me."

The girl's eyes grew wide. "I did no such thing, sir. What are you talking about?"

"I saw you," Eryck said. "I came back into the room early, and you were putting something in my drink. I didn't think anything of it at the time; I assumed that maybe you were just fixing me something. But *now* I know."

"I didn't even come in until you were already in the room,

sir. I swear." The servant wrung her hands tightly.

"But, I saw you," Eryck said, his voice softening. "It was you."

"I was with my sister, sir," the servant said, turning to Roland. "Ask her."

Roland summoned a guard to take the servant away. Then, turning to the others, he said, "We will get to the bottom of this. I saw a shadowy figure running down the stairwell when I heard your servant scream from the hallway. With everything else going on in the Citadel lately, I think we may have an intruder."

The two elder wizards seemed worried but didn't say anything.

"I will bring in additional guards from Whalen for a few days," Roland offered. "We need to figure out what the intruder is after."

Titus paled a bit before speaking. "The room below, sir, the one that was broken into…Someone may be looking for something or have taken something dangerous."

Roland jumped up. "I will go down there right now and ensure that there are enough guards. Titus, get Eryck taken care of, and then make sure the guards are on high alert."

Both wizards nodded, and Roland ran off, heading down toward the stairs to the basement. Opening the basement door, he noticed few lamps burning in the hallways. So he summoned a small flame to his hand to see the way better. Up ahead, he saw a shadowy figure move around a corner.

"Not again!" he whispered out loud and picked up his pace. He would catch the intruder this time.

Coming around the corner, all he saw was a guard, stationed in front of the room he was looking for. Confused, Roland glanced up and down the hall.

"Sir, can I help you?" the guard asked.

"Did you see someone come this way?"

The guard shook his head. "No one here. In fact, hardly anyone ever comes down here, my lord. You are the first in days."

Roland felt a slight breeze move his cloak and spun around, but nothing was there.

"Would you like to see the room, sir?" the guard asked with a smile.

Roland knew that he shouldn't look inside there—it was full of dangerous magic—but he needed to make sure things were all right. He took seriously his position of assumed authority over the safety of the Citadel.

The guard took out a set of keys and placed a key in the keyhole. Then he turned to Roland. "It takes this key and the touch of a wizard, sir."

Roland placed his hand over the man's hand. All at once, multiple things happened: he felt—or, rather, *knew*—that the guard possessed magical powers; the door opened; and the guard shoved him inside.

Roland stumbled to the ground. Turning back around, he saw the face of the guard waver in front of his eyes. Then, in the blink of an eye, the apprentice Celia stood in front of him instead.

"Would you rather I use this face?" she asked.

"What?" Roland didn't understand what was happening,

"Who are you, Celia?"

"I am not Celia just as I am not the guard."

Roland tried to concentrate but, somehow, couldn't stop thinking about how he had kissed Celia. Who was she really? Was she *a man?*

He held his head in his hands and groaned. "What do you want?"

"I am a chameleon and take what I want," Celia said. This time, her full lips and green eyes seemed more like a sneer and a glare. "I will control it all."

"All?" Roland stood up. He needed to get out of here. He tried to bring up the power within him, but nothing happened. He tried harder. What was wrong?

The being that looked like Celia laughed. "You can't use magic in this room, Roland. That is how you wizards made it, to keep all these secrets intact," she said as she spread her arms toward the room that Roland stood in.

Roland considered the artifacts and wondered if there was anything here that would help him. But he couldn't take the chance. He would just need to use his normal strength. It shouldn't be too hard to overpower the young woman. So he charged at her only to find that she had changed once again. Now she appeared as a broad-shouldered, sturdy man, more than a foot taller than Roland. The man brought up a fist and slammed it in Roland's gut, sending him flying backward, onto the floor of the room.

"You can't get away with this," Roland warned. "They will come looking for me. Wizard Titus and Eryck know I came down here."

"Eryck is dead," the man said.

Then Roland understood what had happened. "You were the servant that left the poison. But, you don't know that I healed Eryck."

That made the man stop for a moment. "You are very powerful, Roland Tyre, more than I thought. But it won't matter. They will never find you."

"And, why is that?" Roland asked, raising his eyebrows.

"Because they will never know you are missing." And, with that, the man switched again, this time into an exact duplicate of Roland.

Roland screamed and leaped toward the doorway again. But, before he could get there, the chameleon impostor's Roland shut the door and turned the key in the lock. Roland roared as loudly as he could, but the room was soundproof, magicproof, and dark. And no one heard his yells.

CHAPTER TWELVE

Bakari still couldn't get over this feeling: of flying over the land, sitting on top of a dragon.

It's so wonderful Hold on! Abylar agreed in Bakari's mind. The young dragon found it as invigorating as his rider did, and he flew straight up in the air, turning a quick flip, head over tail, and then came back down.

Abylar, I'm going to get sick if you keep this up!

Sorry, Abylar said, but he made one last swoop before settling down with a loud exhale of fire.

"Young pup," Bakari mumbled under his breath as he shook his head with a broad smile on his face.

Abylar continued flying over the seemingly endless Elvyn Forest, but he kept his acrobatics to a minimum, for the time being.

Bakari watched the overgrown trees race by below them. The Elvyn Forest was the oldest known forest in all of the western lands. Its trees' limbs intertwined with each other, making it very difficult to see anything below them, on the ground. Some of the trees grew hundreds of feet high and just as wide. Villages of elves sat scattered throughout, many of them opting to stay away from the busier city of Lor'l and the border city of Silla.

Bakari searched in his mind for all he knew about the elves. They were usually a quiet kingdom, keeping mostly to themselves. Many of them practiced magic as part of their everyday lives—an outcome of living so long and of being so close to nature—but only a few were equivalent to the wizards of Alaris. These were usually named as protectors and guardians of the land.

The elves had lived in Elvyn for as long as anyone could remember. And it was rare to find one living outside of their kingdom. Though they did trade with others, it was mostly the others who had to do the traveling. In a small book that Bakari had read years ago, he remembered reading something about the elves coming from a faraway land, to escape a horrible war. He would need to ask the king about it when he returned.

Flying northwest from Lor'l, they soon found themselves close to what used to be called the barrier. From their height, Bakari could see the Dunn River, a sparkling ribbon winding its way from north to south. The afternoon sun had moved three-fourths of the way across the autumn sky when they found a patch of land big enough to land on, next to the river.

"River Bend will be just south of here," Bakari said. "A few turns down the river."

This thought made Bakari think of Kharlia again. They had escaped from River Bend about six weeks earlier to make their way to Celestar. The pain of losing her was still present, but the tasks at hand would distract him enough so that he didn't dwell on it too much

"I think we should stay here tonight." Bakari pointed downstream. "I don't think the people of River Bend are ready to see a dragon yet."

Abylar snorted in agreement.

The dragon had informed Bakari that a dragon egg was

near here, but there was no sign of Breelyn yet. She had left Celestar a few days before Bakari and Kharlia had last visited. The king said she had escaped from Silla only two days ago.

The sun had set earlier tonight, and Bakari wanted to get to sleep early and then get a fresh start in the morning, so he started setting up camp. He was feeling anxious about what was happening in Alaris. And they would need his help soon.

While Bakari set up a small fire and fished for some dinner, Abylar took off to find bigger game to fill his growing appetite.

After a nice meal, Bakari settled down on a blanket for the night. It still felt strange to be alone. Over the river, he glimpsed stars in the clear night, but the forest took up most of his vision.

Barely an hour into the night, the howl of a strange beast pierced the darkness. He stood up and threw some more wood on the fire and then grabbed a knife. He was trying to listen again, to figure out what direction the sound had come from, when another, deeper growl sounded directly behind him, just a few feet from the river's edge.

Bringing forth a bright mage light in the air in front of him, Bakari gasped.

An animal—more like a misshapen beast—stood facing him. It was the size of a large wild boar, and, at its core, it resembled one somewhat. But the magic of the barrier must have reformed it, giving it two enormous tusks; a longer snout, full of razor-sharp teeth; and a body and tail covered in spikes.

Before the beast moved any farther, the howl Bakari had heard earlier in the night sounded again now on his other side, somewhere inside the dark trees. Walking out from the forest came a hideous creature on two legs. His head was too big for a man, and his torso was hairy. He walked forward, hunched over.

Bakari thought he remembered reading something about apes living in the Elvyn Forest, but this creature was much more dreadful than an ape. Upon a closer look, the creature's hair appeared more like small, spiked needles and its hands ended in giant claws.

Bakari's first reaction was to fling magic at the beasts. Battle was not his expertise, but he knew how to draw fire and then throw it. He threw fire first at the apelike creature, then at the boar beast. But nothing happened other than him making both of them angrier.

So Bakari moved closer to the river. Maybe they were afraid of the water. He stepped forward carefully holding the knife out in front of him. The two beasts watched him, low growls and groans escaping their jaws.

As Bakari's left foot touched the water's edge, the boar beast let out a ferocious scream and ran at him. That spurred the apelike beast, and it dropped to the ground and ran forward, using all four legs.

Bakari jumped into the water and tripped on a rock. The water was cold, originating in the peaks of the Mahli Mountains. The water was not too deep yet, so he pulled himself up and pulled out his sword. The beasts slowed and paced at the edge of the river. They indeed seemed afraid of the water.

Things had happened so fast that Bakari had forgotten all

about Abylar. Calling to him now, in his mind, Bakari summoned him to come quickly.

The apelike creature took a careful step into the water. Bakari thrust his sword at it, but the apelike creature moved more quickly than Bakari had thought possible. It grabbed the knife out of Bakari's hand, slicing its own beastly claws in the process. That seemed to embolden the boar beast, and it crashed into the water after the young wizard, its hard muscles pushing its bulk through the water.

Bakari waded out farther into the river. His clothes made his movements slow and sluggish. Taking two more steps out, he now stood in waist-high water. The farther out he got, the harder the rushing water began to pull him south.

Then a knotted log came hurtling down the river at him. Bakari tried to move around it, but it hit into him and knocked him down into the water, his hands scraping the bottom. Losing his balance, he was swept along in the current of the fast-moving river.

Overhead, Bakari heard a loud roar and, out of the corner of his eye, saw Abylar swoop down toward the two creatures. Picking each one up separately, he flung them hard, off into the forest.

By now, Bakari had been swept around a bend and farther out into the river. After some minutes of struggling, he finally righted himself. Floating on his back, he let the current carry him along. Abylar flew overhead, trying to figure out how to save Bakari. The river moved too fast for Bakari to stand up in, and he was too small for Abylar to get close enough to lift him directly out of the water.

Bakari sifted back through his mind for an answer. And, once again, his natural instinct was to reach out to an animal. He extended his mind out to call nearby fish to swim under him, buoying him up in the water.

Once the fish were in place, Bakari reached deep down inside himself and tried to get the fish to lift him up. He tried twice but couldn't draw enough power to rise up out of the water—he was only a level two wizard.

Draw on my magic, Dragon Rider, Abylar said to his mind. *I have strength for you.*

Bakari opened his mind more fully to Abylar, delving deep inside his dragon's mind while still keeping a hold on his own, and drew forth additional power. He didn't know how he could do it, but he did. He felt the extra power. It was the power from the guardians, which Abylar had stored away as he had grown and developed.

Water splashed over him, and he lost his concentration for a minute. Then Abylar pushed the magic into him, and it was enough. Bakari began to rise out of the fast-moving water, but his momentum and connection to his magic enabled his body to still rush along at the same speed as if it were on the surface of water.

Abylar flew lower and brought down his two front legs and grabbed Bakari with his claws. The dragon swayed for a moment and almost dropped him, but Bakari steadied himself with the magic. Once Bakari was free of the water, Abylar took him to the nearest bank.

The young dragon rider stayed still and only breathed, trying to recover from the strenuous ordeal, both physically and magically. He was weak and tired and hardly able to concentrate.

Abylar! he called out in fear as he was about to black out. He felt himself sliding into the darkness, clutching onto the grass at the edge of the river. Then drops of rain, from an incoming storm, started to pelt his tired body. He tried to crawl up the bank farther but just couldn't do it. Finally, it was too much, and he passed out.

CHAPTER THIRTEEN

A short time later, Bakari opened his eyes and looked around. He was still on the bank of the river but had been pulled up a bit farther from the water. Abylar stood over him. Bakari sat up too quickly and had to wait a moment before his vision cleared all the way. Shaking his head to get himself thinking again, he scooted closer to Abylar.

Thank you, Abylar. Bakari touched the side of the growing dragon, and the bond flared up brightly in his mind.

You are my dragon rider. I told you I would protect you.

Where can we go? Bakari asked. *The storm is getting worse, and I'm still weak and cold.*

Abylar gazed across the river toward River Bend.

No. Kanzar may still have men there, and I can't risk them knowing about you yet, Bakari said with a groan. *I drained us of too much energy, so we can't get caught unawares right now.*

I saw an overhang of rock, north of here, when I flew back to you, Abylar offered. *It is high enough to keep the beasts away and should be dry.*

So Bakari climbed up onto the dragon and flew the short distance back to their camping spot. Bakari gathered up what the beasts hadn't destroyed, and then they continued back north, flying low over the river. Soon they came to the high rock overhang Abylar had mentioned.

There was a shelf, high up above the river, just big enough for Abylar to land on. As he did so, some of the cliff's face broke off and splashed into the water below. The storm now picked up a notch, but it blew in from the Blue Sea, in the East, so the western-facing cliffs were dry enough still.

Finding a useable cave, Bakari gathered some wood from under the larger trees and then moved into the cave. With a flick of his fingers, he lit the small fire. After a few moments, the cave grew warmer, and Bakari's clothes began to dry. Dawn would arrive in a few hours. Then, rain or not, they would continue looking for the other dragon egg.

Laying his head on his wet pack, Bakari drifted off to sleep while Abylar stood guard.

*   *   *

The next morning dawned dull and gray. The rain had continued, bringing with it a drop in temperature. So Bakari threw some more wood on the fire. The front part of his silk and cotton robes had dried, but the back was still soaked with river water.

His stomach growled, and he dug through his pack to see if he could find something that wasn't soaked. Pulling out a soggy piece of dried meat and a few carrots, he consumed them for the strength that he needed.

"We'll never find the egg in this weather," Bakari mumbled. Then he paced the floor of the cave for a few moments, moving farther back in it.

There's a tunnel here, Abylar, Bakari said. *But you can't fit.*

I can fly overhead and stay with you that way, Abylar voiced to Bakari's mind. *But, if you get into trouble in there, I won't be able to get to you.*

Bakari didn't want to leave the protection of his dragon, but he felt something pulling him to enter into the tunnels. So, picking up his pack and dousing the fire, he began walking, holding a mage light out in front of himself to light the way.

At first, the tunnel stayed fairly straight, with only a few turns. After an hour of walking, he stopped and drank a bit from his waterskin. Bakari stayed in constant contact with Abylar, and the dragon told him that there were people—elves, he thought—traveling not far from them.

As the tunnel branched, a few times, Bakari would stop and push out his mind to see if he could tell where he was and where the dragon egg might be.

Dragon Rider, Abylar spoke suddenly. *The elves are in trouble. A trio of beasts are chasing them. I am going to try and help.*

Bakari took comfort in Abylar's thoughts, but he hated being physically blind to what was happening above. What if his dragon got into trouble? Bakari picked up his pace and started jogging forward through the tunnel. Then the underground space opened up wider, and he found himself in an immense room, filled with old clothes and scattered bones.

Bakari sensed Abylar shooting down fire at the beasts above but could also tell, by Abylar's frustration, that it didn't stop them. And the forest was too thick for him to land.

The elves disappeared, Abylar said. *I can't see them anymore.*

Bakari stumbled against the wall as a loud rumble shook the tunnel. A scattering of dust and rocks fell from overhead. He didn't like being this far below ground. He ran out of the room and back into another tunnel, now sprinting as fast as he could.

Coming to a fork in the tunnel, Bakari abruptly stopped. Breathing hard, he tried to determine which way to go. He felt something pulling him to the left, but then he heard sounds coming from the right. And that was also the direction Abylar was in.

"Which way?" the young wizard voiced out loud. "I feel like I need to go both ways, but I can't."

The noises from the right grew louder. It sounded like people running. Suddenly a bright light erupted down in the tunnel. Into the light came two people—elves, by the way they were dressed. The light grew so bright it was hard to see clearly. They came up in front of Bakari, not seeing him until they had almost run over him.

"Bak!" a woman called out, definitely caught by surprise. "What are you doing here?"

Bakari was also surprised but was happy to see Breelyn, the first elf he had ever met. She held the bright flame of light in front of her slender, but strong body. Her straight, blond hair framed her bright blue eyes and pale face. Next to her stood Alair, sweat glistening off his skin, his muscles held taut.

"I am here looking for you," Bakari notified her.

Surprise flashed across Breelyn's face. "I thought that might be your dragon, trying to help us out there."

"He told me you were running away from three barrier beasts."

Breelyn's eyes widened in awe. "Of course, I should have guessed you can communicate with him."

Alair nodded his head toward Bakari. They had met shortly

after the barrier fell but before Bakari had left Celestar with Abylar for the first time. The man was a guard of sorts for Breelyn, one of King Arrowyn's protectors. He was taller than Bakari or Breelyn, his long dark hair hanging down in Elvyn fashion. He looked like he could wield every one of the numerous weapons hanging from his belt, as well as the bow across his back.

"I collapsed the tunnel opening so that the beasts couldn't follow us, but I am not sure that will stop them for long," Breelyn said in a quick clip. Looking at the other two tunnels, she then turned to Bakari and asked, "Which way?"

Bakari pointed down the other tunnel of the fork.

"Is that the way you came from?" Alair asked, looking down the other fork. "Where does it go?"

"I came from the other direction, from the Dunn River," Bakari said as he started down the other way, taking quick steps in front of the others.

"What's down here?" Alair asked, urgency in his voice. "Where are you leading us?"

Bakari turned back around and shrugged. "I wish I knew, but this is the right way. I can assure you of that."

Breelyn put her hand on Alair's arm. "He is the dragon rider. We can trust him, Alair. You know the histories. He is the first in one hundred and fifty years."

Alair grunted but then fell into line.

Bakari spoke with Abylar, asking him to try and find out where they would be coming out.

"You said you were looking for me?" Breelyn came up behind Bakari. "Why?"

"I've been to see your king," he said, not answering her question. "He thinks highly of you."

"King Arrowyn! You saw him?"

"Yes, and Lan." Bakari turned around and grinned at Breelyn, clearly surprising her with his words. She seemed flustered and stopped talking, and a small laugh came from Alair. "He said he wishes you well until you are reunited again," Bakari added.

Breelyn blushed and turned away from the two men.

Up ahead, Bakari saw the tunnel widening once again into an underground room.

"Do you feel that?" Breelyn whispered with awe.

Bakari only smiled and continued walking. He appreciated what she now felt. It was the same thing that he had felt when he had first come into contract with the Dragon Orb in Celestar. Breelyn was feeling her connection to the next egg. Through his bond with Abylar, Bakari felt the same thing.

Walking into the room, the three of them stopped in silence. Sitting in the middle of the underground room was a light yellow dragon egg about twelve feet tall. It rocked with small movements on a bed of ancient pine needles and dried oak leaves. The cavernous room was about fifty feet wide and at least that tall; its walls, a smooth rock.

"Breelyn," Bakari whispered. "The king suggested for you to be another dragon rider."

Her elf-maiden eyes opened wide, a small tear appearing in the corner.

"But," Bakari continued, "the dragon needs to choose its rider."

Up above them, a scraping sound was made. The group looked up only to have to shield themselves from falling rocks, leaves, and dirt. In a moment, there appeared a wide hole, about five feet in diameter, directly over their heads. In through that opening peered Abylar, his blue skin shining in the firelight that Breelyn continued to keep in front of them. He almost grinned down at Bakari. Their bond shivered with excitement.

No one spoke as Breelyn took a few steps toward the egg. Before reaching it, she turned her head back to look at Bakari, as if for his permission.

He smiled and nodded his head for her to continue. "Go ahead, Breelyn."

As she placed her hand on the egg, it flared so brightly that the two men had to shield their eyes. After a moment, it settled down to a translucent shine. Inside the egg, the outline of a baby dragon appeared, its wings beginning to move. Without warning, the egg cracked, then shattered into hundreds of pieces, shells flying through the air, hitting, but not hurting them.

Standing before them appeared a beautiful yellow dragon, about eight feet tall and already about twenty feet long, including its spiked tail, which saked around the room. Touches of orange and red covered the tips of its beautiful scales.

The three gasped in delight, Breelyn laughing—a musical sound that filled the cave. Reaching up to the dragon, and with a joyful laugh, Breelyn touched its neck just below its substantial jawline.

"She is a female dragon," Breelyn said. "Miriel! I name you Miriel—meaning *jewel*."

The dragon emitted a small purring sound at the mention of her name. Her emerald eyes sparkled in the light.

Abylar roared overhead, and Miriel eyed her fellow dragon up above. Taking a few steps around the room, to strengthen her legs, she flapped her wide, curved wings, and then lifted off the ground. She took one small circle around the room and then flew straight up and out of the hole that Abylar had created – breaking the ground open even further with her massive body.

The room was quiet for a moment.

Then Bakari turned to Breelyn and said with a toothy smile, "Welcome, Dragon Rider."

Tears flowed from Breelyn's beautiful eyes. The feeling of reverence was only broken by the two dragons, squawking above them in the sky.

Breelyn knelt in front of Bakari and, with words thick with emotion, said, "Now I know how you feel. The bond is amazing. I cannot believe I am a dragon rider, Master."

"Rise, Breelyn." Bakari offered her his hand and pulled her up. "I am not your master."

"But you are the first. History is full of stories about the famed dragon riders. Always, the first is the master, referred to as the king or queen, and others come after." She paused for a moment, as if realizing what she had just said. "Others? Oh, Bakari, will there be others?"

Still not used to the deference being given him, Bakari looked around the cave nervously. "Yes, there are more, but time is running out. Alaris is on the brink of war."

"We must leave the cave, Dragon Riders," Alair said with

grave reverence to the two.

Bakari pointed to an opening on the far side of the cave. "It's only a few dozen feet."

Emerging once again into the open air, Bakari breathed in deeply. He didn't like how long he had been underground and away from his dragon. The bond was just as strong, but being able to touch his beautiful blue scales made him feel more comfortable. Looking around, Bakari noted that the rain had stopped, but water still dripped down from the tall trees.

Circling overhead flew two of the most beautiful creatures Bakari had ever seen—blue and yellow—Abylar and Miriel. Bakari asked Abylar to fly high across Alaris and come back by nightfall and report so that they would know what was happening there. Then the three of them found a place to camp for the night, where the dragons could land safely when they returned.

Alair turned to Breelyn with uncommon mirth and a sparkle in his eyes. "Wait until the prince hears of this," he said. His laughter boomed through the looming trees, echoing off into the distance.

CHAPTER FOURTEEN

Erryl Close, a former guardian of the Orb, sat on a white bench in the cool autumn air of the small park in the center of Celestar. He glanced up from the book he was reading—the one Bakari had given him, from Mahli. The leaves on the trees were turning orange and yellow and were starting to fall once again. This far up, toward the mountains, the cool weather began earlier than in the rest of Alaris.

He had been reading about the deserts to the south and could hardly comprehend a land filled with dust, sand, and only a few trees. He stood and stretched his young body. At almost fifteen, he certainly didn't have much experience in the world, outside of the schooling they gave all guardians. But he had touched a real dragon and met a dragon rider. That was something!

A dragon! Abylar! It was still hard to comprehend. The Orb, which Erryl and his family and many before them had guarded and had given their life forces to, had—unknown to them—been a dragon egg.

As he walked around the quiet garden pathways, he thought about the book he held in his hands. Its ancient writings talked about the prophecies of a dragon king. One that would come from Mahli and bring them back into the happenings of the world. But, most importantly, he would bring peace to all lands that he touched. It seemed that the dragon riders came whenever the need for peace was the greatest. So the land of Mahli had regents that watched over the land and waited until the next dragon king arose.

There were multiple stories and historical accounts in the small book, of that same thing happening numerous times over the past thousand years. And, always, the first dragon rider became the leader. Always, he became the dragon king. Never once was there a discrepancy in the order of these things: One dragon rider would emerge. He would then find the others. And, together, they would establish peace and hope among the nations. Then they would name him king—a high king, in fact—one that would rule over all the southern kingdoms on the Western Continent. Erryl knew that this wasn't what Bakari wanted to hear, but it was the truth.

He saw a few elves walking with guardians outside of the garden gate. He liked how the elves treated them, almost reverently, for their part in providing life force to sustain the Dragon Orb. Erryl was thrust into a leadership role, too, with the rest of the guardians, even though he was one of the youngest. His part, in bringing Bakari to Celestar and in freeing the dragon, earned him a position of respect. One that he wasn't all too comfortable with.

He put the book into a small pocket of his white robes and walked back to the building that used to house the Orb. With his thoughts elsewhere, he walked around the corner of a building. Then a strong hand grabbed him from behind and shoved him up against the wall.

"Where are all the guardians, boy?" A man, who was definitely an elf, held Erryl close, but his demeanor didn't seem like that of any elf Erryl had met. The man still had the long hair, slanted eyes, and pointed ears of a typical elf, but his face was harder and cruel looking. And he was looking at Erryl with only a few inches between them.

"The guardians?" Erryl stuttered. "What do you mean?"

The man grabbed Erryl's shoulder harder. "Tell me where they are!"

"You're hurting me, sir," Erryl said, trying to stand up to the man, but Erryl had never been trained in fighting.

"I'll do more than that if you don't tell me."

"They're...they're everywhere, sir. Since the barrier fell, we don't have any other duties, but..." Erryl was cut off by a thin finger pointing in his face.

"You mean you're one of these guardians? So young!"

"I was a guardian, as I said. We don't do a whole lot now that the dragon is gone." Erryl heard a couple of distant screams, and he tried to pull away. But the man held him tight.

"So, there is a dragon...interesting," the man said. Dragging Erryl away, the man continued, "The governor will be interested in you."

As he was pulled down a side road, Erryl thought about the book in his pocket. He didn't know who this man was or what he wanted, but Erryl knew he couldn't let him read what was in that book. Feigning a trip, on the walkway next to the garden gate, Erryl fell down. And, before the man could tell what Erryl was doing, he shoved the small book underneath one of the fence posts.

"Get back up, boy!" the elf yelled, grabbing him roughly.

Coming up to an intersection, Erryl saw some of his fellow guardians and a few elves, walking together, and thought to yell.

But, before he could, a small knife was pushed with a slight jab against his ribs.

He heard more screams, coming from the other side of the city now. Then the air filled with crackles of lightning and fire.

"Wizards attacking!" someone yelled, the sound floating down from a side street.

As Erryl tried to pull away from the elf again, the point of the knife broke the skin on his side. The small slash brought a jab of heat and pain. So he decided to go without any other struggle.

The two walked quickly down the hill, away from Celestar, and across the point that used to be the barrier but that was now only a line of trees. Soon they walked within the thick Elvyn Forest. Erryl heard sounds of fighting behind them and wondered if it was Kanzar's men. Gorn and Bakari had both warned him that Kanzar might attack Celestar. What could Kanzar want now, though? The orb was gone.

After walking for another thirty minutes or so, Erryl began to see other guardians, being escorted in the same manner. Most were older than himself. Erryl thought about his father and wondered where he might be. His mother had passed away a few months ago, not too long before Bakari had shown up. She had given everything to the Orb, including her final act of life.

They walked for another hour. The sun had moved closer to evening. After passing a small stream, in the middle of the forest, they came upon a small gathering of men standing around a group of humongous oak trees.

Looking up high, Erryl noticed platforms and buildings

scattered among their branches, typical of an Elvyn village. When the barrier was still up, Erryl hadn't realized he lived so close to the elves. But these elves didn't seem like those that had come to Celestar to help. These elves seemed intent on causing trouble.

About twenty guardians were corralled together and set up with guards, behind a fenced area. As he was led over to join them, they looked to Erryl for help. Then he saw that his father was among them. Erryl had been out of the city before, on his way to find Bakari, so he had observed how strange the world was outside of Celestar—a city where all their needs were met for them.

Some of the women began to cry, and Erryl moved over to them and tried to comfort them. "Things will be fine," he said. "Gorn and the others will find us."

Gorn was a battle wizard that had been Alli's mentor and had arrived to help right after Bakari had. Gorn had taken a real liking to Celestar and was invaluable to Erryl for helping him to understand his young leadership responsibilities. A fierce battle wizard, Gorn was also a good mentor. And Erryl hoped the fighting in Celestar wouldn't stop the wizard from helping them.

"What about the beasts?" someone asked.

"And, where will we get food and sleep?" questioned another.

These were just some of the questions the other guardians threw at Erryl. He didn't know if he knew all the answers to their questions. The world was a big place.

Erryl scanned the area. A beefy man came to the entrance

of the pen where Erryl and the guardians were being kept. The man was an elf, by the slope of his ears and eyes, but not by his weight. Erryl hadn't seen many elves, but he didn't think they grew so big around. The man's belly pushed out his brown robes way over his toes.

He walked into the pen and grabbed the nearest guardian. "Tell me about the dragon."

The guardian shook his head. "I don't know anything, sir. I only saw it once."

The man then grabbed another guardian and roughly pulled her close to himself. "How many wizards do you have?"

She glanced over at Erryl. But he gave a slight shake of his head to her. They couldn't tell any information to these elves until they understood what was going on.

"My name is Governor Ellian," the fat elf said, pushing the woman he had held to the ground. "I want answers. And I want them now. I want to know about the dragon. Where is it? How many wizards do you have? Where is Breelyn? Have Kanzar's men arrived?"

The guardians stood quietly, but many of them glanced at Erryl for support. These looks were not missed by the governor. He strode over to Erryl.

"These guardians seem to be looking at you, son. What is your name?"

"Erryl Close, sir."

"Well, Erryl, do you have the answers I need to know?"

Erryl had never felt so much fear in his life. His throat went dry, and he barely held himself up.

Then the governor grabbed Erryl's chin and pulled it up.

"We have been waiting years for the barrier to come down and for me to get my due," the governor said. "Some youngster is not going to get in my way."

Digging down deep inside himself, Erryl thought about Bakari, Breelyn, Alli, Gorn, and the others he had met in the last few months. His world had indeed turned exciting, more so than he would have ever thought possible when, as a guardian, he used to dream about leaving Celestar. These new friends had taught him many things, but the one thing that stood out was friendship, that and loyalty to something that was bigger than themselves.

"Like you said, I'm only a youngster. What would I know?" Erryl cringed inside as he said this. It wasn't like him to be combative or rude to someone, but this man was not good. Not good at all.

"If that Breelyn girl hadn't escaped, I would have more answers," the governor mumbled under his breath.

With the mention of Breelyn's escape, Erryl perked back up.

The governor grabbed Erryl, marching him out of the corral. Then Erryl was shoved against a nearby tree, and the governor grabbed his hands, pulling his arms around the back of the tree. The governor used rough vines to tie his wrists around the tree. Erryl cried out in pain as his arms were yanked back tighter. He tried to move, but couldn't, his back pressing against the tree's rough bark. Then tears stung Erryl's eyes as his limbs were pulled back again, tighter. "No!" shouted one of the other guardians. "He's just a boy!"

"Just a boy who defies me!" shouted Governor Ellian, his

face red with exertion. "He knows more than he is willing to tell. So, now we will see how stubborn he can be." The governor then motioned for one of his men to take another guardian, a middle-aged man, out from the others.

"What is your name?" the governor demanded.

"Reese." The guardian hung his head low.

"Well, Reese, there are beasts here by the barrier," the governor continued, "nasty things with sharp teeth and horns. They like to *eat*." He scowled at the group of guardians. "But they do hold on to some kind of intelligence, and we have come to a type of understanding with them. They will leave us alone in these remote villages if we offer up some food to them. Normally, it's a chicken or a dove or maybe a deer. But I think they would indeed take a liking to eating a guardian."

Many of the guardians began to cry and to beg for help from their captors. But Erryl had never seen such evil in his life and didn't know what to do. He just hoped that Gorn would find them soon.

The governor ordered one of his men to take Reese to the beasts. In silence, Erryl and the others watched the two fade into the forest.

Five minutes passed.

Then ten more.

A slight breeze stirred the leaves, and Erryl noticed a few gold and red ones float to the ground at his feet.

Suddenly a horrible sound filled the air—a beastly growl—and Erryl felt his hair stand on end. Then it was silent again. But he feared that this wouldn't last long.

A lonesome, painful cry filled the air.

"Noooooo! Noooooo! Heeeeelllllp!" Reese's scream came, floating over the trees.

The guardians in the corral started yelling at once for someone to help the man, many of them bawling uncontrollably.

Erryl wanted to cover his face, but his hands remained where they were tied. Tears blurred his vision and dropped down onto his check, running down his neck and onto his shirt. But he had kept his mouth closed, and didn't take his eyes off of the governor. Even some of the governor's men turned away.

The yells from Reese abruptly stopped. Erryl heard a few echoes of snarls, and then silence filled the night once again.

Turning to Erryl, the governor's face went hard. "Well, Erryl Close, this is what happens when you defy me. Every four hours until morning, another guardian will be taken and given to the beasts. By noon tomorrow, if I don't have answers from you, then you will be the noon meal—you and the rest of this ragtag lot, all together. Think about it, Erryl. Or, you can talk and be saved."

Erryl didn't know whether he could take the death of even one more guardian, but he also realized that he didn't dare give a man like this such information.

"We serve Alaris," Erryl said. "We serve peace. We were prepared to give our lives to the Orb to protect the land," Erryl continued, his voice coming out strong and clear as the other guardians listened and nodded in agreement. "The barrier is destroyed but not the intent, not the mission, not our responsibility. If we die, we die for something bigger!"

The guardians cheered and reiterated what Erryl had said.

But the governor strode over to Erryl and backhanded him. Then he began hitting Erryl over and over and over.

"Ready to answer yet?" he asked Erryl as blood dripped down the sides of the young guardian's face.

But Erryl said nothing and let his head hang low. He sucked in a brief bit of air to try and still his cries.

"Then you will all die—die for nothing—because I will be king of this land!"

Erryl's vision was blurry, and he could feel blood and spit dripping from his mouth.

"Never," Erryl said in a whisper. "Never."

CHAPTER FIFTEEN

The fighting in Corwan was getting on Alli's nerves. Too many good people were dying and all for the greed of the few individuals wanting power. In just the last hour, the docks had been breached, and Kanzar's men were now advancing into the city. The tail end of a storm had dropped a bit of rain on the desert city the day before, but now the sun shone as brightly as ever, and the sands quickly absorbed any remaining moisture.

Alli stood on the roof of the governor's building, surveying the layout of the city and considering what they could do to hold their defenses. The elves from Mallek were diligent in keeping the opposing army from breaking through the front gates, but Alli wondered how long these elves would allow their ranks to continue to be decimated.

Looking west, she hoped for some sign of Tam, returning with Judge Azeem's army. But nothing yet stirred up any desert dust in that direction. Seeing the enemy coming quicker up from the docks than she had hoped, Alli took a deep breath and then let it out in slow puffs. Then she took the steps by twos back down to the ground floor and ran out into the city. Snaps and flares, from magic being used, scorched the air, so she picked up her pace.

Just before she reached the docks, a man sideswiped her, and she tumbled to the ground. She must be getting tired. She should have anticipated that. Rolling on the ground, she stood back up and faced a man that she recognized. He had fought *with* her and Gorn in Orr only a few months back. He seemed to recognize her also and gave a deep sigh.

"You don't have to do this, Lars," she said, preparing to fight against the man.

He cringed but brought up his sword. "You don't understand, Alli. We belong to Kanzar now."

"He doesn't own you. Be a man, and do what's right."

The sounds of swords and of men yelling were getting closer. Soon they would be breaching the city itself.

"Easy for you to say, Wizard," spat Lars. "You have magic to protect you. I have a wife and my children to think about."

Alli knew that Lars had a good point, but someone needed to stand up to Kanzar.

Then Lars advanced toward her, with his sword out and a determined look on his face. With a sudden jump into the air, Alli spun in an arc around to the side of Lars, kicking the sword out of his hand on the way. Grabbing his other wrist, she twisted it behind him, forcing him to the ground.

"I don't want to kill you," she said. "But I need you to leave."

Digging his heels into the ground, the muscle-bound man tried to push Alli away. So she stepped back and let his momentum send him flying to the ground on the other side of her, knocking him out in the process. Then she kicked his sword away and left him on the ground.

The sounds of fighting grew stronger, and the docks nearest to the river were now burning. Running toward the source of the flames, Alli spun her way through a dozen men, her blue cape swirling around her small body as if it were alive. She dropped men all around her: a sword thrust here, a punch there, or a kick to the head. She tried not to kill them, but sometimes that was hard when they were trying to kill her.

She reached the docks themselves and surveyed the damage. Then she sucked in a quick breath in surprise. Through the smoke and fire, she glimpsed Mericus, talking to someone. Looking more closely, she realized it was one of the enemy soldiers. A young man, not much older than herself, by the looks of him. Mericus seemed to be shouting at him and pointing.

What was the judge doing, talking to the enemy? Was he really who he said he was? Or, was he letting the enemy in through the gates? She never had trusted the man, his smooth talk and good looks. He was more a politician than a soldier for sure. But, was he negotiating his way out of this?

Alli clenched her jaw and turned back to the flames. She would deal with Mericus later. Putting forth her hands, toward the river's water, she drew on her extensive power. She churned the water with wind until it stood up in the air, forming a funnel about ten feet high. But she found her concentration slipping. She was definitely getting tired. So, with one hefty heave, she brought the water crashing over the docks to douse the fire. The water hissed as it hit the burning docks, and a wall of steam flew up in the air.

She heard a mixture of cheers and yells behind her. Glancing over her shoulder, Alli saw two of Kanzar's soldiers running forward to stop her. Turning back toward the water, she pushed her power out again and gathered water into the air.

This time, her arms quivered and her hands shook. Three days of fighting with little rest were taking their toll.

She began to move the water. But, before she could get it completely over the docks again, a man hit her from the side, and she went skidding across the recently burning wood, charcoal and splinters of wood scraping into her thin leather pants. The water she had held in the air began to fall back into the river.

"Nooo!" she yelled and began pulling the water back up into the air. But a second man stood over her now, with his sword held high. She watched in a daze as his arm lowered toward her. Then, using a reserve of strength that she didn't know she still possessed, she pushed herself forward, under the man's legs, pulling the water with her and knocking him down. The soldier's sword hit the dock, and then a wall of water smashed into him, throwing him a dozen feet away.

The rest of the water continued to put out the remaining fire. Alli breathed in deeply, trying to calm her beating heart. It hurt to breathe; she had taken in a lot of smoke and steam.

The first soldier, who had hit her, came back at her again now, rushing toward her. She could hardly gather the strength to stand. She pushed her dark hair out of her eyes and braced herself for the attack. Moments before the soldier reached her, his face registered shock, and he stumbled and fell forward. Alli rolled to the side, and the falling man just missed crushing her.

Looking back at him, she noticed a small knife sticking out of his back. She sat up, got onto her knees, and then scanned the area. Twenty feet away, Mericus stood, looking at her, with a grim smile. He approached and, with an outstretched hand, helped her up.

"Who were you talking to a minute ago, Mericus?"

"Not even a thank-you for saving your life, Wizard?" Mericus smirked, his white teeth perfect and his blue eyes sparkling down at her.

Alli grunted and tried to breathe in deeper. "I'm tired" was all she could say. The smell of burnt wood filled her nose, and her lungs hurt. "Did you let Kanzar's men onto the docks?"

Mericus frowned. "Why would you think that? You need to rest."

Alli grew even more suspicious when Mericus didn't answer her clearly. She couldn't trust anyone. *Well, maybe Bak, and possibly Roland. Roland!* Why did she always seem to think of *him* at the worst times? Maybe it was because he was arrogant and no good for her. But he did allow her to be raised to a full wizard. A level three wizard. And at only fifteen years old.

Now, she stood as the youngest battle wizard. Looking at Mericus, Alli was consoled by the fact that, as a wizard, he was now only her peer, being a level three wizard himself. So, without warning, Alli threw herself against Mericus, taking him to the ground.

He brought up his hands and, with an attack of air, pushed her off of himself. "What are you doing?" He jumped back up from the ground. "Are you insane?"

"I'm tired of being betrayed, and I'm tired of fighting." Alli stood with hands on hips. She licked her lips, wishing for something to drink.

"I haven't betrayed you!" Mericus roared. "I've been fighting with you these past three days, and I just saved your life."

"Why were you talking to that enemy soldier? You pointed at the city. You were giving directions to him."

Mericus took in a deep breath and then let it out slowly. He took a step closer to Alli, and she readied herself. Barely able to stand, she gathered as much power as she could muster.

"That was my nephew, Alli," Mericus said in soft tones. The two stood facing each other, strangely alone, the battle having moved off the burning docks and farther up, into the streets. "He's not even a man yet."

Alli let her power subside and then stumbled into Mericus. He caught her from falling and put an arm around her.

"I can't bear to see him die," Mericus said. "He is the only son of my oldest sister." Mericus looked pained as he kept an eye open for any attacks. "I told him where to go to be safe. He doesn't want to fight us. Most of these men don't, but Kanzar has them so afraid."

Alli felt ashamed. Just moments ago, she, too, let an old friend go free. War did rotten things to people, making friend fight against friend. She held on to Mericus and stared up at his face. It held smudges of ash from the burning docks, and his normally combed-back hair was messed up and singed. Unbidden and sudden, the thought of how handsome he actually was came to her exhausted mind.

Tentatively, Mericus reached up and brushed a stray hair out of Alli's face. Alli wanted to smile at this unanticipated attention, but she was just too tired.

"Sorry" was the only word she said before she collapsed fully into his arms.

* * *

Chief Judge Daymian Khouri sat with his military advisers around a table. His dark tan face was indicative of the people of Orr—his hometown. His hair was still full and dark, but his thin beard and goatee were starting to show signs of gray. Having been a judge of Alaris for twelve years, the last three as Chief Judge, he'd faced difficult circumstances before, but the complete collapse of the government was not one he had been prepared for. He had been considered a good and fair judge, but now, under the pushing of Kanzar Centari, many people wanted a king. Daymian had agreed to stand by the vote of the people, but Kanzar had overpassed that vote and had set himself up as the king already.

Over the last few weeks, support had arrived from all over the kingdom. Those wishing to abide by the law of the land and to keep Kanzar from becoming the king.

"If the people want a king, I will step down," Daymian said to the group, "but I will not—and I repeat—I will not allow Kanzar to be that king."

Cheers and claps sounded around the table. These men and women, a handful of them even wizards themselves, sat in complete agreement: Kanzar had grown too power hungry to be a fair and decent king.

"Reports!" Daymian ordered.

Lenz, A battle wizard in his late twenties answered first. "Kanzar has sent a sizable contingent of soldiers to Corwan. I heard from my sources that Mericus went there and, if it is to be believed, that he defected and didn't take the city as Kanzar had commanded him to do."

"Mericus, huh?" The Chief Judge thought for a moment. "I don't know him well. An opportunist, maybe, but a good sign of weakness in Kanzar's ranks."

"And, it seems that Kanzar is also having trouble in Cassian. The thieves' guild seems to be acting up and causing him trouble," Lenz said, finished now with his report.

"Any mention of Onius?" Daymian asked. He still hoped Onius, his old counselor, had not defected to Kanzar's side.

"He seems to be by Kanzar's side and doing his bidding, but he doesn't seem too happy with things."

"I hope he's feeling guilty," Daymian mumbled under his breath. "Next!" he said more loudly and motioned for the next report.

"The Citadel seems quiet," said Riona, one of the few women among Daymian's military advisers. "More apprentice recruits arrive daily, but there is no sign of preparing for anything, other than wizards teaching them."

"Who runs the place?" the Chief Judge asked, for clarification. "Are they still bowing to Roland Tyre?"

Riona laughed. "Yes, they are, sir. That young wizard has them all doing his bidding. I spent a few days there, and it was quite fun to watch the older wizards deferring to him."

Some of the other wizards in the room frowned at her and seemed to grow concerned.

"Besides that," Riona continued, "there are a few reports of things going missing."

Daymian nodded his head. Taking a drink from a glass goblet in front of him, he motioned for the next report. His throat was always so dry in Orr. The desert dust made him thirsty. He wished for the more northern cities' climate. He smiled to himself at this thought. He had let himself get spoiled through the years.

Before anything else was said, someone burst into the room.

"Tam!" The Chief Judge rose out of his chair. "I didn't expect to see you here."

The young apprentice's clothes were disheveled and looked full of desert sand. He took off his head wrap, and sand fell all over the floor. "Sorry, sir." He looked embarrassed. "I've been on the road from Corwan for days and couldn't wait to get that darn thing off. I know it helps to keep the sun off my head, but it is surely uncomfortable."

"Don't worry," the Chief Judge said. "Where is Alli?"

A servant standing nearby handed Tam a mug, and he gulped its contents down in generous swallows. Wiping his mouth on his sleeve, Tam continued, "Judge Mericus arrived last week with a group of men."

"Yes, I had heard that," Daymian said.

"Don't know much about him, but it seems he's decided to defy Kanzar. Well, it seems Kanzar sent an army to convince him to do otherwise. Judge Azeem left with his battalion right after Mericus arrived. They were marching back here to support you. But I was sent to ask Judge Azeem to return to Corwan to help fight Kanzar's men. Then, I continued on alone to make sure you were aware of their plans."

"Whose authority had you for that, young man?" Lenz spoke up again.

Tam looked at the Chief Judge and then back at Lenz

"Well, Battle Wizard Alli, sir. Kanzar sent his men by land and by river. The Mallek elves are also helping, but it might not be enough."

"That girl doesn't hold any authority," Lenz stood up from his chair.

"What about the elves?" asked Hakim, another of the Chief Judges advisors from Orr.

"What is Mericus doing?" Riona chimed in.

"Quiet, please," the Chief Judge said, raising his voice slightly. "These are difficult times. I trust that if Alli thought additional help was needed, it was. So far, Kanzar has not deigned to attack us directly yet."

Tam then proceeded to tell them about the help from the Mallek elves and that Mericus seemed to be working against Kanzar for now, but that no one truly understood what Mericus's end goal was.

"His end goal is to be king," stated the Chief Judge, frowning. He didn't know if that was good or bad. "For now, we will hold our course and wait to see the outcome in Corwan. In the meantime, we will continue to train here in preparation for Kanzar's attack. It will come. It has to."

CHAPTER SIXTEEN

The darkness seemed to suffocate Roland Tyre, and he grew claustrophobic. And, for the first time in his short life, he was truly afraid. When the creature who was Celia—that Roland now named *the Chameleon*—had closed the door, Roland had stood in the darkness, hoping and even praying that something else would happen: A light would seep underneath the door. Help would come. Or his magic would return. Anything.

But nothing happened. No one came. And his magic—his lifeblood—remained dormant.

Roland had lived a relatively easy life. Sure, when he was younger, he did work on his family's farm and helped his father with his carpentry, but, in the end, it wasn't all that hard. He figured now that, for most of his life, the easiness he'd found had much to do with the magic that had flowed unfettered through his body. He had told Bakari that he didn't just feel the magic but that he *was* the magic. That it was who he was. And that, at sixteen years old, he was one of the most powerful wizards in Alaris.

But now, the magic had left him all alone. If this is what normal humans felt like, Roland never wanted to be *normal*. He felt tired and sluggish, and his senses were dull, but that could be in part due to the dark.

For the first half hour, he had screamed his voice raw. Then extreme anger set in, and he thought of all the harm he would do to the Chameleon when he found her or him or whatever it was. Now despair was beginning to consume him, bit by bit.

What if he never got out? How long could he survive in this dark room with dangerous magical artifacts around him? He slowly sat down on the floor and then scooted himself back until he found a space on the wall to lean against. He closed his eyes, though this didn't matter in the least. Eyes open or closed, it was the same.

Somehow, Roland fell asleep. His slumber was restful and long, filled with dreams of glory and leading other wizards. Upon awakening, he felt a renewed sense of peace and hope.

Wasn't he always bragging about how smart and powerful he was? Well, when he wasn't watching the women. That thought was stopped short. He had liked Celia, and look at what she had done to him. And he had kissed that thing! *Yuck!*

He shook his head to clear his thoughts. Above all else, as a counselor, he had been trained to think clearly. Onius had been relentless in trying to have Roland look at all the possibilities and positions.

He stood back up and began stepping carefully around the small room with his arms outstretched. With only a step or two in each direction his hands met shelves filled with boxes, bottles, and sacks full of strange things. Things he wasn't sure he actually wanted to touch.

What would they do? Did it matter what they did? It couldn't be much worse, could it?

Feeling a small box, he worked to open the lid and began to reach inside. He hesitated for a moment, let out a deep breath, and then plunged ahead. His hands wrapped around a small, round object. It felt cool to his touch, signifying a type of metal. He brought it out in front of him, but, of course, he still wasn't able to see it.

On instinct, he tried to bring forth his magic once again, to study the object. The backlash was severe, knocking him back against another shelf. Objects dropped to the ground, and he waited for something else to happen. But it didn't.

"What was that?" he muttered to himself.

He still held the round object. Even though he couldn't get to his magic, the object had responded to him trying to use it. He reached out blindly for a nearby shelf and set the strange item down. The shock had numbed his fingertips.

More timidly now, he reached forward in the dark once again. This time, he found a sack. Inside, he found a dozen very small blocks of wood. He pulled a few out and ran his fingers over them. Five of their sides were smooth, but one side was rougher, almost as if something was written on it. He fumbled with one for a moment, turning it over, and then it dropped from his hand.

By the time when it would have hit the floor, Roland's feet were sinking into the ground, or rather through the ground. He couldn't see it with his eyes, but somehow he knew his body had just slid through the solid rock floor. His feet finally came to rest on another floor a dozen feet lower.

Roland realized his eyes were still closed as he had handled the small blocks. Now, he opened them and found himself in another room, similar to the one above. Shelves lined with boxes, bottles, and bags of objects stood before him.

"I can see," he said out loud, realizing the truth of it. He smiled broadly and took a deep breath. Light had never seemed so wonderful. He laughed out loud.

Glancing around again, he furrowed his eyebrows. The room appeared identical to what he remembered the room above looking like.

"That's strange."

Roland took a few steps and found the box with the ball inside that he had opened earlier. It was back in its original place, as if he hadn't disturbed it. In fact, everything was back in place except for the two small blocks he still held.

He walked toward the door and pushed. And, to his surprise and relief, it opened wide, letting more light, from the torches lining the hallway, flood in beside him. He had thought he must be down on a lower basement floor, as he remembered passing down through the floor of the dark room, but everything here looked eerily the same as before.

Remembering Celia and what she had done to him, he raced down the corridor until he reached the stairs. Taking them two at a time, he ran to the top. Right before opening the door, he stopped, putting the blocks in a pocket of his robe. Then he combed his hair with his hands and took a deep breath.

Pushing the door open, he found himself on the main floor of the Citadel. Servants were rushing around as if in a hurry to do someone's bidding. So he stepped out of the stairwell to stop one of them.

"What is going on here?" he asked the young woman.

The servant ignored him, not even looking his way, and

continued on her task.

Roland frowned. He hadn't encountered anyone so rude before. Coming down the stairs was Titus. A group of guards walked with him as if guarding him. The wizard's wrinkled face looked even more tired than usual, and his steps were slow.

"Titus?" Roland ran up to him. "What's wrong? What's going on here?"

Once again, Roland was ignored. It didn't seem personal—the man didn't look away from him—but he just continued on as if he couldn't see or hear Roland.

At first, Roland became angry, but then he grew curious. He reached inside himself for his magic, and the blessed power was there again. He felt alive once more. The smell of baked bread from the Citadel kitchens washed over him and made his stomach growl. But he ignored this for now.

He decided to follow Titus's group and see what was going on. Entering the main reception room, Roland saw that a small throne was set at the back. A figure was sitting on it, dressed in blue with a gold cape swirling magically around him. Where had that throne come from?

Roland blinked and let out a small curse. It was himself. *He* was sitting on the throne. It was the impostor, the Chameleon.

"Bring the wizard to me!" shouted the impostor at the guards who held Titus.

Roland moved closer.

The impostor continued, "Titus, there is a new order here now. I know that you plot behind my back. Well, no more!"

It was uncanny: the Chameleon's voice was Roland's own; the face, his; the smirk on his lips, his. But the eyes—those

Roland recognized. They were the Chameleon's eyes. The same green as Celia's. Roland gathered his magic and threw it in the impostor's direction. It swirled right toward the man and then went right through him with no one noticing.

This was maddening. Roland looked down at himself. He looked real, and the floor beneath his feet appeared solid. He was Roland Tyre, but no one else seemed to be able to see him.

"You will be taken to the dungeons and kept there until all the old wizards are rounded up," the Chameleon continued. "There is a new order. A new generation of wizards now." The impostor of Roland laughed. "I will prepare the Citadel for the return of the true king."

The true king? Roland asked himself. What in the world was this crazy impostor talking about?

This must be a dream, he thought to himself.

He put his hand in his robe pocket and pulled out one of the small squares, fingering it in his hand. What kind of magic did it hold? He held it out and dropped it on the floor, as he had done with the first one. As before, the floor softened, and Roland fell down through it into darkness.

"Nooo." Roland yelled, reaching out his hands to try and stay in the room with the impostor.

As his feet hit the ground again, he tried to see, but it was pitch-black once more. He reached for his magic, and it was gone once again.

"Let me out of here!" he yelled. He was back in the dark storage room. No one would ever hear him.

Was what he had witnessed up above real? Was the Chameleon taking his place? Or, was it a glimpse of the future?

Or, could it have been only his imagination? And what was that crazy talk about a real king?

In his anger, he swept his hand to the side and knocked over some unseen items from the shelves. Then he grabbed another shelf in the dark and tried to pull it down. Muscles bulged, but nothing happened.

"I'm going crazy in here," he whispered, his voice raspy. He wondered how long it had been. Was it minutes or hours or days? He had no sense of time. No sense of anything.

Think, think. He needed to stay sane and in control. He tried, unsuccessfully, to slow his breathing. There had to be magic in the room, among the artifacts. Something to help him.

He fumbled with the items around on the floor, where he had knocked them from their shelves. He found a cylinder. It was smooth, and, although it felt like metal, it was warm to the touch. He felt a lid screwed on the top.

Slowly—and pausing a few times, in fear of what might emerge—he unscrewed the lid. The foul smell of rotten garbage emerged. He wrinkled his nose and tried to put the lid back on with one hand but dropped it in the darkness.

"Roland," said a loud and deep voice, echoing in the small room.

Roland whipped his head around. Where did the voice come from?

"You say you are one of the greatest wizards in the land," the voice continued. It sounded slimy and evil. "But you can't even get out of this little room. You're pathetic!"

"Who are you?" Roland called. He was feeling pathetic; the voice was right.

"Who I am is none of your concern. You're no wizard. You cheated in the test," the voice said, moving around the room.

Turning in circles, Roland tried to follow it. "I *am* a wizard!" Roland hollered to the darkness. "I did not cheat. I outsmarted them. There's a difference."

The voice laughed, deep and guttural, oppressive and everywhere at once.

"What do you want with me?" Roland backed up against a wall. "Leave me alone."

"You can't get away from me, Coward," the voice boomed at his right side. "What are you doing, hiding in the Citadel, when your friends are out fighting?"

"What do you mean?" Roland groaned.

"Bak is out flying around on a dragon, a majestic being, trying to save Alaris. Alli is with the Chief Judge, preparing to fight. Even Onius is with Kanzar, hopefully making a difference." The voice reverberated inside Roland's mind. He couldn't escape it.

"But you sit here, all safe in the Citadel. You are weak. A weak, pathetic coward!"

Roland sank to the ground and brought his knees up to his chest, rocking back and forth. He knew the voice was right. He was weak. And he was no wizard! His mind faded into the distance, and hollowness began to grow within him.

* * *

Sometime later, he felt his body twitch. He didn't know if

he had slept or just zoned out. He fingered the cylinder in his hand, and a small, distant thought came back to his mind. He had saved the Chief Judge's life—twice. He had removed poison from Eryck. He wasn't weak. He was strong.

He reached out, feeling around on the floor, blindly trying to find the lid to the cylinder. The voice tried to speak again, but Roland pushed it back.

"I am not weak," he forced himself to say out loud. "I passed the test. I am a wizard. A powerful wizard!" The more positively he talked, the better he felt.

There, finally, he found the lid. Lifting it to the top of the cylinder, he screwed it back on. As soon as he did so, the disturbing voice went silent. Also, the room grew lighter—not from removing darkness but from removing evil. The foul stench had also disappeared. Roland realized then that the voice was his own insecurities, the darkest part of his mind. Everyone had some.

"I am one of the most powerful wizards in the land," Roland repeated to himself. More than ever before he knew that this was true, now that he'd totally vanquished his doubts. He also knew that magic existed in this room; in the artifacts. That meant there should be a way for Roland to reach his magic also. This was a task he could put his mind to. Something to keep him sane.

He sat on the ground and began to think, pushing his mind deeper and deeper, taking himself into a trance. He thought about nothing else. The room seemed to grow more distant, and he felt as if the Citadel did not exist around him any more, Alaris didn't matter, and the world was just a temporary place for people's bodies to reside. He pushed his mind and spirit farther and farther beyond his mere physical existence. To a magical stream of consciousness. He would find his magic again—because *he was magic*!

CHAPTER SEVENTEEN

"I should go with you, Bak," Breelyn argued. "Miriel isn't ready to carry you yet."

"Abylar could take both of us." Breelyn folded her arms across her chest.

Bakari wasn't really comfortable arguing with a woman, especially one that was almost twice his age, but he knew what he needed to do. "Look, Breelyn, you and Miriel need to go back to Lor'l and see the king and the prince. You owe that to them."

"But I am a dragon rider now, not a protector of Elvyn."

Bakari sucked in a deep breath and then pushed it out again. "They need to hear that from you, Breelyn. There will be plenty of time to fight before this battle is over, I am sure. I need to find the other riders, but I am going to Corwan first. We will meet up later."

Abylar was flying back now with Miriel and reported through their bond the intense fighting in Corwan. He had seen no fighting in Orr or even Cassian for now, though Abylar did say both cities showed signs that they were building up for war.

Bakari sensed a force, pulling him toward Corwan. It was time for him to do something to help Alaris. He was a dragon rider, after all!

Alair put his hand on Breelyn's arm. "Dragon Rider Bakari is right, Breelyn. You need to follow his directions."

Breelyn held her mouth tight for a moment. Her green

eyes flashed at the two of them. "Fine, I will do as you say, Dragon Master."

Bakari spread his hands to his sides. "Breelyn, don't call me that. I am still Bak."

The two dragons appeared overhead once again, and Bakari, Breelyn, and Alair all gazed up into the sky. When they looked back at each other again, Breelyn had a large smile plastered on her face.

"This is a lot to take in. I just want to do what is right and protect the land. Sorry about the outburst." She hit Bakari softly in the shoulder and then reached her hand up to touch his hair. "You're all right, Bak, but this hair of yours is getting shaggy."

Bakari laughed. "I'm growing it out. The men of Mahli wear their hair in braids."

Alair raised his eyebrows and cocked his head at Bakari.

"We could braid yours, too, Alair." Breelyn put her hand up to touch her guard's hair. "It's long enough."

With a laugh, Alair pushed her hand away.

They walked over to where the two dragons were landing. But the bond between Bakari and Abylar wavered for a moment, and Bakari stumbled.

Breelyn caught him from falling. "You all right?"

"Yes," Bakari said. "The bond with Abylar is a little strange today. Every few hours, there seems to be a strange loss in his power."

"Maybe he's just tired," Breelyn said. "He is still young."

Bakari walked closer to Abylar and put his hand up to his side, running it lovingly over the growing scales. "But he eats like a pig."

I heard that, Dragon Rider. Abylar turned his neck to look at his rider.

I know, Bakari said through their bond. *I let you hear it.*

I don't eat like a pig, young Dragon Rider, but I like to eat pigs.

Bakari shared what his dragon had said, and Breelyn and Alair laughed.

I could eat one now, but I am too tired to hunt, Abylar spoke again.

Too tired? Bakari grew concerned. *I've never known you to be too tired to eat before, Abylar. Maybe you flew too far last night...but I need you to fly me to Corwan. Can you do that?*

Anything for you, Dragon Rider. Abylar seemed to perk up.

Breelyn stood next to her dragon, rubbing Miriel's bright yellow head. Her snout held a touch of orange that matched the tips of some of her scales. She seemed to grow even brighter in the bright autumn sun.

"I will await you in Lor'l, Bakari," Breelyn said. "You are correct: I need to let the king know what is happening. He needs to send troops to Silla and the border, in case Alaris attacks again."

Abylar knelt down for Bakari to mount up. "I will see you in Lor'l—or sooner, if I finish up in Corwan. We still have more dragon riders to find." He checked his bag. It was full of wooden discs. He might yet use some in the upcoming battle.

Flapping his wings, Abylar almost knocked over the two elves. Soon they flew up above the treetops, the late morning sun just slightly south of directly overhead. Bakari breathed in, then let out a whoop. Flying still amazed him every time.

Everything seemed so small, but marvelous from up above. He watched the Dunn River, winding its way from north to south, and even saw the Corwan River, moving southwest, toward Cassian, before it curved back to Corwan, where they were now going.

Without any warning, Abylar suddenly dropped, and Bakari almost fell out of his seat. Holding on tightly to a nearby scale, in which a tethered strip of leather was held, he was barely staying on.

"Abylar!" Bakari yelled out loud.

It hurts, Abylar moaned. Then the mighty dragon leveled out and continued flying, although more slowly now. *Another loss of energy.*

Hold on. It won't take us long to get there. Bakari pushed his dragon. *You can do it, Abylar. You're strong.*

We're strong together, Dragon Rider.

Bakari tried to figure out what was happening. He hoped it wasn't what his initial thoughts had told him. Then a thought made his stomach sour: Abylar's strength may still be tied to the guardians' strength. If something bad was happening to them, Bakari would be tempted to turn around and fly north— back to Celestar. But he was closer to Corwan now, and they needed him first. He could feel the pull more strongly, the closer they came.

Soon they left the forest behind. Now, the only color threading its way through the brown sands was from the two rivers, which were coming closer together. Off in the distance, Bakari could make out the town of Corwan. He had never been there before. It was the second largest desert city, after Orr.

But being on the convergence of the two rivers had made Corwan a busy fishing and trading town. It might even grow bigger than Orr, now that the barrier had come down. A haze of light smoke hung over the city, indicative of an earlier fire, though Bakari could not see any flames at the moment.

As they came closer, he made out groups of soldiers fighting below. Some were at the gates of the city, and others seemed to have landed in boats, and they now pushed deliberately through the town. Bakari thought about how best to help them. As a scholar wizard, he had never found much need for military training, but he did know tactics from books he had read.

He reached to the side and unlatched his bag. Abylar dipped down lower. Hopefully, just the sight of a dragon would be enough to scare Kanzar's men back.

Flying over the road that led from the North to the gates of the city, Abylar roared. A group of soldiers glanced up into the sky and then almost fell over themselves trying to get out of the way.

As they got closer to the city, the shouting grew more intense. None of these people had ever seen a dragon, and probably very few had even heard there was one in existence now. Bakari noticed the looks from the soldiers on the walls. They too were afraid, too.

A barrage of arrows and wizards' fire were being hurled at the walls from the outside. The gate was half fallen, but men from the city stood defiantly to defend it. Over toward the river, Bakari spotted a contingent of red-haired men fighting together. One saw him, and soon the cry of "Dragon Rider" filled the air.

Bakari smiled. They had realized who he was.

A wizard near the wall hurled a blast of fire up at Bakari. It didn't make it up far enough, but it alarmed him nevertheless. He drew out one of his wooden discs. He had practiced a lot. So he drew a deep breath, concentrating, and hurled the disc forehand, down at the enemy wizard. The disc hit him squarely in the chest and knocked him to the ground. Cheers rose from the city walls as the soldiers inside realized the dragon wasn't there to hurt them.

Bakari threw another disc, down at an attacking soldier that was trying to knock down the gate. Bakari hit the man on the back of the head, and he fell forward. The dragon and its rider gave renewed enthusiasm to the city's soldiers.

Abylar flew back up, over the city, and roared loudly again. Off to the west, not far away, Bakari spotted rising dust high in the sky. Flying Abylar closer, Bakari saw a full battalion of soldiers on the road between Orr and Corwan. He landed Abylar in front of them. They immediately drew their swords and awaited word from their commanders.

Then a man walked out in front of the battalion.

"I am Bakari, a dragon rider, and friend of the Chief Judge," Bakari said.

The men relaxed, and then the man out front spoke. "I am Azeem, southern judge. We were summoned back to Corwan by Battle Wizard Allison Stenos."

"Is Alli in Corwan?"

Azeem nodded his head in the affirmative. "How goes the battle there?" He was a big man with the skin color indicative of the southern desert people. And Bakari had heard the Chief Judge mention Azeem before as a good and fair judge.

"I just arrived," Bakari said. "They are being attacked at the gates and at the river. The city is holding, but just barely. I don't dare get too close with my dragon's fire, or we might hurt the wrong people."

"Give us three hours, and we will be there." Azeem motioned his people to pick up their pace.

Bakari waved, and Abylar lifted back into the sky, the edges of his spikes on his blue body reflecting an orange tint in the bright sunlight. Turning back toward Corwan, they arrived to find intense fighting in about one-third of the city. They flew overhead and spotted a dense pack of Kanzar's men, approaching around a corner.

So they flew low, and Abylar breathed out a roar of fire. Blue and yellow flames flew toward the ground, halting the men from advancing. They turned to go another way, but Abylar spit out another breath of flames on their other side. With Kanzar's men now trapped, soon the city's soldiers arrived and disarmed them.

"Bakari!" a voice called through the afternoon air. Glancing around, Bakari noticed a small figure standing on top of the tallest building in the city.

"Alli," he said out loud and then flew down toward her. He landed Abylar on an enormous rooftop patio, hoping the structure would hold the dragon's weight. Its rock floor groaned but seemed to hold.

The young battle wizard ran up and gave Bakari a hug. "Thank you for coming," Alli said.

"Azeem's battalion is only three hours away," he informed her.

"With you and them, we can end this battle," Alli said seriously.

Out onto the balcony walked Mericus, dressed immaculately in dark fighting gear, black boots, and a red cape. Looking at the dragon, his eyes grew wide. But he seemed to be enough of a politician to maintain his decorum in any circumstance.

"Mericus, this is Bakari," Alli said. "He is a dragon rider and is here to help us."

Mericus gave a short bow. "I think I remember you from River Bend. You were the Chief Judge's scholar wizard that everyone was looking for."

Bakari's face grew hard. Then he said, "And, the last time I saw you—or rather heard you—you took down a man, your mercenary captain, I believe, with little thought. You and Onius were planning your treachery." He dropped down from Abylar's back and walked toward the man, drawing himself up as tall as he could, which was still a good five inches shorter than Mericus.

The judge's jaw dropped, and he looked to be trying to gather his words, but he couldn't find what to say.

"I heard you and Onius talking," Bakari continued, "about a king and about making sure Roland, Alli, and I didn't get in the way of your plans." Bakari stood with his fists clenched. He knew that the dragon standing behind him added weight to his words.

Alli turned to Mericus with a glare and pulled her sword

from her scabbard.

Mericus held his hands up in front of him. "If you had listened to the entire conversation, you would know that Onius didn't like Kanzar's plan and that he tried to convince me to move against our High Wizard."

Before he could say anything more, they heard a loud crashing sound from the front of the city. The three moved over to the edge of the roof and peered out across Corwan. The front gate had been breached, and the enemy—with Alana, Kanzar's wife, leading them—rushed through the gates, slicing right and left as they pushed their way in.

Alli and Mericus turned, as if waiting for direction from Bakari. He wasn't used to being looked at as a leader. He knew his power and rank had as much to do with the dragon he rode as with anything he did personally.

"We can sort out my past follies later, Dragon Rider," Mericus said with a glance back toward the gate. "Suffice it to say, I am as much opposed to Kanzar now as you are."

Bakari nodded. "Very well, then. Let's end this fight before anyone else gets hurt. Azeem will be here soon. Mericus, go and shore up the men coming in from the river. Alli and I will handle the front gates."

They both nodded. And, as Bakari jumped back on Abylar, the two other wizards headed down the stairs and into the city. Before they got too far away, Bakari called to them, "Who are the red-headed ones?"

"Elves," Alli replied. "From Mallek. Mericus brokered a deal with them."

Bakari's eyes opened wider in surprise. He did not expect

elves to act independently from their king, who would not jump into a fight without long consideration and counsel first.

"Well, I'm glad they are on our side then," Bakari said. With a few flaps of his giant blue wings, Abylar lifted off the roof and headed once again toward the city gates.

CHAPTER EIGHTEEN

Erryl was beginning to feel delirious. He had not been given any food or water since the day before and was still tied to the tree. His limbs ached and were now swelling. From this position, he couldn't look away as the slaughter of the guardians continued. But, by now, his body stood empty of tears, though his soul still cried out against the injustice around him. Being raised in Celestar, he had never realized the evil that existed out in the real world. He now questioned his desire to have ever wanted to leave his peaceful city.

Every few hours, as promised, the evil governor of Silla had killed another guardian. Each time, Erryl was first asked to give information the governor assumed Erryl knew. Much of it, unfortunately, Erryl did know, but he wouldn't share it. He loved his fellow guardians, but there was more at stake here— the peace of multiple kingdoms. So, each time the governor had questioned him about the orb, the dragon, Bakari, Breelyn, and other things pertaining to Celestar, Erryl had held his lips tight and had tried to take his mind somewhere else. It was the most difficult task he had ever undertaken. It stretched him to his limits.

The portly governor approached Erryl from the other side of the camp. He walked slowly and deliberately, with a smirk on his full face, his eyes never leaving Erryl's face. Erryl began to pray to a god that he knew must exist. He thought about his deceased mother, who had been gone for a few months. He now believed he would be seeing her again soon.

Erryl looked at the guardians. His father stood with the rest of the guardians and gazed back and forth from the governor to Erryl. Tears filled his father's eyes, but a look of grand respect filled his face, and he nodded encouragingly to Erryl.

"So, Guardian, are you ready to answer my questions?"

Erryl turned his head away from his father. The governor stood a few feet in front of Erryl. A slight breeze blew, and a few autumn leaves floated down between the two of them as Erryl kept his mouth closed and his lips tight.

Then the governor stepped forward and, in a quickness that belied his size, slapped Erryl hard across the face.

"You foolish boy! Do you want them to die?"

"No. But there are worse things than death," Erryl said through gritted teeth.

"Spoken by someone willing to watch others lose their lives for something so stupid. I will kill every one of them and then torture you until you tell me what I need to know!" Spit dribbled out of the side of the governor's mouth.

Silent, Erryl pushed himself up on his toes, trying to stretch his aching back.

In unison, the guardians knelt on the ground and bowed their heads toward him. Tears that, moments before, he had thought already spent now gushed forward again, dropping down from his face onto the leaf-filled ground. He had never been as proud of his people as he was at that moment.

The ring of the governor's sword being drawn filled the afternoon air. Erryl's heart beat through his chest. Erryl knew he and the others would die. One of his biggest regrets now was he wouldn't be able to tell Bakari he was the fulfillment of prophecy.

Without warning, a war cry filled the air, and Gorn came crashing through the trees, his weathered face, full of wrinkles, looking hard and full of intent. His clothes were stained red, and a bleeding gash ran down his left arm. Stretching forth his hands, he sent a whip of lightning toward the governor. A last minute movement by one of the governor's men made it catch a younger soldier rather than the governor himself.

Pouring out of the trees behind Gorn, a group of elves and Celestar protectors followed. They drew swords and attacked the governor's men. Fierce battle ensued around the guardians, none of whom owned any weapons or were trained to use them.

Gorn fought like a madman, using a combination of wizard power and weaponry, slicing down anyone who stood in his way.

Erryl's heart nearly burst with joy. His sudden deliverance, from a certain death to a possibility of life now, lifted his soul. The guardians stood in the middle of their pen, trying to figure out how to help. As a guard fell to the ground next to them, Erryl's father picked up the guard's sword and jumped over the fence. Suddenly, all the guardians roared and swarmed into the battle. All except Erryl. He still stood tied tightly to the tree—a witness to the slaughter..

A few guardians were sliced down easily. They were no match for the seasoned Elvyn soldiers of the governor.

"Get back!" Erryl yelled at them. But they had taken things

into their own hands now, tired of being slaughtered while defenseless. If they died now, at least they would die fighting. Many of them did.

Then Gorn made his way to Erryl and moved behind the tree. He struck his sword against the ropes, and Erryl slumped to the ground.

"Ahhhh!" Erryl cried out as the blood rushed back into his hands and feet with such pain. "You cut things awfully close there, Gorn."

"Rub them," Gorn suggested, referring to Erryl's hands. "We were attacked by a group of Kanzar's men. Luckily, there were only two wizards with the group. The protectors and the few elves with us fought well. We lost a few of our fighters but captured most of the attackers and then came in search of you and the other guardians." The wizard then turned, looking behind him, and took down another soldier. The men and elves from Celestar were outmatched in numbers, but not in skill.

Erryl drew himself back up and began hopping up and down a bit to get the blood flowing again to his feet. He wiped blood off the side of his mouth with the back of his hand.

Suddenly, he was knocked over, from the side, by one of the enemy men. He rolled to the side and, by only a slim margin, missed a sword coming down on him. Before Erryl could move again, one of the elves from Celestar took the other man down. Erryl nodded his thanks and grabbed the man's sword.

A dozen feet away, the governor had beat off one of the Celestar protectors and now stood facing Erryl once again.

"This is your fault, boy. I promised you I would kill you if you didn't give me what I wanted." He took a step toward Erryl with his sword held high. Thankfully, Gorn arrived in time to bring down his own sword, knocking the governor's sword out of his hands.

Standing defenseless now, all the governor could do was watch the next thrust coming from Gorn. The swift stroke into his gut surprised him, and a look of alarm spread across his face. He collapsed to the ground, blood pouring from the wound.

The battle slowed as those with the governor realized the fight to protect him was now over. Gorn turned back around to survey the scene. As he did so, he missed seeing the governor's slight movement, but Erryl had not.

Time seemed to slow for Erryl as Governor Ellian, renegade elf, reached into his boot and, with a smooth motion, grabbed out a small dirk and threw it, with his last ounce of strength, toward Erryl.

He noticed the etching on the knife's handle as it flew, end over end, directly at him. He took a deep breath, breathing in the sweet forest air—towering pines, broad oaks, and small ferns and bushes—it felt wonderful to him and overwhelmed his senses, pushing out the stench of blood and battle. Turning his head, Erryl found his father looking back at him.

"Father!" he began to cry out as Gorn jumped forward to help. Then the world came back to life, yells and shouts filling Erryl's ears as the knife slammed into his chest, digging deep into his internal organs.

Blood started gushing out instantly, and Erryl dropped the sword he was holding and slumped to the ground. A crimson stain spread across his white guardian robes, and everyone shouted at once, but Gorn and Erryl's father were the first to reach him.

"Bakari," Erryl mouthed in barely more than a whisper. He leaned closer to Gorn. "The book…the book…" Blood filled his mouth. "Under the garden gate fence post."

"What book?" Gorn tried to put his hands over Erryl's chest.

Erryl felt a small tingling—his organs trying to heal themselves—but it was not enough. "Tell Bakari, he is…" Erryl coughed up blood and closed his eyes. Then he felt his father's hands on his arm. Opening his eyes, he tried to continue, knowing he must tell Gorn what he had discovered, "Bakari is not just the dragon rider…"

"Yes, Erryl?"

He felt Gorn remove his hand from his chest, as if knowing he could not heal Erryl. Moments passed, Erryl's mind growing foggy. He couldn't think.

"Bakari is the…"

Erryl felt his life force leaving him. Not only his but also, for a brief moment, he felt himself once again connected to Abylar's and knew immediately that the deaths of the guardians were affecting the poor dragon. He sensed the might of the great dragon, its intelligence, but also its pain. *Oh, so much pain!*

"Abylar!" Erryl opened his eyes and screamed. Everyone stopped and stood looking at Erryl, who had given up so much to protect those he admired. His eyes closed one last time, and he saw a light coming for him.

"Oh, Abylar," he said. Then, in a final sigh of breath

before he would let his head loll to the side and would leave everything he had ever known and loved, Erryl said, "Bakari, my friend, I am sorry."

CHAPTER NINETEEN

Soaring over the city of Corwan, Bakari and Abylar flew down closer to the fighting, trying to find where they could be the most useful. The gate was still being overrun. Maybe he could stop more from entering the city.

Pulling two discs out of his side bag, Bakari considered a new idea for a moment. Running his hand over the first disc, he infused it with two spells. Then he directed Abylar down and threw the disc against the outside wall at such an angle that the wooden disc skidded along the wall, spitting out fire at everyone within ten feet of the wall. That was the first spell.

As Kanzar's fighters screamed and backed away from the wall, Bakari stuck his hand out, and the disc flew back to him, having used up its flames. That was the second spell. Casting it would ensure that he didn't use up and lose all his discs. They each took a long time to be carved and sanded by the men of Mahli.

Alli arrived at the top of the wall and waved up at Bakari. "Nice trick," she said loudly enough for him to hear her. "Where did you learn that?"

"I've been practicing," Bakari called back down.

Bakari swooped again and threw out another disc, a roller on the ground, and it cut a path of fire farther out from the wall, pushing Kanzar's fighters back even more. At the same time, Alli jumped down and stood in the opening of the gate itself. Then she spun, around and around, her arms extended with a knife in each hand. As she spun, faster and faster, fire gushed forth from her knives, cutting down the enemy and pushing them back out farther from the gate.

Now the enemy found themselves trapped between the fire of Bakari and Abylar and the danger of Alli. Alli then turned and ran inside the city to continue cleansing the area of the enemy.

Abylar flew up higher so Bakari could see more of what was happening. A few blocks in from the gate, a significant group of Kanzar's men and women, led by Alana, were pushing through the city's defenses. So he flew down to meet them head-on.

Coming in quickly, Abylar was preparing to spit out a flame of blue fire, when instead, he tipped to the right and hit into the side of a building. Bakari was thrown off-balance and fell to the ground. In a daze, the young dragon rider stood up and ran toward Abylar, who was breathing hard.

What's wrong?

My power, Abylar said into Bakari's mind. *My power is leaving me. I don't know what's wrong.*

A few men jumped out at Bakari. One of Kanzar's wizards also threw fire at Abylar, hitting him on his delicate, newly formed scales. The dragon hissed out a breath of fire that consumed the wizard, but it also started a fire behind him on the ground.

Alana arrived and prepared a spell to throw at Bakari, but Abylar moved a wing in front of Bakari in time to intercept her fire. He howled in pain. Alli also arrived on the scene, looking at Bakari and then at Alana.

"Abylar, fly away and stay up higher," Alli said. "I will watch out for Bakari."

So Abylar lifted off from the ground on unsteady wings.

Then Alana turned toward Alli and flipped a knife at her. Alli dodged this easily and then ran up the side of a building, coming back down behind Alana. She let go a bolt of fire, hitting Alana's armor so that she stumbled back a few steps.

Then Alli motioned Bakari to follow her, and they headed deeper into the city. Coming around the corner, they found a man that had fallen to the ground, blood seeping from his side. A hooded figure was kneeling over him, trying to stop the bleeding. Alli leaped over the two, but Bakari stumbled as he was running around them.

Picking himself up off the ground, Bakari gasped. Under the hood was a face that he thought he might never see again. Unbidden tears came to his eyes.

"Bak," Alli yelled. "We need to get back to the castle and regroup."

When Bakari didn't move, Alli turned and ran back toward him, then stopped mid-stride.

"Kharlia?" Bakari's heart lurched. "You are alive. How did you get here?"

"Bak?"

The young woman's soft, dark skin and intelligent brown eyes were exactly how Bakari remembered them. Her hood fell back as she stood up. Her black hair hung behind her, tied back into a ponytail, its tips reaching below her shoulders. He reached out and touched her face. Kharlia shivered with the caress. As another enemy fighter came around the corner, Alli stepped forward to meet the man's charge. "Come on, you two lovebirds, we need to go."

Both Bakari and Kharlia blushed, but Bakari didn't care. Kharlia couldn't keep from smiling as she leaned back down and quickly finished tying up the soldier's gashed side. Then she stood up and faced Bakari. In mere moments, his long-submerged feelings came rushing back to the surface, and Bakari embraced Kharlia in a fierce hug. Her tears soaked his shoulder as she sobbed with the joy of their sudden rejoining.

Alli grabbed Bakari's right hand and pulled them away. With his other hand, he held on to Kharlia and pulled her along with them. He promised himself that he would never let her go again.

Running through twisted alleyways and streets, Alli held back any attackers with one hand and pulled Bakari and Kharlia along with the other. Overhead, Abylar flew over Corwan with a loud wail, spewing blue fire forth toward the ground, heedless of which fighters he hit—friends or foes.

"Abylar!" Bakari screamed upward into the sky and in his mind at the same time. "Stop!"

The dragon had a crazed look in his eyes. As he wobbled in the air, trying to right himself once again, fire sprayed down over the city.

Dragon Rider! Abylar answered Bakari. *What is happening?*

"Bak, who is that?" Kharlia said—her first words since saying his name earlier.

"My dragon." Bakari tried to swallow away a sheepish grin.

"Well, he's going to kill us."

"She's right, Bak," Alli said as she continued to direct them to the castle.

Once there, they ran up the side stairs to the roof to get a better look at the battle. The Mallek elves were fighting valiantly at the riverbanks, pushing back Kanzar's fighters and lighting their ships on fire with burning arrows. The city's front gate seemed to be pulsing back and forth between the city's defenders and Kanzar's troops. And, looking west, Bakari spotted Azeem's forces, entering the battle just outside the city. He realized they would indeed push back Kanzar's troops.

Then he saw Abylar. The dragon was heading down lower, but then stumbled in the air. Flapping wildly, Abylar tried to right himself, but he wasn't able to. Through the bond, Bakari felt Abylar's fear, terror, and loss.

Bakari tried to comfort the mighty beast, but Abylar was falling faster to the ground than he should have been, and his mind was spinning in frenzy. As Bakari tried to grab a hold of his dragon's mind, Abylar growled loudly, spitting out a wall of blue fire, and then Abylar fell.

"Bakari!" Alli screamed above the din. "What is Abylar doing?"

Bakari shook his head and tried again to gain control. *Abylar?* Men and women from both sides of the conflict were nearly burned by Abylar's fire once again and ran screaming down the streets. *Abylar!* Digging deeper into the dragon's mind, Bakari pushed through the magic there and took control of the dragon's mind.

"Noooo!" Bakari screamed out, feeling the pain within his dragon's mind. He stood on the edge of the rooftop and grabbed a hold of an iron railing to keep from falling. He could hardly withstand the pain and the loss himself. His vision darkened, but Bakari delved deeper, to the core of control for the young dragon. Pushing aside the despair, momentarily, Bakari forced Abylar's body to straighten out and fly to himself, on the rooftop of the governor's castle.

Bakari hated controlling his friend this way, and the dragon's mind pushed back against his own. Abylar hit the roof hard, knocking a railing into the street below, while Bakari pulled Kharlia away from the rolling dragon.

Abylar's mind fought Bakari's for control of Abylar's mind. Finally, Bakari let go, letting Abylar roar again.

Stay here, Bakari commanded, brooking no disobedience.

The guardians, Abylar said. *The guardians are dying.*

Bakari put his hand on his dragon and jumped fully into their bond: feeling what the dragon felt, but not controlling him anymore. Part of who Abylar was—part of the life force given to him willingly by the guardians when he was in his egg—was being drained away now.

Then an unexpected lapse in power jolted Abylar's mind, knocking Bakari to the ground. His head throbbed with pain, and his heart almost burst.

"No, no, no!" he yelled. "It can't be."

As Kharlia and Alli came to Bakari's aid, Kharlia kneeled down and put her soft hand on Bakari's chest and said, "Bakari, what's wrong?"

Bakari shook in agony, his mouth open wide and tears pouring down his face. For only a moment, through Abylar's mind, Bakari had seen it all happen as if he *was* Erryl. He had seen the knife flying toward himself and hitting himself in the chest.

The pain! Abylar groaned and rolled over on his side, shaking even the foundations of the building.

"Bakari!" Alli shook him now, tears in her eyes. "Come back! We need you!"

Bakari pulled himself back from Erryl's last moments, but then the dragon lifted his long neck and roared a screeching and painful wail that filled the city with a tone of despair and grief. Fighting stopped on both sides as the wave of pure anguish and sorrow filled the entire city. The magic from the dragon's pain brought all to their knees.

"He's gone," Bakari wailed with his hands over his ears. "He's gone and it's all my fault."

Feeling blackness creep into his vision, Bakari laid his head down on Kharlia's lap.

"Bak, who's gone?" Kharlia asked as she stroked Bakari's hair. Tears ran down and over the side of his face. With slow blinks, Bakari opened his eyes and peered up at Kharlia. Alli was on her knees next to them. "Erryl!" he gasped. "They killed so many guardians, and then they killed Erryl."

Alli moved her hand to her mouth and let out a groan. "No, Bak. No, it can't be."

"Who's Erryl?" Kharlia asked, clearly not understanding what was going on.

Bakari tried to speak, then shook his head, for the words choked in his throat.

"A brave young man who helped Bakari free the dragon," Alli offered as a short explanation.

Bakari sent his mind back to Abylar and tried to comfort

his dragon. Then another, faint voice echoed through their thoughts. It was Miriel's. She shared in Abylar's pain. She also sent her comfort to her dragon kin, and Bakari felt it. It was amazing for one so young to hold so much power and empathy.

After a moment, his tears slowed, and then Bakari took a deep breath. Turning back to Alli and Kharlia, he sat up. "Miriel. Abylar and I can feel her," he said with amazement. "She is so wonderful."

"*She?*" Kharlia said with a tinge of jealousy in her voice.

"Who is Miriel?" Alli asked.

Bakari laughed through his tears, putting a hand on Kharlia's arm. "She's Breelyn's dragon."

Alli opened her eyes wide. "Another dragon rider?"

"Dragon rider?" Kharlia spoke. Turning to Bak, she grabbed his hands in hers. "Seems like all I have been doing is asking questions, but what is a dragon rider?"

"He is." Alli pointed to Bakari. "The first in over one hundred and fifty years. He freed the dragon from the Orb."

Kharlia's eyes lit up, and she wrapped an arm around Bakari.

"And there will be more," Bakari said.

"More what?" someone said, and the three of them turned to see Mericus walking over to join them. "More destruction by this beast?"

Abylar turned his head and growled at Mericus.

"Be careful, Judge," Bakari said.

"That dragon killed some of our own men down there." Mericus stood with one hand clenched over the pommel of his sheathed sword. "If you can't control him, you shouldn't be here."

Alli stood up and walked in slow but even strides toward Mericus. The man stood a good foot taller than she, but he took a step back as he noticed the look on her face.

"Mericus, don't threaten the dragon or his rider," Alli said. "They just suffered a vast blow to their growing power. Some of their guardians were killed."

Mericus glanced at Bakari with a confused look on his face. "I don't know about what you are saying, Alli. All I know is that his dragon went crazy and sent out a wave of terror across the city."

"Has the fighting stopped?" she asked.

"Yes," Mericus said, holding his lips tight.

"Then the dragon and its rider did what was needed. No more lives will be lost."

Bakari stood now and strode the few steps to Mericus while holding on to Kharlia's hand. He wanted to never let her hand go again. "These deaths are on your head, Mericus, not ours."

Mericus jerked straighter. "What are you saying?"

"You were one of Kanzar's fighters. You and Kanzar and maybe even Onius. Any deaths here today are on your heads. If I had my way right now, I would take you captive and try you for your crimes."

"You...you can't..." Mericus said, stumbling on his words.

Then Abylar stood back up and took a giant step toward the humans. His eyes were full of pain, mirroring Bakari's own.

"I could. I am *the* dragon rider!" Bakari pulled rank for the first time since freeing Abylar. He had read the stories and talked to the king of Elvyn and the regent of Mahli. He understood his rights in that role.

Mericus froze. He, too, had been trained in the Citadel and knew the histories. A grim look covered his face, but then he gave in and bowed his head. "Of course. I acknowledge your authority. This battle has us all in knots."

Everyone stood silent, as if waiting for Bakari to speak.

Then Alli laid an arm on his shoulder, "Bak, I believe Mericus is on our side…at least for now." She scrutinized the judge with a solemn look. "Many good people have committed crimes in the past; let's let Mericus prove himself before we dismiss him."

Bakari nodded. "I must go to Celestar. I need to see what has happened." His eyes teared up again. "Oh, Erryl, my friend," he whispered.

"Is Abylar strong enough?" Alli asked, sounding worried.

The dragon snorted, tossing his neck from side to side, as if in answer. A few sounds from the city below floated up to them. Bakari heard a few people clanging swords and yelling.

"Yes," was all he said. But he sent a silent message to Abylar: *We can't take revenge, my friend. That won't solve anything.* Bakari didn't know if he believed this himself, but it was the right thing to say, and he needed a break to think. *We need to go and honor the fallen guardians.*

"May I leave and take care of my troops?" Mericus asked, getting back to the business at hand.

Bakari nodded, so Mericus began walking away. But,

before he left the roof, Bakari called out to him, "Mericus, I will be back. I will accede to Alli's judgment for now, but peace is my goal. Peace for all of Alaris. If that is your end also, I welcome your help. But, if not..." He left the rest of this sentence unsaid.

Mericus nodded and then headed down the stairs to the city below.

Alli put her arm around Bakari. "Bak, you have become a dragon rider indeed."

Bak slumped down on a bench. "Oh, Alli. I don't know what to do. I never asked for this."

"Bak, I always knew you were destined for greatness," Kharlia offered for encouragement. "I must admit, though, I still don't understand half of what is going on. But, I am never leaving my dragon rider again."

Bakari grinned. This was the fierce young woman he remembered. Those few weeks together, with him and Kharlia on the run, had brought them close together, and Bakari now realized how much he had missed having her love and support.

"You are doing well," Alli said. "You stood up to Mericus." Alli smiled, her green eyes sparkling.

Bakari laughed, but the mirth did not reach his heart. "Yes, I did," he said. "Who would have thought I could do that? Roland would be proud of me."

"Oh, yes. I am sure that arrogant boy would be." Alli laughed again, this time more fully.

With this thought of Roland, Bakari felt something else stir inside him. Something was calling to him. He frowned and closed his eyes to concentrate.

"Bak, what's wrong?"

He felt Kharlia touch his arm.

"Is it the guardians again?" Alli asked.

Bakari only shook his head and put up his hand to stop their questions. Then he dove deep inside the power again. There was something there. Something new. Oh, he felt so exhausted. He felt the pain and sorrow from the death of the guardians. Their wounds—still fresh—almost overwhelmed him again. It was all he could do to push them aside.

He also felt Miriel there and even a brief presence of Breelyn. He would need to think more about that relationship later—he was still learning about the powers of a dragon rider. Bakari pushed all those thoughts aside and opened himself up further to the power. He drew on the strength of Abylar—the power of the spirit, a strength that was recently reduced and weakened but still one with a mighty and immense reservoir of power.

He pulled his mind into the stream of magic and chased after...a voice. Memories of Roland popped back into Bakari's mind. Many thought that Roland was only concerned with popularity, women, and power, but Bakari knew—deep down inside—that his friend was compassionate and caring and really did want to do the right thing.

Then Bakari thought he heard Roland's voice.

Bakari, it whispered.

Following the voice deeper, Bakari focused his attention northward, toward the Citadel, and then it came stronger, filling his soul.

Bakari, help me! Roland's voice pleaded in a tone of deep

agony. *Bakari, I need you now!* the voice said louder.

I can't come now! Bakari thought. *I need to go to Celestar.* He needed to see the guardians. They had fed Abylar's life force for years. They deserved Bakari's compassion and support.

Please, Bakari, the voice said with a mournful cry. Then it faded away.

As Bakari opened his eyes, they filled with tears again, an occurrence that seemed to be happening all too often this day. Alli and Kharlia were still sitting next to him, but the sun was now an hour farther down the horizon, so evening was only a short time away.

"Bak?" Kharlia prompted.

"It's Roland," he replied.

Alli stood up.

"He needs me," Bakari said.

"Needs you?" Alli frowned. "I don't understand. I thought you were going to Celestar."

Pain passed through Bakari's heart, and he struggled to hold himself together. He shook his head from side to side. "I'm being torn into pieces, Alli. I can't do this all by myself. I can't."

You are not by yourself. This faraway thought came from Miriel.

Compassion showed in Kharlia's eyes, and then she hugged Bakari, allowing him to stay there, in her arms, for a few moments as he composed himself once again.

"You're not alone, Bak," Alli said. "You have Kharlia, me, Roland, and others. I can go to Roland for you."

Bakari frowned. "Not this time, Alli. I have a feeling that

he really does need *me*. And I need you here, to watch over Mericus. I still don't trust him."

"Alright." Alli sighed and her lips pursed into a faint pout. "I understand."

"Kanzar will attack Orr next. You must be ready," Bakari said. He walked over to Abylar and let go of Kharlia's hand to mount the dragon.

Looking down at Kharlia, he saw the tears running down her brave face. She thought he was leaving her. *No way!*

Bakari stretched his left hand down toward her and grinned. "Get on behind me."

Wide-eyed, she stood for a moment as if not sure of what to do.

"It's wonderful, Kharlia," Alli said. "But don't let Abylar's flying make you sick. He likes to play around up there."

I don't play. Abylar pouted as his words, spoken to Bakari's mind, were related to the two girls.

They both laughed. Alli came over and patted the young dragon tenderly. "He's a fine dragon, Kharlia. I can't imagine his feelings of loss right now. But it really is wonderful to see the world from his back."

Abylar turned his huge head, lifting it to Alli as if nodding his thanks to her. Bakari pulled Kharlia up behind him.

"Tell Roland I said hello," Alli said in a sudden rush of words.

"I'm sure he will like that," Bakari said back.

"What do you mean?" Alli frowned now. "Well, then don't say anything to him. That arrogant wizard…"

"Alli." Bakari stopped her. "As a friend, I will tell him

hello for you."

Alli nodded her head, her cheeks flushing pink.

Then, as Abylar lifted himself up into the air and began the flight northward, toward the Citadel, Bakari wondered what his friend had gotten himself into this time.

CHAPTER TWENTY

Nagasi, current Regent of Mahli, glanced around the table. Sitting with him for the council meeting sat nine people: one elder from each of Mahli's four main cities; Regent Nagasi; his son, Regent-Elect Kolo; Zaire, their military adviser; a scribe; and an elderly wizard named Imari. Except the wizard and the scribe, all wore their dark hair long, hanging down in dozens of braids. Their skin was brown, but their differing shades gave hints to mixed heritages in their pasts.

Nagasi had been regent since his father's death, twenty years earlier. As regent, Nagasi understood that, one day, the true king may appear and retake his throne. This was what the regents did—try to rule fairly while holding the throne in readiness for their king. Sometimes these true kings came once in every few generations; sometimes hundreds of years separated their returns.

The Council of Elders sat in a closed room in the regent's wooden castle in the middle of Amar, the capital city. Mahli was a small kingdom, in terms of numbers. Surrounded by a ring of tall, snowcapped mountains, the isolated kingdom did not have many that ventured in or out of it. The valleys between its tall mountains made for excellent grazing of cattle and contained rich soil for vegetables and fruits, many of which were unique to the mountain kingdom. It was not as large as the kingdoms to the south—Alaris, Elvyn, Tillimot, and Quentis—but it traded mostly with the territories to its north—

Khazer, Turg, and Cyrene—with an annual ocean trip even farther north to Gildan and the Realm.

Being an isolated, yet hard to reach kingdom had kept Mahli at peace for many years. Her people were sturdy, self-sufficient, and hardworking. They were also extremely stubborn. And today was no exception.

"You are all aware of the prophecy as much as I am," Nagasi said, standing to make his point. Out of the corner of his eye he noticed the tips of some of his braids more gray than black. Sometimes he felt he was getting too old to rule a stubborn people. But he worried what his son, the regent-heir, would do to their people.

Looking each participant in the eye, Nagasi continued, "It has been a long time since a dragon rider has appeared in Mahli: over one hundred and fifty years. Never have we gone so long. The world, during this time, has almost forgotten about how great we once were."

"We can be great again, Father!" Kolo said, his face a younger and less-wrinkled version of Nagasi's own, but holding an almost permanent scowl.

Nagasi put his hand up to quiet this outburst, for he was not done speaking yet. "The last prophecy said that a dragon rider would arise when the need was greatest. This man would bring us out of obscurity and into the world and would bring peace to the kingdoms around us."

"And you think this prophesied dragon rider is this boy from Alaris? He wasn't even born here," Kolo said, voicing his opposition again.

Some of Nagasi's other councilors nodded their heads at

that.

"Some of you met Bakari. You cannot deny that his heritage is from Mahli," Zaire said.

"He did not stay here long enough for most of us to meet him," said Tadaaki, one of the elders from the west. "Alaris has been closed off for one hundred and fifty years. Now, all of a sudden, our dragon rider appears from *there*. I don't like it." The man crossed his arms.

Nagasi saw a small smile spread across Kolo's face.

"I have seen him," Kolo said. "And I am still not convinced."

"You saw his dragon, too, Kolo." Zaire's dark brown eyes gazed intently at Kolo. "How can you deny he is a dragon rider?"

"I don't deny he has a dragon—one whose egg seems to have somehow been stolen from us to power the barrier around Alaris!" The veins stood out on Kolo's muscled neck. "Maybe he is out gathering an army now, to overrun Mahli."

"Sit down, Kolo," Nagasi commanded. Kolo slumped back onto his seat. Nagasi turned to his scribe and asked, "Is there anything in the library archives that can help us decipher this mystery?"

"There is a small, ancient book of prophecy," Tuma, the scribe said. "But the dragon rider asked to take it with him to study."

Nagasi watched as his son's eyes grew large and his mouth constricted in anger. Kolo was too temperamental to be regent. Nagasi worried about Kolo's influence on the other councilors. There were at least two councilors that seemed to be in Kolo's pocket.

"Do you know what was in the book?" Nagasi asked Tuma.

The small man nodded. "It is a history of the dragon riders throughout time, as far back as we know. Dozens of occurrences have been documented. Each time a dragon rider has appeared, the first one draws other dragon riders to him. He becomes their leader and ours."

Kolo stood up again, and Nagasi took a deep breath. Looking to the wizard, Nagasi said, "Imari, you have been quiet."

The elderly wizard was the eldest wizard in Mahli. It was rumored that he could remember being there when the barrier first went up. "*Bakari* means *royal promise*. So his name seems to be a portent of the truth."

"Don't hide behind your fancy words and hidden meanings, old man," Kolo said, turning to glare at the man. "What do you know of any of this? You're just a fading wizard."

"That is enough, Kolo," Nagasi said as he slapped his hand on the table. "If you can't be civil here, you will leave."

Imari put his hands up in the air, his colorful wizard robes sliding down his bony arms. "I am fine, Nagasi. Kolo is just young and untrained." A slight smile seemed to be trying to push its way out, but Imari kept his lips under control.

Kolo sat back down and glared at the wizard.

"Go on," Nagasi prompted Imari.

The wizard put his hands together into a steeple on the table in front of him. "Dragon riders have indeed not been seen since the barrier went up. Before then, they came every few generations. And they have always been through the same ancestral line, since the beginning."

"How can this youngster, Bakari, be him then?" Akar, the eastern elder asked. "He's been living behind the barrier."

"Ahh. Now that is my story to tell," Imari said. "I won't go into all the details at this time, but I did play a part in the forming of the barrier. In the end, I took the last descendant of the dragon riders and brought him to Alaris, to a small city north of the wizards' Citadel. I needed to ensure that his posterity would stay safe until dragon riders were needed again."

Kolo grunted in apparent disbelief, and Nagasi silenced him with another look.

"All these years," Imari said to Nagasi, "the bloodline was preserved in that man's descendants, even until Bakari was born. He is a direct descendant of the dragon riders and dragon kings of old, my lord."

As conversations broke out between the elders and Kolo, Nagasi let them talk amongst themselves. He knew that nothing would be resolved that evening anyway. Turning to Imari and Zaire, Nagasi asked, "With the fall of the barrier, do you think we can expect aggression from Alaris again?"

Zaire spoke first. "The dragon rider thought we should expect harm, at some point, if Kanzar wins rule of Alaris. Our forces are small, mainly only trackers and such, with a few trained men on the northern border. We will need to recruit people from Khazer and Turg and maybe Solshi to help us."

Nagasi nodded, signaling for Zaire that they would make

that plan happen.

Imari, the elderly wizard, seemed to take his time answering. The man was so slow sometimes, that he seemed like an elf in his patient and unhurried way of speaking. Maybe just getting old did that – the wizard was the oldest person alive in Mahli.

Eventually, Imari spoke. "I will try to contact the wizard school, in Gildan, or the wizard conclave, in Arc. I've even heard of a new school for wizards, in the Realm, that has existed for the past ten to fifteen years. Ever since the Realm got a new wizard king, more wizards seem to be showing up in the North. Maybe they have also heard of the prophecy and could send reinforcements if needed. Though, I don't truly know if they can arrive in time."

"We are a hard kingdom to reach," Zaire admitted.

"By design, my friends." Nagasi lowered his voice as he continued, "If this Bakari is the dragon rider and will be proclaimed King, he will find the other riders first. Then Kolo and the others won't be able to deny it. If the young man never returns, then maybe my son is correct."

"I will send a messenger bird to them." Wizard Imari nodded. "In the meantime, I think we should reinforce the southern roads, just in case of an invasion."

Nagasi turned back, to take control of the meeting. "In time," he said to all of them, "we will see if this Bakari is the true dragon rider or not. I admit he is young, but age does not determine strength or nobility."

"Father," Kolo said, "we have come up with another plan."

Nagasi raised his eyebrows.

"With the backing of some of our illustrious elders," Kolo continued, "I will lead an expedition to find another dragon egg." Kolo looked smug, as if he was extremely pleased with himself.

Nagasi shook his head in embarrassment for his son. "Kolo, you cannot force yourself to be the dragon rider."

Kolo stood up and moved behind his chair to use his full height and size to his advantage. "I will, Father. I will be the prophecy."

"You cannot force prophecy, boy," Imari said.

Looking around the room, to all present, Kolo puffed his chest out and said, "No one can deny that I am of Mahli. Wouldn't you rather have someone you know as your king?"

Many in the room nodded, but Nagasi didn't know if he could. At this moment, he rather hoped young Bakari was the prophesied one. His son would not be a good regent or king. Too greedy and filled with a thirst for power. But maybe the trip would do him good. When he didn't find a dragon egg, Kolo would then bow to Bakari as Nagasi was sure the rest would do one day.

"You have my leave to do so, Son," Nagasi said, to Kolo's surprise. "Just don't get too frustrated if you don't find one."

"I will find one," Kolo said. Then he turned and commanded the scribe, "Find and document all the books having to do with the dragon riders and their eggs, Tuma. We leave in three days."

The meeting broke up after that, and Nagasi returned to the wing of the building that was his home. Nia, his wife, walked up to him, her hips swaying nicely. After all these years, he loved her fiercely and still found her very attractive. She pulled on his hand to get him to come and sit down next to her. They sat in a comfortable silence for a few minutes.

"Kolo is going in search of a dragon egg," Nagasi finally said.

Nia let out a long breath. "That boy has never been satisfied. He's always been thirsty for more power and influence."

"I've tried to train him well, to be a regent. But, if the dragon rider truly is to be our new king, Kolo won't even have that."

"It will be his downfall, Nagasi," Nia said. Nagasi felt her fingers rubbing his neck, trying to lessen the tension there.

"I know," Nagasi's eyes grew wet, and he blinked a few times to get control. "I love him and have given him so much, but he wants more. Always more."

Nia nodded in agreement.

Then Nagasi leaned back against the cushion and took his wife's hands in his left hand, closing his eyes for a moment. "I fear what Kolo might do if he doesn't find an egg," Nagasi said. "But I fear more what he will do if he does find one."

CHAPTER TWENTY ONE

Bakari and Kharlia flew northwest on Abylar, from Corwan over the warm and sandy desert. There wasn't much to look at besides the Corwan River, running through the edge of the desert. Both Bakari and his dragon were exhausted. Their flight to Corwan, the subsequent fight, finding Kharlia, and then the loss of Erryl and the other guardians had drained them both physically and emotionally.

Abylar was flying high so as not to alarm anyone below. But his strength had waned, and he would need to rest soon. Events had happened so fast that Bakari still didn't know how Kharlia had survived. As soon as they landed he needed to find out. Her small hands encircled his waist, and he patted her hands with one of his.

Bakari. Abylar woke Bakari from his thoughts with this gentle thought. *I need to rest.*

Bakari felt torn now between rushing to Roland and letting Abylar rest. Roland had sounded frantic for help. But, if they arrived too exhausted to help, what good would they be?

Just south of Cassian, between the Corwan and Dunn Rivers, at the edge of the Elvyn Forest, they found a place to land that seemed free of any onlookers. Dragging his wings across the ground, Abylar landed roughly, and then Bakari and Kharlia climbed off. As Abylar settled in for a spell before he would go hunting, Bakari took a small fishing line and decided to catch and cook a few fish for himself and Kharlia before sleeping.

A small stream ran by the edge of the trees, hopefully deep enough for a few fish. Bakari and Kharlia walked the few dozen steps to the stream and settled down on a group of rocks next to the bank. Kharlia sat down next to him, resting her head on his shoulder. The sun would soon be setting, and its orange rays shone in Kharlia's eyes and reflected off the small stream.

As the thick trees of the Elvyn Forest rustled behind them in a slight breeze, Bakari breathed in deeply, relishing the peace. He couldn't remember when he had last felt this relaxed. The last few months had been more of an adventure than he had ever thought a minor scholar like himself would have.

It was now approaching the end of autumn, but Bakari realized that it was only this past summer when he had sat in the library, reading, before Roland ran in with news that the Chief Judge had collapsed. From that moment on, the whirlwind surrounding his life had started: making preparations for the trip to the Citadel, discovering that the Chief Judge had been poisoned again, meeting Kharlia, escaping River Bend in the middle of the night, losing Kharlia, traveling to Celestar, finding the Dragon Orb, becoming a dragon rider, traveling to Mahli and then to Elvyn, and fighting in the battle in Corwan that very day. Bakari admitted to himself that this was definitely not the life he had thought he would live.

"Bak, what's wrong?"

Bakari turned to the side. "Absolutely nothing now, Kharlia. What happened? You know, I searched for you."

Kharlia leaned away from Bakari and punched him softly on the shoulder. "Don't feel guilty. I made the decision, Bak.

The choice was all mine."

Bakari laughed. "It really is good to have you back. How did you survive?"

Kharlia smiled and Bakari's heart melted once again. "After dropping off the cliff I landed in the water and blacked out for a few moments," she explained. "When I came to, I was on my back, spinning down the river. I heard you yelling, but there wasn't anything I could do."

Bakari pulled a fish off the line and Kharlia paused for a moment while he set the line to catch another one. "Where did you go?"

"I grabbed a log and floated for hours as the water carried me farther south. I had passed River Bend before I could climb out. In a small village, an elderly couple had compassion on me and fed me and let me rest. They were taking some hand-carved furniture down to Corwan, on a riverboat, and offered me a job if I would go with them."

Bakari nodded.

Kharlia laid her head on Bakari's shoulder, "Oh Bak, I wanted to go back and find you, I truly did." Tears glistened in the corners of her eyes. "But I had no way of getting back there alone or of knowing where to even go. I asked people about Celestar, but no one knew about any city in the northeast of Alaris."

"I understand, Kharlia. I really do. I barely knew where I was going. I'm just glad you are safe. I wondered so many times if...if..." He stopped, tears gathering in the corner of his eyes.

Kharlia put a hand on Bakari's arm. "I never stopped thinking about you either, Bak. I just didn't know how to ever find you again. Once I arrived in Corwan, I found the city healer. And, after showing him my knowledge of herbs and healing, he let me stay in a small loft above his home and work for him. Shortly after I arrived, I learned that the barrier had come down."

Bakari laughed and felt embarrassed. "That was because of me. A Dragon Orb—or egg—powered the barrier. When I touched it, it shattered, and Abylar came out."

Kharlia glanced to her side and laughed, her voice carrying through the forest. "Oh, Bak, that must have been exciting."

Bak pursed his lips for a moment. "Well, it was unexpected, to say the least."

When his fishing line tugged, Bakari turned his attention back to the small stream. He could have coaxed the fish to him, with his powers, but that seemed like cheating. His powers were there to be used to help others, not himself. As he pulled the string back, he realized how clear the scales of the fish were to him now. It was a reminder of the heightened senses he had received since bonding with Abylar. The glasses he had fashioned for himself were now becoming only a distant memory.

Kharlia sighed in contentment next to him.

Soon they finished catching enough fish and headed back to the camp. Working together to prepare and cook the fish seemed natural for the pair. Bakari and her had been on the run for a week before they had been split apart.

The smells of the cooking fish roused Abylar from his sleep.

He stretched his neck close to Bakari. *Smells good, Rider.*

Not much here for you. Bakari laughed. *But you can have one if you'd like.*

The dragon snorted, and a drop of blue flame sizzled the leaves on the ground. *One of those fish aren't even a small bite. How do you survive on such little food?*

Bakari glanced down at his still thin frame. His muscles had developed in the last few weeks, with all the walking, riding, and practicing the disc weapons, but he was still just a skinny young man with not much meat on his bones. His robes were getting a little shorter on his arms and legs, signifying a recent growth spurt, but his size would never get him noticed.

I need real food, not boy food. Abylar snorted again, and Bakari thought his dragon was actually laughing at him.

"Hey!" Bakari said out loud. "That's not nice!"

A deep rumble ensued from the dragon, and he flapped his wings a few times as he lifted off the ground. *Hunger makes me cranky,* he said to Bakari. With that, Abylar flew off to find something more filling than the few bites of fish they were eating.

After cleaning up a bit from cooking, Bakari pulled a small blanket out of his bag, and then he sat with Kharlia again and told her his own tale, from the time she had fallen into the Dunn River to the present. She lovingly ran her fingers through his hair.

"Your hair is getting longer, Bak," Kharlia said and then smiled mischievously. "Why don't we put it in braids, like you saw in Mahli?"

Bakari's eyes went wide. How would he look in braids?

"Do you think it's long enough?"

Kharlia walked over to a tree and pulled off some thin vines. Stretching them out and pulling them as straight as she could, she tore them into pieces a few inches long. Then, pouring a little water on her hands, she ran them through his hair, trying to straighten out the curls. Over the next few hours, as Bakari talked about visiting Mahli, she made dozens of braids throughout his hair, tying them off with the vines. They were short but would hold for now.

Then, moving back a few feet, she admired her handiwork. "Oh," she said, clapping her hands in delight. "You look so exotic, Dragon Rider."

Bakari rolled his eyes. "I'm not sure I want to be *exotic*." He would have to wait until daylight to see his reflection in the river.

Kharlia leaned in and gave Bakari a soft kiss on the lips.

His body quaked, and his heart fluttered. He remembered their first kiss and had wondered so many times if he would ever feel her lips again. He kissed her back now, running his hands through her soft brown hair.

Feeling both surprise and delight through the bond with Abylar, Bakari pushed his dragon away before pulling back from Kharlia. He couldn't stop smiling.

"What?" Kharlia asked, and her cheeks flushed.

"I'm just so happy, Kharlia. This is nice."

They talked for a few more minutes, but the activities of the day and the food in his stomach started to make Bakari sleepy. He felt Abylar giving chase to a small animal. The dragon warned Bakari that he himself might get sleepy after he ate. Bakari forgot sometimes how young Abylar was. Only a few weeks old. He still needed his sleep, just like any baby.

I'm not a baby! A low growl through their bond.

Bakari laughed out loud and then said back to his dragon, *I just meant you are young and still growing.*

Settling down on a blanket, next to the dying fire, Bakari grasped Kharlia's hand. He still couldn't believe she was back in his life. With Kharlia being a few years younger than himself, Bakari was still amazed at how much she had survived in her young life.

After a few hours of sleep for all of them, they would need to be on their way once again. So they should arrive at the Citadel early in the morning. The last time Bakari had seen Roland was when he had flown there on Abylar, to warn Roland of the barrier falling.

Kanzar had taken most of his loyal followers to Cassian, to battle the Chief Judge, and Roland had nicely taken control of the Citadel. An accomplishment that was indeed quite rare for a sixteen-year-old. Roland always had set his sights high in life, not like Bakari.

Bakari's reflections then moved back to Kharlia, and he settled down to sleep. The night was quiet and calm, darkness settling in nicely. His last thoughts were of her, snuggling up next to him, and of him feeling her warmth and comfort.

A few hours later, in the still of the night, Bakari was woken up by the snap of a twig, and he carefully opened one of his eyes. He flinched as the point of a sword appeared, only inches away from his opened eye.

"Well, what have we here?" said a thin man with a cruel face under his dirty brown hair.

Kharlia sat up and screamed. Bakari tried to rise, but the sword's blade moved closer to his throat.

Then the man continued, "Are you a runaway from the king's army, finding a few nights warmth with a girl?"

Bakari felt confused and was still trying to wake up. "What king?"

The man kicked Bakari in the side. "Kanzar, stupid boy!"

"Kanzar is king?" Bakari asked.

"He really is stupid," someone else said. Another man must have stood off to the side. But Bakari couldn't see him.

"He might as well be king, boy," the first man said. "It's only a matter of time. You must have run away from his army. All boys your age have been called into the service in Cassian."

Bakari didn't know what to say. Nothing that he might say would placate these men. They were probably looking for a reward by turning him in.

As if in answer to Bakari's thoughts, the second man spoke again. "He's nice and healthy. Should fetch us a nice price for bringing him back."

"I'm a wizard, if you didn't know," Bakari said. He knew it had sounded as lame to them as it had to himself. So he reached out his mind to Abylar, but the young beast must have been in a heavy slumber as Bakari couldn't rouse him. Bakari was on his own for now. He needed to establish himself quickly in order to protect Kharlia.

The two men laughed, clearly in doubt of his wizard abilities. Then they grabbed Kharlia roughly, and she tried to swat their hands away, but they held her arms still.

Bakari was just about to use his powers against them,

when one of the men spoke. "If he's a wizard, maybe we should take him to Wizard Onius instead," the first man said.

"Onius?" Bakari said out loud.

The men turned back toward him, loosening their grip on Kharlia. She pulled her arms away and ran to Bakari's side.

The second man grinned. "I like that idea better than going to Kanzar."

Bakari got a good look at the second man now. He was heavier than the first and was shaved bald. Both men looked to be in their late twenties, and they nodded their heads to each other.

Bakari wouldn't mind seeing Onius again. The Chief Judge had wondered where Onius's loyalties lay, but Bakari trusted the old wizard. If going with these men now would get Bakari and Kharlia to Onius, then Abylar could pick them up later, and they would get to Roland soon. Also, information from Cassian would be important to have.

Drawing on a simple spell, from the back of his mind, Bakari brought out a globe of magic in front of them, to light their way in the dark night. The second man jumped at this show of power, and the first man moved behind Bakari and stuck the cold point of his blade against the back of Bakari's neck.

"Nothing funny, boy. Trying to show off isn't going to scare us," the first man said. "One wrong move by you and your sweetie's pretty neck gets sliced before you can summon any of your power. Understand?"

Bakari did understand. The man's words made him realize their safety depended on himself. He needed to be careful if he was going to get them to Roland in time.

* * *

A few hours into their walk, they came to the Corwan River. The two men had others waiting for them on a medium-sized barge. Cowering next to those men sat three other young men, all younger than Bakari.

"We got us a wizard," his captors said to one man, who was obviously in charge. This man was larger and wore nicer clothes than the rest of the crew.

"Nothing more than an apprentice, by his looks," said the apparent leader. "We got us three other youngster's who be escaping our master's army. We will fetch us some good gold tonight, men."

The men cheered and tied down the young men to a railing in the barge. But they kept Kharlia closer to their sides.

"What can we fetch for this one, men?" another man said.

Kharlia snarled and kicked her feet out at them.

"Ooh, a feisty one." One of the men laughed and moved over next to her. Then he ran his grimy hands down her shoulders. Kharlia jerked her head forward and butted him in the head.

"Stop that!" Bakari shouted, a golden glow beginning to surround him. He wouldn't stand for them hurting her, but he still couldn't contact Abylar—so this group of mercenaries was their best bet to get back to civilization. "She will sit by me."

The man brought back his hand to hit Kharlia, but then the man in charged stopped him.

"Leave the girl alone," their leader said, giving a hard, but respectful look at Bakari. He motioned his head for the men to move Kharlia next to Bakari.

She scooted up as close to him as he could.

"I won't let anything happen to you." Bakari whispered.

"I would rather see you show these men a lesson, Bak."

Bakari smiled. He really did miss having Kharlia's feistiness around. The leader of the group told them to be quiet so they just sat still and looked around.

Bakari wiggled his fingers to keep the circulation flowing and thought about what he should do.

He could easily slide out of his bonds, but then what? They would need to swim across the river. Bakari had swum in the Corwan River many times during the summer to cool off at the end of the day, but it wouldn't gain him anything at the moment. Finding Onius was his best chance. What would he say to the former counselor to the Chief Judge?

Getting across the river took longer than Bakari thought it would. With the walking and the time spent on the river, the eastern sky now approached the earliest signs of dawn. The captives were taken onto the river docks and into the port gate into the city. Early morning bakers were up baking their breads for the day. The sweet smells in the air made Bakari's stomach grumble.

Soon they came to the castle itself. A lump formed in Bakari's throat. He was not expecting to feel this sentimental. But the castle had been his home for two years before leaving with the Chief Judge to follow Kanzar's summons to the Citadel. Now Kanzar ruled here instead.

After disembarking, the entire group of young men and Kharlia were handed off to a steward, who seemed to hold heavy disdain for their captors but paid them the gold nevertheless.

"Smelly boys!" the man said with his nose held. "And a pretty girl." When one of the young men's stomachs growled, the steward laughed. "Hungry too, are we?" He sneered at the five of them, his vicious face in contrast to his nice, crisp, and clean uniform.

"Yes," the young man said.

"Too bad," the steward said. "You are to be taken to the barracks."

Bakari spoke up for the first time. "I was told I would be taken to Onius."

The steward rounded on him, his face and foul breath only inches from Bakari's nose. "And why would I let a runaway see one of Kanzar's wizard council members?" His face was not familiar to Bakari, and he figured the steward must be one of Kanzar's men.

"Because I am a wizard, sir." Bakari tried to act calm.

"You don't look much older than a boy," the steward said, "and an unsightly, dark-skinned one at that."

Bakari blinked hard and tried to hold his tongue, but he had been through a lot lately and wasn't in the mood to be insulted now. He summoned a thread of magic and broke his bands. Then, waving his hands in the air, Bakari sent the rope to tie itself around the steward. Bakari took the steward to a small column and tied him there, hands behind his back, facing away from the other three young men, Kharlia, and himself.

The steward yelled. So Bakari gagged him but realized they might be in bigger trouble now. Others might come, maybe even wizards, and Bakari wouldn't be able to stand up to all of them. Being here this early in the morning would mean having extra time until any reinforcements came. It was probably all that had saved them so far.

"Run," he told the other three young men. "Go outside and back into the city, and be more careful."

"Thank you, sir," one of the young men said and then bowed before running off. "You really are a wizard."

Bakari snorted a laugh. *A wizard, a dragon rider, and maybe a king*, he thought, *and I can barely get past a steward*. Then he smiled to himself, despite the danger of the situation, for he knew the entire layout of the castle: secret passages and all. He had it all memorized.

"Bak, we need to hurry." Kharlia grabbed him and began to run outside with the other young men.

Bakari pulled his hand back and stopped them from running. "This way, Kharlia."

Bakari pulled Kharlia over near a floor-to-ceiling tapestry on the wall. Looking to the right and to the left, to make sure no one was coming for them yet, he slid behind the tapestry and pushed on a specific brick. Then a portion of the wall swung inward, and Bakari and Kharlia jumped through, closing the wall back up again.

Listening for a moment in the darkness, he now heard other voices, responding to the steward's yell. The voices began arguing, and then he heard the voice of the steward again.

"He is a runaway wizard with a girl," the steward said. "Both dark and dangerous."

Bakari smiled to himself, glancing up at Kharlia. *Dark? Yes.*

Dangerous? Hardly. Now, if he could summon Abylar, that might cause some fear. So he reached out with his inner bond. Feeling that Abylar was sleeping, Bakari mentally poked him a few times.

Abylar. Abylar! Wake up! He was finally able to rouse the sleeping dragon.

Explaining what had happened, Bakari said, *Abylar, come close to the city, and wait for me to summon you.* Bakari would need to see Onius first.

"What now?" Kharlia asked, still gripping his hand tightly.

As the voices faded, Bakari brought up a light; though he would hardly need it to get through the hidden passages, Kharlia would need to see.

"This way." Bakari began to run through the secret passage and up two flights of stairs. "Onius will be quite surprised!"

CHAPTER TWENTY TWO

Bakari and Kharlia were standing in the secret passageway outside of Onius's private rooms. They could hear two voices talking.

"You shouldn't come here, Gideon," Onius said, his voice low and threatening. "You endanger our plan and my position here."

"Your position?" Gideon replied, his voice a deeper, older-sounding sneer. "And what position is that, these days, oh great wizard? Are you Kanzar's right-hand man, a traitor, a kingmaker, or a loyal counselor to the Chief Judge?"

Bakari and Kharlia listened intently. They didn't know who the other man was, but this was indeed a dangerous discussion to have *anywhere*, let alone in this castle.

"You go too far!" they heard Onius say. Then Bakari and Kharlia heard something crash to the floor. "I have been counseling the leaders of Alaris for decades."

"And I have been running the underground here even longer," Gideon said.

Breathing in deeply, Bakari realized that this other man must be the head of the thieves' guild. What was Onius doing with him?

Then it was quiet for a moment.

When the conversation resumed, Onius was speaking more softly. "Things got out of control. That's why I came to you. We are on the same side in this, Gideon. I know that I have things to atone for and that I can't predict what will become of me after all of this is over—if I live that long—but Alaris cannot survive with Kanzar as king."

"My men are taking greater risks here," they heard Gideon say. "The trouble they stir up is dangerous. Already, some have been caught."

"I will take care of their families for them—I told you that," Onius said. "You didn't need to come here. This is dangerous. If Kanzar finds out what we are doing here, I don't know if I can control his wrath. The man is so unstable already."

"How much longer until he falls?" Gideon asked.

"I don't think it will take much more," Onius said. "It depends on how his attack at Corwan went."

Bakari grinned at Kharlia. With the mage light between them, he could see concern on Kharlia's face. Kanzar wouldn't be very happy with what had happened in Corwan—that's for sure. Bakari had known Kanzar since Bakari was five years old. The man had always been polite and respectful around Bakari, even encouraging him on his studying when Bakari was younger. So Bakari had always looked up to the wizard. But Bakari knew now that Kanzar was consumed with the need for power and that his greed had taken Kanzar over the edge.

"And what happens to the city after Kanzar falls?" asked the guild leader. "A city in anarchy is only good for business for so long. What do you intend to do then?"

"You know the authority I hold. I will do what I must do," answered Onius gruffly.

A long silence followed.

Then, barely audible, Onius whispered, "But don't look to me as your next king."

"What are you not telling me, old wizard?"

"Nothing. Nothing concrete," Onius said. "There are others vying for the kingship, but there is also a rumor floating on the wind of the rise of a dragon."

"A dragon!" Gideon snorted. "Fairy tales and folklore."

"Maybe," conceded Onius, "and maybe not. There is a long tradition of dragon riders preceding the rise of a dragon king. And both seem to appear at times of immense peril."

"Like I said: fairy tales."

Silence followed this, and Bakari felt his heart pounding. He took a few steps back, taking Kharlia's hand, and wondered what he, a dragon rider, was doing here, in the heart of the enemy camp. Bakari still couldn't tell if he should trust Onius or not. If rumors were already spreading about Abylar, then Bakari needed to be careful. Now there was Miriel to think about, too. She was still young and could be hurt easily.

And don't forget about the other dragons, whispered Abylar to Bakari's mind. *We must hurry. Their time is almost here, and we must be there to match each rider to their dragon.*

Bakari nodded to himself. There was that, too. The other dragons. Could he find them in time to stop this war, which could ravish the land?

Just be ready to come and get me soon, he told Abylar.

I am close, Abylar said. *I will be there when you need me.*

"Abylar is close." Bakari said to Kharlia.

"What are we doing here, Bak? This is dangerous for you." Kharlia glanced back toward Onius's rooms, and Bakari realized that it had grown quiet on the other side of the wall.

"I just need to talk to Onius." Bakari motioned to the door. He stepped forward and pushed his hand against the wall, preparing to open it, when, at that same time, it opened inward instead, almost knocking him and Kharlia over.

In front of them appeared the man Bakari supposed was Gideon, the leader of the thieves' guild. Without warning, the old man pulled out a knife and lunged at Bakari, at the same time calling a warning to Onius.

Bakari moved to the side, shielding Kharlia with his body, but the knife still cut across his forearm. The wound burned horribly, but it didn't stop him from bringing up his hands in front of him as he began to form a wall of air.

"Onius," Bakari called out. "It's me!"

Onius stuck his head into the small passageway. Then his eyes bulged larger, and he reached a hand out to Gideon and said, "Stop."

All four stared at each other for a moment in surprise, Kharlia moving back out from behind Bakari and standing next to him.

Onius then turned to Gideon. "Leave. I will take care of this."

Gideon frowned, then slithered off through the dark passageways. Onius pulled Bakari and Kharlia into the room and, with a stern frown, studied the blood running down the young wizard's arm. Without a word, Onius pulled Bakari over to a washbasin to clean the wound.

With a soft shove, Kharlia moved the old wizard out of the way and reached into her bag, pulling out a yarrow leaf to stop the bleeding. Then, ripping a piece of cloth off a small towel, she wrapped Bakari's arm, then moved over to stand by his side.

Onius glared down at Bakari and Kharlia.

As Bakari examined the old wizard, he wasn't sure what to say or how much to tell Onius. The old counselor wizard was at least eighty years old but appeared younger. His long, graying hair and swirling blue robes made sure that no one missed knowing he was a wizard. He looked the part from head to toe.

Then, with a quick step forward, Onius put his arms out and brought Bakari in for a long hug.

"Bak, where have you been?" Onius asked. "Last time we saw or heard of you two was in River Bend." He paused his questions as he brought Bakari back out in front of himself. Then Onius asked, "How much did you hear in the passageway?"

Bakari was nervous around the wizard. Onius was a legend in Alaris, counselor to many chief judges. Should Bakari admit what they had overheard? Or, could they even trust Onius? Would he help them?

"Why give that man the use of the passageways?" was what Bakari asked instead. He needed a few more minutes to collect his thoughts.

Onius lowered his eyes for a moment. Finally looking back up, he met Bakari's gaze. "Dangerous times, Bakari. We all do what we must."

Yes, we do, thought Bakari, and he found strength now through his bond with Abylar. So Bakari pulled himself up straighter, but he was still quite a bit shorter than Onius. Then

Bakari said, "Kanzar's men failed in Corwan."

Onius's eyes bulged, and Bakari saw more wrinkles on his forehead than he remembered seeing there before. "How do you know?" Onius asked. "Where have you been?"

"I was there," Bakari said, evading the second question.

"So are Alli and Mericus," Kharlia said.

"And Judge Azeem's battalion returned from going toward Orr soon enough to help also."

Onius nodded. "So, Mericus defected from Kanzar's group after all. I didn't know if he would actually have the strength to do it or not."

Bakari frowned. "I'm not sure if I can trust him or not, but Mericus did seem to help secure Corwan, and Alli trusts him, and I do trust her."

"Yes. Yes." Onius seemed to be thinking about something else. "Mericus is capable."

"And, where do you stand, Onius?" Bakari met the counselor's eye.

"Getting bolder now, are we?" Onius asked, then waved his hand, indicating that he meant no offense. "You seem different, Bak—no glasses and a new hair style—but there is also sadness in your eyes."

Bakari took Kharlia's hand in his, and his mind went to Erryl and the guardians. He pushed these thoughts away. He couldn't afford to think too deeply on that right now.

"I have seen a lot, Onius."

Onius nodded and then walked over and grabbed a glass of wine. Drinking it down quickly, he then offered, "Bakari and Kharlia, would you like a portion?"

Bakari glanced at Kharlia but, seeing her expression, he declined for both of them. He needed a clear head right now.

Before anything else could be said, a knock came to the door. Onius frowned, took a step forward, then turned back to Bakari and Kharlia, motioning them to hide behind another door, in his bedchamber. Kharlia nodded and pulled Bakari in after herself.

Bakari could hear a servant speaking at the door, informing Onius that Kanzar was coming to see him.

"There seems to have been a disturbance this morning," the servant explained, "in which, it is rumored, a young wizard had tied up a steward and then escaped from him."

Onius closed the door and then quietly called Bakari and Kharlia back out.

"Kanzar is coming here?" Kharlia seemed to look around for an exit. "I've never met the man, and I don't intend to now."

A moment of silence filled the room. Bakari thought about what to do.

"You never answered our question, Onius," Kharlia broke the silence.

Onius gave a quick glance around the room, then the corners of his mouth turned down. His eyes flashed at Kharlia. "Why does everyone question my loyalty?"

Seeing this, Bakari let his own anger build. He had seen too much loss and fighting in recent days. "Don't jump on her, Onius. Maybe your loyalty is questioned due to your own actions. You gave up the Chief Judge and worked behind his back to strengthen Kanzar and his King-men."

Onius's face grew red with anger. Then, in one quick moment, it changed and lost all its color. "Bakari, please. You have no idea how bad I feel. I never realized Kanzar's full intentions. I had not been around him recently then. The Chief Judge is a good man, which is why I warned him and didn't kill him as Kanzar wanted me to. You must believe me. I am doing what I can to fix the situation."

"Like working with the thieves' guild?" Kharlia said.

Glancing from her to Bakari and then back, Onius nodded. "Yes, like working with the thieves' guild. I am trying to breed instability here so that Kanzar can't focus on his war. It's working, for that man is at a tipping point now."

Bakari looked at Onius, a man he had respected his entire life, and then breathed out a sigh. "It's good to hear that, Onius. The Chief Judge is building an army in Orr. He will attack here soon. The elves are also involved."

"You're getting around quite a bit for a young scholar, aren't you, son?" Onius said as if fishing for more information.

"I can't tell you all, Onius," Bakari said. "Not now. But you must trust me."

Just then, Bakari heard a faint echo of a voice calling for help once again.

Roland! Bakari knew that they needed to leave.

Abylar, come now!

Bakari had too many things to worry about: Celestar, Orr, Corwan, Elvyn, the Citadel, and—not least of all—his ancestral kingdom of Mahli.

Drawing strength from Abylar, he prepared himself to give his last words of command to Onius. Then, in a tone full of authority, he said to Onius, "Hold on, and keep doing whatever you can here to destabilize Kanzar. Help is on the way. I'll be doing all I can to stop this war, but I need to gather more help. I'm going to the Citadel now, to help Roland. He's in some type of trouble there. Get word to Orr or Corwan if you need anything, and I will receive it."

Kharlia smiled encouragingly at Bakari, but Onius just stood there and nodded, apparently not used to being given orders from others. But Bakari had not been speaking as a level two scholar wizard but as a dragon rider. Even though his status was still unknown to Onius, Bakari's new authority came through, nonetheless.

Yells came up from outside the castle, and Onius frowned and then moved over to his balcony. Opening its double doors, Onius went out, and Bakari and Kharlia followed him, walking together to the edge of the balcony.

Turning back to Onius one final time, Bakari said, "Gather those who are faithful around you, Onius. War is coming, but hopefully I can limit the damage. I hope to see you again."

Then a knock came at the door, and Bakari knew they needed to leave immediately. Turning, Bakari saw Abylar coming down from up above the castle's roofs. His enormous, beautiful, and noble blue dragon lowered himself down until his back was even with the balcony, a wing held out for them. Bakari held Kharlia's hand as they climbed onto the railing and then walked out on his wing, moved quickly to Abylar's back and settled themselves in the saddle.

"Bakari!" Onius said, his eyes opened wide. "*You* are the dragon rider?"

Bakari shrugged his shoulders. "Yes, sir. That's me."

Then the door to the wizard's chambers flew open, and Kanzar ran in with heavy steps toward the open balcony, a permanent scowl on his large face.

As Abylar lifted himself up into the air, Bakari gave Onius one last look and said, "Good luck." Then he waved.

"Tell Roland hello for me," Onius said and then added, in a softer voice, "and tell him I'm sorry."

With a rush of air, Abylar took off in the early morning light just as Kanzar stepped out onto the balcony. Without a moment's hesitation, Kanzar threw a bolt of lightning toward them and the young dragon.

Dodging it deftly, Abylar turned in a wide circle and spit out whirring flames of blue fire into the morning sky.

The frustrated bellows of Kanzar were drowned out by the cheers of wonder and optimism from the people of Cassian below them, on the ground. They were seeing a dragon and its rider for the first time in living memory. Bakari hoped that maybe his appearance that day would spur action and excitement among the people—a catalyst for them to know that things would get better.

Abylar dipped his wings in the air to wave to the people, then shot off in the clear blue sky, carrying Bakari and Kharlia away safely toward the Citadel.

CHAPTER TWENTY THREE

Flying north, from Cassian to the Citadel, Bakari and Kharlia watched the grasslands below flash by in a blur. After food and sleep, Abylar was as strong as ever, and he flew faster than he ever had before. Time had been lost in Cassian, and Bakari hoped all would be well at the Citadel. Through Abylar, Bakari felt overly anxious to find the next dragon egg and dragon rider. His mind pulled him to the south, toward Quentis, and he knew he didn't have long to gather another rider to him.

With Abylar in almost constant connection to Miriel, Bakari checked on Breelyn and Alair's progress toward Lor'l. They would be there in the next day or two, and by then, hopefully Miriel would be strong enough to fly with Breelyn on her back.

Kharlia sat behind Bakari, holding on to him around his waist. It was hard for him to concentrate with her warm breath on the back of his neck. It reminded him of their last kiss.

"The land is so beautiful from up here." Kharlia observed and Bakari smiled at her excitement.

Soon Bakari saw Whalen in the distance, and the Citadel wasn't much farther than that. He wondered how Whalen fared, with the strife between Kanzar and the Chief Judge. Being so close to the Citadel, their destiny was usually tied up with that wizarding city.

As they flew, Bakari did nothing to hide the presence of

his dragon. The people in this land needed to find hope in knowing there was a dragon rider again to protect them. News of their sightings in Corwan and then in Cassian would spread rapidly.

Bakari saw the farmers outside of Whalen gathered in their last harvesting of the fall, to begin preparing for winter, but he saw nothing to overly worry himself about. Some people ran for safety, while others stood around and pointed to the great blue beast flying in the autumn sky.

Soon the spires of the Citadel rose before them. And, once again, a longing filled Bakari's breast. The Citadel had been his home from the time when Bakari was five up until two years ago. He knew the Citadel's layout even more fully than the castle's layout in Cassian.

The Citadel itself was a significant stone structure with beautiful balconies and ornamental spires rising high into the air. Many different gardens, courtyards, and practice yards surrounded it, with a small town, which had grown up around it, providing the short-term needs of the Citadel wizards. And the markets in Whalen provided the rest.

Unlike Whalen, the Citadel did look different now than it had before. Even in midday, the gates stood closed and more guards than usual stood in front of them. The only people that Bakari could see on the castle grounds were in the practice yards. Pairs of what looked to be battle wizards were standing there and fighting each other to practice their skills. But the ferocity with which they clashed surprised Bakari.

Once Abylar's shadow fell over the Citadel, many wizards stopped fighting and pointed up into the sky. Some had seen

Abylar before, just briefly after the barrier had fallen. But, if word was true, Roland had gathered dozens of more apprentices since then.

Lowering down, Abylar came to rest in one of the reception courtyards. *I saw a nice herd of wild buffalo not too far back. Hungry again, my friend?*

Hearing the dragon's stomach rumble made both Kharlia and Bakari laugh.

Based on what happened yesterday, Abylar, I would ask for you to stay on the ground until we find out what is going on. Bakari patted his dragon on the neck.

A puff of smoke came from the growing dragon's mouth, but he assented to remain.

Bakari climbed down off the dragon, noticing he was farther off the ground than he had previously been. As he wondered how big Abylar would grow, Bakari helped Kharlia down off the dragon. She took a minute to smooth down her rumpled clothes, which Bakari now noticed were badly in need of cleaning and repair. He smiled at her, and she grinned back, grasping his hand in hers.

Bakari's short braids blew against his face in the growing wind. And the sky was becoming gray with an approaching storm.

People began to gather around them, and Bakari noticed their mood was more somber than before. Coming out of the Citadel strode Roland, with guards on each side and a contingent of young apprentices, dressed for battle, following behind him. Something indeed had changed.

"Roland!" Bakari shouted out to his friend as he

approached. "I received your message. It sounded dire."

A flash of annoyance and possibly anger flew across Roland's face but, in a flash, was replaced with a smooth smile. "Everything is fine here, Dragon Rider. No need to worry about us."

Bakari frowned, alarms going off in his head. His friend Roland would never have referred to Bakari as *Dragon Rider*; it would have been too much for Roland to acknowledge that someone else could do something better than himself. Bakari glanced at the guards to Roland's sides and recognized a few of them. As they nodded briefly to Bakari, one leaned in and whispered something to Roland.

"Bakari," Roland said, nodding to his old friend.

Bakari was confused. But the leader of the Citadel stood in all his perfection before him. Roland's blond hair still hung into his eyes, and his square chin carried his newfound authority well. And Bakari opened his eyes wider as he considered the golden cloak that now floated around Roland's shoulders.

"Wizards are always welcomed here, at the Citadel," Roland said. "You and this young woman may dine with me this afternoon as our special guests. The food will be ready soon, and my guards will escort you in."

Bakari stiffened. Something was definitely wrong. Roland was never this formal. "You remember my friend Kharlia, don't you?"

Roland's eyes squinted, and he appeared deep in thought. Turning to one of the other wizards, he whispered something to the man, but the man just shook his head. Then Roland strode forward and lifted up Kharlia's hand. "I didn't recognize you, Kharlia. Your beauty has increased since we last met."

Then Roland gawked appraisingly at Abylar and strode forward a few more steps, toward the dragon. "A beautiful creature," he said, his eyes turning dreamy. "Oh, to be able to fly over the land and see everyone so small scampering around." Turning back to Bakari, he continued, "Wizard Bakari, Dragon Rider, your dragon is a prize indeed." As Roland reached his hand out toward Abylar, the dragon growled deeply, and Roland pulled his hand back.

That man is dangerous, Abylar said silently to Bakari.

Bakari nodded in silent agreement.

Soon they were escorted inside and seated around a long rectangular table at the south end of the dining room. Polished wooden floors and high ceilings with low hanging chandelier lamps ran the length of the room. The other wizards and apprentices in the room were quiet and looked only at the food on their plates. At the table where Bakari and Kharlia sat, there were no elderly wizards. The guards around Roland were in their twenties, and the other apprentices with Roland seemed to gaze at him with worshipful looks in their eyes.

Substantial platters of roasted pork, fresh bread, and fried vegetables were brought out, and the group began to eat.

"So, what news of the outside world, Bakari?" Roland said.

The voice seemed like his, but his speech patterns surely didn't. Was Roland under someone's spell? Bakari glanced around the room, trying to find someone powerful enough to put a spell on his friend.

"Kanzar is gathering his forces in Cassian, while the Chief Judge gathers his own in Orr," Bakari answered vaguely.

"Has there been fighting yet?" Roland asked.

Bakari nodded. They would find out here eventually anyway. "In Corwan."

Roland nodded then leaned in closer to Bakari. "You have a great gift in that dragon. It, of course, should be housed here, in the Citadel."

"But Bakari is a dragon rider. He is needed all over Alaris to help establish peace," Kharlia said to defend Bakari. "You can't keep his dragon here."

"He is still a young and weak wizard." Roland waved his hand in the air and then pushed his hair back. "I'm sure you both understand."

Inwardly, Bakari jumped back. It wasn't just the words coming out of Roland's mouth that seemed wrong, it was his eyes. As Roland had pushed his hair back, Bakari had noticed two bright green eyes staring back at him.

Green! Roland's eyes were supposed to be blue. Bright blue.

Bakari realized now that his suspicion that someone had put a spell on Roland was incorrect. Instead, someone had replaced Roland. While this Roland turned and spoke instructions to one of his guards, Bakari pushed his own thoughts deep into his memory. Were there spells that could do this? He sorted through all he could remember from reading on the subject of taking someone's physical identity. He remembered a temporary spell that would give off an illusion but would not hold up if touched. So Bakari reached out his hand and touched Roland's arm casually.

Roland turned, simultaneously with Bakari, pulling a knife from his waistband, and, before anyone could notice, stabbed it forward toward Bakari's throat.

"Roland!" Bakari said, moving his head sideways to be missed by the knife. "I just touched your arm to get your attention."

Everyone at the table froze. But most just stared at the food on their plates.

Roland's eyes softened, and he seemed to regain control. "Sorry. Old habits, you know," he said, trying to play it down as an overreaction based on prior experience.

But Bakari knew that Roland did not ever overreact. There were no old habits to overcome here.

Soon the awkward dinner was over, and then men and women started leaving the table.

"I have business to attend to, Dragon Rider," the pretender Roland said. "I'm sure you must be tired."

Bakari decided that he should try to placate the impostor. "Of course," he said. "You run a tight Citadel here. It all looks very well cared for."

The pretender smiled and seemed to relax. "We are trying to build the most powerful place in the world, Bakari. I hope you will join us. I would appoint you to care for our dragon."

Our dragon! thought Bakari. He would never share Abylar with this impostor.

The false Roland excused himself, and Bakari sat, thinking for a few minutes.

Soon most of the others left the table, leaving only Kharlia, himself, and one lone young man, someone that Bakari remembered from his stay at the Citadel.

The young man was two years older than Bakari. Glancing

around, he leaned in toward Bakari and spoke quietly over the table.

"Things are not right here, sir." The young man, although older than Bakari, showed deference to him for his position as a dragon rider.

Bakari nodded his head and glanced around himself.

"Reese, isn't it?" Bakari never did forget a name.

Reese nodded and continued, "They locked up the older wizards—Eryck and Titus." He sat back when a serving boy came in and started to clean the dirty dishes off the table. Once the boy had left, with a pile stacked on his arms, Reese leaned in toward Bakari once again and said, "You must help us. Roland is not himself lately."

"What do you mean?" Kharlia asked, looking from Reese to Bakari for confirmation. "Bak?"

Bakari held his lips tightly as he thought about what to do. He needed to go down to the dungeons and check on Eryck and Titus. Maybe they had seen the real Roland. That would also be the logical place for him to be held captive.

Getting up from the table, Bakari held Kharlia's hand as they walked behind Reese. Then Bakari patted his shoulder with the assurance that something would be done.

He feigned tiredness and asked which rooms would be theirs. Soon a Citadel steward appeared and then directed them to the west wing, opposite of where Roland kept his own rooms and offices. Bakari smiled at their luck.

No one knew this castle like he did. As they walked to their rooms, Bakari ran his hand along the brown stone walls and recalled the escapades of a young boy—himself. His thirst for knowledge had not been limited to books but to a desire to know everything around him. That had included exploring to learn every inch of the Citadel. Bakari now ventured that, maybe only outside of Kanzar himself, Bakari knew the secrets of this castle as no other did.

When they reached their adjoining rooms, they were left there by the steward. Kharlia wanted to go into hers to freshen up, so Bakari asked a servant to bring her some new clothes and warm water for her to bathe in.

Before heading in, she turned to Bakari, "Everything all right? You've been awfully quiet since dinner."

"I'm fine." Bakari waved a hand in the air, "Just tired."

"What about all that talk about Roland? Is something wrong?" Kharlia put her hand on Bakari's arm.

"I'm sure everything is fine." Bakari said the words, but didn't really believe what he said. He wanted to keep Kharlia safe.

"Bak!" Kharlia's brown eyes flashed. "Don't hide things from me."

Just then a servant came back with some new clothes for Kharlia and ushered her inside her room. Before the door closed Bakari saw Kharlia's stern look directed at him. He sighed and turned away. *I have to keep her safe.*

Bakari peered up and down the hall. *Empty.* He then continued walking toward the end of the west wing, where he could take a way down to the dungeon that would keep him from being seen. He was sure that was where the older wizards would be held, and if Roland was still here and held prisoner, that's where Bakari would find his friend also.

Opening the barely used door there, he began to climb down the servants' stairs. But, halfway down one flight, he stopped at a specific spot. Reaching across the wall, he touched a few particular blocks of stone in the right succession. A small, two-foot door swung open. The door had seemed much bigger when Bakari was seven years old and had discovered this entrance to the floors beneath the Citadel.

Crouching down now, he entered through it, scraping his back on the top of the opening. He stood up in the narrow passage on the other side, swung the door back into place, and then brought up a small flame in his hand to light the way. He didn't need much light to see. The hidden hallways were narrow, touching his thin body on both sides, the top strands of his hair grazing the ceiling.

After a few turns, he came to a narrow set of stairs and descended down them, past the ground floor, and continued going deeper, into the passages under the Wizard Citadel.

The Citadel had been a home to wizards for over a thousand years. So it was built to last, the walls made thick and fused together with magic. The deeper Bakari went, the more power that came to him. He sent his mind out to Abylar to make sure he was being taken care of.

They brought me food, a happy Abylar almost purred. *Three tasty cows.*

The dragon seemed content for the time being, and Bakari marveled once again at his ability to communicate with a dragon. He shook his head in bewilderment at the luck of having a young scholar wizard be the one to find the first dragon egg.

The steps continued down even farther, but Bakari stopped descending for now to push on another set of stones, revealing another hidden door not much bigger than the previous one. Ducking through it, he entered a small closet and then shut the door behind him. Bakari stretched for a moment and then put his ear to the door as he heard sounds from someone on the other side of the door. A few bored guards were talking from not far away. Looking around the closet, he spotted a pair of old servant's clothes, their coarse wool dirtied by time. He breathed deeply, pulled the clothes on, draping a cowl over his head, and then exited the closet quietly.

Coming upon two guards, Bakari pretended to trip. The commotion made the guards jump.

"Who are you?" asked one of the guards. "And what are you doing here?"

Bakari put on his dumbest face to act the part of an errand boy. "The master wants to see you."

"Who?" asked the second guard, a man a few inches taller and wider than the first.

"Master Wizard Roland," Bakari said.

When the guards looked at each other nervously, Bakari saw he had guessed right. The false Roland had instilled fear in the men.

"You go see what he wants," the first guard ordered the second.

"Me?" the larger one said. "Why?"

"Because I'm in charge."

The two glared at each other, neither wanting to face whatever it was that Roland might have wanted. Finally, the larger man shuffled away, leaving the keys with the first guard. Once the second guard was a few turns away, Bakari turned to the remaining guard and grinned dumbly.

"Why are you still here?" the guard said, kicking Bakari in the shins. "Run along."

"I also wanted to see the prisoners," Bakari said, trying to sound like an excited apprentice. "The filthy traitors. I want to see them suffering."

The guard smiled and laughed, clapping Bakari on the back. "Like to see them punished, huh? Maybe you'll be a guard someday."

The man led Bakari forward to the cell and held up a torch. In the back of the small cell sat two old men, their clothes tattered and soiled. An empty plate sat on the ground in front of them. Bakari held his nose at the stench.

"They don't look so mighty, do they?" Bakari said, forcing a laugh and drawing the guard in closer to himself.

The guard laughed with him and, with a wicked gleam in his eye, turned to Bakari and asked, "Want to get closer, little man?"

"Oh no!" Bakari backed up, pretending to be afraid.

"Scared?" taunted the guard.

"No!" Bakari puffed out his chest and then felt amusement through the bond from Abylar. He pushed Abylar's thoughts away because he didn't want to get distracted.

The guard took his keys out and opened the metal door, its hinges creaking loudly in the lonely dungeon. The guard put his hand on Bakari's back, pushing him forward, and then followed him inside.

"See," the guard said. "They are chained. They can't hurt you."

As Bakari and the guard walked closer to the men, Bakari tried not to react to the poor conditions. Bakari felt sorry for them. The old wizards glanced up at Bakari, not recognizing him, and Eryck tried to kick his leg out at the guard. So Bakari knew that Eryck still had some fight left in him.

The guard moved forward and seemed about to kick Eryck. But, with the guard's back turned, Bakari took this chance to draw upon his power. His hard push of air knocked the guard forward, dropping him to the floor, where his forehead hit the hard ground. He slumped down, unconscious.

Bakari saw that the two wizards now held hope in their eyes. Bakari grabbed the guard's keys and undid the chains that bound them. Standing up warily, the two wizards thanked Bakari.

"Spelled chains," Eryck said. "Couldn't work our magic."

Bakari nodded. He knew that a lot of old magic existed in the lower levels of the Citadel. In fact, the rooms one level lower held artifacts that were not to be messed with.

Bakari removed his hood, and the two men finally recognized him.

"Young Dragon Rider." Titus bowed his head to Bakari. "Thank you for coming, however you did it."

"Have you seen Roland?" Eryck asked. "He threw us in here. I don't understand why. Just a day earlier, he had healed me."

"It isn't Roland—but an impostor," Bakari said. "But we need to get out of here before the other guard comes back."

The wizards agreed. So they chained the guard and locked him inside the cell.

Bakari stood there, momentarily, trying to figure out where to go. He closed his eyes and breathed in deeply. Then he thought about how Roland had communicated with him before and tried the same thing now.

Roland? he asked in his mind.

Nothing came to him, and so he pushed down deeper.

Eryck tapped Bakari on the shoulder. "Hurry. I hear the sounds of boots coming down the stone stairway."

Bakari thought about how he communicated easily with Abylar. The dragons had the power to bind things together. That was how they spoke across distances to their riders and to the other dragons. So Bakari pulled upon Abylar's power, amplifying his own and then brought it all together inside of himself.

Roland? he thought again.

But there was no response.

His friend had to be here somewhere. Bakari tightened his focus on only the few floors below the Citadel and called out again in his mind, *Roland, where are you?*

A faint thought tugged at his mind, and Bakari chased its path down to below where they stood.

Bakari!

Bakari felt relief and exhaustion fill Roland's mind, then the connection abruptly dropped away.

Bakari pulled the two men with him, down the hall, in the direction of the stairs.

"They'll catch us!" Titus said.

The approaching sounds grew louder as multiple pairs of boots clunked down the stairs toward them. Bakari could also hear the gruff voices of those guards, talking and arguing, as they came closer. So, before getting to the stairs, Bakari stopped and pushed on the secret places in the wall, and another passageway opened up, this one taller than the others had been.

He pushed the two wizards inside, in front of himself, and then turned, closing the door just as the guards came walking by. Their voices rose in alarm when they soon discovered their prisoners missing and the guard locked in the cell.

Bringing up a flame in his hand to see more clearly, Eryck turned with a stern look toward Bakari. "Do you really know what you are doing, Scholar?"

Bakari pointed to a dark space on the other side of the room. Eryck shoved the light inside to look within the small opening. It was a stone slide, the only way for them to leave the hidden room without being caught.

"You can't be serious?" Titus said, himself a scholar wizard also.

"Better hurry if you want to help me save Roland, our illustrious Citadel leader. He's down here," Bakari said before he jumped through the opening and then slid down the dark, stone slide. Memories of his childhood surfaced then, and Bakari laughed.

CHAPTER TWENTY FOUR

Onius Neeland sat in a room with the rest of Kanzar's Wizard Council. At the front of the room, Kanzar sat fuming behind a desk but, as of yet, had stayed silent. Onius touched the bruise on his cheek, where Kanzar had hit him, but it was hard for Onius not to grin when he thought about Bakari flying off on that dragon. *Bakari!* Of all the scholar wizards—or even among all wizards, young and old—Bakari was the last one Onius would have guessed to become one of the fabled dragon riders. The young man retained a fabulous memory for facts and figures and historical events, but Bakari was relatively weak as far as being a wizard goes.

Following Bakari's escape on the dragon, Kanzar had stood next to Onius. The would-be king was livid, and his screams had filled the air as Bakari flew off. But Abylar's final display, the dragon turning around and breathing fire out toward the castle, sent Kanzar over the edge. And he, a man Onius had known for decades, hit Onius hard on the face, knocking him to the ground. It had taken all the control that Onius had not to retaliate.

Maybe I should have, he thought now. Something would need to be done soon about Kanzar.

The last wizard entered, and Kanzar stood up. His face looked stern, as if his anger was barely in control. His tight lips quivered as he said, "I am convening this council to declare open war on not only the Chief Judge but the dragon rider also."

That comment brought chaos to the room. Some of the wizards had seen the dragon's display as he had flown off. But many had only heard of the spectacle secondhand. And a few, by the looks of them, had heard nothing yet, so they questioned what Kanzar was even talking about.

"Earlier today, a dragon rider and some girl snuck into the castle," Kanzar informed the small group. "His dragon awaited him outside. As they left, the dragon shot fire toward the castle, a sign of the rider's intention to declare open war."

"If he had wanted to do any damage, he would have hit the castle, I am sure," said one of the elder council members, a counselor wizard. Some of the other wizards nodded in agreement. Onius understood why, since the dragon riders had always promoted peace.

"This order is not open for debate," Kanzar said. "This dragon and its rider are our enemies." Kanzar stood up from his desk's chair and paced across the front of the room. "He was last seen flying north. I want to send a delegation back to the Citadel, to protect it from the dragon."

"What about Corwan, sir?" asked a younger battle wizard that seemed eager for war. "Have you heard if we have captured the city yet?"

Kanzar shook his head.

Onius stood and, without looking at Kanzar, said, "We lost Corwan."

This news once again brought panic and side conversations to the room. And it took Kanzar a moment to regain control.

"Onius, how did you come by this information?" Kanzar asked as he walked up to within inches of Onius.

"From the dragon rider," Onius said with complete control. "Bakari told me that elves from Mallek and a battalion of the local judge's men fought hard against our forces. Though, I would bet the dragon rider himself did some considerable damage, too."

The veins on Kanzar's neck pulsed, and his lip rose into a snarl. "The dragon rider was Bakari—the boy scholar that went missing in River Bend?" he demanded as he grabbed Onius by the front of his robes and shook him.

Onius saw others in the room put their hands on their swords.

"Why did he come and see you?" Kanzar bellowed, his face contorted. "I've known the boy since he was five."

"He and I became close in Cassian." Onius tried to shrug, but Kanzar still held tight. "I was trying to get more information, but you interrupted by trying to kill him."

"You go too far, Onius!" Kanzar yelled, moving to backhand him again. But two other wizards intervened, so Kanzar turned on them and said, "What is the meaning of this?"

"You are acting unstable, Kanzar. We are not your enemies here. We are your Council," said one of the other level four wizards, speaking for the rest of the group. "Let us in on your plans, and use us. We sit around here, wondering what is going on. You can't seem to keep Cassian safe from the thieves; they steal and spread disruption at every turn. Even the army is getting spooked, for you underestimated Corwan and sent only a small contingent there. Now, you worry about a lone dragon rider—a boy with little power of his own?"

Kanzar stared hard at the man but said nothing.

Then another wizard stepped forward, one of the older counselor wizards, only slightly younger than Onius himself. "Focus, Kanzar," the wizard said. "We are with you, on having a king for Alaris. That is the goal, remember? While we sit here and argue and play games, the Chief Judge, the largest threat to our plan, builds up his army from deserters and sympathizers. Let us make some plans. We can still succeed, but only if we work together."

Since Onius was now away from Kanzar's grip, he took a couple of steps backward and surveyed the faces in the room. Not all seemed in agreement with the last speech by the older counselor wizard. Some glanced toward Onius with questions apparent in their eyes. Onius decided that he needed to do something to find out who would side with him against Kanzar if need be and who might be having second thoughts about Kanzar being king.

"Let us send a delegation to the Citadel, Kanzar, as you had mentioned," Onius said. "We can get more information on the dragon rider as well as ascertain how many more apprentices are available to fight for us. Roland Tyre has been left there alone too long." Onius eyed some of the wizards in the room that he thought would take his hint. "Who here will volunteer for that?"

Four Council members came forward—three older and one younger—a mix of battle, counselor, and scholar wizards. Onius looked to Kanzar for confirmation.

As Kanzar nodded his approval, Onius realized that the man was blind to what went on around him.

"We will then send a small group to spy on Orr," Onius continued, "a mixture of wizards and other men and women. We need to know the enemy's strengths and where to attack first."

Kanzar nodded again and scanned the group. Then he chose four men that were extremely loyal to him. Onius nodded, secretly smiling at his luck. That would leave only three Council members in Cassian, besides Onius and Kanzar, wizards who were on the fence and, hopefully, could be trusted to leave Kanzar's side once they saw him fall.

Kanzar then pointed to one wizard that he had chosen. "You, Stephen, I want you instead to go to Celestar. I have not heard from Gorn or the others I sent later to reclaim the city. I want to know what is going on there. Take more soldiers with you, and secure the town. Then bring me back anyone that knows what has happened there. I have allies there that I haven't heard from."

That detail surprised Onius. He thought he had kept abreast of all of Kanzar's plans. But, ever since the barrier came down, Onius hadn't thought about Celestar or his old friend Gorn.

"I will be king!" Kanzar said, after a brief pause, as if trying to once again find his dignity. The councilors gave short bows—each in turn—and then left the room.

Kanzar called to Onius to stay behind a moment. Hearing the sound of boots on the stone floor fading as the wooden door closed behind him, Onius stood still. He tried to appear unbothered by Kanzar's beckoning, but Onius was terrified to be alone with the crazed wizard.

"Onius, I saw what you did," Kanzar said without any other preamble, once the door had closed, "sending those men to the Citadel."

Onius began to grow worried. Did Kanzar know about his plans? Did he know Onius's intentions? *I have been so careful.*

Kanzar continued, "You must think that one of those men is the traitor, and you planned it well to get them out of my midst."

Onius took a silent breath. "Yes, Kanzar. That's why. It must be one of them."

Kanzar nodded. "Good. Good." His face softened, and he placed a hand up on Onius's shoulder. "And, Onius, you must forgive me. I lost control. That shouldn't happen."

Onius tried not to flinch with the contact but smiled instead, rubbing his fingers over his goatee. "I understand, Kanzar." He spoke more smoothly than he felt. It gave credence to his years as a counselor. Onius decided to stroke Kanzar's ego with his next words. "You are under a lot of pressure, and many look up to you. It's hard when not everyone understands that you want the best for them and that a strong king that will lead us back out into the world."

Kanzar did smile now, the gleam of power in his eyes as big as ever. Then he clapped his hands together in delight. "I do wish the people could understand that, my old friend. Sadly, I will have to convince some of my intent. Sometimes that convincing has to be harsher than what we would like."

Just then, Onius noticed something outside. In a distant

quarter of the city, smoke was rising into the sky—another sign of Gideon's men causing havoc. But, with his back to the window, Kanzar did not see this newest sign of trouble in his city. So Onius kept his own face passive. One more leaf to fuel the raging fire inside Kanzar, a fire that soon would either burn itself out or need to be extinguished.

With a short bow, they parted ways, and Onius returned to his own rooms.

CHAPTER TWENTY FIVE

Breelyn was tired of walking. The events since Celestar and Silla had been trying and tiring. But she and Alair kept glancing up into the sky for a glimpse of Miriel. The yellow and orange dragon was one of the most beautiful things she had ever beheld. Already, the bond shared between them was growing stronger. Breelyn felt power, peace, and drive from the dragon, and she immensely enjoyed the little conversations they briefly held.

The ability to communicate with other dragon riders through their dragons was simply amazing. From studying and through oral histories, Breelyn was familiar with the concept of dragon riders, though it had been before her father's lifetime, over one hundred and fifty years ago, when they were last seen. She wondered if the old king knew anything more he might share.

Entering the outskirts of Lor'l, Breelyn stopped and peered longingly up into the tall trees. *Home again.*

Alair touched her arm and motioned with his head for her to continue forward as more and more elves came out of the trees. They bowed their greetings to Breelyn, the youngest protector to be chosen in decades. She smiled at each one.

Soon she found herself before the great tree, where King Arrowyn Soliel resided. Alair motioned for a lift, and then he and Breelyn stood silently as they rode up, high into the tree complex. Stepping off the lift onto a platform, they were met by two guards.

"Greetings, Protector," the guards said as they bowed their heads at both Breelyn and Alair.

Then another man came up behind the guards, Lanwaithian Soliel, prince and heir to the Elvyn throne. His long, brown hair and piercing gray eyes caught Breelyn unawares. She had been gone from Lor'l for a few months and had left on the king's orders without saying goodbye to Lan.

"Breelyn," Lan said. His voice was deep for an elf, and it carried deep emotion. "I am so glad you are safe."

She stood formally in front of him while others were looking on. So Lan motioned her to follow him, allowing Alair to go his own way. Once they had found a bit of privacy, Lan turned to her with a gentle touch on her arm.

"Are you all right?" he said. "The king told me about Silla."

Breelyn shivered at the memory but pulled on Miriel's strength and then nodded her head, her long blond hair swinging down around her tired face.

The prince held his arms wide, and she moved into his embrace. She stayed there, feeling safe near the warmth of his body. She breathed deeply and let her body relax. Finally, she emerged from his arms.

"What now?" Lan asked. "You are hiding something. I can tell. That familiar twinkle is in your clear blue eyes."

"You always could." She pouted for a moment but then grinned wide.

Just then, a loud roar sounded above them and the trees, so Breelyn pulled Lan up a flight of stairs to an overlook that stood out on a broad, naturally occurring branch. Looking east, the sea sparkled off in the distance, a twinge of salted air reaching them. And then Breelyn pointed her finger out.

With a questioning look, Lan followed the direction of her finger and then gasped. Coming right toward them was Miriel.

"A dragon?" Lan said. Then his mouth hung open.

"Miriel is her name. Isn't she beautiful?" Breelyn watched the golden sunlight sparkle off Miriel's scales and settled her mind on their bond.

I will be with you shortly, my lovely dragon, Breelyn said to Miriel.

Miriel stretched her wings in the air and blew out a breath of hot flames, yellow and orange. *I am strong enough to ride on now, Dragon Rider.*

As tears came to Breelyn's eyes, Lan turned to her and asked, "What's wrong, Breelyn?"

"Nothing, Lan. Nothing is wrong." She paused and then turned toward him and grabbed both of the prince's hands in hers. "Lan, I am a dragon rider."

Lan's eyes opened wide, and he laughed, the wind blowing his long hair around his face. A beautiful laugh of pure delight. "You are an amazing woman, Breelyn. Here I was, worried about you going off on such a dangerous mission, and then you come back with a dragon. The tales you must have to tell."

Breelyn smiled at Lan's excitement. "First, I need to see the king and tell him many things."

Lan's face dropped. "Breelyn, he is not well. Be prepared."

"Bakari told me." Breelyn was saddened by this reminder that their beloved king was failing.

"Bakari?" Lan said. "That boy sure gets around."

"It is easier when you have a dragon to ride on." Breelyn laughed. "And, Lan, I must follow him."

Lan frowned. "What do you mean, *follow him?*"

Then the two moved back from the overlook, with Breelyn looking back once more to see her dragon. As they continued walking toward the king's chambers, Breelyn lovingly ran her hand across the wood of the mighty tree. She was comforted with the touch of its familiar magic.

To continue their conversation, Breelyn said, "Bakari is the first dragon rider. If history and tradition hold, he will be a dragon king. As the first dragon rider, he is my master. So I will follow him."

"What about us?" Lan's eyes grew dark. "You and me. We are set to be married in the spring."

Breelyn placed her hand on Lan's arm. "I still love you, Lanwaithian. We will be married," she said fiercely. "But I need to help Bakari establish peace first, so the ceremony may need to be postponed. I don't know right now."

Lan's lips were held tight. Then he said, "You might follow him, but you are still an elf, Breelyn, a protector of the king."

Breelyn shook her head. "I don't know if I can be both a protector and a dragon rider, Lan."

They had reached the king's chambers, so the rest of their conversation would need to wait. Something that Breelyn was fine with. She was still coming to grips with who she was and what being a dragon rider might mean. A servant opened up the cloth door for them to pass through. The room was dark, and it took a moment for Breelyn's eyes to adjust. When they did, the sight that met them made her heart fall.

Rushing to the king's bedside, she knelt down next to him. "My King," she whispered in pain. His face was thin and pale. His soft, pure white hair framed his wrinkled cheeks.

After a few labored breaths, the old king opened his eyes. A thin film covered them, and it took a moment for him to focus. "Protector."

Breelyn smiled through her tears. "My lord, I returned."

The king patted her hand. "Did you return with something new?" His eyes regained their old sparkle for a moment.

"Yes." Breelyn beamed. "A dragon, my lord. I am a dragon rider."

"I told Bakari you would be a good fit," the king whispered, his voice raspy and low. "But it is always up to the dragon."

Breelyn poured him a glass of water, and he took a few sips.

"What color is your dragon?" The king's eyes brightened.

"Yellow, like a sunrise." Breelyn felt joy infuse into her bond. "Her name is Miriel."

As the king smiled and closed his eyes, Breelyn glanced up at Lan. Lan's eyes barely concealed the sadness Breelyn knew he felt over the obvious failing of his father's health.

The king spoke again without opening his eyes. "Bakari will need your guidance, Breelyn. He is young and not accustomed to things of the world outside of Alaris. Protect him, and stay by him."

With that, Breelyn looked up at Lan once more. His face was stern and unreadable.

"Lan, my son?" the king said, opening his eyes as he called to the prince.

Lan stepped forward, closer to his father.

"Don't be jealous," the old king said.

Lan opened his mouth, as if to argue.

But the king cut him off. "Breelyn will be by your side as queen, Lanwaithian. Have no doubt of that."

Lan let out a held breath.

The king moved his hand, picking up Lan's and bringing it to Breelyn's hand. Holding both hands together, he gazed intently into their eyes. "There is an evil brewing in the land. As I sleep, the borders of this world and the next seem blurred, and I see things happening. Events unfolding.

Breelyn flashed a worried look at Lan and then asked, "What things, my king?"

"Just shadows and portents, nothing concrete, but..." The king opened his eyes wide, and then his voice grew stronger as he said, "There is more at stake here than our Elvyn land. We have kept ourselves away from others for too long. The western lands need our guidance and our knowledge. And Bakari has more in front of him than he knows."

"Kanzar, one of their top wizards, is greedy, sire," Breelyn said. "He stirred up trouble in Alaris and, somehow, infected the governor and his men in Silla."

The king waved his other hand weakly in the air. "That is of no concern. I see the worry on your face, Protector. Yes, it is serious, but I think Bakari and his dragon riders will prevail in this. But there is more. A horrible evil is coming that threatens all magic. A man who twists magic to his own bidding and who means to harm us all. He has followers that are preparing a way for him to return to the world of the living: men and women that distort the true use of magic. *That* is what you must fight, not as a protector but as a dragon rider."

"What can you tell us about this evil?" Lan asked. "We can send our armies to fight it."

The king shook his head. "It is not an evil you can fight with a physical battle but a dark abomination that has to be fought with magic. It will take all the knowledge from all the lands, Lan. So you will need to let Breelyn go for a time. That is what I wanted to tell you."

Lan nodded, and Breelyn glanced at Lan in concern.

"Don't keep her from her destiny," the king said. Then he closed his eyes once again and appeared to be falling back into sleep.

Breelyn and Lan stood up and walked quietly toward the doorway. As they reached the opening, the king stirred again and opened his eyes, fixing them on Breelyn. Then he nodded his head to her and said, "Hail, the dragon rider."

Lan repeated the sentiment. "Hail, the dragon rider."

Soon the word spread from there, each tree hearing the news in turn: a dragon rider was among them again.

* * *

Breelyn left a short time later, saying goodbye privately to Lan before speaking with Alair. Soon Breelyn stood between the trees and the Blue Sea next to Miriel. A crowd of onlookers had formed behind them, which included the prince. As she mounted the growing dragon for the first time, Breelyn lovingly ran her fingers over Miriel's rough scales.

Ready? said the dragon to Breelyn's mind.

"Ready," Breelyn said out loud as she held tightly to a spike directly behind the dragon's long neck.

As Miriel lifted Breelyn up into the air, the watching elves clapped and shouted.

Hail, the dragon rider, Miriel sang out in Breelyn's mind, bringing tears to Breelyn's eyes.

Her soul was infused with joy. And then, to the delight of the onlookers and the slight embarrassment of their prince, Breelyn blew Lan a kiss as she swooped back over the crowd. When Lanwaithian blushed, the crowd cheered even louder.

Then, with a few larger flaps of her wings, Miriel circled around the group once more and flew out over the sea. Climbing even higher, Miriel turned again and took off over the Elvyn Forest.

To Bakari, Breelyn directed.

To Abylar, Miriel answered, and Breelyn laughed in delight.

CHAPTER TWENTY SIX

Suddenly, the two elderly wizards, Eryck and Titus, fell on top of Bakari in a room on the lowest level of the Citadel. The slide they had just gone down was a long-lost laundry chute, from the days when the Citadel had first been built. Bakari knew about it but had never actually slid down it until now.

Standing up, the three wizards found themselves in an old, dusty room, filled with shelves that were decaying and falling over. Putting one hand to the door, Bakari pushed it open slowly and looked down the long hallway. His mage light gave a ghostly blue tint to the worn floors and battered stone walls as they walked down them.

"There should be a guard down here," Titus said. "These rooms hold artifacts that are not safe."

Eryck nodded his agreement. "After healing me, Roland mentioned he was going down here to check on things. The next time we saw him, he ordered us to be taken to the dungeons."

"Roland is here somewhere." Bakari tried to listen for Roland with his mind.

A distant yell from up above them pushed the three men to move more quickly. As they walked by the numerous doors, Bakari put his hand on each door, to the apparent surprise of the older wizards.

"Titus, tell me about each room," Bakari said. "You've been here a long time."

"And I studied many of these artifacts enough to know how dangerous they are, Bakari," Titus said. "You mustn't touch any more of the doors. Some have wards of protection on them that might hurt you."

Bakari gave Titus a questioning look. "Why didn't you tell me that before now?"

Louder noises gathered above them, and Bakari was sure the false Roland would be on his way down here soon.

"Roland called to me before, but I can't sense him anymore." Bakari quickened his pace. "We must find him soon. He could be in mortal danger."

"We are all in danger," Eryck said. "We should be leaving."

Bakari was growing tired of these two men, cowering before their task. He understood they were old and had been locked in the dungeons, but they needed to help him find Roland. Bakari gathered in strength from Abylar's bond and felt himself grow stronger.

"Your irises have taken on a blue hint," Eryck said, and he and Titus stepped away from Bakari.

"We will find Roland Tyre," Bakari said, his voice deepening and his tone brooking no argument.

So, as the two men reached out with their own powers and examined each door, Bakari tried to reach Roland again with his mind.

But he couldn't find anything.

Down the stairs came a contingent of guards with the false Roland. They stood at the far end of the shadowed hall, and Bakari wondered how he had ever thought that man was Roland. The man's eyes, his sneer, the whole way he held his body now—these looked nothing like the real Roland's features. Only the face and the body size reminded Bakari of his friend.

"Dragon Rider," the man said, his voice echoing down the hall, "what are you doing down here? These rooms are forbidden and dangerous."

"What did you do with Roland Tyre?" Bakari shouted back with anger.

The man walked forward to stand in front of his guards a few steps. "What do you mean, Bakari? I am Roland Tyre. You must not be feeling well. Come with us, and I will forget this ever happened. I will even allow Eryck and Titus to return to their rooms. But you must return with me now."

"And why are you in such a hurry to have me leave? What are you hiding down here?" Bakari said as he continued to walk along the hallway, putting his hands on various doors to see whether he could feel anything that would alert him to Roland's presence.

"Guards," the false Roland said. "Bring me those three wizards."

Three guards, clothed in chain mail, their swords drawn, advanced on Bakari and the two wizards. One guard moved out in front and threw an exploding ball of fire down the hallway. Bakari ducked, the fire barely missing his hair, but Eryck was not so lucky. He was thrown to the ground by the blast and then yelled out in pain.

The other two guards, which obviously weren't wizards, ran down the hall toward them with quick steps, reaching Bakari and Titus in mere moments. But Titus pushed Bakari behind him and brought up his palms, shooting a stream of fire from each. He hit the two guards. One was lucky enough though to block most of the fire with his sword, and he kept coming forward, slicing Titus down the forearm.

Bakari! Abylar spoke to his mind. *You are in danger. That man is evil.*

As Bakari studied the man with Roland's face, he briefly saw the visage slip to something older and evil. "Who are you?" he asked, knowing the man probably wouldn't answer. But he was trying to stall anyway as he continued to walk backward down the hall, toward the last few doors.

The false Roland took a few steps closer to Bakari. "I am whoever I want to be." In the blink of an eye, the man changed to look like Bakari himself.

Bakari gasped. "How?"

"There is much you do not know about magic. Your group of wizards are weak and pathetic. I hold the true power." The man then changed again, now looking like one of his guards.

Bakari felt something slippery beneath his feet and took a second to glance down. A small smear of grease ran along the front of a door, with a light footprint smudged into it. This was the only door Bakari saw a footprint in front of.

Looking back up, Bakari realized now that he couldn't tell one guard from the other. The false man blended in, and there were too many shadows now for Bakari to see the man's eyes.

"Titus?" Bakari yelled. "Who has the keys for this door?"

"Kanzar always had one." Titus held his arm, which still dripped with blood. "A guard was stationed down here with one, and I kept one in my rooms, as head scholar."

Bakari brought up a brighter flame in front of himself and sent it down the hallway, lighting up the shadows so as to see each man's eyes. There were three men standing there. But, as they walked steadily down the hallway, all three held their eyes down, so Bakari still couldn't tell.

Abylar, I need your strength. Bakari dove deeper into the bond and encountered a stream of immense power and intelligence, flowing in and around his young dragon. He had to get the door opened and get to Roland. He reached out to the door, but, even with all the power he held, the protected door threw him back.

Picking himself up off of the ground, he pulled in more strength from Abylar. *There is so much power.*

Abylar chuckled in his mind. *And I am just a young pup? I wonder what Kharlia would say.*

Kharlia! Bakari thought. He hoped she was still safe upstairs.

Looking at the door again he put his mind to the task of trying to figure out how to get it open. Titus and Eryck kept the guards busy as Bakari worked on the problem. Finally gathering his powers again, he shot a large stream of fire at the door with such force than it threw him and the others to the ground. *Nothing's working!*

He thought once again and decided to use more finesse this time. He brought up a small sliver of power and tried to work it down under the door. A small space separated the door from the ground, and Bakari pushed his slender power through it. He felt it give slightly and smiled, but then he heard a scream inside and pulled his power back inside him. *Roland!*

"You need a key, Bakari!" Titus yelled to him. "The special key and the power of two wizards are needed to open this door. Is there anyone here you trust to get my key?"

Kharlia! No, no, no. He didn't want to send her back into danger again.

A blast from two of the guards knocked Titus down. "Bakari!"

With the three men approaching again, their swords drawn in front of them, Bakari reached out his mind to find Kharlia. He had never done this with anyone besides Roland—and his friend was also a wizard. But Bakari tried anyway. It was evening now, and the last time he had seen Kharlia, she was entering her rooms to get cleaned up and to rest.

Suddenly, one of the men jumped toward him and tried to grab Bakari. This move so surprised Bakari that he stumbled back and fell. It was difficult to split his mind between the current situation and trying to reach Kharlia, all the while keeping his contact with Abylar steady.

Pulling in more power, Bakari realized how little power he possessed on his own. But, now he was a dragon rider, and he pulled on his dragon's magic, letting it flow through him. Looking up, Bakari saw the guard that had tripped him staring down at him now. By seeing the guard's eyes, now flashing yellow, Bakari could tell it was the impostor.

Kharlia! he called as he found her. She was lying on a bed, resting. He nudged her awake, careful not to hurt her mind or to take control.

Bak? she thought as she awakened. *What are you doing?*

How he hated to involve her in this, but she was their only hope.

Bakari became distracted as the impostor reached toward him, and he briefly lost contact with Kharlia.

"You are actually harder than Roland was to detain," the impostor spat. "You should be proud of that fact."

Bakari scooted back, bumping into the nearest door. As his back touched the door's cool metal, scenes flashed through his head. He saw himself riding Abylar, with Abylar spitting fire down on a village of people. In the image, he saw himself throw back his head and laugh at the destruction.

Bakari! a voice called to his mind.

He shook his head, finding familiarity in the voice. *Kharlia?* he whispered in his mind. Then he saw a brief image of her, standing up in her room. She had donned clean clothes in a light blue that set off her darker skin, eyes, and hair beautifully.

Once again his mind wavered, and he saw himself standing in front of the Chief Judge. Daymian appeared afraid, and he bowed his entire body down in front of Bakari. Bakari then saw himself sneer and reach out his hands, wrapping sizzling fire around the Chief Judge, squeezing the life from him.

Bakari! another voice called to him. This was a deep and powerful voice. One that infused his body and mind with power. *Come back*, it pleaded with worry.

Bakari opened his eyes and moved his back away from the door, finding that only a second of time had elapsed. He wondered what power had possessed him. The impostor was still moving toward him, his green eyes looking wild.

"See what you can become, Bakari?" The impostor's voice was smooth and oily. "You can be the greatest wizard of all time. With the power of the dragon, you can decimate the people of this land and raise yourself up as a mighty king."

As Bakari put his hand out to attack the approaching man, the impostor changed his image again. Bakari cried out. It was a dark-skinned woman now, black hair curling around her head, with a red scarf holding it back from her forehead. Feelings that he hadn't thought about in years flooded back through Bakari's mind.

"Mother?" Bakari moved his hand up toward the woman's face. He barely had any memory of the woman who had loved him but had given him up to the Citadel at five years old.

Bakari? a voice came into his mind one more time. It seemed tired and weak, but close by.

Roland? Bakari replied, trying to remember where he was.

Then the visage of his mother in front of him flashed away, and the guard resumed reaching his hands toward Bakari's throat. Fear and anger grabbed Bakari all at once. This was not how he was going to die! He had just become a dragon rider and still had a lot to accomplish.

"Titus!" he shouted to the old wizard.

Then Titus, despite his age and injury, jumped onto the back of the impostor, taking him to the floor mere inches in front of Bakari. The other two guards jumped in, but Titus held his ground.

In those few, precious moments, Bakari took a deep breath

and reached out to draw strength from Abylar, to tell Kharlia where to find the key and how to bring it to him, and to inform Roland, on the other side of the metal door, that he would be freed soon. With that done, Bakari stood back up to help the elderly wizard while awaiting Kharlia. Pushing a wall of air out against the two guards, he threw them down the hall, their heads hitting against stone walls.

The impostor threw off Titus and the old wizard flew through the air. A sickening crack ensued when his head hit the stone wall. Bakari watched as the wizard's limp body fell to the floor. "Titus?" he yelled, but there was no response. A puddle of blood began to pool around his head.

Bakari turned back around and their attacker once again, changed his appearance, this time to a young woman not much older than Bakari. She stood still, tall and curvy, her brown hair hanging beautifully over her shoulders.

Bakari hesitated for a moment.

"My name is Celia," said the now beautiful impostor. "Roland couldn't keep his eyes off me either." She reached her hand out and held on to Bakari's arm.

Bakari yelped in pain. His skin began to blacken, and his life force began to drain out of him. He drew some more of the dragon's power into himself.

Be careful, Dragon Rider, Abylar warned. *I cannot get to you in the dungeons. Don't draw too much power.*

Bakari used his other hand and put it on the young woman's chest, pushing Celia back as hard as he could. She dragged Bakari down on top of her, but he scrambled out of her hold and then stood over her.

"Bak!" Kharlia called from down the hall.

Bakari turned Kharlia's way and then looked back at the impostor, who once again shifted its shape.

"Oh, Bak," the impostor said. "Don't hurt me."

Bakari stared in horror. She had now taken on the face of Kharlia. It was unnerving.

"You can't hurt me now, can you, oh mighty dragon rider?" the false Kharlia said.

"He can't, but I can," the real Kharlia said. Running up next to the impostor Kharlia kicked her hard in the side of her head. "Stay away from him!"

The kick surprised both Bakari and the impostor. The imposter's eyes flashed yellow, and the face its face of Kharlia dropped away, revealing the visage of an ugly old man, his lips almost white and his cheeks sunken in. He held his hand up to his head and moaned.

"Ah, your true face, I see," Bakari said as he used his dragon's power to quickly encircle the old man within a shield of air. Then he took the key from Kharlia and put it in the keyhole of the door.

Nothing happened.

Eryck stepped forward. "I've heard Titus say that it needs wizard power along with the key."

Bakari and Eryck both brought their power to bear and pushed it into the keyhole along with turning the key. Unlocked, the door swung open, allowing their mage lights to flood into the small room, dissipating the shadows inside.

Then Bakari saw someone. Sitting curled up in the corner, arms wrapped around his knees, was Roland. His wizard robes were tattered, and the floor was littered with magical artifacts. Their spells and magic filled the air, threatening to distract Bakari. His nose wrinkled in reaction to the odor of sickness and human waste.

"Bak, is that you? Really you?" Roland's face looked gaunt, and his eyes, wild and momentarily blinded.

"Roland!" Bakari rushed in and fell down on his knees in front of his friend.

Roland reached his arms around Bakari and hugged him fiercely, sobbing, his tears streaming down his dirty face. "Oh, Bak, you heard me. You actually heard me!"

Eryck came in behind Bakari. "We should get him out of this room." He touched Bakari on his back.

Bakari nodded. Reaching over to Roland, Bakari took his hands and pulled Roland up with him. Then, with one arm around his friend, Bakari led him out of the cursed room.

After crossing the threshold, everyone looked relieved. Breathing deeply, Roland stood straighter. He then noticed the ugly old man sitting on the floor.

"You?" Roland seemed surprised.

The old man sneered. "Yes, me. Your whole lot of wizards are pathetic, Roland."

"You're the one that looks pathetic to me," Kharlia said and Roland snorted a small laugh.

"What will you do with him, Roland?" Bakari asked.

Roland's glazed eyes glanced around the hallway for the first time. His attention turned to Titus, lying still on the floor among the guards, blood running along the stone. Sadness crept across his face.

Roland then turned to look at Kharlia, who stood protectively close to Bakari.

"What did you do to your hair, Bak?" Roland pointed. "Is this Kharlia's doing?" Turning to the young woman, Roland bobbed his head to her. "Nice to see you again, Kharlia. Glad you are back with us. Bak needs someone to look after him. He's always getting in trouble."

Bakari was happy to see that Roland still held a semblance of his old humor. Bakari glared at the impostor once again and then turned back to Roland with a questioning look.

"The Chameleon," whispered Roland to no one in particular.

"An ancient, evil magic," Eryck said.

Roland looked directly into Bakari's eyes, as if thinking over something in his own mind. Without any words of preamble, Roland knelt—one knee on the floor and no guile in his face—and gazed up at Bakari as he said, "Dragon Rider, I submit to your authority in this and all things from this time forth."

Kharlia put her hand over her mouth as she gasped.

Bakari blinked and Roland gasped. "Your eyes, Bak...your irises are deep blue—the color of your dragon." He bowed again.

"Roland?" Bakari said. He couldn't believe what his friend was doing. "Get up off the floor. You don't need to bow to *me!*"

Dragon Rider, Abylar said into his mind. *It is your right. All will kneel to you in time.*

"This is not what I want," Bakari voiced out loud and to

Abylar.

But it is what you are destined for, Abylar said.

"But I do this, nonetheless," Roland replied. "I can never repay you for what you have done today. You have no idea what I went through in there."

Bakari nodded, not yet sure of the portent of this moment. "Is that room totally secure?"

"What do you think?" Roland snapped back, a little of his old arrogance returning. "Would I have called you here if it wasn't?"

Looking at the Chameleon, Bakari motioned for Eryck to pick him up. The imposter's magic was spent for now it seemed. "Until we figure out a more permanent solution," Bakari said, "this man will stay as you did, hidden and confined to this room."

The Chameleon seemed to blanch at this idea. "Nothing can hold my power, young wizard. And I am just one...soon there will be more."

"Shut up, old man!" Roland kicked him hard.

"He will be guarded night and day by three guards that you personally trust," Bakari said to Roland. "Food will be brought in, and waste brought out. But, any time the door is opened, no less than three wizards will be present to help watch over him."

"What about the artifacts?" Eryck asked.

Roland gave the room a hard look. "Let them torture him as they tortured me. He deserves it."

Bakari nodded. "I see no harm in keeping him here for now. Though, once we have settled the dispute in Alaris, we will come back and try him for his crimes."

Eryck dragged the Chameleon into the dark room and threw him on the floor. As Bakari began to close the door, Roland took once last glance inside and then, with a determined look, turned away.

Helping Roland back up the stairs, Bakari asked Eryck that, after Eryck saw to himself, if he would organize the cleanup down below and that Titus would then be given a funeral with full honors for what he had done to help free Roland.

Coming to Roland's rooms, Kharlia opened the door and they entered.

"Roland, take care," Bakari said.

"Leaving so soon?" Roland asked.

"I must go south, to find another dragon rider," Bakari said. "There is still much to do. Mericus rules in Corwan and desires to be the king. The Chief Judge still gathers followers to himself in Orr. And Onius is working with us, behind the scenes, to destroy Kanzar in Cassian."

"Nice to know the old counselor came to his senses." Roland smiled, walking over to sit on the edge of a chair. Servants began trying immediately to take off his dirtied clothes and bring him food.

"Onius said hello and that he is sorry for any trouble he has caused you."

Roland waved his hand in the air. "No problem. I'm sure I've caused that old man more trouble than he's caused me."

Bakari laughed. "That I am sure of."

"And, Bak…" Roland looked around him, waving away his servants for a moment before lowering his voice to say, "I can't ever repay you for what you have done for me." The old Roland twinkle came to his eyes once again as he added, "But don't you ever tell anyone I cried on your shoulder."

Kharlia, who stood nearby, put a thin finger over her closed lips, her eyes bright with laughter. Bak laughed and then hugged Roland one last time before heading to the doorway.

Bakari turned around one more time. "Oh, I almost forgot. Alli said hello, too."

Roland blushed and smiled. "What is that fetching battle wizard up to anyway?"

Bak laughed out loud. "Oh, you know, taking as many enemies down as she can."

Roland sighed. "And she does it so beautifully, too."

Bakari and Kharlia left Roland's rooms and went outside to find Abylar. He was finishing up another meal.

Eating again? Bakari asked.

Can't eat too much, Dragon Rider, Abylar said. *You never know when your next meal will be.*

I swear you have grown again. Bakari laughed and told Kharlia what was being discussed.

Abylar puffed his chest out proudly. *Climb on, Dragon Rider. We ride south, to the mountains of Quentis. The next dragon egg awaits us.*

CHAPTER TWENTY SEVEN

Bakari and Kharlia were enjoying their flight south, over the heartland of Alaris. Abylar had regained most of his earlier strength and flew with new determination now toward the mountains of Quentis.

That night, they stopped and rested on the plains northeast of Targon. Early the next morning, they awoke and left because Bakari was feeling the pressure to hurry. Soon they were flying over the snowcapped mountains that formed the boundary between Alaris, Quentis, and South Solshi. A few clouds from an overnight storm lingered below them. But, atop Abylar, everything looked clear and blue.

When Bakari saw a flat spot in a small valley between two peaks, it caught his attention, and he directed Abylar to land there. As they touched the ground, the light snow puffed up into the air around them.

"It sure beats walking or riding a horse," Kharlia said.

Bakari and Abylar laughed, and the dragon gave off a snort of steam. It was colder up in the mountains, so Bakari wrapped an extra cloak around Kharlia. Roland had supplied them both with new clothes before they had left the Citadel, but Roland did not have much to protect them against the colder weather here.

Bakari closed his eyes and tried to get a sense of his surroundings. Drawing upon his dragon's magic, he sensed another dragon egg nearby. Opening his eyes, he pointed up into the rocks a few hundred feet higher than where they now stood.

"We need to climb higher," Bakari told Kharlia.

"Up there?" Kharlia sighed deeply. "Well, let's get started then."

They left Abylar to rest by a small stream as they began the hike up. Bakari enjoyed how the early morning sun broke through the clouds and began to warm the air, but the few inches of fresh snow covering the ground made the climbing feel strenuous. More than once, they hit a dead end and had to go back down and then try another path. What should have taken only a short time was turning into hours of climbing, and they both were becoming tired.

Grabbing hold of another ledge, Bakari pushed Kharlia up in front of him as she climbed. Then he climbed up himself.

"Hey, who are you?" a young man said, greeting them so suddenly that Bakari almost fell backward off the rock. But another youth, with long, dark hair hanging down his back in a ponytail, grabbed Bakari's hand and steadied him.

After gathering his breath, Bakari looked around briefly and then back at the two young men. "My name is Bakari, and this is Kharlia," he finally said.

They looked at him and Kharlia suspiciously. Then the one with the long, dark hair said, "My name is Jaimon Schafer, and this is Bug."

Kharlia gave Jaimon a questioning look.

So Jaimon explained, "He used to like bugs when he was little."

Bug nodded and then turned red at receiving Kharlia's

attention.

Bakari took a few steps in a circle and studied the ground. The two young men were watching him, but they seemed not quite sure what to say.

Abylar, Bakari thought. *I need your help finding the egg. I know it is close, but I can't see over all these rocks.*

"Sir," Jaimon said, "what are you looking for?"

Before Bakari could answer, Abylar rose up in front of them, his bright blue scales reflecting the morning sunlight, his tail wrapping around the air behind him. Then his giant wings sent a gust of cold wind flowing over the four youths.

Bug screamed, "What is that thing?" Then he went running back inside a nearby cave. But Jaimon had kept perfectly still, only moving his blue eyes to follow the path of the dragon.

"He's beautiful," Jaimon said.

"His name is Abylar," Bakari said.

"Bakari is a wizard," added Kharlia, "and a dragon rider."

Jaimon stood quietly, but his eyes were intelligent and attentive.

Getting down to business, Bakari said, "I am here to find a dragon egg."

Bug walked tentatively back out of the cave, his eyes as big as saucers. He motioned with his head to Jaimon, who looked over at Bug, then back to Bakari again.

The egg is in the cave, Abylar told Bakari, flapping his wings around in excitement.

"You've seen it already, haven't you?" Bakari asked Jaimon.

"But we didn't touch it," Bug said as he waved his skinny arms around. "I promise you, we didn't."

Bakari smiled and motioned with his hand for the two young men to lead him and Kharlia to the egg. It was dark in the back of the cave, so Bakari held his hand out and created a flame to see by. Both Jaimon and Bug gazed at Bakari with apparent amazement. In the light of the flame, Bakari saw the egg, sitting on a small patch of straw at the back of the cave.

"It grew since last night," Jaimon said.

Bakari nodded. He knew how fast the egg would grow right at the end, before the dragon was ready to come out. This egg wasn't as big as Abylar's had been, but it was still a good three feet taller than Bakari. He closed his eyes momentarily and reached his mind out to the egg. He sensed the dragon inside. It was almost time.

"What are you two doing here?" Kharlia asked.

Jaimon looked down as if embarrassed. "We were tending our flocks of sheep in the valley below and decided to climb up here for a better look. A sudden storm caught us here last night."

"I told you we shouldn't have come here." Bug butted in. "We are going to get in so much trouble.

Looking at Jaimon, Bakari tried to make him and Bug feel more relaxed. Bakari laughed inside, remembering how he had been the first time he'd laid eyes on the Dragon Orb; and, being a wizard, he had already witnessed many marvelous things. But these two, Bakari surmised, were quite a bit out of their element here. There was no magic power coming from either one of them, but there was something special about one of them.

"Jaimon," Bakari said, turning to the seemingly more mature of the two. "Touch the egg, please."

Jaimon's eyes opened wide, and he glanced at his friend. Bug shook his head back and forth at Jaimon, telling him not to, but Jaimon seemed calm and took a step forward.

"Go on," Bakari said. There was a feeling of peace as Bakari looked from the egg to Jaimon. He was young and untrained, but he was the one the egg had chosen. The thought had come quickly to him, and he felt it as true. Not all dragon riders had to be wizards.

Bakari felt Kharlia grab his hand and heard her whisper, "Is this how it was with you?" Then she leaned in next to him.

"Yes," Bakari said quietly. "Except I am a wizard, too, so I think I could feel more of the power."

"Feel anything yet?" Bakari asked Jaimon as he walked toward the egg.

Jaimon shook his head but continued walking.

Bakari held his breath tight inside him. *A third dragon!*

Reaching the egg, Jaimon turned his head and, with a quick gaze, took in each person's face. Turning back to the egg, he reached his hand out and touched the solid surface. A bright light flared out from this egg, as it had with the two previous eggs for Bakari and Breelyn.

Jaimon gasped and then said, "It's a dragon." Inside the egg, the shadowy outline of a dragon became apparent to the small group.

Bakari smiled. This was the third dragon egg he had seen in the last few months. And there would be two more, if the old king was right: one, just across the border of Alaris, in Turg; and the other, farther north, in the Realm.

Keeping his hand on the egg, Jaimon closed his eyes briefly. Then he opened them, and, as he slowly backed up, the egg began to crack. Thousands of small pieces of shell fell from the egg, and then a small, green dragon stumbled forward.

The dragon gave a loud squawk, which was answered back by Abylar's mighty roar from outside the cave's entrance. The young dragon stretched its wings out a dozen feet to either side and took a few hesitant steps. Its neck moved around, and then its giant head settled on Jaimon. The young man took a step forward and extended his hand tentatively to the new creature, touching the deep green scales.

After a silent moment, Jaimon spoke softly, "Cholena. I name her Cholena, meaning *she who soars.*"

The young green dragon blinked her light red eyes and emitted a deep purr.

"I can feel her in my mind!" Jaimon exclaimed to Bakari. "All her thoughts and strength."

Bakari understood the feeling well. "Welcome to our ranks, Dragon Rider."

Then Bug collapsed to the floor. "You mean Jaimon's going to ride that thing?"

Bakari and Kharlia laughed.

"I knew climbing up here was the right thing to do, Bug," Jaimon said. "But I really don't know what a dragon rider is," Jaimon said as he turned to Bakari.

"I'm still learning that also," Bakari said. "But dragon riders have appeared throughout history when the need for peace is greatest."

Jaimon looked deep in thought.

"The barrier around Alaris is down," Kharlia said. "And Bakari needs your help to reestablish peace in the land."

"The barrier is down?" Jaimon asked, seeming surprised. "You mean you are from Alaris?"

"I grew up in Alaris, but my heritage is from Mahli."

"This makes three dragon riders," Kharlia added. "Bak was the first, an elf named Breelyn was the second, and you are the third."

Jaimon pulled his long ponytail forward and draped it over his shoulder. Then, he kneeled down on one knee, and bowed his head to Bakari.

"I will serve as a dragon rider," Jaimon said solemnly. "But you must teach me what I need to know. I'm only a sheepherder."

"Don't worry," Bakari said. "We are all learning. You'll do fine."

Cholena squawked again and moved toward the mouth of the cave.

Jaimon stood up. "She's hungry."

Abylar flew by, outside of the cave, and beckoned the young dragon to follow him.

"Abylar will help her find food," Bakari said as he motioned the group to follow him back out of the mountain cave. "Dragons are always hungry."

You need to eat more, Dragon Rider, Abylar admonished Bakari as he flew out of sight. *You're too skinny.*

Ha, Bakari said to Abylar. *Just don't get so fat that you can't carry me anymore.*

I can always carry a stick on my back.

Bakari related this conversation to the group.

"Dragons have a sense of humor?" Bug asked, looking perplexed. "Those big things?"

"Oh yes," Bakari said with a laugh. "They think very highly of themselves."

I heard that! Abylar said to Bakari's mind.

Bakari led the group back down the rocks to the valley that he and Kharlia had landed in earlier. The sun had warmed things up, and the early snow was beginning to melt, leaving the rocky terrain wet. Still, it took them a much shorter time to climb down.

"Kharlia and I will need to fly north to find the next dragon rider," Bakari declared to the group. "Then we will be ready."

"Our parents must be worried about us," Jaimon said. "I need to check on the sheep also."

Bakari was pleased with Jaimon's sense of honor and caring. He would make a fine dragon rider. "Once the dragons eat," Bakari said, "we can all fly back to your town on Abylar. You can stay there for a bit. It will take a week or so for your dragon to be strong enough to carry you. Then we will all gather and do what we must to bring peace to the land."

Bakari's ominous tone quieted everyone down and left them in their own thoughts for a few minutes.

They all turned as Bug began making a strange sound. He had put his hand on a rock and looked sick now. "You mean I'm going to fly on that...that big blue thing?"

Jaimon slapped his best friend on the back. "Yep, and I bet you'll be telling the story to your grandkids until the day you die."

They all had a good laugh and then settled down to wait for the dragons to return from eating.

CHAPTER TWENTY EIGHT

Kolo, the son of the regent of Mahli, was hiking through the mountains that separated their isolated country from Turg, their western neighbor. Turg was one of the United Territories, along with Khazer, to their north, and Cyrene, to the northwest. These three sparsely populated kingdoms had joined together years earlier under three relatively weak leaders. By banding together, they had staved off troubles caused by other, larger neighboring kingdoms.

Kolo was accompanied by three other men and horses for each. The small group had set off from the city of Amar a week earlier. For Kolo had determined, after much threatening to their chief librarian, that one of the dragon eggs had to be in Turg.

"We may need to leave the horses soon, sir," said Talib, one of Kolo's three men. A multitude of weapons hung from Talib's belt. "The snow is getting too thick."

Kolo motioned for the men to push on. "I don't care about the horses. We are almost at the summit."

The two other men, Isooba and Jabari, pulled their horses along, their faces red with exertion.

Kolo didn't care about the horses or these men. So he would drive them as hard as he could. His mind felt giddy in his anticipation of finding a dragon of his own. A dragon he could control and pull power from. There were already relatively few wizards or people with magical powers in Mahli, and being a dragon rider would put Kolo far above even any of those. He would be king!

Three hours later, they reached the top of the mountain. Clouds held to the tips of the peaks, and small flakes of snow drifted down onto Kolo's clothing. Layered with tanned leather over wool, Kolo was still warm underneath. He saw a broad overhang close by, and he and the other men trudged over to it and escaped most of the snow under its protective roof.

"There is nothing to light for a fire," Jabari said.

"So, after feeding some oats to the horses," Kolo said to the three men, "pull out your food rations and chew them in silence."

Not long after they had returned and started eating, Jabari asked, "How much farther, Kolo?" Jabari's hair hung down in braids like the hair of the rest of their party, though Jabari's braids were colored at the tips, in red, signifying he had recently had a newborn child—his first.

"As far as we need to go," Kolo mumbled, and then he saw Jabari shoot him a dark look. "Is there a problem with that?" Kolo stood up and walked closer to Jabari.

Isooba nudged Jabari, and so the man only shook his head.

"Good," Kolo said. "When I find the dragon and become king, those who have helped me will be rewarded well."

"Maybe my own place to rule?" asked Talib, one of Kolo's trusted advisers. "And a few women?"

Kolo laughed. "Talib, you may have whatever you want—once we find the cursed dragon egg."

The group settled down for the evening, using the heat from the horses to warm the small area. As Kolo laid his head back onto his pack and closed his eyes, he thought about Bakari and his blasted dragon. Kolo hated the young man. The dragon rider had embarrassed him, and Kolo was sure Bakari was trying to take Kolo's place. Bakari was not much more than a boy—a skinny specimen of a man—and was born in another country. So Kolo decided he would destroy Bakari the first chance he got.

Sleep began to take over, but then Kolo felt a slight nudge in his mind. A presence that was hardly more than a thought at first. It seemed to be feeding and agreeing with Kolo's thoughts regarding Bakari and his dragon.

Who are you? Kolo thought to the voice inside his head.

I can be anyone you want me to be, it answered back. *But, most importantly, I can help you become a dragon rider.*

Now Kolo didn't care who the voice was, and he asked, *How?*

The voice laughed, a haunting, low sound that shook the depths of Kolo's dreams. *Open your mind to me, and tell me your name.*

My name is Kolo, regent-heir of Mahli and the next dragon king, Kolo said firmly.

Good. Good. You have aspirations, the voice said, speaking louder now. *Names have power, especially dragons' names.*

Kolo was intrigued. *Where is the dragon egg, Master?*

Master? the voice echoed. *I like that. A half day's ride into Turg, you will find a lake with a river leading to it. Up the river is a waterfall, and behind the falls, a cave. There you will find the dragon egg.*

Will you be with us? Kolo asked.

I will be here, in your mind. I have a magical artifact that allows me to search you out and be with you, but my body is trapped in a cold, dark room.

Anger had flared in the voice's last sentence, and Kolo's mind recoiled from it.

After you find the dragon, the voice continued, *you will free me, and together we will rule the entire Western Continent.*

Kolo smirked. He would take advantage now of any help he could get, but he was not going to share his rule later with the voice inside his head.

Suddenly, pain exploded in Kolo's mind, and he screamed out. Sitting up around him, the others must have heard his scream and woken up also. Kolo assured them he was all right and then settled back down to sleep again.

After a few moments, the voice came to Kolo's mind again, but, this time, with more force and determination. *Don't think that you can double-cross me, Kolo. Now that I know your name, I can find you anywhere. I can even become you if I want to.*

Kolo didn't quite know what the voice meant, but the pain in his head got his attention. Then Kolo realized that he now couldn't think anything without the source of this voice hearing him. So Kolo held at bay any thoughts of leaving the voice and going off on his own, making sure that these didn't develop into actual thoughts that could be heard by the voice.

What do I call you? Kolo asked.

I have gone by many names, through the years, as I have gathered my power. Call me the Chameleon, Kolo. This is not my real name, of course. Knowing that would give you too much power over me. But this is what you may call me.

Kolo lay in silence for a few minutes, thinking about the

Chameleon. Then he finally drifted off to sleep, thinking, *Tomorrow, I will be a dragon rider.*

* * *

"Chief Judge?" a man called to Daymian down the hallway of the governor's castle in Orr.

Daymian turned toward him and smiled. "Marco, I haven't seen you for a while."

Marco shook the Chief Judge's hand. "Is there somewhere we can speak privately?" He glanced around himself anxiously.

"Yes." Daymian led Marco to a small private chamber, telling the guard there to stay alert. He kept a table with a few chairs in the small room. They seated themselves across the table from each other.

"Onius sent me." Marco came straight to the point.

Daymian raised his eyebrows, but he let the man continue. Marco had been one of his stewards in the castle at Cassian. A very capable man, who had many friends and connections.

"Kanzar is unstable, sir," Marco continued. "Onius has been pushing him slowly toward the edge. It is dangerous for Onius to maintain a connection with Kanzar while working against him. Only a few others besides me know of Onius's true intentions. Now Kanzar has sent a delegation of wizards here, to Orr, in secret. They are to report back to him on the strength of your army and by what means they might attack."

Daymian sat with his fingers held under his chin, his dark beard tickling his hand. "Kanzar is getting ready to attack."

"Yes, we believe so," Marco said. "He lost in Corwan, and there is unrest in Cassian. Unless he wins a decisive victory soon, the other wizards will turn away from him. There has already been a break in their ranks."

"I believe I might have an idea," the Chief Judge began, but, before any of his plans could be revealed, they heard yells fill the hallway outside of the room.

Standing up quickly, Daymian reached toward the door and flung it open. A group of his military advisers came marching down the hallway toward him, their faces flushed with obvious excitement.

"What is it?" Daymian asked. "Are we under attack already?"

"No, sir," said one of the women in the lead. "It's a dragon, sir. I think you better come with us."

"A dragon?" Daymian smiled. It must be Bakari returning. That would surely help their odds against Kanzar. He picked up his pace, following the group back outside, with Marco on his heels.

Coming outside into the town square, Daymian stopped. It was not Bakari, as he'd supposed, but a woman instead. This beautiful woman, with long, blond hair and high cheekbones, sat atop a yellow dragon, its orange and yellow scales reflecting the afternoon sun. Never in his entire life could Daymian have anticipated seeing something so exotic and grand.

The yellow dragon lifted its head and roared, a flame of yellow and orange spilling out into the nearby air. Daymian stepped back from the flame's heat and frowned.

"Are you Daymian Khouri, Chief Judge of Alaris?" the women asked. Her voice had a lovely musical quality.

Daymian nodded his head. "I am. And, who are you?"

"I am Breelyn Mier, protector of Elvyn, the betrothed of

Prince Soliel, and a newly named dragon rider."

Daymian paused, wondering at all those titles for a moment. The woman could be dangerous indeed. "And, do you know my friend Bakari?"

Breelyn's face lit up, and everyone stood mesmerized as she said, "Yes, he is my master."

The Chief Judge felt himself relax and then held his hand out to her. "Then, I bid you welcome, Dragon Rider. Will you join me?"

Breelyn nodded and slid gracefully down off of her dragon. She walked with poise and grace over to the Chief Judge. "Bakari asked me to meet with you on my way to meet up with him. There is much to discuss if we are to ensure the peace of our two lands."

Daymian nodded and led Breelyn into the castle, thinking that his plans might come together even better now.

CHAPTER TWENTY NINE

Alli watched Mericus out of the corner of her eye. He was delegating the task of rebuilding the portions of the docks destroyed in the fire to a group of men. She wanted to hate the guy, but a grudging respect for him was slowly building inside her—he actually was good at what he did.

He glanced over at her and smiled, as if to say, *See, I told you that I care.* Was there something else in that look also? Or, was Alli seeing things that weren't there? She turned her head to the side to hide her blush. The man was at least ten years older than her.

Soon all the visitors departed, and Mericus strode over to the chair that Alli sat slumped in, against the wall. Mericus seemed to like wearing black, and today was no exception: dark shirt, tucked into black pants, which, in turn, were tucked into black boots. A black-handled dagger hanging at his side.

"Bored?" Mericus asked.

Alli sat up a bit in the old stuffed chair. "Yes, I am—if you must know. I should be with the Chief Judge, preparing for the next battle, not here..." She stopped speaking, not quite knowing the right words to say.

"Not here, watching over me, like a babysitter?" Mericus said and then laughed, his dark eyes opening wider. "Then, why are you?"

"Because Bakari asked," she mumbled, feeling heat creeping up her cheeks again.

"Ahh, the dragon rider." Mericus stroked his short, dark beard with his fingers. "Quite a thing, to see a dragon, isn't it? I've got to admit, I wouldn't have believed it if I hadn't seen it."

Voices picked up outside, and then they heard a loud thud on the roof. Alli jumped up and pulled out a short knife, heading toward the door.

"Expecting trouble?" Mericus asked as he followed her to the stairwell leading to the roof.

"I'm always expecting trouble."

They emerged from the stairs and peeked around the top of the building and together let out a concerted gasp.

"Not another one," Mericus groaned.

In front of them stood a bright yellow dragon, its scales tipped with orange. Sliding down it was the exquisite, long-haired elf woman named Breelyn.

"Her name is Miriel," Breelyn said. Then she gave a slight nod to Alli and added, "Nice to see you again, Allison. I hear you are a wizard now."

Alli gave her a broad grin. At fifteen, Alli had needed Roland's generosity to be tested and named a full wizard. Thoughts of that arrogant Roland made her almost blush again. She had to get hold of herself. Alli wouldn't let these men around her cause her to act like a weak, infatuated girl—she was a battle wizard!

"Not that I could have doubted it at all," continued the elf, "from the way I saw you fight." Turning to Mericus, Breelyn said, "Alli is a marvel to watch in a battle." She took a few steps forward and added, "My name is Breelyn."

"Mericus."

"Breelyn, what are you doing here?" Alli asked. "Is everything all right with Bak?"

"Can we talk inside, with some refreshments?" Breelyn asked. "I am famished and sore from riding my dragon."

Alli noticed that Mericus had not said much, but he ushered the two of them inside.

Alli took one more look back at the beautiful creature. "She is like the sunlight. So, you are a dragon rider also, like Bak?"

Breelyn nodded. "Dragon Rider Bakari is my master." The elf took the steps two at a time, and Alli and Mericus had a hard time following her as quickly.

Arriving downstairs, they went into the judge's office, and Mericus offered Breelyn a drink. She downed it in one long gulp. Sitting themselves down, Alli and Mericus waited for Breelyn to begin.

"The Chief Judge has a plan to trap Kanzar," she started off, without any other preamble. Her soft blue eyes glittered with enthusiasm.

"What about Bak?" Alli asked again.

Breelyn turned to Alli. "Oh, I'm sorry. It's just that being a dragon rider is so exhilarating; I hardly have time to think."

"I thought elves were more deliberate in their natures," muttered Mericus.

Breelyn laughed, and it was as if music filled the room. "We are, usually, though I'm not. Rushing into things headlong got me into trouble many times as a youth."

Mericus smiled and started to relax.

"Bakari sent me a message," Breelyn said. "He saved

Roland, found another dragon, in Quentis, and is now flying north, to Turg, to find another one there."

"Is Roland all right?" Alli felt her face redden.

"I'm not sure of all the details." Breelyn furrowed her light eyebrows. "But someone had impersonated him and had trapped him in a room where his magic couldn't be used."

"Someone should take care of that boy." Alli said, then realized she had spoken the thought out loud. So she tried to change the subject. "So, about the plan?"

Breelyn put her cup on a small side table and began to explain. "Kanzar is sending spies to Orr. When they arrive, the Chief Judge will hide most of his troops. Thinking the city is not fortified well will embolden Kanzar, and he will send his troops there. When he does, you will march from Corwan and come up behind his army—on the plains south of Cassian. The Chief Judge's troops will then come out, and we will surround Kanzar's army."

"That will not stop Kanzar," Mericus stated. "He cares little for his troops—or anyone, for that matter." Mericus seemed bitter and a look of disgust spread across his face. "The only way to stop this madness is to kill Kanzar himself."

"Leave that to the dragon riders," Breelyn said.

"It's about time we do something," Alli answered back. "I will inform the troops and get them ready." Mericus raised an eyebrow at her, so Alli shot him back a dark look. "I *am* the most senior battle wizard in the city." She shrugged.

Then Mericus raised both his eyebrows and laughed. "And a feisty one at that." Growing more serious, he said, "I appreciate any help you can give us, Breelyn. I will inform the governor of these plans. We will be ready to march soon."

Breelyn took her leave, and they returned with her to the rooftop. Alli saw that quite a crowd had gathered below, in the streets, and Miriel seemed to be enjoying the attention, roaring and preening in front of them. Alli and Mericus stood next to Breelyn as she mounted the dragon.

"We will meet on the battle field!" Breelyn said as Miriel took off into the air.

* * *

Roland was still recovering from his recent ordeal. The effects of being around the strange magical artifacts still disturbed him. He had called a meeting of all those in the Citadel and had explained what had happened, but the mood was still tense, and no one seemed to trust one another now.

Sitting at his desk, he put his head in his hands. He was more shaken up than he had admitted to anyone. Being locked in that dark, magicless room for days had stretched him beyond his normal limits. His thoughts often became dark, and he would shake his head to try and concentrate on running the Citadel once again. His goal of becoming the most powerful wizard was also set back once he had realized how much magic existed that he knew nothing about. And he couldn't seem to keep his mind from thinking about all the magical artifacts locked behind the doors in the lower levels.

A knock sounded at his door, bringing Roland out of his musings. In walked one of the administrators. He was an older, serious man with only a few wisps of hair, who did his work quite well. The man approached the desk and cleared his throat.

"A group of wizards from Cassian have arrived at the front

gates." The man's face was tight and brooked no smile.

Roland jumped up out of his seat. "From Cassian? Have they stated their intentions?"

"They asked to speak with you and are not very happy about being held at the front gates," the administrator said.

Roland managed a smile. "I bet not." He wondered who the wizards were and if this was Kanzar's way of trying to rope him back into his plans. "Show them to the ready room. I will be with them shortly."

The man bowed, and Roland went through a side door to his own set of rooms. He dug through his clothes for the appropriate attire. Black boots, black pants, with a white shirt and red cape caught his attention. After dressing, he rounded up a contingent of guards to walk with him. After letting the wizards wait for a few more minutes, Roland entered the room, making two of his guards open the double wooden doors in front of him.

Strutting into the room, Roland gazed around at the dark, wooden décor and the golden lamps lighting the room. With a flick of his hands, he turned up the flames on the lamps.

"Greetings, wizards," he said, bobbing his head to them. One woman and three men; none of them were wizards Roland knew well.

An older man stepped forward. Roland remembered Lyman from his own wizard test. The man was a member of Kanzar's Council. Bowing his head to Roland, as was befitting of a level three wizard, the man cleared his throat.

"Sir," Lyman began nervously, looking back at the other three wizards before he continued. "We have come to discuss the…um, current situation."

Roland called for refreshments to be brought in. "Please be seated," Roland said, offering the wizards seats in huge, overstuffed chairs.

Before beginning, Roland also called Eryck in to join them. The old wizard had been through a lot, but Roland owed it to him to be a part of these proceedings. Eryck walked around and greeted each of the visiting wizards personally.

Roland watched the four unfamiliar wizards carefully for any sign of deceit or danger. He reached his mind out and felt each one's power. Three were level three wizards, and one, a level two. All weaker than himself, but together they could possibly overwhelm him. Two were counselor wizards, and two were scholar wizards—battle wizards were still in short supply and, most likely, were being kept close to Kanzar in his bid to take over the kingdom.

Once everyone was settled, Roland began. "What can I do for you?"

"My name is Gavin," said another one of the men. "We come at the request of Kanzar to look in on things here, at the Citadel, and make sure everything is all right."

Roland kept a straight face. There was no way they could know about the Chameleon and the havoc that impostor had caused. They were fishing for something.

All businesslike, Roland stood, his cape floating around his body. "We have received new recruits—of those wishing to be made apprentices—every day. Training goes well, and the Citadel is in good hands."

"There haven't been any new wizards raised, have there?"

asked the woman, her expression not very friendly, and not bothering to state her name.

Roland started to report in the negative, but then he remembered Alli and felt no need to hide what he had done. "I raised Allison Stenos to battle wizard level three."

All four let out gasps.

Gavin stood up and waved his hands around. "You do not have authority to do that, young man. You are barely a wizard yourself. And, if I remember correctly, she is only a young girl."

Roland moved forward two steps in quick succession to stand in front of Gavin. He must show his authority now, or they would never let him be.

"The highest ranking wizard at the Citadel has the right to raise an apprentice," Roland said. "That is in Citadel law. Eryck was there and can confirm it was all held according to our laws."

Eryck nodded his head but didn't speak.

Eryck had helped to free Roland, but he was still a rather timid wizard, even more so now, it seemed, with these other wizards in the room.

"And that *young girl* could run circles around all of you—at the same time." Roland thought of Alli, remembering how he became mesmerized each time he saw her fight or train as she created a deadly dance that flowed from one position to another with such accuracy and grace that it almost made him jealous. And he wouldn't mind a nice peck from those pouty lips of hers.

"What are your intentions here, young man?" the woman asked, pulling Roland out of his thoughts.

"And what is your name, wizard?" Roland asked. "I have not met you before, but I take it you were trained as a counselor wizard like myself."

The woman tightened her lips. "My name is Rosilyn. I trained here many years before you were even born."

Roland was getting tired of being treated like a youngster. And so he turned the question back on the group of wizards. "What are *your* intentions? And, what does Kanzar want?" he demanded, his voice roaring with power.

The visiting wizards stood up, and Roland's guards moved behind him, their leader. Power crackled in the room. Lyman brought his hand out to gather his power.

One hand in his pocket, Roland moved his fingers over a small cube he had taken from the room below the Citadel. He then moved his hand next to it as he felt something else. It was a small cylinder. He didn't remember taking this with him from the room. He wondered what it was. The room had been full of powerful objects.

Running his fingers around the edge of the metal, he tried to sense what it was. His fingers sizzled with its power. Wrapping his hand around it, he tried to push his power into it. For a brief moment, nothing happened.

"Roland!" he heard Eryck yell.

Roland felt *invincible*. He brought his hands out, one hand holding on to the cylinder. They had threatened his power and authority. Now they would learn what he could do. A sweet, dark power filled him. The power wanted to protect him from these wizards, who would try to take his place in the Citadel. They didn't trust him and only wanted his power for themselves.

Take them down! a voice rumbled inside Roland's head.

He raised his hands out in front of him, a black snaking smoke rising from the cylinder, winding its way around up his arm and around his red cape, growing bigger and darker. It filled his mind with heady thoughts of power and destruction.

The blackness gathered around his hands, and crackles of lightning came through his fingers. All four visiting wizards drew on their powers and stood ready to attack him.

Attack them before they attack you. They want to steal your power, the voice said more clearly to Roland. *They want what you have. They are Kanzar's men.*

Then he felt a hand on his shoulder. Turning around, he saw Eryck, in all his frailty, trying to stop him.

"Roland, let go," Eryck said. "This isn't you."

Not me? Roland's eyes filled with darkness and then, with only a blink, sent a tendril of black smoke toward the old wizard.

Somehow, a brief thought deep in his mind made him think of the room he had been sealed up in, and fear gripped his heart once again. He remembered Bakari saving him. And he thought of Alli and her ability to so precisely control her powers. Then he thought of Onius and his teachings. Finally, he thought of the Chameleon and then heard a cackle of laughter rip through his mind.

So weak…so weak…and pathetic.

Roland clenched his fist and brought the tendrils of smoke back into his hand as Eryck fell back onto his chair. Turning to the remaining wizards, Roland gritted his teeth and fought for control.

"Stand down," Roland ordered the wizards. "Pull your magic back."

Gavin looked at the other wizards, fear evident in their eyes.

"Now!" Roland roared, and the power in his voice spoke deep into the wizards' souls and brooked no disagreement. As their powers receded, Roland continued to fight for control of his own.

He pushed the Chameleon out of his mind and thought about his own magic. He had bested Kanzar and his cronies in the wizard test, and he now controlled the Citadel, the magical seat of power in Alaris. He realized then that he was more powerful than the evil trying to permeate him.

"I...am...magic."

Roland finally dropped the cylinder from his hand back into his pocket, and the blackness receded instantly. It was all Roland could do to remain standing, but stand he did. Feeling determined, his own power crackling around him, Roland faced the four wizards.

"You now see what I can do," he said through gritted teeth. His head pounded, and he was on the verge of collapse. "Why are you here?" he roared, his voice shaking the windows of the room.

The visiting wizard's faces looked haggard, as if they had aged ten years in those two minutes. Lyman was the first to speak. "We are here to help take down High Wizard Kanzar Centari. He must be stopped."

Roland let go of his power, and he slumped back into his

chair. "Why didn't you say so at the first?" He tried to smile, but it came out more like a sneer. "That would have prevented quite a bit of trouble."

All four bowed their heads in apology and sat back down. Nothing was said for a few minutes while everyone collected their thoughts.

Roland wondered, briefly, how the evil cylinder got in his pocket, but he realized it must have been from the Chameleon. The man was powerful. Roland would need to put more guards on his room, but obviously the Chameleon had found an artifact that projected his thoughts beyond the barriers of that room. That could mean trouble for all of them.

Roland called for the servants to bring in more drink. After a few sips, to calm his nerves, he resumed the conversation.

"I have been trying to stay neutral in this conflict over Alaris," Roland began, "but I see now I won't be able to enjoy any peace at the Citadel until it is resolved."

"Onius hoped you would say that." Gavin smiled for the first time. "You are a very dangerous man, Roland Tyre. I hope his confidence in you is not misplaced."

Roland felt better after a few bites of food. His head cleared, and his strength returned. "So, the old counselor is behind this after all. The sly fox."

"Kanzar is out of control and must be stopped," said Rosilyn. "He is obsessed with power and doesn't care who stands in his way."

"So, control of Alaris goes back to the Chief Judge?" Roland asked.

"Not exactly," Gavin said.

"I won't fight the Chief Judge, if that is your plan." Roland felt a strange sense of loyalty to that man. Roland had always looked upon Daymian as weak and boring. But, in trying to run the Citadel, Roland had realized the skills and abilities the Chief Judge must have possessed to run all of Alaris. Daymian was a good man and, whether he ended up leading Alaris or not, Roland would do what he could to ensure Daymian's safety.

"Very well. Then you should come with us," a wizard said.

Roland nodded his head. "Yes, I guess I must." Turning to Eryck, Roland saw that the old man was looking better already. "Eryck, ready the advanced apprentices; we march in two days."

"Sir?" asked Lyman. "The apprentices?"

Roland grinned. "You don't think I'm going down into that mess—of men vying for power—without my own army, do you?"

CHAPTER THIRTY

Bakari and Kharlia soared high in the air on the back of Abylar. After staying in Westridge for two nights, due to a harsh storm, they now flew farther north, into North Solshi, to avoid any other delays. They didn't bother to hide themselves now, as time was a more important factor than stealth. As they neared the mountains on the border of Turg, they settled down for the night.

Abylar, can you go and search the mountains for us? Bakari asked his dragon. *The egg must be close.*

I will pick up a few extra animals to eat on my way. Abylar snorted a puff of smoke out of his large nostrils.

Bakari rolled his eyes at the dragon. He had never thought of animals as having senses of humor. He said as much to Abylar.

I am not an animal. Abylar flapped his wings twice and rose up into the crisp mountain air. *I am a dragon.* With that, he flew off, leaving Bakari alone with Kharlia.

They sat down against a tree, shoulders touching and fingers intertwined.

"Quite a dragon you have there, Dragon Rider." The campfire reflected orange in Kharlia's eyes.

Bakari chuckled. "Remember sitting against that tree after leaving Forest View, before the bandits attacked us?"

"Yes, Bak," Kharlia said. "Seems like so long ago."

"I still can't believe it."

"Believe what? That you are a dragon rider?"

"All of it," Bakari said. "I'm only a weak scholar wizard. How did all this happen?"

Kharlia's eyes flashed as she turned her head. Her lips only inches away from Bakari's. "You are a mighty wizard, Bakari."

"I don't think you understand how wizard power works, Kharlia. I am a level two wizard. Yes, I have a great memory. But, in terms of sheer power, many apprentices are more powerful than I am. Look at Roland and Alli. They both passed me right up." Bakari looked at her lips, so smooth and inviting. He had relished every touch from them.

Kharlia's face flushed, and her breathing quickened. "A weak wizard you may be, Bak." Her breath was soft and husky. "But you are *my* wizard."

Bakari grinned, his heart full of joy.

He felt Abylar through the bond, but he was miles away now, roaming over the mountain peaks in search of the next egg. So Bakari leaned his head down and gently pressed his lips against hers. Fire seemed to fill his soul as she let out a soft sigh. Then she kissed him back, hungrily, and Bakari felt distant laughter from Abylar. Pushing the dragon farther from his mind, Bakari kissed Kharlia back with similar feelings.

After a few minutes, they pulled back from each other, and Kharlia laid her head on Bakari's shoulder. Within minutes, they both slipped off into a restful sleep.

Early in the morning, Abylar flew back down into their camp.

I have found two groups of people, Dragon Rider, and one includes Kolo.

That thought woke Bakari at once. He nudged Kharlia and told her about Kolo.

"He is searching for the dragon egg?" Kharlia asked.

Where are they? Bakari asked Abylar.

Both groups are heading toward the same spot, Abylar said, lowering his body to the ground next to them. *The dragon egg is located between them.*

Gathering up their packs and kicking snow over the fire, Kharlia and Bakari mounted the dragon, and then they took off over the mountains.

The mountains here were similar in size to those in Quentis, where they had found Jaimon and his dragon: quite a bit smaller than those encircling Mahli. Still, their peaks held snow, and the deciduous trees had lost most of their leaves. A few birds were scattered in the air around them, most likely wondering what kind of oversized bird Abylar was. He enjoyed roaring at them and chasing them off.

"Can you tell your child to settle down, Bak?" Kharlia groaned. "I'm going to get sick."

Bakari laughed but patted Abylar with his hand. *Relax, Abylar. We're back here, remember?*

Abylar slowed down. Way down. Until they were barely staying in the air.

Kharlia rolled her eyes at the dragon, and Bakari tapped him with his feet lovingly and said, *Not that slow.*

Abylar roared and sped back up, this time keeping his acrobatics and turns to a minimum.

They continued their ride up over the mountain peaks. Bakari saw a picturesque lake, surrounded by snow, with a half frozen river winding its way from the mountain peaks, down to its shore, and then out again on the other side. Soon they spotted a small group of people, hiking in a small valley between two mountains. Pointing up at the large beast, they pulled their swords out in defense. One began to gather a fireball in his hands, signifying that at least one of them was a wizard. He threw the fireball up at the dragon, but it was a pathetic attempt compared to the might of Abylar and the height they were flying at.

Bakari raised his hands in greeting. "We come as friends," he shouted down to them.

The three people stopped running but didn't sheathe their swords. So Bakari asked Abylar to find a place to land, and then Bakari and Kharlia hopped off the dragon and approached the group.

There were two men and one woman. All had dark hair, and they were wrapped in warm parkas of white fur. All three appeared to be about a dozen of years older than Bakari or Kharlia. But he and Kharlia walked deliberately forward through the snow and stopped twenty feet away.

"I am Bakari, Dragon Rider," he said, for he couldn't hide from who he was anymore, and he needed to get it out in the open.

The three opened their eyes wide. The woman stepped a few feet out in front of the other two. She removed her hood, and long, brown hair cascaded down over her shoulders. Her eyes were brown, and her skin looked weathered, but she exuded an aura of power.

After a brief nod of greeting, she said, "I am Delia, wizard of Turg." Her voice held a heavy accent, and Bakari listened carefully. "The Oracle of Turg has foreseen this day. We are here to search for a great power."

"The Oracle?" Bakari asked.

Delia frowned at Bakari's apparent lack of knowledge. "Our supreme leader. He is a seer and sees the future."

Bakari nodded in understanding. "A powerful wizard gift."

The two other men walked up to stand even with Delia. "Seth and Milo," Delia said, introducing them. "Seth is the oldest of us three."

"This is Kharlia," Bakari said. Then he turned his head toward his dragon and added, "And this is Abylar, the first dragon. And, of the dragon riders, I also am the first. There are two more pairs, and I have been directed here to find the fourth."

"The power we seek," Delia said. "Maybe it is a dragon. Our Oracle was not clear on that fact."

"There is a dragon egg close to here," Bakari said. "Abylar senses it. But there is also another group approaching it, which I am sure, is up to no good. We must find the egg before they do."

"The Oracle directed us to a waterfall," offered Delia.

There is a waterfall at the head of this river, up into these mountains, Abylar said to Bakari.

Bakari related this information, and then the group began to walk north, following the stream.

"You can speak with it?" Seth asked.

Bakari smiled. "Yes, I can speak with him in my mind."

"You truly are a dragon rider," Milo said.

Delia looked Bakari up and down. "So young," she said with almost a sneer.

Bakari blushed with frustration. "A friend of mine told me that a wizard's level should not be determined by age but by power. I assume that is the way with dragon riders also. The dragon chooses the rider, not the other way around."

Delia took a step back at the forcefulness of Bakari's words. "I meant no offense to you," Delia said. "My first language is not the common tongue you speak. I only meant it as an observation. In Turg, a wizard cannot be named until his twenty-fifth birthing day."

Bakari's eyes brightened. "Yes. In a ceremony called *The Acceptance*, if I remember correctly."

"You know of Turg?" Milo asked. "And our ceremonies? You are correct. I was accepted just last week. This is my first mission."

"Bak remembers everything he reads," Kharlia said. "It is amazing." She took hold of Bakari's hand and led him to walk quicker. Once out of earshot of the others, she turned to Bakari and whispered, "Do you trust them?"

"I see no reason not to," Bakari said.

"You trust too easily, Bak," Kharlia censured him. "You must be more careful. What if the wrong person got hold of the dragon egg?"

"Like Kolo," Bakari said. Motioning to the others, he said, "Hurry. We must reach the egg before the others do."

Abylar flew overhead and related information back to Bakari about the approach of the others.

Soon their party began ascending a hill, still following the creek, which now crashed over rocks, spraying a cold mist in their faces. After another hour, the climbing became steeper. The steep face of the mountain loomed up in front of them. Stopping to catch their breaths, they saw the head of the waterfall, a thousand feet above them.

Milo and Seth groaned.

"How are we going to get there?" Delia asked. She turned to Bakari. "Why are you smiling, Dragon Rider? Have you brought us here to fail?"

Kharlia moved in front of Bakari, to defend him. But, with a gentle touch, Bakari held her back.

"It is only the way they speak, Kharlia," Bakari said.

"Well, I don't like it." She folded her arms in front of herself and took a stance of defense. "I don't like it when they don't respect you for who you are, Bak."

"Respect must be earned," Bakari said. "They are only testing me." Turning back to Delia, Bakari pointed up at his dragon. "Abylar can take us."

Delia's brown eyes opened wide, and then she threw back her head and laughed. "Of course! But how?"

Bak took a rope from his bag. "I will toss this end to Abylar. He will hold on to it, while two or three of us at a time will hold on to the other end."

Now it was Kharlia's turn to stand up to Bakari. "You mean we will be pulled up a thousand feet into the air with only that rope to hold on to?"

"Yes," Bakari said, directing Abylar to come down closer to them.

Bakari spent a few moments tying loops and knots in the

thick rope. Then, first, Seth and Milo grabbed the rope and were lifted up into the air. With a whoop of excitement, the two men were pulled up through the air and then dropped off a few dozen feet away from the head of the waterfall. Then Abylar returned for the rest of them.

Bakari motioned for Delia to grab the rope. "You go first, Delia. Then Kharlia and I will follow." Turning to Kharlia, he whispered, "I'm not letting you go alone this time."

Kharlia leaned in and gave him a quick kiss on the cheek.

Delia raised her eyebrows at the two.

"Just hold on tight," Bakari said.

As Delia was lifted up through the air, Abylar flew quicker than he had the time before.

"You crazy dragon," Delia shouted at the top of her lungs.

Bakari reached out to tell him to slow down.

I don't like her, Abylar said.

"Slow down, or I'll blast you away," Delia yelled. In her hand, she gathered a fireball, preparing to use it.

But Abylar roared and blasted blue fire out into the air in front of them. The wind from the blast put out Delia's fireball.

"Abylar, behave," Bakari said out loud. In his mind, he continued with, *She may be the next dragon rider.*

The dragon slowed down but ran Delia right through the waterfall itself before dropping her off on the landing spot. Then he returned for Bakari and Kharlia. Bakari got a firm hold on the rope, placing one arm around Kharlia for support.

That wasn't very nice, Bakari said to Abylar. *Now she will think I can't control my dragon.*

Abylar's reaction was one of satisfaction, with only a minor amount of shame. But Bakari assured Abylar that it was fine and that he wasn't mad.

Kharlia laughed, and Bakari pulled her closer as he gave her a stern look, which only made her laugh more.

"I thought it was funny," she said as they continued to be lifted higher.

"Kharlia!"

"Well, I did."

Soon they landed, and Delia marched up to Bakari, fire blazing in her eyes.

Before she could say anything, Bakari put up his hand. "My dragon is still a child, in many ways," Bakari said. "He is still learning. He is only two months old."

"That thing is only two months old?" Milo exclaimed. "How big will he grow?"

Big enough to eat your whole town, little man, Abylar said, but only to Bakari.

Trying to stifle a laugh, Bakari motioned them forward. "We must hurry," he said. "Behind the waterfall. Something is there."

Delia wiped the remaining water off her face and then continued forward with the rest of the group.

CHAPTER THIRTY ONE

As Bakari and the others entered the cave behind the waterfall in the mountains of Turg, the five travelers stopped to let their eyes adjust to the dimming light. Climbing through a narrow opening, they found themselves inside a huge, cavernous room. Bakari, Milo, and Delia lit mage lights in front of themselves so they could all move farther into the shadows.

"It's here," Delia squealed in delight. "It's really here."

Bakari nodded. Sitting in front of them was a huge egg, not unlike the previous three. But this one stood even larger than Abylar's egg had and almost hit the twenty-foot-high roof in the room. The shell looked rougher and thicker than the other eggs' shells, most likely to shelter it from the cold climate of the high mountains.

Bakari and Delia walked toward it.

"Can you feel it?" Bakari asked, turning to the older woman.

Delia nodded. "It is amazing. Peace, love, intelligence, and power." She reached her hand forward and touched the egg. Upon contact, the egg let off a stream of light, making Delia and Bakari shade their eyes for a moment. Then the light receded somewhat, and the egg was transparent. A white dragon with red eyes sat inside.

"It is beautiful," Delia whispered.

"It's yours," Bakari said. The more times he had helped

match an egg to its rider the more sure Bakari was of the feelings that had guided him.

Delia placed both her hands on the egg, and it began to crack, swirls of light breaking through and shining out into the cave. Then Delia stepped back, next to Bakari. The entire group watched as the enormous dragon almost filled the entire cave, its bright white wings spreading, touching the walls on either side.

Outside the cave, Abylar roared, and the new dragon answered back, its head swinging down to look at Delia. She gazed into its eyes and reached a hand out, touching its head lovingly.

"This dragon has called you, Delia," Bakari said. "But you must name it. That cements the bond. In dragon lore, this is called *the naming ceremony.*"

Delia pursed her lips in thought and then opened her mouth.

But a scuffle had ensued behind them. Bakari turned around to find Kolo and three other men emerge from the cave entrance. Kharlia screamed, and Delia's companions drew their swords, but Bakari called out to Abylar.

Kolo jumped up on a small rock and, before anyone else could speak, yelled out over the din. "I name you Sephtis Kerboros."

The white dragon swung his head back and forth with a painful howl, the tips of his white spikes and wings turning as black as coal.

"You are mine now!" Kolo rushed forward, pushing the other men to the side. Delia and her men moved to block him.

But, before they could, Kolo placed his hand on the dragon's head and forced him to look into his eyes. The dragon moaned and roared, but Kolo kept his stance.

Bakari! Abylar roared in his mind. *Get out of there. Now!*

Bakari took Kharlia's hand and ran, motioning for the others to follow. If the now crazed dragon shot out fire toward the small cave opening, they would all die inside.

"Noooo!" Delia shot her hands forward, ready to blast Kolo.

"No, Delia," Bakari called out. "There is not enough room in here. You might hurt the dragon!"

She relented with a grunt but then jumped onto the back of Kolo instead, wrapping her hands around his throat.

Glancing back as he hurried forward still, Bakari saw Kolo's men jump in to help as Kolo reached back and tried to grab Delia off of his back.

"I am a dragon rider now. Sephtis will obey me. I have bound him with his name," Kolo croaked out, gasping for breath.

"That is not how it works," Bakari said to Kharlia as they turned back around at the mouth of the cave, motioning the others behind him to keep moving.

Kolo's eyes went black with an abomination of the dragon's power. Sephtis roared again and scratched his claws into the ground. Swaying his head back and forth, the dragon tried to shake off the bond with Kolo, but it seemed to be too strong.

"Kill her!" Kolo directed the dragon, and Sephtis tried to swat Delia with his claw. But she jumped off of Kolo just in time, rolling to the floor of the cave.

Milo hurried back to help Delia up and then ran with her to the cave entrance to join the others again.

"Get them!" Kolo directed to his two companions.

Abylar, get ready, Bakari said.

For what, Dragon Rider?

Bakari motioned Delia, Milo, and Seth to follow him as he and Kharlia moved closer to the edge of the waterfall.

"We need to jump," Bakari told them.

Argument seemed about to break out among the group. Delia and her men clearly wanted to fight Kolo's approaching men.

"You can't fight them," Bakari yelled over the sound of the waterfall. "Kolo will be too powerful now, with the dragon doing his bidding." Then, making his decision, Bakari moved next to Milo and pushed him through the waterfall off the cliff. Before anyone else could react, he had pushed Seth and Delia off also, signaling to Abylar to catch them. Then he turned to defend himself and Kharlia against Kolo's approaching men.

"I am the rightful dragon rider," Bakari shouted to Kolo's men. "You know that what Kolo has done is not right."

The men turned, looking back toward their leader. Kolo's eyes were black, his dragon now half black itself. Bakari hoped their hesitation would buy a few precious seconds for himself and Kharlia to escape.

I have them, Abylar said to Bakari.

"Our turn," Bakari said and then reached around Kharlia, grasping her tightly as the two of them jumped through the waterfall off the cliff's edge.

Free-falling in front of the waterfall felt strange. He had been able to see the snow-covered mountain through the water.

Kharlia screamed in his ear and grabbed on to him tighter.

"Abylar!" Bakari yelled, his voice echoing.

He felt a sudden change in the wind and then saw the dragon appear beside them, timing his drop to match their fall. The three riders on Abylar's back reached over and grabbed Bakari and Kharlia out of the air, bringing them onto the back of Abylar.

Straightening himself up, Bakari took his rightful seat behind Abylar's neck, the other four riders sitting behind him. Then Bakari motioned his dragon back up in the air, and they watched as Sephtis Kerboros, with Kolo on his back, crashed out of the narrow cave opening through the waterfall. Sephtis soared up into the open air, leaving the two other Mahlians stranded on the hilltop.

Kolo yelled and struggled for control. Sephtis roared, black fire rolling over the air in front of them, and then tried to throw Kolo off. But Kolo held on tight.

"I will kill you, Bakari," Kolo yelled, "and return as dragon rider and king!" Then Kolo headed straight for Abylar by forcing Sephtis to obey.

Bakari knew he had to do something. He couldn't put all of his passengers at risk. He wished Breelyn and Jaimon were here to help him. Then he remembered what both of them had done after their bondings. They had each bowed to Bakari and called him *master*.

Bakari knew he was young and untrained in fighting, but he was the first dragon rider, the master of them all. So Bakari drew strength from Abylar through the bond and opened up communications to the other dragon.

To both Kolo and Sephtis, Bakari spoke out loud and in his mind. "Kolo, if you really call yourself a dragon rider, you will obey me. Regardless of whatever evil means you have used to capture and bond with the dragon, I am still the rightful dragon rider master."

Sephtis rose up in the air above them and screeched, so Bakari directed Abylar to rise up even higher.

"I will never follow your command, Bakari," Kolo said, his long, braided hair swinging around his head.

Bakari closed his eyes and drew more of Abylar's power into himself. Then, opening himself up to Breelyn, he pulled upon Miriel's strength also. Jaimon and Cholena were still too new, but Bakari felt their distinctive and faint presence already growing through the dragon bond.

"Bak!" Kharlia yelled.

Bakari opened his eyes as Kolo, sitting atop Sephtis, dove down toward them. But Abylar swerved just in time, almost losing Delia off his back.

Bakari stood up on the back of Abylar's neck. Kharlia looked up at him, holding on to his legs. "Bakari, your eyes!" she exclaimed. "There are swirls of blue in them."

"The power is so strong," Bakari said and then had to clench his jaw to keep from fainting. Stretching forth his hands, he shot a blue flame across the air with all the power he held. It streamed toward Kolo and enveloped both him and his dragon.

"As your master, I command you to turn away from us and pursue us no more," Bakari said, his voice booming unnaturally, echoing off the walls of the valley.

The black dragon roared and put his claws up in the air, Kolo holding on for dear life. Turning around in the air, the two were forced away, the blue flame's power still surrounding them. Bakari heard Kolo screaming as Kolo and his dragon became just a black speck in the sky over the distant mountain peaks. Then Bakari sat back down and directed Abylar to return to the top of the waterfall.

Kolo's three companions stood there, glaring at the blue dragon and its riders.

From the air, Bakari called to them. "What Kolo did is an abomination to the dragons! He took control of a dragon that was not meant for him," Bakari shouted. "You must warn the regent that Kolo is dangerous."

Kolo's men didn't say anything back. Bakari felt bad about leaving them here, but they had gotten themselves to the cave somehow and should be able to get back to Mahli that same way.

"I will return to Mahli after Alaris is at peace," Bakari said.

Two of the three men *did* bow their heads slightly to Bakari before they turned and left.

* * *

Carrying five people soon became taxing for Abylar. So he flew a few miles west from the mountains into Turg and then settled back down onto the ground. The group stayed there the rest of the night, resting and letting Abylar eat.

The next morning, Kharlia and Bakari climbed back up onto the growing dragon, his blue scales sparkling in the early morning light.

"What will happen now?" Delia said, her voice almost pleading.

Bakari tried to imagine how she must feel. She had just begun to feel the bond only to have it snatched from her grasp by Kolo.

"I don't know, Delia," Bakari said. "I am so sorry. I need to return to Alaris. There is danger there that might spill over into all the neighboring kingdoms. After taking care of that, I will go to Mahli to try to rein in Kolo. If I can free the dragon from his bond, I will return him to you."

Delia nodded, but her eyes seemed to reveal that Delia knew the odds were very slim now that she would actually become a dragon rider.

"We must return to the Oracle," Delia said, "and let him know what has happened."

"Good luck," Bakari said. "Hopefully we will meet again." Bakari's heart broke for Delia. He knew what bonding with a dragon was like. And she had been so close. He hoped she would be all right.

Abylar lifted off with Bakari and Kharlia on his back.

I'm hungry again, Abylar said to Bakari.

Bakari grinned. *Of course you are, my friend. Of course you are.*

CHAPTER THIRTY TWO

Onius rode up next to Kanzar, who was flanked by wizards dressed for a war. They were heading south, from Cassian, to attack the Chief Judge in Orr.

"You don't need to march with us, Kanzar," Onius said.

Kanzar sneered at him with a dangerous spark in his eyes. "I want to see Daymian Khouri get crushed with my own eyes."

"But you put yourself in needless danger." Onius would rather have had Kanzar stay in Cassian. It would be easier to take him down if he was separated from his cronies. But, maybe in battle, an accident could occur.

"I am not in danger." Kanzar spread his arms around him. "I am protected by the greatest wizards in Alaris, including you, my friend."

Onius just grunted.

"Anyway," Kanzar continued, "this will be easy. My spies said there were few men with the Chief Judge."

Onius almost smiled but bit his cheek instead. A messenger pigeon had arrived the night before with news from the spies. These had reached the outskirts of Orr and had seen very little evidence of any sizable army. Marco, Onius's messenger to the Chief Judge had indeed done what he was supposed to do.

Turning around on his horse, Onius surveyed the group of at least a thousand men and women marching behind them, with Alana, Kanzar's wife, in the lead. Alana did not look very happy. Seeing that she had caught Onius's eye, she rode forward to meet him. So he hung back from Kanzar.

"It's a trap," Alana said. "There is no way there are as few men as the message said."

Onius just nodded, not wanting to give away anything about the plan that he already knew of.

"He won't listen to me anymore," Alana said and then let out a deep sigh. She had returned from Corwan and had reported their losses, including the death of the Battlemaster, and Kanzar had gone wild with anger once again. He had killed two of her captains, and the bruises on the side of her face now stood as apparent evidence of Kanzar's displeasure with her.

"He won't listen to anyone," Onius added.

She directed her horse even closer to Onius. "He is obsessed and unstable, Onius," she said, lowering her voice. "He will kill us all in his ambition to be king."

As if he could hear their conversation, Kanzar turned around then, from atop his horse, and glared at Onius and Alana. Crooking his finger, he motioned for them to join him up front.

"What are you two discussing?" Kanzar asked, his eyes darting back and forth between them. "Are you plotting behind my back?"

Onius saw the nervous twitch of Kanzar's mouth and knew that their leader had almost hit his tipping point.

"If we march to Orr, we will die," Alana said, holding her head high and proud. "This mission is suicide. We need more men."

"We would have more men if you hadn't failed in Corwan!" Kanzar bellowed, his spittle hitting Alana's leather armor.

"We were surprised there," Alana said, "just like we will be in Orr." A strong battle wizard in her own right, Alana wouldn't back down.

Kanzar stopped his horse—mere inches now from Alana—and grabbed her horse's reins in his gloved hand, jerking Alana's horse to a stop.

"I am in charge here." Kanzar's face had turned red. "You will follow my orders."

Alana appeared cowed for a moment, then lifted her chin high to meet Kanzar's gaze with her steely eyes and said, "I am in charge of this battalion. As the lead battle wizard, I will not direct my soldiers to march to their deaths."

Kanzar's eyes bulged, and his jaw tightened. With blinding speed, he hit Alana in the jaw, the force almost knocking her off her horse. In an instant, power flared around her, and she threw a ball of fire at her crazed husband.

Onius directed his horse back a few steps and only observed. Two of Kanzar's guards moved their horses between the two and absorbed the blow from Alana's fireball.

Kanzar drew his sword and pointed it at Alana as he said, "Traitor."

She stood up in her stirrups and yelled back to the soldiers, "I give you a choice. You may choose to follow Kanzar and most likely meet your deaths or choose to return to Cassian while we make more informed plans."

The soldiers were confused. Conversations, then

arguments broke out among them. Onius moved back further, not wanting to get caught in Kanzar's rage.

Kanzar turned to his other wizards and said, "Bind her." Then, turning to one of his other advisers, he said, "Baylor, you are now my general and are in charge of this army."

"No. You can't do that," Alana howled. "I'm more powerful than he is."

She drew her sword and began to fight off the other wizards, who were now approaching. They seemed to be conserving their wizard strength for the upcoming battle, but they did as Kanzar commanded and tried to take Alana down to bind her.

But subduing Alana wasn't easy. She sheathed her sword and did a flip off her horse, landing on the ground as she pulled out a pair of knives and then threw them at the guards and wizards approaching her. One knife hit its mark and took the man down. The other bounced off of a guard's armor.

Sending bolts of lightning from each hand, Alana tried to take down the wizards. They went on the defensive, as if letting her tire herself out.

Then Onius saw that some of the soldiers began to turn around. Baylor, a dark-haired, stocky man, stood up higher in his stirrups and, with power bellowing from his mouth, yelled, "Anyone leaving this army will be court-martialed and either killed or sent to the dungeons."

Onius knew that this was not a normal army. Many of these men were mercenaries, here for the pay only. So they were not sure how to handle these threats.

Turning back, Onius saw one of Kanzar's wizards get his

sword inside Alana's defenses, slicing her thigh open. Blood spurted forth immediately, and she fell to the ground. Then, by forcing a bitter liquid down Alana's throat, Kanzar's men took her remaining wizard powers away.

"What do we do with her, sir?" Baylor asked Kanzar. "It is too far to go back."

"Bring her with us," Kanzar said. "She will witness the destruction of the Chief Judge and my rise to power. Then we will kill her for her treachery."

As they began moving forward again, Baylor, a level three battle wizard, now led the soldiers, and he pushed them hard.

Onius noticed that not all the wizards or soldiers in attendance seemed happy at Kanzar's capture of Alana, his own wife. Onius took a deep breath. Soon this would all be over. One way or the other.

* * *

Two days later, Onius paused with the rest of the army. They glimpsed Orr in the distance, its rounded roofs rising up over the flat, sandy ground. Dust blew in the air, making their eyes water. Kanzar drew in Onius and the rest of his council into his command tent. But there was still no sign of an approaching army.

It was late in the afternoon when Kanzar gave the order to attack the city. First, the cavalry; next, the foot soldiers; and then, the wizards—they marched down the road and to the city's gates.

All was quiet. The city looked deserted.

"Where are they?" Kanzar bellowed.

"Maybe your wife is correct," Onius said.

Kanzar turned to him, murder in his eyes. "Are you in league with that traitor?"

Onius stood his ground. He realized he might die—probably would die—in this battle, but, in doing so, he would bring Kanzar down with him. So Onius pushed Kanzar harder.

"I am not in league with her, no," Onius said. "But, Kanzar, you continue to ignore the experience of those around you." Onius stood in his wizard robes, his thin arms waving in the air as he added, "Look around you. What does common sense tell you?"

"Bind him, too," Kanzar bellowed to some nearby guards.

But they hesitated. Onius was known as Kanzar's right-hand man, a very powerful wizard in his own right, counselor to chief judges.

Onius shook his head. "No more binding, Kanzar. This is a trap."

As if to give truth to Onius's words, hundreds of soldiers rose up out of the desert sand right then and began to strike down Kanzar's army. This attack had caught them so much by surprise that hundreds were killed before Kanzar or Baylor could issue any orders.

When they finally did, chaos ensued. More and more enemy soldiers rose up from under the sand all along the road, as far back as anyone could see, the wind blowing the upturned sand into the air, creating a storm of sand, blinding Kanzar's troops.

But the attackers from Orr had thin cloths around their eyes and had swords in their hands as they swept through the ranks, taking down horses and soldiers alike. Then, over the city walls burning sand and pitch were catapulted far into Kanzar's ranks. This was followed by screams and soldiers catching fire and grabbing their faces.

In the midst of this chaos, Onius saw a lone man stand up on the city walls. Daymian Khouri, Chief Judge of Alaris.

"Surrender Kanzar," the Chief Judge called out. "Or all your men will be killed."

Kanzar glared up at his enemy. "We will not surrender," Kanzar called back. "We have a hundred soldiers to your one. We will battle to the death and will destroy your pathetic city."

Then Baylor motioned for the cavalry to ride hard into the city.

Crashing through the city gates, the cavalry began to cut down anyone they found. New hope seemed to surge through Kanzar's army, and they began to take down the Chief Judge's soldiers.

In the rear, soldiers screamed, and fireballs from wizards were being hurtled through the air. But these were not aimed toward Orr—they were from behind them. Onius turned back and then pointed.

Kanzar followed Onius's finger and roared, "A dragon!" Then Kanzar bellowed, "I will kill that boy and his dragon, once and for all!"

"I don't think that's Bakari, sir," Onius said, wonder filling his voice. "That dragon is yellow."

As the dragon flew closer, its orange and yellow scales reflecting the bright, late-afternoon sunlight, Onius saw that the rider was a woman. Her long, unbound, blond hair flowed back behind her head, revealing her pointed ears.

"An elf," remarked one of Kanzar's soldiers, fighting beside Onius and Kanzar.

Kanzar shot fire out of his hands, and the dragon swerved, its tail knocking down dozens of soldiers on the ground. So Kanzar kicked his horse hard, motioning Onius and others to follow him toward the back, to fend off this new attack. As Kanzar neared the back of his army, fire and lightning filled the sky.

His wizards threw fire at the dragon and at the attackers, but their opponents continued to push forward. At their head, Onius saw a blur of a wizard spinning, jumping, and twirling through the air, taking down dozens of soldiers.

"Alli?" Onius said softly, feeling awe as he watched her fighting skills. They were mesmerizing.

"Onius," Kanzar said, bringing him out of his stupor. "Did you know about this? Are *you* the traitor in our midst?" Dark veins stood out on his bald head, ready to burst. Turning sideways, Kanzar clobbered a man with one fist and sent out a bolt of lightning with the other, taking out a half dozen opponents.

Onius decided it was time to tell him. "Kanzar, you have lost sight of what we wanted. We talked for years of a king. A glorious king with the power to make Alaris bright again. A king that would be a beacon for the southern lands. But you took too much power to yourself."

Kanzar shook his head back and forth with rage, his breath quickening and his muscles tightening. An aura of power gathered around Kanzar. Onius braced himself for death.

But, as Kanzar brought his hands out, another voice

pierced the battlefield. "Surrender, Kanzar, and we will discuss terms."

Onius realized that it was Mericus that had roared this over the fray. He was riding on an enormous black horse. With black armor on and a black wizard cloak billowing behind him, Mericus looked like Death itself, on a rampage.

Kanzar moved toward Mericus, but Onius was still in the way. Leaning over on his horse, Kanzar put his hand on Onius's chest and, using the full force of his power, threw Onius twenty feet into the air. Onius fell hard and crumpled to the ground, his arm twisting dangerously behind his back.

Mericus continued to barrel through the melee, power crackling around him.

Kanzar had jumped off his horse now and ran with increasing speed toward Mericus, gathering power to himself.

"Mericus!" Kanzar yelled, his frustrated voice traveling with power over the entire battlefield.

Mericus threw a bolt of blue fire toward his former leader, catching Kanzar in the shoulder. Kanzar stumbled back but stayed upright, blood gushing down his arm.

Onius, breathing deeply and trying not to pass out, scooted further away from the battle. The yellow dragon flew overhead once again, orange and yellow flames pouring out of its massive jaws. Its magnificent and elegant rider flashed her own brand of magic down in quick bolts of lightning, taking out Kanzar's guards.

"I am Breelyn, protector of Elvyn and a dragon rider of all lands," she called down. "By the voice of my master, I command you to surrender now." Then Breelyn and her dragon swooped down lower, stopping in the air just over Kanzar's head.

Onius stood slowly, holding his right arm in his left hand. He stumbled forward, closer to Kanzar. Then Mericus stopped his horse beside Onius, and the two watched the exchange between Kanzar and the dragon rider with interest.

Kanzar turned his attention to the sky. "And where is your master?" he asked. "Is the boy hiding? Afraid to meet me?"

Breelyn flew up into the air and took another pass over the army and then came back around, hovering above Kanzar once again. "Bakari has other matters to attend to, but his command is still the same. Surrender now, and, as Mericus said, we can discuss terms."

The fighting slowed, and soldiers, mercenaries, and wizards alike were looking at Kanzar for his answer. The field became eerily quiet, with only the sounds of the wind-blown sand and the flap of the dragon's wings filling the air.

Onius studied Kanzar's body language and his stomach fell. The High Wizard would never surrender.

Flicking his wrist, Kanzar drew forth an enormous amount of power and, with a flash of light, sent fire hurtling toward Breelyn and her dragon.

Out of nowhere, Onius heard a loud roar and felt a gust of wind blow between the ground and the sky, pushing Kanzar's attacking fire away from the dragon and out into the empty air. The crowd looked up in the sky, gasping and pointing.

"Another dragon?" Onius mumbled, wondering where Bakari was finding them all.

Flying over them and joining Breelyn was a green dragon,

smaller than the first. On its back was a young man, his long, black hair wrapped in a ponytail, flying out behind him.

"I am Jaimon Schafer from Quentis," he said to Breelyn.

"Welcome, Dragon Rider." The elf woman laughed, her voice melodically filling the air around them.

Kanzar, however, wasn't done. "Attack!" he ordered, gathering more power and then flinging it at the new dragon. It swerved, the fire catching only the tip of its tail.

In the rising cacophony, Onius heard a familiar woman's voice.

"Onius, drop to the ground."

He spun around.

"Now!" Alli said.

Onius obeyed and went down on all fours, almost falling to the ground as the pain flared in his arm. With wizard robes swirling around her and a sword in her hand, Alli ran at full speed toward Onius and jumped up on Onius's back, using it as a springboard to launch herself ten feet into the air. Flipping twice in the air, she came back down, her sword in front of her, and landed on Kanzar, bashing his head with her sword hilt, and he collapsed to the ground.

Mericus rode up next to Alli. "You took all the fun out of it." He smiled wickedly at Alli.

As Onius saw their eyes lock on to each other, he wondered what sort of relationship Alli and Mericus held there.

"I wanted to put the other end of the sword in him," Alli said, a grim look on her face, "but I am tired of all the violence. This needs to stop."

Mericus nodded as if he understood her frustration.

Turning to the crowd, he waved his sword in the air and yelled, "This battle is over! Round up Kanzar's troops. We march back to Cassian."

The Chief Judge limped over to join the two wizards, his sword hanging down in his right hand. "Who put you in charge, Mericus?"

The two men glared at each other for a moment.

Then the two dragons flew overhead once again, and Breelyn called down to the group, "Settle your differences later, men. Mericus is right; we must march back to Cassian. Bakari will meet us there."

The Chief Judge signaled to his troops, and Mericus rode out in front of his own.

"Alli," Onius said, coming forward, "Gorn would be pleased with you."

The young battle wizard smiled back and took a deep breath. "I was just getting started."

Onius laughed. "Speaking of Gorn, do you know where he is?"

"Last time I saw him, he was still in Celestar, but..." Alli grew serious. "Bakari said many of the guardians were killed, and I don't know if Gorn has survived or not."

"He is a tough old wizard," Onius said.

Soon Kanzar's soldiers and wizards were rounded up, and Onius found himself standing alone for a strange moment, wondering what would happen now. Kanzar was caught, but the decision of who would be the leader of Alaris had still not been made. As Onius surveyed the field of battle and picked out the grave faces of both Mericus and Daymian, a deep sigh escaped his lips. His greatest work as counselor may just be beginning.

"Daymian," Onius called to his old friend, "we have much to talk about."

CHAPTER THIRTY THREE

Bakari and Kharlia flew on Abylar over the western fields and farms of Alaris, seeing the sprawling city of Cassian in the distance. The beginning of winter was just around the corner, and acres of dried cornstalks and hay lay across the land.

Through the bond, Bakari communicated with Breelyn and Miriel and learned what had occurred between the armies of Cassian and Orr. The first of those armies would be arriving soon in Cassian.

What should I do? he asked Abylar.

What you must do, Bakari, Abylar answered. *It is your responsibility to establish peace.*

But how? I am just a boy. Bakari was feeling the weight of the day begin to settle on his shoulders.

You are not a boy. You are a dragon rider! Abylar roared and then dove down closer to the ground.

Just north of Cassian, Bakari spied a large group approaching the city. He bonded closer with Abylar to see through the dragon's eyes. It was Roland, riding with a group of wizards, and a trail of apprentices behind him. Abylar circled twice, and then Bakari directed Abylar lower.

"Roland!" Bakari yelled down toward the ground.

Roland's face split into a grin. Pushing the hair out of his eyes, he turned his neck up at his friend. "Bak!"

"What are you doing here?" Bakari asked.

"I was convinced by members of the Council that I shouldn't miss the party." He laughed. "Why don't you come down here so we can talk like normal men? It's quite intimidating to have you up on that dragon of yours."

Abylar roared, and Bakari saw fear cross the faces of those on the ground.

"See you in Cassian, Roland." Bakari waved, and Abylar flew back up higher in the air, resuming their short flight toward the capital city. Looking south, Bakari glimpsed the first line of soldiers approaching in the distance. Those on horses were riding in front, while the soldiers on foot dragged endlessly into the distance. In the air above the soldiers flew Breelyn and Jaimon on their dragons. Bakari grinned, and Abylar flew to join them.

To the apparent amazement of all those on the ground, the three dragons—blue, yellow, and green—circled around and greeted one another, playing in the air. Cholena and Miriel both seemed to vie for Abylar's attention.

"Abylar!" shrieked Kharlia, holding on tightly behind Bakari as the dragon made a high loop into the sky. "I'm going to fall off," she told Bakari.

Bakari patted his dragon on the side and asked him to settle down.

You're no fun! Abylar said.

You can play after we land.

Excitement grew through the bond. It was hard for Bakari to remember sometimes how young their dragons were. Highly intelligent and powerful with their minds, their bodies were only like children's, and each dragon still held the appetite and playfulness of a child.

"Bakari," Jaimon called to him through the air, his ponytail blowing in the wind behind him. "This is so wonderful." Jaimon spread his arms to either side, only holding on with his knees and then added, "I'm actually flying."

Bakari heard Kharlia laughing behind him. What a joyous sound it was. But now he had to concentrate on the task at hand.

Soon the dragons reached Cassian, and they landed outside of the city gates. Bakari had Kharlia move off to the side to a spot of relative safety. He didn't know how this would play out, and he didn't want Kharlia in any crossfire.

As the army approached, Bakari stood at the opening of the gate, with Breelyn and Jaimon on either side. Bakari realized that they were three people with no outward similarities—one, a blond elf woman; one, a dark-skinned young man from Alaris, with Mahli heritage; and one, a young man from Quentis, with a dark ponytail hanging down to his waist. Their three dragons stood next to each of them—their connection to each other.

"Dragon Riders." Bakari grabbed the others' attention with a soft voice and a nod of his head. "Be ready."

Bakari stood up straighter, brushing his colorful robes with his hands and drew additional confidence from Abylar's strength. When he looked at Breelyn and Jaimon, to either side of himself, they both smiled and gave a slight nod of their heads back to him. He was their master, and they would follow his lead.

The first group to approach consisted of the Chief Judge,

Onius, Mericus, Alli, and Azeem. The Chief Judge's face was hard for Bakari to read, but Onius appeared exhausted. Mericus, in his usual black robes, held an air of confidence. Alli smiled at Bak and seemed ready to fight, as always, and Azeem, a gentleman Bakari had never met but knew by reputation, appeared nervous.

Then Bakari saw Kanzar, chained up tight, standing behind the first group, his eyes blazing with hatred for everyone.

"Dragon Rider," Kanzar spat. "So you are behind my defeat, it seems."

Bakari held back a stronger retort and only said, "We come in peace."

"The soldiers lying on the ground," Kanzar said, "and their families might think otherwise." Kanzar flexed his muscles against his bonds.

Bakari knew Kanzar could use his power to break free, but Kanzar seemed to understand that, with all the other wizards' power around him, he would not get far. Bakari guessed, however, that at some point, it would come down to that.

"Their blood is on your hands, Kanzar," Bakari said. "From the moment you tried to usurp the authority of the rightful government of Alaris, all these deaths became your doing. That is why you are not fit to be king."

"And you are?" Kanzar pushed against his captors, but they held him tight. "Is that your game, Dragon Rider, to become the Dragon King?"

Bakari's mind reeled and he tried not to stumble backward. Kanzar's accusation had hit closer to home than he realized. Was Bakari the prophesied one? The Dragon King? Bakari knew that he may be, but not right now, and definitely not the King of Alaris.

Before Bakari could say anything more, another group of people approached from inside the city, behind him and the dragon riders.

"Roland Tyre." Kanzar saw the young man in the lead and then laughed. "I have heard—and now see—you have made quite the name for yourself." Kanzar's former council members stood with Roland, as well as a group of apprentices, all looking ready to fight.

"I tried to stay out of these affairs, Kanzar," Roland said. "I have been quite clear that I don't care whether we have a king or a chief judge." He turned his attention to Daymian and nodded his head at the Chief Judge as he said, "No offense to your leadership, sir."

The Chief Judge nodded back, a slight smile cracking his otherwise stoic expression. "So," the Chief Judge said, "what is your intention here?"

"Yes," Kanzar said. "What is your intention here, young wizard? Have you had a change of mind? Or, do you want to rule Alaris, also, along with Bakari, Onius, and Mericus? The list is growing longer."

Roland shook his head. "I represent the Citadel."

"How dare you?" Kanzar's eyes bulged.

Roland stepped forward, and a glow surrounded him. "You have no idea what I would dare do, Kanzar. Once you declared your intent to be a king, you forfeited your authority as the High Wizard. The leadership of the Citadel must be separate from the government of Alaris. The Citadel is bigger than Alaris; we represent many lands."

Bakari wondered what Roland was saying.

"In front of all these witnesses," Roland continued in a strong voice, "I declare myself now the High Wizard and ruler of the Citadel." Roland stood forth with power, his golden wizard robes swaying around him in the breeze. Looking young but regal, he continued, "I further declare the Citadel to be separate from Alaris—open to wizards and apprentices of all lands, wherever they may be from."

The crowd was quiet, as if no one knew who should speak, but Bakari suspected they were all thinking the same. Suddenly, the Chief Judge, Mericus, and Onius all spoke at once. But Onius's voice prevailed as the loudest.

"You have no right to declare yourself as being above the law of the land, Roland," Onius said, his voice growing louder. "Gosh, boy, you were only an apprentice a few months ago. What makes you think you can lead the Citadel?"

Roland looked over at Bakari, who had stayed silent so far during Roland's declaration. To Bakari, something in all of this seemed right.

"In the past," Roland continued, as if teaching all present, "the leader of the Citadel was someone that was not from any one discipline of magic, but from all three. A leader who not only held magical power but was magic itself. That is how they always recognized who their leader should be. I declare today, in front of the Wizard Council and all other wizards and apprentices present, that I AM MAGIC." He paused to let the fact sink in. "And, by virtue of that fact, I do officially declare myself the High Wizard."

Onius held his hand up, to speak again, but Roland overrode him.

"I know your worries," Roland continued, "about me not being beholden to the laws of this land or to—what I surmise will soon be—a king of Alaris." He gazed at them, one at a time, Onius, Daymian, and Mericus, and then actually winked at Alli, who jumped in surprise. Then Roland said, "But, with my authority, I *will* bow to one man."

Roland turned toward Bakari and knelt down on one knee, staring up into his eyes. Bakari's stomach churned—he wasn't ready for this. Bakari realized what Roland was about to do, and, even though Bakari didn't want this, he accepted it. In the blink of an eye, as Bakari gazed deeply into his friend's eyes, it was as if Roland's soul was laid bare for him to discern. With all of Roland's arrogance and greed for power, Bakari could see that his soul was good.

"I yield myself," Roland continued, "and by virtue of my role as High Wizard do also submit all wizards of this land to the authority of Bakari, Dragon Rider, and now also named the High Dragon King." Power filled the air, and a brief silence blanketed all present—but only for a brief moment.

Then chaos broke out.

Kanzar and his other captured renegade wizards started yelling and building up their power. And Bakari saw Onius glare at Roland, but Onius kept his mouth closed.

Then Bakari put his hand forward and raised Roland from the ground. "You have quite the flair for dramatics, Roland."

Roland laughed. "Hey, I'm not the one flying around on a dragon."

Bakari raised his eyebrows and turned his hand toward the group in front of him. "And what did you hope to accomplish by this display?"

"To give you a chance to show everyone who you really are, Bak," Roland said.

Bakari nodded to Roland, then turned to the other dragon riders and motioned for them to mount their dragons. Kharlia stepped forward, but as much as Bakari wanted her with him, he needed to do this with the dragon riders alone. He motioned her back to safety.

Kharlia growled her displeasure but did Bakari's bidding nevertheless and stood watching Bakari as he lifted up into the air with the other dragon riders.

*   *   *

Onius shook his head and tried to clear his thinking. Events were moving faster than he had ever anticipated. *Roland as High Wizard and Bakari as a Dragon King*; the thoughts were almost beyond his comprehension.

Looking around him arguments ensued and fights broke out on the ground, as the three dragons lifted up into the sky and began circling around the gathering—blue, yellow, and green.

Then Kanzar roared and broke free of his captors. Daymian was standing close by him, so Kanzar ripped into the Chief Judge first, slicing his arm with a blade of fire and punching him hard in the chest.

"This is all your fault!" Kanzar yelled. "If you had just stepped down, none of this would have happened." Then his rage exploded into bursts of fire around himself.

Alana was standing next to him, and she put a hand on his arm to stop him. He turned to her and blasted her with fire, throwing his wife into a crumpled heap on the ground. Onius doubted Alana would ever get up again. Four of Kanzar's other captured wizards broke free and joined in his battle.

Onius looked up at the sound of a mighty roar. Blue, yellow, and green—the dragons began moving faster and faster in the sky. The wind built up, making it harder for people to stand straight on the ground.

Kanzar turned back to the Chief Judge, but Mericus placed himself as a shield between the two. Pushing his hands out in front of him, Mericus tried to push Kanzar back with a pulse of air, but Mericus was not a battle wizard nor as strong as Kanzar. So the Chief Judge moved out of the way, to safety.

Onius turned and battled Kanzar's other wizards, who had somehow gotten hold of swords. Back and forth they dueled, but he was working with one arm and was exhausted beyond all reason. A cut here and a cut there. His body was going to give out soon.

Alli joined in and leaped onto the back of one of the wizards, knocking him to the ground. Then, sliding under another wizard, she lifted him up into the air and spun him around, knocking over other wizards who came too close to the young battle wizard. Onius shook his head slightly. *Did that woman ever get tired?*

The blue, yellow, and green streaks now swirled together, forming a turquoise blur across the sky outside of Cassian. Many of its citizens stood on their housetops and walls, watching the spectacle. Bakari put forth his hand and drew power from each dragon—physically discernible to those below by a blur of light. Onius made his way toward Kanzar, blood still dripping down his arm. Kanzar was sweating and tiring with all the fighting, but he held incredible strength. Kanzar punched out toward Onius, so the counselor didn't have time to move. He felt something crack in his ribs, and he made an awful noise and fell down.

Alli finished off the other wizards, while Mericus pushed himself between Kanzar and Onius.

"You, again!" Kanzar bellowed.

Mericus brought a sword around and thrust it toward the crazed wizard. But, with a flick of Kanzar's hand, the sword went flying, landing at the feet of Daymian. The Chief Judge picked it up and advanced on Kanzar instead.

"No, Daymian," Onius yelled. "You can't beat him."

"Shut up, Onius," Kanzar said, turning to his former friend. "You are the biggest traitor of all. Helping me to plan this for years, then, at the end, you scurry back to your pathetic judge. Serving him made you weak." He stepped hard on Onius's chest and crushed it further.

Onius screamed out in agony. He tried to breathe but couldn't get a full breath of air— and his mind began to grow dark. He used all the magic at his disposal to stay alive.

The wind picked up more as the dragons continued to spin around the group. Onius watched Bakari reach inside his leather pack and pull out two wooden discs. Power from his hand seemed to gather around the disc themselves. Then Bakari threw them down and over the crowd.

The discs spun down in a wide arc, swirls of turquoise power following in their wake. They spun down and flew straight through the group of soldiers.

Onius's pain grew deeper as his magic suddenly drained away. By the look of others around him, all the wizards had somehow lost their powers. With awe he looked up at Bakari.

Hearing an animalistic growl, Onius turned his attention back to the ground around him. Daymian Khouri did not hold any powers but had a sword in his hand, and it was already in motion.

Kanzar stepped back, off of Onius's crushed body, and Mericus let his hands fall to his sides, but Daymian's sword continued to move. Without the ability or time to block it, Kanzar opened his eyes wider as Daymian plunged the sharp end of the sword deep into the former High Wizard's chest, driving its tip through his chest and out of the back side. Kanzar wobbled for an instant. Then his eyes froze and his body fell backward to the ground, dead.

Onius tried to get up on his knees, but he fell back down again. Bakari's young friend Kharlia ran to his side, trying to offer help. Silence filled the air, and the two of them looked up into the sky.

Bakari had jumped off of Abylar while the dragon was still in the air and, with the power he held, pulled the discs back to himself and continued to float toward the ground, landing next to Roland.

"Talk about dramatic," Roland mumbled next to Bakari, having stayed out of most of the fight himself. "How did you do that?"

Onius tried desperately to push the blackness from overcoming his mind. He, too, was interested in the answer that Roland sought.

Bakari's cheeks reddened. "The power of the spirit, Roland, the fourth power, the power to bind all other powers. It is the power the dragons hold. With it, I blocked all the wizards from using their powers."

The power of the spirit! Onius had never imagined such power. He closed his eyes and let Kharlia try to tend his wounds. Her touch was gentle and her heart was good, but Onius feared he would not live out the day—let alone the next hour.

CHAPTER THIRTY FOUR

Roland stood next to Alli and, with affection, looked down at Onius. The old counselor's breathing was labored, and blood dripped from the corners of his mouth. Kharlia had bandaged him up and given him some sedative to dull the pain. Onius reached up one bony arm toward Roland.

"You were a good apprentice," Onius whispered. "Be a good wizard and High Wizard also."

Roland knelt down next to him. "I can heal you, Onius."

Onius shook his head. "It's my time. This is an era of change. My season of influence is over." His sentences were short, his breathing growing shallower with each breath.

Roland turned his head to watch Daymian limp up next to them, blood and dirt covering his armor. "Counselor," he said, his voice thick with emotion, "thank you for all you have done."

"I wish I could've done more," Onius said. "I wish Kanzar wouldn't have gotten this far."

"So do we all, old friend." Daymian knelt down and grasped his old counselor's hand.

Onius took a breath, smiled briefly, and then closed his eyes. One last breath followed, and then Onius Neeland, mighty counselor wizard to three chief judges, passed on.

Roland closed his eyes for a moment. He felt more fondness for his old master than he had shown. The wisdom of Onius would be missed. As Roland stood back up, he reached over and helped the Chief Judge to his feet.

The group stood silent for a moment, each seeming to give personal thought to the impact that the famous wizard had had on their lives.

Alli, watching from a few feet away, caught Roland's eye and moved closer. He put his arm around her and drew her in nearer to himself. Her small body molded into his.

Daymian took a step back, toward Mericus who had also been watching the exchange, and Roland leaned closer to listen.

"Thank you for saving my life." Daymian's eyes still glistened from losing his old friend and counselor. "I may have misjudged you."

"I have done things I am not proud of, Daymian," Mericus admitted, wiping at some blood on his outer armor. "And I admit that I may have received my judgeship from Kanzar stretching the law."

"And you took advantage of the situation," Daymian added, his face grim.

Mericus nodded. "But," he added, putting his finger up in the air, "Kanzar pushed me too far, and I changed sides."

"Have you?" Daymian said, and Roland saw anger flash across Daymian's face.

"What are you implying?" Mericus stood dressed in black, his face a mask of emotions. "I have been doing all I can for Alaris since the time I made my decision to leave Kanzar's employ. Don't you believe in redemption, Chief Judge? Don't you believe a man can change?"

Without replying to these questions, Daymian asked one of his own. "Mericus, you just referred to me as *Chief Judge*.

Does that mean you still recognize my leadership?"

Mericus thought for a moment.

Then, with a swipe of his arm toward Roland, Mericus answered, "Our friend Roland, here, just pledged himself and all of the wizards to the Dragon King. But, as a judge, my accounting should be to you. That puts me in a very difficult situation. I do indeed proclaim my allegiance to Bakari as High King through Roland, but Alaris needs a king, too, sir. No disrespect to your leadership, but, as Onius said with his last breaths, this is a time of change."

"And you would be that king?" Daymian let out a long breath.

Mericus only nodded.

Then Roland took a step forward, to put forth a plan. "Sirs, the original agreement was to put the choice to a vote. As High Wizard, I will monitor the voting. With the help of the dragon riders, we can gather each city's votes in a manner of days and get the answer quickly. The worst thing for Alaris would be to have no leadership."

Daymian put his hand on Roland's arm. "The counselor in you still shines through, Roland. Onius did a good job of teaching you. I will honor those terms as I did before."

"As will I," Mericus agreed.

Then the Chief Judge, along with the help of Mericus, took charge of gathering the troops back into Cassian, sorting through who would be let go and who needed to be held and tried in court for crimes. Whether a king or chief judge prevailed in Alaris, Roland knew that it would still take some time for events to be settled.

* * *

Bakari knew that soon the riders would begin to disperse across the country, to gather the vote and learn the will of the people for the future of Alaris. So Kharlia had decided to stay in Cassian and help tend the injuries from the battle. He was moved once again by her compassion and desire to help others.

Bakari saw Roland walking over to him and the dragon riders with Alli next to him. So Bakari pulled Roland and Alli aside.

"I have a small gift for you, Roland," Bakari said. Roland raised his brows but said nothing.

"How would you like to ride on a dragon?" Bakari motioned toward Abylar.

Roland opened his mouth but didn't seem to know what to say.

"As a friend and High Wizard," Bakari clarified. "Not as a dragon rider."

"I guess I can't have everything, huh?" Roland winked at Bakari.

"No, but close," Bakari said. "How about I take you and Alli up on Abylar and back to the Citadel? Roland, you need to form a new Council."

"And I do need a battle wizard to teach the apprentices." Roland winked at Alli.

Bakari noticed Alli look over at Mericus briefly; Roland followed her gaze also, and his lips tightened. Alli seemed to come to a quick decision and turned back to Bakari and Roland.

"I…I guess I could manage being around you for a while,"

Alli said to Roland. Then her pouting lips turned up into a full grin. "But only if I am made Battlemaster."

"Done." Roland laughed and took a deep breath. "This is going to be fun!"

All three laughed as they walked back over to Abylar. Bakari excused himself for a moment and moved toward Kharlia.

Kharlia reached out and held Bakari's hand. "I'm so proud of you, Bak."

Bakari looked down in embarrassment. Kharlia reached over, and putting a finger under his chin, raised it back up. She leaned in and gave him a small kiss on the lips.

Bakari's stomach fluttered and his heart raced. "Will you be all right here, Kharlia?"

Kharlia's eyes flashed. "I can survive without you, Bak." Then she softened her tone. "But not for long. Hurry back, please."

Bakari gave her a hug and turned to walk back to Abylar. After a few steps, he turned around halfway. "You really are amazing, Kharlia."

Her grin stretched wide, and she wiped a tear from her eye and waved for him to get going.

Reaching Abylar, Bakari seated himself first. Then Alli and Roland climbed up behind him.

"Hold on tight!" Bakari yelled over his shoulder. Then, to Abylar, he instructed, *Have as much fun as you want, my friend.*

Soon after taking off, Abylar flew straight up and turned hard, at full speed, until they were facing north. Roland was screaming—at first, with obvious fear, then with apparent delight. Then Bakari heard Roland groaning as if he was feeling sick.

So Bakari asked Abylar to slow down.

"What's the matter, High Wizard?" Alli purred over her shoulder. "Stomach can't take the heights?"

Bakari turned in his seat and saw that Roland's face had turned pale.

"If you want to know," Roland said, "I didn't eat much today, and I am hungry. It is so wonderful—seeing Alaris from so high—but now my stomach is roiling with discomfort. It isn't fair, Bakari. I don't see you getting sick."

Bakari just laughed and enjoyed the freedom of flying over the land on his dragon.

Soon the Citadel became visible as a small speck in the distance.

Alli pointed at something above the Citadel. "Bakari, what is that?"

Bakari peered closer, pulled on the dragon's powers, and then groaned.

"It's Kolo and his abomination." His words turned hard.

As they came closer, Bakari saw that Kolo and his dragon were flying around the top of the Citadel. Then Sephtis Kerboros breathed out flames of black fire down on the Citadel, bursting through its roof and burning many of the top floors.

Abylar! Fly faster, Bakari directed the dragon.

Coming up to Kolo and his dragon, Abylar reached his claws out toward the other dragon, which was now almost all black.

Sephtis screamed, and Kolo turned to Bakari and said, "I am freeing him."

"Who?" Bakari asked. "Who are you freeing, Kolo?"

"The man that gave me this dragon," he said. "The most powerful man alive."

Sephtis blew out more flames of black fire, and the men and women of the Citadel began to scatter out of the building.

Roland groaned, as if his stomach had turned over again. But Bakari guessed that it was not from the flight but from the realization of what was happening.

"The Chameleon," Roland yelled to Bakari. "He intends to free the Chameleon from the dungeon. I guess we underestimated his power."

Now it was Bakari's turn to groan. He had indeed underestimated the man, but he was in such a hurry to find the other dragons and settle the war that he hadn't thought clearly regarding the dangerous man.

The black flames of Sephtis went deeper, toward the Citadel's dungeons. Men and women continued to run out of the building and into the practice yards as dark black smoke billowed from the center of the Citadel.

Abylar dove for Sephtis again, knocked him to the side, for Abylar's strength was twice that of the younger dragon's.

"Bak, can you reach his mind?" Roland asked.

Bakari closed his eyes, trying for a brief moment. There was an evil barrier blocking the dragon's mind. He pushed on it further, but the mind of Sephtis made him sick to touch. He shook his head. "There is too much evil there. Kolo controls him with the power of the Chameleon."

Bakari directed Abylar to the ground, and they landed fast and hard.

"I need you two off." With this command, Bakari almost threw off Roland and Alli. "I need all my attention on Sephtis."

The dragon and Bakari rose back up in the air.

Circling the black dragon, Abylar dove in for another attack. At the last minute, Sephtis rolled to the side, Kolo barely staying on. But Abylar's claws scraped its side. Then Kolo brought his dragon back around and, with surprising agility, came up under Abylar, butting his head into Abylar's stomach.

The force of this blow caused Bakari to lose his balance, and he began to tip. Throwing up a wall of air, he pushed against it and righted himself once again. Back and forth, the two dragons screeched and roared, with the black one spitting out more black flames down into the center of the Citadel any chance that he got.

* * *

My Citadel! Roland thought, pulling Alli forward with him.

They ran up outside stairs to a balcony portion of the Citadel that was not burning yet. Standing as close as possible to where the dragons were fighting, Roland and Alli brought forth streams of fire, aimed directly at the black dragon's belly. Roaring, it turned toward them. But, as it did, Abylar reached down from above and dug his claws into Sephtis's fresh scales. Sephtis wailed and flapped his enormous black wings harder in an attempt to get away from Abylar. Then Sephtis flew straight up in the air, Kolo barely hanging on.

A deep rumble from under the ground made the Citadel's

walls shake. Then they heard a loud shriek emerge from deep inside the underground rooms. Roland wondered what might happen if all the strange magical artifacts got loose. He realized that he might not have to wonder for long.

A white billow of smoke rose from the depths. Then Roland heard voices, externally and internally. Alli covered her ears, shaking her head, and Roland knew full well what those voices could do to a person.

The voices eventually stopped, and Roland grabbed Alli's hand. "We need to fight together."

Alli nodded her head. "We are two of the most powerful wizards around; an evil dragon shouldn't be a problem for us."

Roland knew she was boasting as a means of coping with the situation, but he also knew that their powers together could indeed rival that of a newly hatched dragon.

Roland and Alli gathered their significant strength and signaled to Bakari that they were ready for one final strike.

Bakari flew down closer to the two, and power crackled in the air around him. Roland saw Bakari's irises turn blue once again, and then he nodded to Roland. All at once, the three young but now powerful wizards threw their combined force toward the black dragon, hitting him over and over, in the chest, stomach, tail, and face.

Fire, wind, and lightning tore into the evil dragon. Sephtis faltered, trying to flap his wings to stay aloft.

Roland reached deep into the recesses of his own mind, where he wanted to never go again, where only magic existed. This is where he had found his redemption in the dungeon of the citadel. He could feel the artifacts, down under the Citadel, and he felt the Chameleon emerging. Then he sensed Bakari's mind and even that of his dragon. He could see sparks of light in the darkness of the magic stream. Bright flares that represented Bakari, Alli, and Abylar.

I WILL NOT LOSE THE CITADEL!

Roland grabbed hold once again of the cylinder in his pocket and then let it loose. A dark, black power emerged. Wrestling with this power for a few moments, Roland gained control and then tossed the cylinder high up into the air, trails of black smoke flying toward the black dragon. The cylinder hit the dragon and enveloped him. Sephtis bucked and Kolo went flying through the air, falling hundreds of feet down to his death in the midst of the burning Citadel. The dragon turned to midnight black and then began to break into a million pieces.

Suddenly, Roland felt Alli grab his arm and slap his face.

"Roland. Come back," she screamed at him.

Roland felt the pull of Alli's voice and let go of the dark, black power. Looking up into the sky they watched Sephtis continue to explode. Roland sank to his knees. As he did so, he heard a loud roar from deep below.

Out of the destruction at the center of the Citadel, from deep down underneath it, an immense black dragon arose, flying straight up into the air. It swooped back down lower and glared at Roland. Then, with a loud roar, it sent fire rushing out of its great mouth.

Alli hastily threw up a barrier of air that blocked all of the fire and most of the heat. Still, she and Roland turned their faces away, but not before Roland saw the yellow eyes of the evil dragon.

"The Chameleon," Roland screamed to Bakari.

But Bakari was too far away to hear him.

Roland watched his friend try to race back toward the new black dragon, but Abylar was too tired.

With one final roar, the Chameleon—in the guise of the dragon, turned and flew off east as speedily as he could.

As Abylar landed on a stone patio nearby, it groaned with his weight. Then Bakari came running over to Roland and Alli.

"It's him, isn't it?" Bakari asked.

Roland put his hands on his knees, trying to catch his breath, and nodded his head. "Yes, the Chameleon has now taken the form of the black dragon."

"He could be very dangerous," Bakari said.

"We should go after them." Alli pointed east.

Bakari shook his head and said, "No. We need the other dragon riders with us. First, we need to settle the peace in Alaris; and then, we will take care of the Chameleon." Turning to Roland, he asked, "What was that power you used to destroy Sephtis? It felt *evil*."

"It was evil," Roland said. "Sometimes you have to fight evil with evil."

"Just be careful, Roland. Be very careful." Bakari looked like he wanted to say more, but he didn't.

Alli harrumphed. "He doesn't know how to be careful," she said, moving up closer to Roland. "But I will stay here and make sure he doesn't get into any trouble, even though our new High Wizard does seem to have a flair for dramatics."

"What happened to Kolo, the dragon's rider?" Bakari asked Roland.

Roland shook his head. "He fell from the sky. I don't think anyone could have survived that fall."

"I will need to inform his father." Bakari said sadly. "Greed killed Kolo, but his father will still grieve for him. Find the body if you can and have it sent to Mahli."

"Sure." Roland agreed.

"I will return to the Citadel after the king question is settled," Bakari said to Roland. "Then we need to discuss the terms of your oath and allegiance to me."

"I knew that moment would come back to haunt me." Roland patted Bakari on the back. "Just remember, Bak, who is more powerful."

Abylar roared, and Roland turned his head to the growing beast.

"Remember, I have a few dragons as my friends now, Roland." Bakari laughed.

Roland rolled his eyes. "I will begin to research how to rid this world of the Chameleon. I don't think he is done causing trouble yet."

Bakari jumped back on Abylar. "Let us help, Roland. The purpose of the dragon riders is to help establish peace: Alaris today, the Chameleon tomorrow. We will have peace again." With a wave of his hand, the young Dragon King flew off into the air. Roland knew that there was one other place Bakari needed to visit.

CHAPTER THIRTY FIVE

Four days later, Bakari stood outside the city of Celestar. Breelyn and Jaimon had just landed with their dragons and were walking toward him. In the background, all three dragons flew off together now, over the Elvyn Forest, looking for something to eat. Their colors of blue, green and yellow forming a spectacular sight in the clear sky.

After the dragons flew out of view, the three dragon riders looked back down at the ground in front of them. Bakari pondered over the rows of freshly dug graves that stood only a few feet from them. Then Gorn and another man walked up next to the three dragon riders.

"Welcome back, Bakari," Gorn said. The old battle wizard appeared more worn now and walked with a limp. "This is Erryl's father, Derek." He motioned a hand toward the thin man standing next to him.

"Pleased to meet you, sir." Bakari put forth his hand to shake the hand of the father of his friend. He vowed that the sacrifice of the guardians would never be forgotten.

"Breelyn," Gorn said, nodding his head to the elf, "I see you have picked up a dragon also."

"This is Jaimon," Bakari said, introducing the youngest dragon rider.

Gorn shook his head. "And three of you are dragon riders. I would have never believed it. Will there be more?"

Bakari thought of Kolo and Sephtis. *What a tragedy to lose a dragon so soon.* "I do have a feeling that there may be one more, far to the north," Bakari said.

There was a calm silence for a moment, then Derek turned to Bakari. "My son, Erryl thought very highly of you, Dragon Rider."

"And I, him." Bakari's words were thick with emotion. He turned back toward the graves and thought about his young friend.

Erryl had been so excited to learn and to see the dragon that the guardian had helped to bring forth. Listening to Abylar's call from the Dragon Orb he had helped to find Bakari. From what Bakari had heard, in the end, this young man had defied the crazed governor of Silla and held to his principles as a guardian.

"He will be missed," Bakari said. "Anything you need here in Silla. Anything at all. You let me know. Erryl Close will live on as a hero to all of Alaris. I will make sure of that." Bakari wiped his eyes on his sleeve and then hesitated a moment, remembering the book Erryl was studying and wondering if he should say something.

But Gorn put his hand on Bakari's arm and said, "The book? You are wondering about the book?"

Bakari nodded.

"Erryl had told me where to find it," Gorn said. "I have been studying it, and, though I don't pretend to understand it all, it does have a few surprises." He raised his eyebrows at Bakari.

"About me," Bakari said, feeling depressed.

Gorn dropped his voice so those outside of the dragon

riders and Erryl's father couldn't hear him. "It seems, Dragon Rider, that you are meant to be a king."

Breelyn spoke up before Bakari could answer. "It has already been declared, in Cassian. Roland Tyre, newly elevated High Wizard, declared his allegiance to no other but Bakari, the Dragon King."

Gorn's face seemed troubled. "And Alaris? Who rules our land now?"

The three dragon riders glanced at one another. They had been out tallying votes for the last few days. The people of Alaris had taken it seriously and the majority had voted their desire.

Breelyn spoke for all of them. "It seems that Alaris will have a new king, sir."

Gorn held his lips together tightly. Then he said, "So Kanzar will get his way, it seems. What about the Chief Judge? What will happen to him now?"

"Kanzar is dead, and Onius is dead," Jaimon said, speaking up for the first time, his voice sounding higher and more timid than the other riders. "And Mericus will be the new king of Alaris."

Gorn's face grew gray with a flash of anger. "But Mericus was one of Kanzar's wizards. Surely the Chief Judge would not stand for this."

"Mericus proved himself worthy, Gorn. He has changed," Bakari said. "The Chief Judge and Mericus came to terms, agreeing to abide by a vote of the people. And the people want a king."

"But you..." Gorn paced around and appeared confused.

Bakari felt self-conscious, for this would be the first time that he would acknowledge it himself. "Each land will continue to have a king. But, as leader of the dragon riders, I will need to be proclaimed by each kingdom as High Dragon King of the western lands."

Gorn was silent.

Bakari could feel his face burning. "I never asked for this, Gorn," Bakari said in almost a whisper. "I only wanted to be a scholar and pass on the knowledge I gained to others."

Gorn nodded and seemed to think for a moment. "Then, good luck to you, Dragon King. For, not wanting it makes you a greater king than most would be. The duty will be heavy at times, but there are many who want to see peace in the land. If you can be the means of that, you will indeed be known as a great king."

Bakari's gaze was drawn back to the graves. He walked over to them by himself. He knelt down and touched the dirt, letting his tears fall to the ground. It was hard for Bakari to believe how wicked some people could be. He shook his head at the thought of Ellian, the governor of Silla, Kanzar, and Kolo. Bakari wondered how a young man like himself, barely sixteen years old, could keep the peace.

His thoughts moved to Kharlia, still in Cassian. With so many hurt in the battle and the loss of many wizards—either from the conflict or from treason, her skills with herbs and healing were making a difference. He missed her greatly and had promised to return soon. Bakari let out a great sigh. *At least she is safe where she is at now!*

After another moment by himself, he stood up straight

with a new resolve. He looked each of the other dragon riders firmly in the eye. The dragons returned, flying over the edge of the Elvyn Forest. Bakari took strength from both their physical presence and through the magical bond.

"Dragon Riders," Bakari said firmly, "mount up. We fly together. Peace will yet prevail."

# # #

Read THE DRAGON KING,
book III in The Alaris Chronicles
to continue the magical adventures of
Bakari, Alli, and Roland.
Coming Summer 2017

About the Author

Mike was born in California and has lived in multiple states from the west coast to the east coast. He cannot remember a time when he wasn't reading a book. At school, home, on vacation, at work at lunch time, and yes even a few pages in the car (at times when he just couldn't put that great book down). Though he has read all sorts of genres he has always been drawn to fantasy. It is his way of escaping to a simpler time filled with magic, wonders and heroics of young men and women.

Other than reading, Mike has always enjoyed the outdoors. From the beaches in Southern California to the warm waters of North Carolina. From the waterfalls in the Northwest to the Rocky Mountains in Utah. Mike has appreciated the beauty that God provides for us. He also enjoys hiking, discovering nature, playing a little basketball or volleyball, and most recently disc golf. He has a lovely wife who has always supported him, and three beautiful children who have been the center of his life.

Mike began writing stories in elementary school and moved on to larger novels in his early adult years. He has worked in corporate finance for most of his career. That, along with spending time with his wonderful family and obligations at church has made it difficult to find the time to truly dedicate to writing. In the last few years as his children have become older he has returned to doing what he truly enjoys – writing!

www.MichaelSheltonBooks.com

Other Series By Mike Shelton

The Cremelino Prophecy

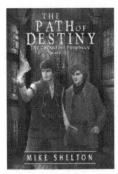  

A powerful sword, magical horses, lost love, and revenge against nobility. These are just a few of the struggles Darius faces in The Cremelino Prophecy, a teen/young adult series consisting of The Path Of Destiny, The Path Of Decisions, and The Path Of Peace.

"Forgotten lines of ancient magic and the power of the throne. One will make them both his own if his heart sees the true power. . ." So begins The Cremelino Prophecy!

In this Young Adult/Teen sword and sorcery fantasy series, Darius San Williams, son of one of King Edward's councilors, cares little for his father's politics and vows to leave the city of Anikari to protect and bring glory to the Realm. But when a new-found and ancient power emerges from within him, he and his friends Christine and Kelln are faced with decisions that could shatter or fulfill the prophecy and the lives of all those they know. Wizards and magic have long been looked down upon in the Realm, but Darius learns that no matter where he goes, prophecy and destiny are waiting to find him.

Sign up on Mike's website at www.MichaelSheltonBooks.com and get a copy of the prequel novella e-book to The Cremelino Prophecy, The Blade and The Bow.

Follow Darius and Kelln in one of their more fantastic adventures prior to The Path Of Destiny.

Made in the USA
Lexington, KY
13 May 2017